December S

Part Three of the Lyndf...

A Saga of Shropshire and the Welsh Marches

December Song

Part Three of the Lyndford story
A Saga of Shropshire and the Welsh Marches

Francis John Simcock

To the memory of my first wife, Hilda; and with grateful thanks to my second, Joan, who has transformed years of desolation into decades of happiness; and who throughout has encouraged and helped with the writing of these books; not least in bringing some wilder flights of a fanciful pen down to earth.

YouCaxton Publications

24 High Street, Bishop's Castle, Shropshire. SY3 8JX
www.youCaxton.co.uk

Published in Great Britain by
Francis John Simcock

The Author asserts the moral right to
be identified as the author of this work.

ISBN 978-1-909644-04-5

Cover Design: YouCaxton from original artwork by Raymond Gordon

Set in Adobe Garamond Pro.

Printed and bound in Great Britain.

Acknowledgement

I am indebted to a number of sources for background information on the terrible, and apparently senseless conflicts in the Balkans, the Bosnian wars. And in particular to Laura Silber and Allan Little for their work of penetrating dissection, The Death of Yugoslavia.

Francis John Simcock

One

Charles and Maria

It was his habit, most Sunday mornings, to walk as much as he could of Lyndford Home Farm's 700 acres, partly for pleasure, partly to see fields, and stock, with which he had not been in contact during the working week. Sometimes, if time was short before he had to be back for lunch, or the weather was particularly unpleasant, he drove round in the Land Rover. But mostly he walked, like today. Usually alone except for Mima, the Border Collie bitch, and sometimes Maria's terrier, Jack. When they were first married and took over the farm, Maria walked with him, but now, with three young children at her apron strings, as often as not his mother and father or others of the family coming for lunch, and a new au pair still being broken in to British farm life, she had to obey the demands of the kitchen.

He started off through the churchyard, stopping as always at the grave of his grandparents, his namesake Charles, and Emily Jane (brackets Dolly), from which he cleared half-dead roses and made a mental note to make sure they were replaced. His great-grandparents' grave was close by, and he noted appreciatively that the blooms there were beautifully fresh. His mother and father made that one their special responsibility.

The churchyard was half full of Jameson graves, ranging from sepulchral-scale structures dating back to the 18th Century to the curbed plot where lay the great-grandparents, Alastair and Dorothea, the last of the family to lay claim to the title of squire and lady of the manor. Charles and Dolly's resting place, from which he removed the dying roses, was marked by a plain upright slab of granite, modestly lettered. But he stopped there only for brief moments before crossing the lane on the other side of the church and turning towards the hillside fields pasturing some of his 500 sheep.

Charles was his own shepherd, making a point however of employing a youngster as his assistant and bringing up him (and, this year, her) into his ways. His father always said Charles had inherited his love for and skill with sheep from his West Indian mother – "the best shepherd in Shropshire and the Marches," according to Dad. She still lent a hand, at lambing time, and sometimes joined him on his Sunday morning walk, if his father was indulging in his new hobby of golf, usually with Uncle Peter. This morning though he was alone. His mother and father had gone to Derby, to a motorcycle club lunch marking the racing achievements of their other son, Edward, recently retired after bringing many honours to the club.

He walked through the ewes in the first field, noting how well they looked, and on to the next, containing a score of suckler cows and calves, some more than half as big as their mothers, and all in the peak of condition. What superb beef they were going to make in another eight or nine months time, he thought. Then, still climbing steadily with the road on his left, to another enclosure, this one containing the tail end of the year's crop of lambs, which would be going to a wholesale butcher in a few days, before crossing the road to take a look at a 30-acre field of wheat, one of the objects of today's inspection, for it was just about ready for the combine.

The wheat was on some of the farm's highest ground and Charles took a few minutes to lean on a gate and savour the view, westwards into Wales, north towards the Long Mynd and Shrewsbury. He did not know it, but he was leaning on the very gate, or its successor, where Grandfather and his sister, Great Aunt Billie, had stopped one Christmas nearly seventy years before to reveal to each other the secret loves that were to bring so many changes to the Jameson family. Charles knew much of the history, but on this Sunday the magnificence of the vista, and the prospect of the wheat, steered his thoughts in another direction: across the Atlantic, to the Caribbean, and the plots of land which put together would have amounted to little more than a third of the wheatfield, but from which his other grandfather had wrested a living. Charles had never been to Masterman Creek, Jamaica, but his father had, and the stories of his visits to the island were littered with praise and admiration for his parents-in-law and the way they had survived and conquered hardship and poverty.

He knew though that Alastair himself, and Debra, had struggled through years of hard work before they had finally lifted their heads clear of the muddy financial waters of their early years. They spoke little, to the children, of how she came to Britain, although they could not completely hide all the grim truth. For one thing, the long scar on her cheek, visible all her life, had to prompt questions, which must be answered without subterfuge, for if there was anything Debra abhorred, it was lying; and Charles himself could clearly remember how he, his sister and brother were at one time not allowed to cycle home from school, because "some very bad men had come, who Mum had helped put in prison." That was when they lived at Forest Farm, ten miles away, which Alastair still owned and Charles nominally farmed but was looked after day to day by his father's old employees and friends, "Erbie" Johnson and his wife Connie.

His thoughts meandered back across the ocean, via his mother's early life, to Forest Farm, and to wondering how long Erbie and Connie would want to stay there. They were well into their sixties, and between them milked nearly 100 cows twice every day, as well as supervising all the other work on the farm's 230 acres.

When Alastair retired and had mooted the idea that they might like to have things a little easier – he knew they had not taken more than one holiday in ten years – Erbie had rejected it with vigour.

"Aren't you 'appy wiv the way we're doin' 'ere, then, Ally?" was his first rejoinder – he never lost his strong Cockney accent.

And on receiving assurance on that score: "Look, Ally, you did me the best turn anybody could when you took me out o' London and give me a job. You know what it was like for me in them days. An' when you went to Lyndford and left me runnin' fings 'ere, that put the top 'at on it. No, we're orlright as we are."

So "fings" were left alone, and Forest Farm largely to the Johnsons. But that was five years ago, they were now approaching pension age, and Charles had one or two ideas, which he worked out as he looked over the wheat, and resolved to put to them, and his father, very soon.

There was another bunch of cattle he had not personally seen for two or three weeks, and they were his next call before moving downwards and along a woodland track that, even more than the gate into the wheatfield, had marked the scene of hugely significant developments in the family history. It was where his namesake grandfather had first openly declared his love for the housemaid who became his wife, and which led directly to his father disinheriting him, more or less losing his mind and eventually committing suicide. Charles did not know about the woodland tryst, but he was well aware of the main burden of the story.

Lyndford had been a substantial estate in those days, just after the first war, and for more than two centuries before. Home Farm was all that was left. But whether the locality of the little-changed woodland path somehow communicated a message to a mind ready, that morning, to wander in different directions, he found his thoughts going back again to his Jamaican grandparents, descended from slaves within a handful of generations, although his grandmother was hardly coloured, his father had told him – no doubt the long term effect of some white slaveowner's excursions into his servants' quarters. Or more likely his orders to the servant girl to warm his own bed.

Not for the first time, ruminations about his Caribbean grandparents left him pondering, marvelling almost, how he had been brought to the ownership, or potential ownership, of nearly 1,000 of the most beautiful acres in Britain.

He knew all about the racial prejudice that pervaded much British life and although his mother had been liked and respected at both Cravenbury and Lyndford, when he took over Home Farm one or two newspapers got hold of it and made hay of the fact that the remnants of an estate that for nearly three centuries had nurtured a family of the type which "made Britain great" were now in the hands of a "black" immigrant. Not of course forgetting to mention the shadows over his father's own past. Alastair had been as angry as he ever became about anything, not because of what was written about him, but about the racial slurs. And wrote to the editor of the worst offending paper telling him that "my father-in-law and mother-in-law put in more effort in one day than many of this country's layabouts expend in a week." And that while his grandmother had been the daughter of a baronet, his mother had been a kitchen maid and he was proud of it.

However it had all come about, Charles, thought, here he was. He had never wanted to be anything but a farmer, and meant to be, and was, a good one. His father, foreseeing the hard times that would beset dairy farmers as the supermarkets and the quest for cheap food drove milk prices down and the size of herds ever upwards, agreed to scrap the seven days a week, 52 weeks a year business of milk production. The monthly cheque had been essential to Alastair and Debra when they were struggling to make Forest Farm viable, but the enterprise was now big enough and well-enough capitalised for it to be no longer necessary. And ending milk production at Forest Farm was part of the plan for an easier life for Erbie and Connie that Charles had worked out through his wheatfield cogitations.

But all that was not what was passing through his mind as he walked through the wood, stopping to fondle Mima and sit on a fallen tree – not the one that other Charles, and Dolly, had occupied; that had gone the way of all fallen trees, over 70 years. The theme of his thought was a straightforward recognition of how good life was. Here he was, barely 34 years old, with a lovely wife and three small but lovely children; a farm that would surely provide them all with a comfortable living, as long as he worked reasonably hard with head and hands, both of which he enjoyed; a mother and father not quarter of a mile away, looking forward to many more well-earned years of retirement; a recently-married brother, who was making a big mark in advanced technological development; and a sister who was doing just as well as a research-orientated doctor.

A tiny question mark formed in his mind as he thought of Edward, and his marriage. He hoped it would work out. Stella was beautiful, poised and self-possessed. But was she a bit hard, a little too much of a career girl, he wondered.

Edward himself was a complex character, Charles knew. He had a brain like a razor, when he applied it to his own ideas, alongside a most likeable personality. Did he not need a partner, a mate, who would balance her husband's qualities, potentialities and perhaps eccentricities with a straightforward and yes, not quite so brilliant steadfastness which would base its raison d'etre on her family?

Em – Emily Jane – too. Charles somehow could not think of her as having the clinical detachment he thought necessary for a medical researcher. As a child, between him and Ed in age, she had always seemed so warm and cuddly, although ever ready to join in rumbustious activities. She had never had any boy friends, he believed, and her friendships with girls had come and gone. He hoped she would meet someone with whom she could share her life. It may be seen that Charles thought a life-partner of the kind who lit up his own days was essential for happiness and fulfillment.

By now he was a mile from home, and he must get there in time to have a little play before lunch with Alastair, who would have his fourth birthday next month, and Dorothy; number three, Douglas, was only a month old. Emerging from the woodland and back on to the metalled road, he took only a minor detour to check that the field of maize, a crop he was growing for the first time this year, looked healthy. Jasmine Cottage, his parents' home, came into view .... at the same time as his own Land Rover. He stared, wondering, as it came nearer and stopped. Maria tumbled out, leaving the door swinging open, and threw her arms round him.

"Charles," she gasped. "Oh, Charles ...."

"Whatever's the matter, sweetheart? What's the matter?"

"Oh, Charles .... it's your Mum, and Dad .... they've ...."

"What, love, what ...."

"They've had an accident .... your mum .... oh, Charles .... she's .... been killed .... Charles ...."

His knees buckled. Maria, the Land Rover, the little dog she'd not been able to keep out of the vehicle almost swam before his eyes.

"What .... how .... oh my god ...."

She caught his arm.

"Sit down, darling. Get in the car."

She shepherded him to the passenger side of the vehicle, opened the door and he got in. She stood beside him with the door still open. Jack the terrier scrambled on to his knee and he fondled him, as always.

"What about Dad? Is he alright?"

"They've taken him to hospital. I don't know any more. The police told Edward, and he rang, a few minutes ago."

"Where was it?"

"At a level crossing somewhere near Wolverhampton. They've taken Dad to Birmingham, I think."

"Is he badly hurt?"

"I don't know. Ed said something about 'multiple injuries.'"

"Are you sure about Mum?"

"Ed said it was instantaneous. Oh, darling ...."

"Does Em know?"

"He was trying to get hold of her."

"Let's get back to the house. Somebody might ring."

She drove on until they reached a gateway to turn round. As they went back to the farm, past Jasmine Cottage and its flower-decked garden, his mother's pride and joy, the tears could not be held back. But as they turned into their own yard, he asked:

"Did Ed say what happened?"

"It seems they were pushed into a train by a big lorry. That's about as much as he knew."

They went into the kitchen, where Evinka, the Czech au pair, was struggling to further the preparation of lunch at the same time as looking after the three children.

"Thanks, Eva," Maria said. "I'll finish that. You take the children into the sitting room. I'll call you when it's ready."

The girl looked at her, reluctant to go when she knew something terrible had hit them.

"I'll bring the children's lunch, and yours, in there. Lay a cloth on that little table. It'll be better if they have it there. I'll tell you about it just now," Maria said.

When they had gone, Alastair said: "I'm going to try to get hold of somebody. I'll try Ed."

He went into his office, but came back only a minute or two later.

"There's no reply. I'll try Em." But the result was the same. "I wonder if it's the big hospital at Birmingham they've taken him to. What is it, the Royal Birmingham?"

"Yes. But please, darling, just have something to eat, and drink. You need it."

"I'm going to find that hospital's number and see what they can tell me, if he's there."

He went in to the office again, and this time was longer. When he came out he said: "Yes, he's there. And Ed. I spoke to him."

She looked at him.

"He's smashed up pretty badly. And he's unconscious. Oh, lord, Mia, I'm going. I'll have to go."

"Darling, you can't go without something to eat. You'll be ill, and that won't do Dad any good."

"I'm going now. I've got to go."

"Just let me make you a sandwich of that beef. And a flask of coffee."

"Alright. I'll just change my shoes."

As he got into the car, no more than ten minutes later, she put the hot beef sandwich, wrapped in a white napkin, on the seat beside him, with the small flask. As she leaned over to kiss him, she said: "I expect you'll eat that as you go, but please be careful. Don't try to drink the coffee while you're driving. Pull in somewhere." And as her own tears came to the surface, she pleaded: "Please, darling, be careful. Phone me as soon as you can."

She watched the Ford out of the yard and down the road. Back in the house, she went straight to Evinka and the children.

"What is it, Mrs Jameson?" the girl asked. "What's happened?"

"Come into the kitchen a moment," she said, very quietly. And once there told her, tremulously, as much as she knew.

*****

She and Charles had been married for nearly five years, and "together" for three times as long. They were at the same grammar school, she a year younger, but in the way it is with schoolchildren in different year groups, they had very little contact until they graduated to the sixth form, although she had admired him from a distance, chiefly for his athleticism and good looks.

"He's dishy," she told her bosom friend Belinda, in one of the many inquests on opposite sexes of their acquaintance that help keep 14-year-old girls from dying of boredom.

"Oh, he's good looking alright. But could you really fancy one of them? His mother's West Indian or something, isn't she?"

"I don't care, I still think he's dishy."

Her friend's mild objection to Charles' dark complexion did not detract from her admiration of him, in fact it tended to have the opposite effect. She would sometimes break ranks with her friends to watch rugby and cricket matches in which he was taking part, often with distinction. A few times over the next couple of years he actually noticed her, which was not difficult because spectators at those events, especially girls, were not numerous. But his rather diffident "hello" sent her home with a little thrill coursing round her body.

When she entered the sixth form, the lower sixth as it was still called in those days, Charles was in the upper sixth, a year ahead, captain of the rugby first fifteen and a shining light in many school activities. But there was quite a lot of actual contact between upper and lower; for example they shared what in former days would have been called a common room. Boys and girls had also reached the stage of being well aware of each other sexually and attachments were not uncommon. Maria, not the prettiest of her cohort, was at 16 by no means the least attractive, either, and more than one would-be Romeo paid her attention. Charles was not one of them, although they would exchange smiles when they met. But it was the activities of one such pursuer that brought them closer together.

A boy by the name of Mark Sydnam, the son of a businessman in the town, Ludstone, where Maria and her family also lived, had latched himself on to her, or tried to. He would make a point of emerging from the building, or the school gates, at the same time. While being somewhat flattered by his attentions, for the adjective she applied to Charles was used by many of the girls about Sydnam, she did not find herself attracted to him Was in fact distinctly put off when he started to take the attentions further than acceptance of flattery permitted. His arm went round her waist on only the second occasion he waylaid her and walked into the town with her. Next time the hand on the end of it pressed on a breast that had only comparatively recently found itself promoted to the dignity of a bra. She shrugged him off, but he responded by pulling her more closely towards him and planting a kiss on her lips. She tried to pull free but he persisted

It happened that Charles and two younger boys, who travelled by rail to their station at Cravenbury, from where he cycled home, were not many yards behind, and saw what happened. It also happened that he disliked Sydnam, who he had been told had once described him as "that bloody nigger," and who he himself had seen, in an inter-house rugby match, deliberately kick an opposing player in the private parts.

He strode up to the couple, grabbed Sydnam by the arm, and told him: "That's enough of that. She doesn't like it."

Sydnam, taken by surprise, blustered: "What's it got to do with you, you fucking wog," backing up the words with a swing aimed at Charles' face – which however missed by a margin.

"Just leave her alone" Charles said, offering no response to the attempted blow. "If you touch her again I'll report you to the head first thing in the morning. That's what it's got to do with me."

"I'll kick your fucking head in," was the response "but here, take the bloody tart – if she's prepared to go with a frigging nigger." And he pushed Maria towards Charles and stalked off down the road.

"Oh, thank you," she said. "He was being horrible."

"Have you been going out with him?" he asked.

"No, I don't think I'd even spoken to him before this week. He just started following me around."

"Does he live near you?"

"I don't know exactly, but I've seen him in the road."

"I think I'd better come home with you, to make sure he doesn't try anything again."

"Oh, no, I'll be alright. You'd miss your train."

"There's another." And telling his young companions to make haste to the station, he set off with her on what turned out to be a twenty minute walk to a housing estate on the south side of the town.

As they walked, he said: "Your name's Maria, isn't it? I've heard you called that."

"Yes, Maria Edgerton."

"Mine's Charles. Charles Jameson."

"Yes, I know."

He did not feign any surprise. He knew he was well enough known in the school for slightly younger pupils to be aware of who he was, and false modesty was not one of his failings. He did not know that she had been aware of much about him for a year and more, although he had seen her watching sports events and vaguely wondered why. And still less did he realise how her heart was beating a little faster as they walked. Instead he asked her what her subjects were, and led on to talk about what she wanted to do after school. Did she want to go on to university?

"I'm not clever enough," she said. "I only got Bs and Cs in O-levels. But I'm trying to get some decent A-levels. I thought I ought to leave and earn some money but my dad didn't want that. He says you can never get too much education, and he's giving me good pocket money. And I work Saturdays in the market, on a fruit and vegetable stall.

"Do you want to go to university" she asked.

"No, I'm going to Harper Adams, if they'll have me."

"The agricultural college?"

"Yes. I'm going to be a farmer, like Dad. He agrees it's the best thing, for me."

Charles arrived home an hour and a half later than normal, but that was not so unusual for he often had sport and other commitments after school. His mother, Debra said: "Didn' know you'd got anythin' on after school today," and when he said nothing, looked at him quizzically, making him feel he had to offer some explanation. He said: "Oh, there was a bit of bother I had to sort out. I had to go home with someone."

"Was he bein' bullied or somethin'?" Debra had never quite lost her Jamaican way of speech.

"In a way."

"Come on, tell me a bit more. You got me wonderin'."

"It was a girl. This fellow was, oh, trying to kiss her and that and she didn't want it. He's not a nice guy, Mum. I told him to leave her alone and he didn't like it. I thought I'd better take her home."

Debra left it at that. But although she knew very well that the action was typical of her elder son, the son of his father, she felt a thrill of pride for him, as she told Alastair later that evening. She would have been even prouder if she had known what occurred at school next day, when Charles made a point of seeking out Mark Sydnam with no-one else around.

"Sydnam, just listen to this," he said. "If you ever try that on with Maria Edgerton again, I'll either have you up before the head or I'll give you the hiding of your life. Probably both." And Sydnam, an inch taller and half a stone heavier than a boy who had never hit anyone in his life, glared but said nothing.

*****

Although Maria's sensations of pleasure whenever Charles paid her any attention continued through the rest of the school year, there were no noticeable developments in their relationship until his A-level courses had been completed and the end of the final term approached. He occasionally spoke to her, made sure there had been no repeat of the previous trouble, asked how her work was going and – once – helped her with a problem revealed as a result. But with the exams completed, and attendance at school becoming more formality than necessity, he talked to her from time to time, often enough for her girl friends to begin to look on them as an item. It was however the end of year sixth-form hop, glorified by the title of "ball," with a live band, buffet supper and young swells in bow ties and black or white jackets that marked the first major step towards Maria becoming Mrs Jameson. Most of the boys wanted to take their out-of-school girlfriends, or young ladies recruited for the occasion, to the ball, to show they had graduated beyond the level of schoolgirls. A few offered their sisters as candidate companions for their friends. One, or two perhaps, even took their own sister as their lady guest.

Charles was very fond of Emily Jane, but he did not want a fifth former as his partner. He knew who he wanted to take to the ball, schoolgirl though she was.

"Are you going to the ball?" he asked her.

"Nobody's asked me," she said.

"Would you come with me?"

Oh dear, the not-quite-so-little tummy wobble.

"They'll all be in glamorous gowns and things. I've not got anything like that. I'd let you down."

"I bet you wouldn't. You'd look good in whatever you wore."

It was the first time he had said anything even vaguely romantic to her, and the wobble assumed larger proportions.

"Are you sure, and you won't be upset if I'm not very smart?"

"I'm asking you because I'd like your company, not because I want to show off a glamour-girl," realising as he said it that he was implying she was not one, and hastily adding, genuinely if somewhat clumsily: "You'll look as good as anyone."

"Thank you, Charles" - the first time she had used his name. "I'll try not to let you down."

Maria's father was a self-employed lorry driver struggling to pay off the mortgage on a modest semi-detached house, the hire-purchase on his one truck, and keep his family of five including himself and his wife Gwen reasonably fed and clothed. Gwen worked as an office cleaner. They gave Maria, the eldest, pocket money enough to allow her to hold her head up with her grammar school companions although she did not take it when she had work like the Saturday job. Ball gowns and the like, or even hiring them were outside their range. But she had an idea.

"Mum, couldn't I make something?" she asked when she told her mother she had been asked to the school ball by the boy many of her friends would have given their eye teeth to accompany.

"I've got a better idea, p'raps," said her mother. "My wedding dress is still in the wardrobe. Let's have a look at it and see what we can do."

First sight of the 20-year-old garment was not encouraging. For a start, it was white, and very long, with a rear that followed behind, almost like a train. But Gwen said: "We can shorten it, no problem. And we can take that back part off. And we can make a little cape thing, or something in a different colour, so it isna all white. A sash, p'raps."

They toiled away through a week of evenings, without a sewing machine and on the kitchen table, until Gwen pronounced the dress ready for a try-on. Maria took it upstairs and came down just as her father returned from a trip to France.

"Bloody 'ell," he came out with, breaking his rule of not swearing in front of his family.. "Wherever'd you get that from? I 'ope you 'avena paid what it looks like."

"We've made it," Maria said. "It's for our school ball. Do you like it?"

"It's terrific, love. My word, you look like a million dollars. You'll be the belle o' the ball."

Gwen said: "We made it out of my wedding dress. You don't mind, do you?"

"Course not. Time it was done summat with."

Maria said nothing to Charles about her dress through the few remaining days of the term. He said to her however: "Can I pick you up on Friday? Mum says I can have her car." He had recently passed his driving test.

Friday night came. Slightly early, he knocked on the front door. He heard: "Martin, come back," before the door was opened by Gwen.

"Hullo. I'm Charles. I've come to take Maria to the dance, at school."

"Yes, she's expecting you. Come in, she won't be a minute. My, you look smart." As indeed he did, in full dance dress including white jacket and black trousers. Ten year old Martin's eyes nearly popped out of his head. But they were nothing to Charles' optics as, a few seconds later, Maria came down the stairs, looking like every one of her father's million dollars in the dress with a slinky little jacket over her shoulders and her mother's one piece of jewellery round her neck. Nobody was to know that the jacket had come from a second hand shop. Charles could hardly speak, and Gwen saw it.

"Doesn't she look nice?" she prompted.

"She looks beautiful," he managed.

"Well, enjoy yourselves. And don't be too late, please."

When her husband came in later and asked what "the lad" was like, she almost sighed: "Oh Den, he seems so nice. You should have seen them. They looked like something out of a fairy tale."

The ball was like most such school-orientated affairs. Charles enjoyed it, and was happy to find his normal position as a centre of attention usurped by his stunning companion, off whom many of the boys could not keep their eyes. But it was more than pride of possession. He came to know, not completely on that night but it was when it started, that Maria saw him in a special light. Talking in a group of friends over supper, he caught her looking at him in a way he had never known any girl eye him before. She coloured and took her gaze away, but the damage, if it could be called that, was done.

When he delivered her home just after midnight, she said: "Come in and have a cup of coffee. I don't think anyone's up."

Feeling quite grown up and sophisticated, he accepted. As they were drinking, she said: "You don't know how much I enjoyed tonight. Thank you very much."

"I don't think you can have enjoyed it more than I did. Thank you for coming."

And after a slightly embarrassed silence, for both knew it was not going to be left there, he said: "I won't be seeing you at school now. Could you perhaps come out with me sometime."

"Yes, alright." And realising that perhaps she had not sounded enthusiastic, she added: "I'd like that."

And that was it. Maria knew she loved him, had known for some time, or that she could love him if he would allow it. With Charles it was a slower growth. But from that point he looked forward to seeing her as often as he could, and during the first few weeks after the ball, through the school's long summer holiday and before he left home for Harper Adams, they saw each other quite a lot, usually going to the cinema, once to a pop concert at the Castle, although it was harvest time and Charles was kept busy on the farm. By then, his father had only two employees, his old friend Erbie and the dairy herdsman, George, so that family help at that time was invaluable.

He did not tell his parents about her, although when he asked to borrow the car or Land Rover about twice a week, saying only that he was going to see an old school friend in Ludford, they began to suspect that the OSF might be female.

"Never mind, it'll either come to nothing when he goes to Harper Adams, or it'll come out into the open, sooner or later," Alastair assured his wife.

Charles thoroughly enjoyed Harper Adams, and became immersed in college activities, including sport. He found himself missing Maria, how much he hardly realised until half the first term had gone by without seeing her. He had never put any of the affection he was now feeling into words. They exchanged several letters during that half term, but his began only with "Dear Maria" and ended with nothing more endearing than "Looking forward to seeing you." And as hers adopted a similar tone he began to wonder whether she cared for him as he now hoped. It was a matter of absence making the heart have its doubts. As the half-term holiday approached however he decided he must find out. In his letter arranging to meet her, he wrote: "Could we just go for a walk, or a picnic or something? I want to talk to you?" On reading the letter, Maria trembled and did not quite know what to make of the suggestion. One half of her said he wanted to tell her he loved her, the other half feared he was going to say he did not want to see her any more. But whichever it was, it had to be faced. She asked him to meet her at home on the Sunday before he had to go back to the college.

It was a wet day, not conducive to walking, or a picnic, and she said: "Let's go up into the Chase. It's nice there, even when it's wet, and you can see over the town." When they parked up in a hillside clearing with the Castle peering through the murk below them, she took the initiative, quite against her instinct.

"What do you want to talk about?" she asked, very quietly.

"You and me," he said, after a pause. And she thought then that it was going to be alright.

"I want to know whether you think about me like I think about you."

An 18-year-old teenager, now quite sure, opted for a little mischief, even when the target was the boy she loved and meant to marry, one day.

"I don't know how you think about me. You've never told me."

So in spite of feeling about 14, having to force to the surface words that only months before he'd have called soppy, he told her.

"I love you, that's all."

"Oh, Charles." And softly but firmly: "I love you. I've loved you for a long time." And she leaned over to kiss him, on the lips.

From that point, it was as though they were betrothed. Periods apart imposed no strain on their relationship, although as the years went on they missed each other more and more. Their letters opened "Darling Maria" and "Dearest Charles" and ended with variations of "Love You" but the casual reader would find little of the love letter in the words between. They would be about what they were doing, or thinking, or wondering. The love was there between the lines, and grew with time.

And there were a great many letters, for there was a considerable amount of time. Charles was at Harper Adams for two years, and at the end of her time at school Maria made a decision which did not make getting together any easier. Although her A-levels turned out to be good enough to take her to university, and her parents, father especially, wanted her to go – she would be the first member of his family to do so – she decided against it. She wanted to start to earn some money, to relieve some of the financial burden on them, and anyway she did not think she was an academic type. Study was harder work than anything physical. She opted for nursing which, she reasoned, would always be a useful skill whatever happened to her in the future. And she knew very well what she wanted that ultimate future to be – wife to Charles and mother to their children.

She applied for and obtained a place in the Birmingham hospital which a few years later was to play a dramatic part in the life of the family to which she would become allied. Her nursing course, with its associated study, allowed little time for social life, and she hardly saw Charles on more than one occasion a month while he was at college and she on the course.

At the end of his time at Harper Adams, Charles returned home to Cravenbury and divided his time between working for his father and his great-uncle Giles at the 700-acre Lyndford Home Farm. Forest Farm could not really justify another full-time member of staff, and as Giles said: "I expect you'll be helping your dad run this place, Charles, when I'm not here, so it'll be a good thing if you get your hand in now." And before long, Charles was spending most of his time at getting his hand in and taking some of the pressure off his great-uncle, who was not far from completing his eighth decade, and had no children, having married late in life.

His own parents had by then, inevitably, realised that there was a young lady in his life. In fact he told them, when he saw the parental eyebrows raised by requests for a family vehicle to take him to Birmingham. They wanted to know who she was, how long he had known her, what she was doing, etc, etc., and Charles, by now fully committed and proud of it, had no hesitation in telling them. He showed his mother a photograph of Maria, in the home-made ball gown that had been such a hit. Debra wanted to know when he was going to bring her to meet her and Alastair, and Charles, delighted, said he would arrange it as soon as possible, by which he meant, in the next few weeks.

It took longer, because extended time off was difficult to come by, for Maria. But when she eventually arrived at Forest Farm, Debra took to her immediately, Alastair however taking a little longer. He thought she talked too much, but it was really a slight inferiority complex. He still spoke with the remains of the Jamesons' upper-crust accent, giving her the idea that he was both intellectually and socially superior. But his tales of the farm, and showing her round it, soon put her at ease. He told her stories of Debra in the lambing shed and the milking parlour and, making assumptions that he only realised with hindsight should not have been made at that stage in the young peoples' lives, asked how she liked the idea of being a farmer's wife.

"I don't know, Mr Jameson," she said "but I do know one thing. I want to be Charles's wife."

"Has he – have you .... ?"

"Not in those words, no. But I'm sure it's what he wants, as well."

"It's often hard work, you know."

"I'm not afraid of that."

And he was sure she meant it. But it was to be years before she was put to that particular test. Within two years, Giles died and Home Farm passed into other Jameson family ownership, involving much legal and financial to-ing and fro-ing, none of it ill-natured or fractious, but which had to be done before Alastair could assume that the farm was his. Then Maria, who alongside her commitment to Charles had become enthusiastically involved in her nursing career, found herself in stages of it which she could not easily abandon, and did not want to.

Added to which, they had arrived at, or rather created, a situation that did away with, or at least reduced, one of the urges that made them eager to be married. She installed herself in a flat, away from the hospital, put herself on the by-then-readily-available contraceptive pill, purchased a three-quarter size "double" bed, and took Charles into it as often as he could get there.

They were married when his father decided, at the age of 65, to retire and keep only a watching brief on the farm. The pill was abandoned and Alastair and Debra, Dennis and Gwen were made grandparents, three times over.

Two

Star Quality

Stella Hardy could not have been more aptly named. Star quality showed even in her years at a Salford primary school. Along with resilience, determination and an ability to pick out her targets and see the way to hit them.

In the playground and the street, she could hold her own with any of the young toughs of either sex who tried to dominate her world. But it was in the classroom that she shone brightest. She was usually the one to have her "compositions" read out, her drawings pinned on the notice boards. Her hand was invariably the first to go up in mental arithmetic sessions. And when the eleven-plus came along she sailed through to a place at the girls' high school.

Within her family, the achievement was not universally welcomed. Jud Hardy, a labourer at an aluminium smelting plant, had ambitions, but they did not extend to wishing for a better education for his daughter and son. Their high point would be winning the pools, owning a car and a colour television, backing the winner of the National or the Derby. He had never read a book in his life, and pronounced himself proud of it. Literacy and numeracy were needed only to understand race cards or pools sheets.

When the education authority wrote with news of Stella's success, and informed him and his wife of the school she would go to, he said only: "I 'ope that dunna give you big ideas, miss." And when it also became known to him that she must have costly school uniform, sports kit and other extras so far not needed, he went further.

"What'n yer want to go there for, anyroad? What's wrong wi' Waggs Road?" - the local secondary modern.

Stella's mother, Margaret, was of a different calibre. She married Jud when she was 19 and pregnant by the son of the greengrocer for whom she worked. It had come about one morning when she had been sent with him to fetch a load of vegetables from one of the shop's suppliers. She liked him and though he forced himself on her to a degree, she hardly resisted. Showing a worldly perspicacity which would emerge in her daughter, she thought a liaison with him might be good for her.

When she missed her "monthly" she tackled the youth, fully expecting the result to be an offer of marriage, if a reluctant one. But to her surprise the family trio, dominated by the mother, refused to hear anything about it. She had never liked having the good-looking Margaret work with her husband and son, and thought the girl was way below what she wanted for the boy. She told her husband and son that Margaret was trying to put one over on them, persuaded her husband and bullied their son into falling into line approach. No paternity tests were available for such as Margaret, and the upshot was she found herself out of a job, with a flea in her ear.

Jud Hardy lived a few doors away and had been trying to get her to go out with him for some time. She refused because although she did not dislike him and he was personable enough in looks and general behaviour, he was at least two levels below her in terms of intellect. But now she turned her rebuttals into encouragement, quickly accepted his sexual advances and within weeks of the incident that had started it all, she had told him she was pregnant and they were married.

Jud never knew the truth about Stella's parentage. The young greengrocer kept his mouth shut, partly because he knew that the consequences for him could be unpleasant if the facts came to Jud's ears. And the fact that Stella was born barely seven months after their marriage was either ignored or explained in the usual way – she was premature.

Margaret buckled down to the job of being married to a man with whom she had little in common. In fact she was not really unhappy, taking pleasure in bringing up and encouraging a daughter who was obviously bright and talented, and a son who followed Stella quite quickly and if not quite in the girl's class intellectually was well above average that way. And Jud was not unkind to her, even if he did not understand why she always wanted her daughter and son to be able to move away from the level in which she and her husband were obviously fixed. It never occurred to him to wonder where the childrens' gifts came from.

Without much education herself, Margaret could see its value. She worked as a cleaner in the offices of her husband's employers, and when it became clear that Stella's schooling would indeed entail extra spending, she found more work of the same kind, enduring Jud''s complaints when his tea was not ready on his return from work.

So the girl went to the high school. She was good looking, like her mother, quite good at sport, and in the upper echelons academically, but the qualities did not translate to being well-liked, by either pupils or staff. She was "prickly" they might have said if asked why. Really it was that she developed an inferiority complex. She hated being one of the handful of "free school meals" children on whom, she believed, not altogether without reason, many of her schoolmates looked down. And her abilities, which at her primary school had lifted her clear of all, at St Winifred's did not make her so supreme. The academic star still shone, but not quite as brilliantly, compared with a few others among her fellow pupils.

However, the resilience and determination were still there. She worked hard, and did well, always at or near the top of her form. But halfway through the two years leading up to O levels, the family was hit by the first of two blows that came in quick succession. Her father was killed in an accident at work.

Her mother took on more work in an effort to keep the wolf from the door, and her children decently fed and clad. Stella's younger brother also winning a grammar school place increased the financial pressure. Their father's employers, and his trade union, helped, but the family income was greatly reduced. Then came the second blow. Even as they laid her husband in the ground, Margaret started to develop a double cancer – breast and lung. She ignored the symptoms and after the inevitable diagnosis, still kept it from the children for months, until in fact Stella had completed the O-levels. But, just before her daughter's sixteenth birthday, she died, at the obscenely early age of 36.

Stella and her brother were left without any close relatives. Cousins of her mother were the nearest, many miles away, and she and her brother were taken into care by the local authority. But she resisted attempts to part them, or move them from their council house home.

"My dear," said the social worker under whom they were placed. "You cannot possibly manage on your own, and look after your brother."

"Yes I can," insisted Stella, who had already been given advice as to what she could and could not do, or ask for, by her school head and advisory staff. "I know I can get a job, and you've got to provide money for Clive, haven't you?"

"Yes, but we shall want him to live under our care. Probably with a foster-family. And you – wouldn't it be better if you were to go to foster care, and continue your education? That would be much better for your future, surely, rather than having to spend all your spare time cooking and cleaning, and working in some dead-end job. Your school says you're very able, and you ought to go on into the sixth form, perhaps even university."

Stella understood the argument, but dug in her toes.

"No. I'd rather start to earn my own living," she insisted. In the end, a compromise was reached. Clive would go to foster-parents, she to accommodation provided for her by social services, to whose supervision she knew she was obliged to submit until she was 18.

They placed her in a hostel, and she took up the job she knew was on offer, with a locally based mail order firm. It was pretty mundane work, but before she had been there many months her potential was realised and she transferred to the accounts department, with an increase in wages. The resilient toughness of her character had already been made plain by her decision to stand on her own independent feet; and now she began to formulate the personal philosophy that would drive her for years to come.

"I am going to make my way in the world," was the (nearly) subconscious resolve. "One way or another. I will never lead the kind of life my mother did."

The first step was to enrol on an accountancy course at the local college, choosing the most intensive of three options. It meant attending classes three nights a week, working on her own for most of three more, eschewing the pleasures held out to her by her colleagues. But in a year she had gained an important qualification, one that would have taken her well on the road to becoming a chartered accountant. And she was only seventeen and a half.

Next she embarked on a business secretarial course – shorthand, typing and business practice. Another year, of work at the same intensive level, and she had added that qualification to the accountancy and her six excellent O-level GCSEs.

By then her stay in the hostel had come to an end, because she was no longer in the official care of the local authority. Not that "care" amounted to much in practical terms, for the social workers soon realised that she was fully capable of looking after herself, and was unlikely to go off the rails.

Her decision to go it alone had worked out well in another way. Her conscience had pricked over separation from her brother, and she wondered for some time whether she had done the right thing. But it seemed to have turned out satisfactorily.

"Are you sure you're alright here?" she asked on one of the first of her visits to him, when the foster parents left them alone. "Are they OK?"

He hardly needed to assure her. Anyone could see that he was happy in the security of a stable environment and comfortable home. By the time of his own O-levels the couple, both middle-aged and with no children of their own, were telling him they would like to adopt him and continue his education. Stella's conscience was assuaged, even quelled, and she could concentrate on her own needs and ambitions.

The YWCA hostel was comfortable enough, but she wanted somewhere unassociated with the past that she so passionately wanted to leave behind, and was pleased when she was pointed to a small flat that she could – just – afford. By now she was beginning to develop herself in ways other than educational. A natural sense of what was needed in dress and deportment if she was to "get on" was helped along by the contents of up-market women's magazines, deliberately chosen with that end in view. So before she reached her twentieth birthday she looked, and was, an assured, attractive and coolly confident young woman.

Her next step towards making her way in the world was not immediately clear, however. She scoured the local and regional newspapers, and appropriate periodicals, for jobs that would take her forward, but for some time found nothing she thought worth pursuing, especially as her mail order employers gave her another promotion.

Then the way opened via a route she had not thought of. Her mother's cousin, Rhoda, who lived with her husband at Coventry, in the Midlands, had kept in touch ever since Margaret's death. They had come to the funeral, and did their best to assure the girl that they would like to help her and her brother, Clive, but Stella, while thanking them for their kindness, was determined to pursue her own course.

Rhoda however wrote regularly over the next three years, and made efforts to see Stella and Clive when she visited her own mother, who still lived at Manchester. Stella always said she was getting along quite well, thank you, but Rhoda, who felt a degree of responsibility for her young relatives, persisted in staying in contact. And when the mother died, just as Stella was starting to think she really must move on, the funeral gave Rhoda and her husband a chance to offer practical help of a kind that would appeal to the girl.

They stayed the night at an hotel and insisted that Stella join them for a meal there, taking the opportunity of fleshing out the bones of what they already knew about her life and hopes. They had been told of her work and promotions, but were impressed when she told them, after some quizzing, of her college courses and qualifications.

"Aunt" Rhoda – Stella always called her so – said: "I don't think we need have been so worried about you, need we? I can see you're a worker, and you can stand on your own feet. Have you any idea what you want to do now?"

"I want to get on a bit, if I can. I don't want the kind of life mother had."

"Yes, your mother had it hard. I'd have liked to help, but we were so far away. And she was pretty independent, you know – I expect that's where you get it from. And your dad and Joe couldn't stand each other. Have you got something in mind? Or do you think you're best staying where you are?"

"No, I can't see much prospect there. I think I ought to be able to get something better, now."

"Yes, with those qualifications I think you should. Are you going to try?"

"I've been looking in all the papers, but I've not found anything yet that I think's worth leaving Salmail for, especially since I got my last rise."

They went on to talk of other things. But Joe was quiet for ten minutes or more, before he asked: "Are you prepared to move away from Manchester, Stella?"

"Oh, yes, anywhere, really."

"I think I might be able to put you on to somethin', our way. Would you be interested? You could stay with us – couldn't she, Mother?"

Which was how she came to meet Edward Jameson.

*****

She became the junior of three clerks handling the business, wages and other commercial accounts of Protechno, a pace-setting research and development firm founded thirty years before by a small group of engineering-based scientists after their work, which had helped win the war, but was let slip into the hands of American colleagues who had not done much of the real work but had a better eye for the business opportunities. The three Brits who were left with the dregs of the wartime efforts were however some of the unit's best technological and scientific brains. They decided that not only did their ideas have potential, they were going to try to exploit them themselves.

Two of the three had gone their separate ways by the time Stella joined the firm, but the other, Keith Parkinson, was at its head as chairman and managing director. He had seen the concern grow from its three founders plus a dogsbody clerk-secretary to one employing a hundred scientists, researchers, technicians and back-up staff, these last making up a third of the workforce by the time she arrived.

Uncle Joe's brother, George Stanley, was foreman in the fabrication shop, and only a week before the visit to Salford had been on the receiving end of comments by his own boss, bemoaning the quality of some of the administrative staff now being recruited, and had told Joe about it. The brothers correctly believed that the management would snap up a girl with Stella's obvious talents and qualifications.

She found her work more demanding than in her Salford job, but at the same time more interesting, even from the perspective of number three in the department. But as soon as she was on top of the work, she decided to go for a further qualification – a diploma in economics. She enrolled for an evening course at a local college, which as at Salford meant three nights a week in the classroom and another three evenings doing her "homework."

In the meantime, she had found herself a small flat, in the ground floor of an old Victorian house, much nearer to work then her aunt's. She was offered a more modern apartment, but the rent was almost twice as much, and Stella needed to retrench. She only kept her financial head above water by being innovative with her dress – although always maintaining an elegant and sophisticated result – doing her own hairdressing, and practising severe economy in her housekeeping. The only luxuries she allowed herself were visits to her aunt and uncle – which in fact cost her very little, because they always insisted on giving her a meal, and usually a useful present – and buying a few second hand books. She read a great deal, anything from better-quality fiction to biographies and travel books.

She spent a year in her original position at Protechno, by when she had completed the course and obtained the diploma, passing the tests with flying colours – nearly 100 per cent marks in some papers. Fixing her eyes on the future again, she made sure the success became known in the firm, which paid off when "No 2" left on becoming pregnant and getting married, and Stella was promoted to take her place with a welcome increase in salary. She was still only 21.

Another year on, and her big chance arrived. Mr Parkinson's secretary took a long leave to have a baby. Both Stella and her immediate superior asked to be considered for the temporary position, which was as much personal assistant as secretary. The MD had had his eye on her for some time, however, and it was no contest. Her appearance and carefully-nurtured cool poise, on top of her abilities, assured him. And long before the young lady she was deputising for returned, he was almost wishing she would decide not to come back. When she did, she found her nose had been put out somewhat, in her absence. Stella had made such a mark in the office that Mr Parkinson sometimes found himself referring to her in glowing terms, which did Mrs Secretary's ego no good at all and, becoming pregnant again, she decided to leave.

At the age of 25, then, Stella had become personal assistant – for her boss soon decided that a junior secretary was needed so she could devote more time to helping him in some of his own work – to a businessman and technological entrepreneur who was taking the concern he had founded to a position near the leading edge of British industry and expertise. She felt she was beginning to "get on."

As at her secondary school, Stella was not hugely popular with her fellow employees. Some of them resented her rapid rise, others her air of cool sophistication, although she had a ready smile and tried to avoid giving the impression of superiority she knew would be counter-productive. She made one or two good friends however among the clerical workforce and researchers. And on the rare occasions she had to visit the workshops, on some errand or other for Mr Parkinson, she found herself running the gauntlet of whistles and all kinds of invitation, sometimes slightly improper, to which she would respond with an unfazed smile which could be and usually was interpreted as an ironical "and the best of luck;" a unanimous view among the lads was that there were no flies on that one, mate; and advice from them to anyone who appeared to fancy his chances would run along the lines of "don't get out of your depth."

Her position made her party to all the developments at Protechno, including appointments to the more senior jobs. Which was how Edward Jameson first came to her notice – in fact she arranged his interviews and meetings with Mr Parkinson. He was head-hunted when he was on the verge of making a name for himself, despite his youth, with his forward thinking in applying computerised technology to jet units, at one of the world's biggest aero-engine firms. Even on those first encounters, Edward found himself impressed by the pretty and coolly but pleasantly efficient young woman who offered him coffee and chatted knowledgably during the few minutes he was waiting for the MD. On her part, Stella thought the new recruit was a pleasant young man, a shade foreign-looking perhaps.

A friendship with a colleague, formed before her elevation to the PA spot, furnished information that made her take more interest in him. Pauline, secretary to the director in charge of the workshop end of the operations, was something of a gossip, dissipating material that was often but not always well founded. She had a relative at the firm where Edward then was, and even before his appointment was finalised, she was adding personal details about him to the information to which Stella was already, although confidentially, a legitimate party.

"They've offered him lord knows what to stay," Pauline confided. "Goodness knows what our lot must be paying him. Not that it matters all that much to him. His family's as rich as Croesus – got a big estate, in Shropshire or somewhere."

In fact, Stella knew all about Edward's salary, and that he was not leaving the aero-engine concern for more money. His salary at Protechno would mean only a modest increase. But the information about "the big estate in Shropshire" was new and intriguing, and immediately made him more interesting to a mind still intent on "getting on in the world." It was not that she immediately began to think of him as a potential rich husband. She was not thinking of husbands at all. Still, it was interesting.

Pauline also explained the slightly foreign look. "There's what my father used to call 'a touch of the tar-brush,'" she said. "In fact it's more than a touch – his mother's West Indian, they tell me. Seems a bit odd."

Mr Jameson, as the girls of course knew him, was installed in a new office next door to the managing director's, indicating his important status. He was to have his own secretary, but she had to be someone out of the common secretarial run, someone with a scientific or technical bent, and secretaries of that type did not grow on trees, then or now. There was therefore a delay in finding her – or him – and in the meantime he was thrown more into contact with Stella and Rosemary, her "junior." Rosemary typed his letters, and Stella his technical documents, which began to give her an insight into his work, not that any degree of understanding of it came easily. Edward enjoyed the contact with her. Their relations were of a formal, Miss Hardy and Mr Jameson, kind, but from the start she usually brought his coffee or tea, rather than leave it to Rosemary, and the few words involved developed into little chats.

One day when he had been there about three months, Edward was approaching the culmination of his first big development project. Despite much of his work being done via computer, at that stage there was also much use of pencil and paper. With Mr Parkinson's agreement, Stella was recruited to help him get it into presentational form, which meant working with her in her own office, and staying after normal hours. It also meant a degree of physical proximity, which Edward could not help finding pleasurable. She soon became "Stella" to him.

Demand and pressure for the completed project mounted and to finish it meant spending most of a weekend in the office. Both normally had meals in the staff canteen, but it did not operate on Saturdays.

"Can you suggest anywhere we can get a bite to eat?" Edward asked as lunchtime approached. She led him to a nearby cafe.

They went back to the office and worked hard again for several hours. Some time after five o'clock, he said: "Stella, if we pressed on I think we could finish this tonight, but I don't think that would be a good idea. I think we're both tired – I know I am – and when you're tired you don't do a good job. You did say you'd work tomorrow, if necessary. Are you prepared to come back in the morning?"

"Yes, of course."

"Can I suggest then that we make a good early start – say half past eight. That will mean we can be sure of finishing by midday. Then I'd like to take you somewhere for a good old-fashioned Sunday lunch – or one that isn't so old-fashioned if you'd prefer. You've earned it, and a great deal more. What do you say?"

"It's very kind of you, Mr Jameson, but there's no need. I'm only doing my job."

"You know as well as I do that you've been doing far more than your job could expect of you. I'll take you home now, so I can see where you live, and I'll pick you up at 8.30 in the morning. Is there anywhere particular you'd like to go for lunch?"

"I don't know anywhere, I'm afraid, but I've heard Pauline say the Swan at Henley-in-Arden is nice, and not expensive."

"Good. I'll ring them now and see if they can accommodate us. Can you find the number?"

*****

Choosing to call it a day on Saturday and resume the job on Sunday morning was the right move. Both fresh, they had the work wrapped up before noon and were at The Swan in plenty of time for a one o'clock meal. Stella was looking her best, and plenty of eyes were on her as they took a pre-meal drink. Edward found his pulses stirring.

Like his father and most Jamesons, he had never been a woman-chaser. After Loughborough University, at work on the aero-engines and when he was racing motorcycles, there had been "moments." One or two turned into hours, nights. He even moved into one young lady's flat, and was there for best part of a week, until it became obvious he was only one of a good many who had sampled the delights of her bed and breakfast provisions, and he decided he was not hungry enough for that kind of fare.

The ruling passion of his life was his work. Nothing turned him on, even the motorcycle racing, like the idea that either sprang directly from his brain, or from what he was already doing. Academically, while at school, he was rather behind his brother Charles and sister Emily Jane, but face him with a technical problem and his inner eyes lit up. At home on the farm where they had all been born and reared, he had devised and installed improvements to many machines. A computerised system of recording milk yields and breeding records was in place before such developments had left the research establishments of the wider agricultural world.

At Loughborough, there was enough opportunity for the employment of his talent to ensure that it remained, was not atrophied by the influence of commercial necessity or personal involvements. But at Derby he found himself, as he later explained to Stella, pigeonholed into projects for which he was felt to be suited, and told to work out answers to questions asked by others, rather than given any real range for his own ideas. He came to the bike racing by the accident of fixing one of his housemates' machines, being offered an illegal ride, blowing his meagre savings on a machine of his own, and finding an amazing affinity between his brain, his throttle hand and the power unit, wheels and tyres, and the tarmac road. An open day at the Donington Park race circuit led to the racing, at which he became very successful and which helped fill some of the void created by the frustrations at work; and which led to the "moments" among the girls who flocked round the younger riders.

At work, his abilities were noticed, to such an extent that the firm's American rival was told, via the gossip-cum-espionage channels running through big scale industry, that here was a young guy to whom they ought to pay attention. The result was a trip to the west coast of the States, an offer of a job there, but with a warning that he would have to give up the racing. Edward turned down the job, but also decided he had done enough motorcycling, and resolved to try to break away from his present employment. So that when Keith Parkinson, who also had his contacts and had made inquiries, let it be known that there might be a place for him at Protechno, he was immediately receptive. Personal interviews left Parkinson convinced that this young man was exactly what he wanted to help lead his firm still further at the top of the burgeoning world of computerised research and development.

Physically, Edward was anything but most people's idea of the bespectacled, absent minded boffin. His features showed no more than a hint of his mother's West Indian origin, giving the "slightly foreign" look noticed by Stella. His hair was gently curly but fairly light in colour; his nose straight and narrow, his lips only moderately full. Blue-grey eyes needed no glasses at that stage in his life. He was almost a two-generations-later copy of his great-uncle Giles, whose Greek god-like features made him attractive to the opposite sex all through his life. He had never been as keen on sport as his brother and sister, but put a cricket bat or tennis racquet in his hand, or a ball at his feet and he could give a good account of himself. He read, not quite as avidly as his mother and grandmother, but still a great deal. Although, at least in his younger days, it was more from a wish to acquire knowledge than to entertain himself or even to expand a mind already occupied with the things that made him so valuable to the world of high level R and D. Nonetheless, his somewhat limited ventures into the world of fiction, poetry and philosophy did a great deal to stimulate that mind, to balance the practicalities and science which dominated, and help him become a rounded individual.

Whatever may have stimulated Stella's initial interest in him, his for her was in finding a girl who was utterly different from any he had previously known, even his sister. She was aeons apart from the ones who had featured in the "moments" of a few years before, and of which he realised he was ashamed even on his first contacts with her. The idea of involving a girl like Stella in hasty grapples in the back of a race van was impossible. The cool yet pleasant assurance, the air of sophistication that was so obviously a natural part of her, her ability to chat on so many subjects, were all missing from the girls he had known.

Edward did not of course know, then, that the cool poise, the sophisticated air, even the ability to converse knowledgeably were all products of her determination to hoist herself into a different sphere, the world of business success. Her position of personal assistant to Keith Parkinson, at the age of 25, may have been seen as a crowning triumph by most young women. But to her it was a staging post along the road to much bigger things. To a world where newspapers, radio and television programmes would quote: "Miss Stella Hardy, chief executive of the multi-million XYZ company."

For the moment she was just Stella who had helped him with an important project, and in the process had made him aware of her as an intelligent as well as an attractive individual. She had shown much interest in what they were doing, although never letting her questions interfere with getting the job done. It all made him want to know more about her.

While they were waiting for the call to their table, he asked as an opener: "You're happy at Protechno, Stella?"

"Oh, yes. Mr Parkinson's very good to work for."

"You came from the accounts department, didn't you?"

"Yes, I was there for three years."

"And where were you before that?"

She looked at him. She was not keen on talking too personally about herself.

"I worked for a mail order firm near Manchester."

"Had you been there long?"

"Three years. Since I left school."

"And what brought you down here?"

"I wanted a better job."

"Why this firm? It's a long way from Manchester."

"It was through Mr Stanley, George Stanley, the foreman in the fabrication shop. He's my uncle's brother."

At that point they were called to their table, and paying attention to the menu, and the subsequent food restricted the opportunity for conversation. But Edward had caught on to the reluctance to talk about herself. He was intrigued. And the feeling that he really did want to know more about this poised, attractive and capable young woman was growing. Over coffee, he started again.

"Are your parents still in Manchester?"

"No.They're both dead."

"Oh, I'm terribly sorry. Have they died recently?"

"I was 15 when my father died. My mother was a year later."

Edward sensed that behind the poise there were events, tragedies she preferred to keep to herself. Perhaps the aloof coolness was a result.

"Have you any brothers or sisters?" he asked.

"One brother. Two years younger."

"So you and he must have been left as orphans when you were both very young."

"Yes."

"Did you go to relatives?"

"No. We hadn't any that we knew of, except my Aunt Rhoda, who isn't my aunt really. She's my mother's cousin. And she was so far away."

"So what happened?"

"We were taken over by the council – social services. Clive was fostered. I stayed in council care and lived in a YWCA hostel, until I was 18."

"Was it a bad time?"

"It wasn't very good."

Edward was quite delighted with the progress he thought he was now making. Her answers were expanding, and the information reinforced the opinion he had already formed – that this young woman he was quickly growing to like and admire was of a definite and determined character. But as they finished their coffee, he had an idea, not unconnected with getting her to talk.

"Stella," he said as they walked towards his car. "How about going to have a look at Stratford? I've been meaning to ever since I've been here. Would you like to?"

She hardly knew why the suggestion prompted a little flutter of pleasure. But: "If you're sure you can spare the time, I'd love to."

"If I can't spare the time today, it's a poor show. After all, it is Sunday afternoon."

They visited the theatre, saw the tentative plans for its renewal which were to take so many years to be brought to fruition; along with dozens of other tourists, saw Shakespeare's birthplace and Anne Hathaway's cottage; had tea at "Falstaff's Ale Shoppe" and strolled along the Avon. Where Edward renewed his attack.

"What's your brother doing now?"

"He's a teacher. In his first post. His foster-parents adopted him. He's very fond of them."

"And you - how did you get the qualifications I know you have, if you left school and started work at 16?"

"I went to night school."

"In Manchester?"

"Salford, actually. And when I first came here."

"It must have been very hard work."

"Yes, I suppose it was, but ...."

"Yes?"

"I needed to .... You see ...."

And, although she did not know why she was doing it, she started to tell him how she determined to get away from the struggles and poverty of her early days. She had kept it hidden from everyone but Rhoda and Joe for nearly ten years. It was not part of the world she determined to inhabit. What it was about Edward Jameson that loosened her tongue she could not have said. As she concluded, they came to a seat, and sat down. She gazed at the softly-flowing brown water, and a mother duck with her half-grown brood of six, as they plunged their heads under the water, tails in the air.

She said: "I'd be grateful if you didn't tell anyone else about all that, Mr Jameson."

"I won't. But I don't think you should be ashamed of it. What you've achieved up to now, never mind what you can achieve in the future, is something to be proud of, surely. People like me have it easy, encouraged and helped by our parents. You've pulled yourself up by your bootstraps."

"I'm not ashamed. And it wasn't all bad. My mother gave me all the help and encouragement she could. And my brother. And she had to work terribly hard to do it.

"It's just that I wouldn't want people – Mr Parkinson for instance, or you – to think I was just looking on them as a stepping stone in my career."

"Stella, I think Mr Parkinson will realise that if he wants the best people close to him, he will get people with ambition. But don't worry, I won't say anything to anybody."

As he dropped her off at her flat, she said: "Thank you for today, Mr Jameson. I've enjoyed it very much."

"So have I. Do you think we could do something like it again? I mean the outing, not all the work."

"Please don't think you have to, just because I've put in a bit of time helping you. I enjoyed that, too."

"That's nothing to do with it, Stella. I enjoyed your company. Perhaps we could go to a theatre."

"Thank you very much. I'd love to."

"And please, call me Edward. Out of the office, anyway."

THREE

Tremors

Back in the solitude of her flat, Stella's mind began to analyse the implications of the last few hours' events. Why had she allowed Edward Jameson to worm his way into her confidence to the extent of persuading her to tell him things about her that she had never before talked of to anyone, except her "aunt" and "uncle?" Surely she was not falling for him. Surely she would not allow any man to deflect her from the life course she had set herself. When she told him she had enjoyed that day, and helping him in his work, she had told the truth. She had enjoyed it. But then she found there was another truth, and she could not avoid it. Although she had certainly found the lunch, the visit to Stratford, the whole afternoon, pleasant and rewarding, the kernel of the enjoyment was not the meal in the slightly up-market hotel, nor the Shakespearean experience, nor the walk along the Avon. She found herself having to admit that what she had enjoyed most of all was Edward's company. The straightforward truth was, she could not deny, that she simply liked being with him, at work and away from it.

Poor Stella. For nearly a decade the driving force in her life had been the urge to better herself. At 16, it had been a simple demand that she get out of the world that had made her mother a short-lived slave to need; to make enough by her own work-battered hands to keep her daughter and son fed, clothed and educated. Now, well away from that world, by no means rich but prosperous in a job where she was respected, her aims had developed into something far more. She knew she was capable of higher things. The business side of Protechno came easily to her. She had already helped point her boss, a man twice her age and with a reputation in the worlds of business, science and engineering, towards decisions which had proved the right ones. She was coming to the point where in a year or two she could be looking for a position offering greater opportunities, which she knew she was capable of exploiting.

Not once in her 25 years to date had she met a man on anything but the most casual basis who was not slottable into a pigeonhole of usefulness. Even her "uncle" and his brother stood in her regard as people who had done her a service rather than as men for whom she felt affection for their own sake. But now along came Edward Jameson to start an assault on the self-assured bastion rock of her ambition. Not that she saw him like that as she surveyed the events of the past day. She just wondered whether she had done right in talking about her early life to him, and agreeing to go out with him again. And finding herself doing so with pleasure.

"I must not allow myself to change my ideas just because I'm enjoying his company," she said to herself that evening. "I must keep him at a proper distance so that he doesn't get wrong ideas. Starting tomorrow morning."

One problem with such resolve was that she barely saw Edward next morning, or the one after. Phone calls which sent him off hot foot to consultations with colleagues in Ireland were waiting for him. His absence did the resolve no good. She found herself wondering where he was; to the extent that made her remark on it, casually she hoped, and to receive the explanation from her boss. But she still kept looking for him, and listening for his voice, which she heard only on Wednesday morning, telling Mr Parkinson about his trip.

Limited encounters during the rest of that day brought only pleasant smiles and social banalities. But on Thursday afternoon he took the opportunity of finding her on her own to ask: "There's a play at Birmingham I wouldn't mind seeing. Would you like to come, on Saturday?"

Privately chastising her stomach for its flutter, she forced herself to say: "Oh, thank you very much, Mr Jameson, but I'm afraid I can't. I've already promised to go somewhere else." And to go away congratulating herself on the barefaced lie. For about ten minutes. Next morning she very nearly decided to tell him another – that her previous engagement had fallen through and she would like to go to the theatre, if his offer was still on. But she did not. And again spent a little time, a little longer this time, congratulating herself on her ability to act sensibly.

Oh dear, Stella. You are just learning what most of us learn sometime or other. That even the best regulated brain cannot always dictate what the heart must feel, as so many, from monarchs and prime ministers down have found. Even you, Stella, who have thought yourself insulated from such emotions by your determination to succeed in the material world. You will not spend the happiest of weekends, as you fluctuate between self-congratulation and wishing you had not been quite so sensible.

Back at work, Edward said nothing more about theatre or other outings until a week later, when he asked as she brought his afternoon tea: "You enjoyed our little trip to Stratford, didn't you, Stella?"

"Yes, very much," she answered, slightly wondering.

"Well, I've just been reading Kenilworth – you know, Scott – and I'd rather like to see Kenilworth Castle. Would you like to come? On Sunday?"

"Yes, I'd like to. I've never been there."

Again she found herself looking forward to the weekend, between intervals of questioning her wisdom. But the doubts were swept aside by an enjoyable day, including tea in the castle grounds. Edward asked no more questions, instead they talked about Amy Robsart, Robert Leicester and Queen Elizabeth, and he asked whether she would like to read the book.

"It's pretty heavy going," he said. "It's taken me a month to get through it."

Again Stella wondered whether she was doing the right thing, and whether if she asked about his life and background the way he had questioned her, he would think she was pursuing him. But whatever it was made her want to do it got the better of what she thought of then as better judgement. She began with his work at Derby.

"It was alright," he said. "The idea of working on development of the best aero engines in the world was exciting, of course. But you're limited in what you can do. If you have an idea that's outside what they think you're there for, at any one time, you find it's hard to get any notice taken of it. It's how it is in a big firm – you're put in a pigeon hole and you can only get out when someone else decides they want to put you in a different pigeon hole."

"I've been told though that they thought very highly of you, and they offered you a lot of money to stay."

"Ah, yes, they did ask me to stay. Depends what you mean by 'a lot of money' though. But that was after I'd had an offer from America because one of my ideas, that I'd actually done some work on myself, was leaked to them. Not by me," he added quickly.

"So why didn't you go there – to Boeing I suppose it was?"

"I've been there. I didn't like what I saw."

"Why not?"

"I thought I'd be in exactly the same situation as here. Only God knows how many thousand miles from home. And I didn't like America, what I saw of it, although I have to admit I didn't see all that much."

Stella spotted an opening to ask him about home – and that "big estate."

"You'd miss England?"

"I would, and especially Shropshire, where I was brought up."

"In the country?"

"It's difficult not to be in the country, in Shropshire. But yes, on a farm."

That didn't sound exactly like a big estate, she thought. But perhaps he was being modest.

"So you came to Protechno?"

"Yes. Smaller pond, but bigger fish, I suppose. No, that's not the real story. Protechno may be smaller in size, but it's not in importance. And it's getting more important every year."

He could have quoted the other reason – that he was being given a free hand, within the limits of the company's activities, and perhaps even beyond. They sat, drinking their tea and gazing at the castle walls.

Stella said: "I hope you don't think this is impertinent, but .... you dragged my past out of me last week. Won't you tell me a bit more about your self? I mean – I know some of it, don't I, because I had to handle the correspondence when you came – but about your family and things."

"I might say the same as you told me – it's not very interesting. But I won't. I hope it is interesting, to you. Like yours was to me. And it's certainly not impertinent, Stella. What do you want to know?"

"Whereabouts in Shropshire?"

"It's a little village called Lyndford, not far from the Welsh border, in the south of the county. I wasn't born there, though – that was a place called Forest Farm, near Cravenbury, about ten miles away. My father and mother still own it, but they've lived at another farm, at Lyndford, for some time. Dad's just retired though, and my brother Charles has taken over the farms."

Stella smiled inwardly. That was where the "big estate" came from. Still, it sounded impressive enough, by the standards of her background.

"Have you just the one brother?"

"And a sister, Em – Emily Jane. She's between us."

"What does she do?"

"She's a doctor, in London."

"Are you very fond of your family, Mr Jameson?"

He paused a moment or two.

"We're very close. And before they died, I thought the same about my grandfather and grandmother. I'll tell you all about them, sometime, if you'll allow me. And I asked you to cut out the Mr Jameson, didn't I, when we're out of the office. Please, call me Edward."

His next invitation, issued the very next day, was to the theatre the following weekend. This time she hardly questioned the wisdom of accepting.

With an early and rather hasty dinner before they saw the play, a Birmingham repertory performance of A Doll's House, there was no opportunity for conversation of any depth. But it was an enjoyable outing, and both enjoyed the production. Stella was not a virulent feminist, but the idea that a woman's place was only in the home, let alone treated like a captive doll, clashed violently with what she wanted for herself, and raised her hackles, and she said so, when he asked her how she had liked the play, as they drove home.

"I'm with you there, all the way," he said. "We didn't see much of that attitude in our family, though. My mother was happiest when she was out working with animals. Dad tells a story about how she was helping him in the lambing shed, and he went to sleep because he was exhausted. When he woke up she had seen to the delivery of several lambs – he was so fast asleep she couldn't wake him so she just got on with the job. She was only about 18. He was so impressed he asked her to marry him!"

There was an opening there to ascertain the truth about the "touch of the tar brush," Stella realised. But while she was wondering exactly how to go about it, Edward did it for her.

"What's your view on that other prejudice – I mean colour – race - Stella?" he asked. "I have a personal reason for asking."

"I haven't thought much about it," she answered. "I've had very little to do with coloured people. There were a couple of Indian girls at school, and I worked with a West Indian boy at Salford. I don't think I've any prejudice."

"Good," he said. "Do you know why I ask? What my personal reason is?"

She pondered. Should she tell him she thought she did know? No, she decided, and said so. It was only gossip, after all.

"My mother's from the West Indies. My grandfather on that side's nearly as black as this car. Any of my children could be nearer his colour than.. ...than .... yours, for instance. Or mine. My brother's darker than me."

There it was. He was telling her he wanted her to become closer to him. Marry him and have his children, perhaps. But making sure first that she knew this particular truth.

"It doesn't make any difference to me, Edward. It would certainly not make me want to stop working for you, if that's what you mean. In fact, I already knew about your mother. At least I'd been told, but only as a bit of gossip. You know how it is in offices."

He said no more, and talk through the rest of the homeward journey was about the play, and other aspects of the arts; music from rock to classical, books, films, paintings, sculpture. Stella's tastes had developed considerably over the years.

As they rolled up outside her flat, she asked: "Would you like to come in for a cup of coffee or something, if you can put up with two grotty rooms?"

She had no fear that Edward might "try it on." And in fact the flat, although small, was anything but grotty. Stella's taste in décor and furnishing came up to the same standard as her dress, Edward noted.

As he was leaving, he caught her hand and, still holding it, he said: "I'd like to ask if we could do something tomorrow, but I've got another project I must make a start on, and it's going to take me all day. Would you have come, if I could have asked you?"

"Yes." Very calmly and matter of factly.

He pulled her towards him, gently and only by the hand he was holding. She offered no resistance, nor to the kiss planted, just as gently, on her lips. Careful though, to remain passive herself.

But Stella, careful or not – what is the meaning of the tremor that runs down to those elegantly shod toes?

*****

Whatever the meaning, the pattern continued. They usually spent at least one day of the weekend together, the occasional evening, although Edward worked long hours, starting earlier and finishing later, even after the promised secretary was at last recruited. He always kissed her as they parted, but she did her best to make it seem like a sisterly salute, sometimes turning her cheek to receive it. It must not develop into anything, she kept telling herself. The last thing she wanted to be was a housewife. But still the trembles continued. He soon asked her into his own flat, a modest apartment not much bigger than her own. It was one Sunday morning when he had planned a trip into the Cotswolds and it started to rain as they passed near to where he lived, a twenty minute drive away from their office.

"I don't think this is going to be much of a day for Broadway Tower," he said. "Shall we go to my place? I can rustle up a bit of lunch and we can decide then what we want to do."

She was quite happy with the idea. She was not in the least concerned that he might be planning anything physical – was as sure as she could be that he would not, without encouragement from her.

The furnished apartment, although bigger, was not as tastefully turned out as her own, she soon saw. But then, he was a man, and had taken it as it was.

"It's not as nice as yours," he said "but I don't intend to be here very long. I really ought to buy a house, my father says."

"So why don't you?"

"Well, I've not much time for house-hunting, have I? And I can't be sure that I'll want to stay in this area permanently."

"You mean you don't want to stay with Protechno?"

"No, I don't mean that, although you can't be sure, can you? But I think we'll grow. That might mean going to live abroad. One of the projects I'm working on now is to do with a development in Germany. I can see that it might mean having to spend time there, p'raps set up a separate company."

"A company of your own?"

"No, I wouldn't think so. More likely an offshoot of this one."

"So if Protechno grows like you think it will, you might end up in America after all, thousands of miles from Shropshire."

"I wouldn't want to live there permanently, though. I don't think I'd care for it."

Stella thought she had as clear a picture of his ambitions as she was likely to find. They were more to do with his work, the products of his brain, than of any yearning for power or wealth in themselves. She was almost ready to decide. Would she marry him if, or rather when, he asked her? She was sure he would go places, one way or another, whatever the forces that drove him. But that would only leave her as his wife, not as Stella Hardy, the Salford girl who had dragged herself up by her bootstraps to become one of Britain's leading businesswomen. Passionate love did not come into it, she thought, despite the trembles. She liked Edward very much; was happy in his company; shared most of his interests; enjoyed their conversation; had no fears arising from the prospect of sex with him. She had no great desire for sex, although she expected, in a detached kind of way, that she would enjoy that too. And in the same detached way, she had taken precautions just in case – put herself on the pill.

A trip on a canal narrowboat, theatre and cinema visits preceded another planned Cotswold trip. But this time the heavens opened as he picked her up from her own flat.

It was she who said: "Shall we go and have some lunch at Henley? Then we can decide whether it's worth going on."

And when it was still raining after they had eaten, Edward asked: "Your place or mine? There's a film we could watch on television."

The film turned out below par, and Stella readily agreed that it should be switched off. But as she brought back a new pot of tea, she said: "Edward, you said once you'd tell me all about your mother. I'd like to hear it."

He stared at the carpet.

"There are parts of it that aren't very pleasant. I was waiting to tell you until .....but perhaps I should tell you now ...."

"Not if you don't want to ...."

"I do want to. I want you to know all about me."

She knew she should stop him there and then if she was to keep up any idea of not getting in too deep. Instead she said: "Go on."

"My mother was brought over from Jamaica by a gang who wanted to make her into a prostitute, when she was 17. When she wouldn't go along with them, they beat her up and raped her. More than beat her up, one of them knifed her. I think they thought they'd killed her and they put her in the boot of a car – this was in Wolverhampton – and took her off to Shropshire. They were obviously intending to dispose of her, but she managed to get out, and my dad found her and took her into his cottage, and looked after her until he could get her to hospital."

"Oh, Edward, how awful. But she got better, obviously."

"Yes, and she went to stay with my grandmother, and eventually she married Dad, and had Charles, and Em, and me.

"Did your grandparents live at the farm where you said you were born?"

"No, that was Dad's. My grandfather helped him buy it, I think. But he was living temporarily in one of the cottages, because he'd only just bought the farm and the previous owners hadn't moved out. That time I told you about when she was helping with the lambing, she'd gone to Forest Farm with my grandparents, to help out."

She was silent. Before: "Thank you for telling me all that, Edward. Your mother and father sound nice. But they don't live at that farm now, I think you said."

"No, they moved to a big farm that had been in the family a long time, when my grandfather's brother died. Then they retired to a cottage on the farm, and my brother Charles took it over. They kept the one where I was born, though, and farmed them both."

"Was your grandfather very rich, that he could help your father buy a farm?"

"He'd been the steward on a big estate in Leicestershire, and had saved quite a lot of money, I suppose. I wouldn't have called him very rich – depends what you're comparing it with. There's a lot more to tell you, about my grandparents. Not now though."

"Why not now, Edward? I'm going to get us some dinner, if you'll risk my cooking, but there's plenty of time."

"Not now because I made up my mind a while ago that I was going to ask you something. Can you guess what it is?"

She looked straight at him. They were sitting on her settee, almost touching.

"Yes, I probably can," she said quietly, trembling so he could almost see it "but I wish you wouldn't."

"I'm going to ask you, though."

"Please don't, Edward."

"Why?"

"I don't know .... yes I do .... I don't want to hurt you ...."

"I won't ask you then. But I'll tell you. I love you and I want us to be married. I want it desperately, Stella."

She said nothing, only stared at his shoes. This was the moment she knew would come. And she did not know how to deal with it. Amazingly, she thought, I don't know what to say. She was facing the career woman's eternal dilemma, and all it entailed. One which a woman she had yet to meet, but to whom she would become close, had faced thirty years before. In Stella's case, it was the determination to succeed for herself, that she had always thought the most important feature in her life, that had to be balanced against a sincere liking for Edward and the acquired knowledge that they did and would get on well together. Perhaps even that she loved him, whatever that meant.

After a few moments, she said: "I don't think you know me well enough to want to marry me. I'm very self-centred, you know. Before my mother died, I'd made up my mind that I was not going to put up with the kind of life we all had. I meant to get on in the world. I still mean to. I think I've made a good start, but I want go a lot further, and I think I can ...."

He interrupted: "Yes, I'm sure you can ...."

"I don't want to be tied to any man by apron strings, Edward. Even to you. I believe we would be happy together, as people. I like you very much. But if I was married I'd want to be free to pursue a career of my own, as far as it took me, and it might take me away from you, sometimes. That doesn't mean I wouldn't want children. I've never thought much about it, but I think there's enough of the mother in me to believe I would.

"Do you understand what I'm saying? If I married you, it would have to be an equal partnership in every way. I won't be just a housewife. I like being with you, very much, but I think the most important person in my life is me. It's selfish, I suppose. But that's how it is."

"Stella, Stella my dear, I accept everything you say. More than accept it. I welcome it. It would make me happy to see you pursuing your own career. We would fit things together. I'd be proud of you. But I promise you I would never expect you to be just a housewife. I promise."

Another pause, before: "Have I got to tell you now?"

"You haven't got to do anything, my love. You're a free agent and always will be, whether you're married to me or not. But even if you say no, I won't go away. Not until you make it impossible to stay, by marrying someone else or something."

"I don't think I'll ever do that, Edward. I don't think I'll ever like anyone better than I like you."

Three months later, they were married. And she knew, in spite of all her struggles against it, that there had never been a happier day in her life.

Four

Michael and Kathleen

Michael Housman never really wanted to be a lawyer. In the sixth form of his Home Counties grammar school he studied English literature, history and German. His school was unusual in those pre-war days for including German in its syllabus, and Michael equally unusual in being interested. It had arisen through music, for which he also had a modest talent, as a pianist, and found himself delighted by the lieder of Schubert and some other composers. It was history however that took him to Cambridge, via a scholarship open to sons of clergy. His father was vicar of a large parish in the Chilterns. He would have liked his son to go for the church, but Michael, although he attended services as a filial duty, and became a member of the choir, was about as sceptical as was possible for a parson's son who could not and did not care to display open agnosticism. His parent, a mild and gentle man whose own religious beliefs stemmed more from convention than anything in the way of glorious revelation, wisely refrained from pushing the church option.

Before Cambridge however came the war. He was 19 when Hitler's troops marched into Poland and Neville Chamberlain "had to tell us all that we were now at war with Germany," and had left school only weeks before. Michael's Higher School Certificate studies had included modern history and current affairs and left him in no doubt about the nature of the Nazi regime. Within weeks he had enlisted in the army, in the ranks, and after basic training and being spotted as a young man with potential and a knowledge of the German language he was invited to join the budding Intelligence Corps, which although a successor to previous intelligence units, was only formally establised in June 1940, when the Germans were already in Paris. The British military establishment, apparently still with its head in the sands of the Sudan and South Africa, disliked such Johnny Foreigner tactics as intelligence and disbanded the units in peacetime.

Michael had to learn to parachute, at Ringway, now the site of Manchester Airport, but he never took part in any of the unit's activities behind enemy lines, beloved of Winston Churchill. After some intensive furtherance of his German however he showed a talent for extracting information from enemy prisoners of war, doing it by persuasive subtlety rather than physical or mental torture, neither of which was outside the range of techniques employed by some of his colleagues. Over the next two years, a series of promotions left him with the rank of sergeant. He and an officer colleague were particularly successful in obtaining data from a number of German airmen who baled out during the Battle of Britain, and he was offered, and accepted, a commission. Later he was sent to North Africa, where more promotions followed and he ended the war as a major.

Back in Britain, he took up his place at Cambridge, opting to read law, on his father's suggestion but mostly because he could not think of anything better to do. The leftward surge which was by then sweeping the country fitted well with Michael's philosophical inclinations, he voted Labour in the 1945 election, joined the party and became involved in university politics.

He got a good degree, but found he could not quite stomach the idea of being a solicitor, occupied in making wills, conveyancing property, and the like. His wartime activities had left him with the idea that he had powers of persuasion which might be useful in the field of advocacy. He was not without funds, and managed to get himself into one of the inns of court to train as a barrister.

After he was called to the bar, he found, like hundreds of his opposite numbers over the years, that advocacy was anything but an easy route to either fame or fortune. Briefs justified their name by coming briefly, and being not very rewarding financially, and by then his own resources had almost disappeared. He also found that persuading minor judges, magistrates and occasionally juries was quite different from getting information out of POWs.

It was through his work in court that he met Kathleen Jameson, when a trade union engaged him to argue the case of a young woman ambulance driver who had been dismissed on the grounds of unsuitability for the job but who was convinced that it was because of sex-based hostility from male colleagues including her supervisors. Kathleen was by then a features writer on a big Midlands evening paper and was developing a quite virulent dislike of male dominance in the professions, in fact anywhere, following the example of her suffragette aunt.

Michael lost the case, basically because not enough evidence could be marshalled to support it. The distressed young plaintiff fled the court before he had a chance to talk further with her. Needing refreshment, he sought it in the small tea-room adjoining the court, and sat down at the only vacant table. A moment later, a young woman he had briefly noticed on the Press bench joined him.

"Do you mind?" Kathleen asked.

"No, of course not."

"Actually, I followed you in here, Mr Housman. I needed to ask you how you spell your name. The clerk didn't know. Is it with an 'e' or without?"

"Without, actually."

She spelt it out. "H-O-U-S-M-A-N ? Like the poet? Any relation?"

"Yes, that's correct. But no. 'Fraid not."

"Oh, well, always worth a try. But thank you very much. And hard luck with the result in there. I'm sure she ought to have won. Those guys were thugs." And she got up to go.

He rose, politely. "Thank you. I'm sorry, I mustn't express an opinion, out here. And I don't suppose you should. You are reporting it, I suppose?"

"Yes. Wolverhampton Guardian."

"Have you got an urgent deadline? Would you join me in a cup of tea? Or something else?"

"Well, that's very kind of you. I must admit tea would be lovely. It's dry in that court, isn't it?"

When he came back, bearing a tray with pot, two cups, milk, sugar and two muffins, she said: "Really, you shouldn't. But thank you very much."

He said: "I'll be mother. How do you like it? Milk first? Sugar?"

"Not too much milk, please. No sugar."

"Just like me. Have a bun?"

"Thanks."

"So you haven't an urgent deadline?"

"No, I have to write it up tonight, but it won't get dealt with by the subs and news desk until tomorrow morning, so there's plenty of time."

"Subs?"

"Sub-editors. They check it for what we call literals, and factual errors if they think they spot any, and write headlines."

"So if a headline tomorrow says 'Feeble barrister fails to save woman's job' I can't blame you?"

"Well, you could, actually, if the sub's done his job properly, because his headline should reflect what I've written. But surely you don't think you did a bad job there, did you, Mr Housman? If you don't mind my saying so, I thought you made the most of what you'd got to work with."

"It's very kind of you to say so. But I'm a little fed up with losing cases. That's the third in a row."

There was a little silence.

She asked: "Are you based in London?"

"Yes. Grays Inn. I live in Lambeth.

"Have you worked for your paper long, Miss – oh, sorry, I don't know your name."

"Jameson, Kathleen. Yes, since I left school, almost, except for two years in the air force. I was on a weekly paper in the same group, at first."

"And do you mostly cover courts?"

"Oh, no. I'm on the features desk. I'm doing this one because it's about sex discrimination and I'm gathering material for a feature on that. I shall do a straight news report, of course, for tomorrow's paper, but it will also go into my file for possible use in my feature."

"Do you enjoy your work?"

"Very much. I wouldn't want to do anything else. I want to move on, though. I've got an interview in London next week, for a similar job on one of the big dailies."

"And you have to write your article about this case tonight, do you?"

"Yes. I shall go to the office from here, before I go home."

"So it will be quite late before you get anything to eat, apart from that muffin – which I'm sorry to say I didn't find very good."

"Oh, it won't be too late. I should be home by seven or half past. And please don't apologise for the muffin. It wasn't bad."

"Do you live with parents, or anyone?"

"No, I live alone. I have a flat just outside town."

"So you have to cook for yourself when you get in."

"Yes, unless I'm lazy and go to a cafe. Or a fish and chip shop if I'm very naughty."

"I've got a better idea than any of those. Let me buy you dinner. If you don't, I'll have to eat on my own, you'll have to do the same. Cook it, as well."

"Oh, Mr Housman, it really is kind of you. But I couldn't allow you to ….."

"Nonsense. You'll be doing me a favour – saving me from a lonely evening in a town I know nothing about. No strings – you can reward me by filling in my lamentable lack of knowledge about the workings of the Press. Tell me where your office is and I'll meet you there at whatever time you say. Then you can tell me where you want to eat. I'm sure you know somewhere."

Michael never knew quite what got into him to prompt that spur-of-the-moment invitation. He'd instantly liked her, but he liked many women who he would never have dreamed of asking to dinner on half an hour's acquaintance. He was anything but a womaniser. There had been a couple of times in the army when an ostensibly casual relationship had gone all the way, but women were not very available most of the time. Michael and his companions were too busy and too pre-occupied to spend much time pursuing them.

Kathleen too. She was a 29-year-old virgin, neither proud of it nor otherwise. There had been a few dates, but they had led to nothing further. It was not that she was unattractive, in fact the reverse. The few people who knew them both said she looked very like her grandmother, Dorothea. Not as tall, but with the same auburn hair and hazel eyes, although she had also inherited some of her mother Dolly's lovely features.

She was sent to a girls' boarding school when she was 12, leaving a year before the war broke out with good HSC results and a firm idea of what she wanted to do. "I want to write," she told her father, Charles.

"Very good, my dear. But do you think you can make a living at it? I've always understood it's difficult. You can stay at home while you get started, of course."

"Oh no, Dad. I don't want to do that. I'll never make anything of it if I'm mollycoddled. I must stand on my own feet. I'm going to be a journalist."

That was something way out of the Jameson norm, but as her brother was to say years later, more recent female recruits had brought different new blood, and genes, into the family, than the earlier ladies who had been accepted, often hand-picked, as being the right sort for sons of a long-established squirearchy. Charles himself had aided the process by marrying one of his parents' servant maids, bringing tragedy to his home but leading to a long and happy union. His sister Billie, the suffragette, likewise married a relatively poor tenant farmer's son and for a time lived in a cottage with a tin bath, and a lavatory down the garden.

Kathleen applied for jobs on newspapers round the country, was offered more than one, but as her step-niece Josie was to do 40 years later, opted for one with a good reputation for training recruits, spent two years on one of the group's weeklies before graduating to the evening paper. In 1943 she decided she ought to do more for the war effort and joined the WAAF with an assurance from her paper that a job would be there for her when she returned.

She had no qualms, no ideas that having a meal with Michael Housman would lead to more, either. She finished her writing, in an almost deserted news room, in time to call the restaurant she had decided upon and reserve a table.

*****

They both enjoyed the dinner. As he had said he would, Michael quizzed her about newspaper procedures and she answered as well as she could, failing only when he wanted to know about the broader aspects of Press finance.

"All I know is that advertising brings in much more than the cover price –

the sale price," she said. "There was a fear that commercial television would hit the ads, but it doesn't seem to have happened, to any extent. Not yet, anyway."

They were still only in the early stages of the meal, and she made a tit-for-tat decision to ask him a little about his own profession, particularly what had to be done to get into it and how the briefing system worked.

"As far as I'm concerned, it doesn't seem to be working very well," he said. "That is, I'm not getting much work. But please, don't spread that about. In fact, I shouldn't say it. It's about perception, you see. If you're busy, even if you're a lousy barrister, you get lots of work. If you need it because you're not getting it, you get less."

"Vicious circle. How do you break out?"

"Wish I knew. Just keep hope springing eternal, I suppose."

The main course arrived, and she insisted on buying wine.

"Miss Jameson, that's the first time that's happened to me – a lady buying the wine, I mean.

I hope you haven't done it because I've been giving the impression that I'm hard up."

"No, of course not," she smiled. "It's just that I believe in equality between the sexes. That's why I was covering that case today. You see, I knew a bit about it beforehand. She really was treated very badly."

"But of course you can't say anything like that in your report."

"No, I can only report what happens in court."

"What's brought you to believe in equality as strongly as I can see you do?"

"I don't know, really. I just do .... although ...."

He put down his knife and fork and looked at her.

"I've an aunt who was a suffragette. Went to prison for it. She's a lovely person, and I see quite a lot of her. I suppose she's had a bit to do with it."

"Is she still active?"

"To some extent. She's still very active. Pillar of the community, and all that. She's a bit of a dragon, but she's very well liked."

"Do you come from round here – Midlands, I mean."

"My parents live in a village called Netherton, in Leicestershire, or rather did. My father's just retired and he and Mum have moved back to his family's home, in Shropshire."

"Have you any brothers or sisters? Or a boyfriend?"

"Two brothers. No boyfriend."

"Are they in newspapers?"

"No."

He looked at her, wondering whether he was approaching things she did not want to talk about. She looked back.

"Sorry, Mr Housman. One of my brothers has just set up as an estate and land agent, at Shrewsbury. The other's just starting out as a farmer."

"Are they as happy with what they're doing as you seem to be?"

"Oh, yes, I think so. Now."

"Have they changed course or something?"

She hesitated a moment.

"Peter – the land agent – was quite happy. My father helped him set up when he came out of the air force. Alastair went off the rails a bit. He was in prison for nearly four years."

"I'm terribly sorry. I shouldn't have pried."

"It really doesn't matter. It was in all the papers."

She did not know why she had said as much as she had. It really was not fair to reveal things about Alastair, to an almost complete stranger. But there was something about this man that made her ready to.

"I don't talk about it. But I shouldn't mind, really. He's not bad, although he shouldn't have done what he did, and he knew he shouldn't. He ...."

"Leave it alone – Kathleen. It's none of my business."

There was another pause, and the waitress came to offer dessert.

"What would you like?" Michael asked.

"Oh, nothing for me, thank you."

"Or for me. Coffee though?"

"Yes please."

Silence again, before she said: "I'll tell you about Alastair – my brother."

"There's no need, you know. I just said, it's none of my business."

"He was a bomber pilot in the war and he had a friend, another pilot, who was a reckless daredevil. After the war this chap, Steve, asked Alastair to fly a plane with drugs and arms from Egypt. He didn't know about the drugs, Alastair that is, or the arms, at least not that there were so many. They were for the IRA. But the police found out and they were all arrested. The judge said he should have known it was illegal and sentenced him to five years. The others all got much longer. He came out last year and Dad helped him buy a farm. There's quite a lot more to it but that's the essence. He wasn't bad. Just a bit wild and looking for excitement. Now he wants to work hard and make something of himself. Dad reckons he's going to be OK. I think so too."

"I'm terribly sorry. It must have been awful for all of you."

"Yes, especially Mum and Dad. Visiting him in prison must have been awful for them. It was bad enough for me, and I only went once. They've stuck to him, though, and now they're helping him. He's working terribly hard."

The coffee arrived.

Michael said: "You said you're going to London for a job interview next week. Would you like to repeat this, if the timing for both of us allows it? I'd like to."

"Yes. Thank you, Mr Housman. So would I."

"Please call me Michael."

Kathleen got the job and they had the dinner, the first of many. She told him the rest of Alastair's story up to date, and all about the family, including Grandfather Alastair's suicide after Charles married the servant, her mother. And Michael told her his own history, and confided his doubts about whether he was in the right profession. But his briefs were coming somewhat more frequently, and he had one or two successes. He decided he must carry on.

Kathleen's new job went well, and within two years her paper, The Monitor, gave her a regular column of her own, which she was able to use to help the campaign for women's rights and equality. By then she and Michael were living together. It had come about quite naturally, more in the nature of consummating a friendship than a passionate love. But they both knew there would not be anyone else. They felt utterly happy and at ease with each other. Both sets of parents tut-tutted mildly, Rev and Mrs Housman rather less mildly than Charles and Dolly, but were assured that they would get round to marriage "soon," and did. But although they never took active precautions, it was seven years before the advent of their first and only child, Jonathan. They meant to have another, but it never happened.

Jonathan was a troublesome baby, succumbing to all the normal early years ailments plus one or two less usual, and Mum and Dad sometimes wondered about his future. But by the time he was through toddler stage and ready for school he had left them behind. He went to a local infants' school at Lambeth, then to the same establishment's junior section. Neither Michael nor Kathleen, who had both received upper-spectrum educations, were in favour of fee-paying establishments, and felt they could make up for any shortcomings in the schools' provisions.

Michael was by then well established in local Labour Party activities and, encouraged by Kathleen, put himself forward as a potential parliamentary candidate. He was adopted for the constituency in which his father's parish was located, with no hope of success for if ever there was a true blue area, it was the rural Chilterns. He managed however to reduce the Tory majority by three thousand, thereby attracting notice in the party ranks and being tagged as a potential winner in more favourable surroundings. The result was adoption for a South London marginal, which he failed to secure by a narrow margin in the 1964 election which left Harold Wilson struggling to govern with a tiny majority. The inevitable re-run two years later brought the seat to Michael and a majority of almost 100 for Labour, in the Commons.

He held on to the seat for nearly 30 years, winning even in 1979 when Margaret Thatcher came to power, and more remarkably against her Tory landslide four years later. He did it by the strength and likeable nature of his personality, and his consistent record of hard work for all in the constituency, whether or not they were Labour voters. Although he was also well-liked and respected within the parliamentary party, and chaired more than one committee at various intervals, he was never a candidate for ministerial office. Leaders and Michael himself knew he was not a man to make a splash on TV channels, although physically he was quite acceptable at five foot ten, with no paunch, even into his sixties, abundant slightly curly hair, wide-apart grey eyes, and a ready smile.

His undoing, if it could be so called, came when the party, under Michael Foot and Tony Benn, lurched leftward in the belief that such a policy was the only way to counter the virulent anti-union, anti-paternalism, anti-European attitudes and what they saw as every-man-for-himself philosophy of the iron lady. Michael, who was not a virulent anything, liked Benn personally but not his branch of Labour politics, and thought Foot an intellectual clown, whose ideas were far too big for any pragmatic or even political belly. He joined the middle-of-the road group which broke away to form the SDP.

"I'm afraid I've consigned myself to the wilderness," he told Kathleen when he confirmed that he had agreed to join the new party and stand under its banner at the next election. And he had. Leaving Labour for a wishy-washy group, neither one thing nor the other as they saw it, was too much for most of even the most personally loyal of his constituents, and Michael's political career ended with nearly losing his deposit.

He accepted the situation philosophically. He had made sure of good financial provisions for old age, and carried on working to help get the new party off the ground until it all culminated in the merger with the Liberals in 1988. He was offered a place on the list of possible parliamentary candidates but decided he was too long in the tooth, at 69, to start out in that direction, and in any case bright new youngsters were emerging who would serve the cause better and for longer.

Kathleen, by now quite famous for her newspaper columns and television and radio appearances, had also invested wisely, and was still earning substantially. But they were soon to encounter a development which changed their lives completely.

Jonathan had gone to London University for a degree in anthropology, where he met a girl from the Hebrides, Catriona McArthur, studying the same subject. She was a fiesty little redhead from the tiny island of Vatersay, where her father wrested a living of sorts as a crofter, and offering accommodation to tourists. At that time Vatersay had no physical connection with any other land, although a causeway to neighbouring Barra was planned and built, soon after. She went to the ten-pupil island school. Then, exceptionally bright, to a secondary school far away on the Scottish mainland, going so far because she could stay with her mother's sister. Her mother developed a brain tumour during her years there, and died when Catriona was only 18. She had seen her only once since leaving the island . She said it was because her parents' finances were stretched to breaking point simply by having to pay for her keep and school expenses, making costly trips home impossible, but Michael and Kathleen would eventually learn that that was less than the whole story. Her father and her aunt kept the dreadful news from her for as long as they could but in any case she was not a girl to allow family circumstances, even tragedies, to divert her from her chosen course. Her results in her "Highers" would have taken her to almost any university in the world. Her father, who only saw her at her mother's funeral, would have liked her to go to Edinburgh, but Catriona had by then discovered an interest in people who were even poorer than her parents, and was told that London was the place to further it. She was by then so far removed from meaningful contact with her father, who was not even convinced that anthropology was a career worth pursuing, even less that it should be pursued in far away London, that his opinion was hardly considered.

Almost from the day she met him – the day she joined her college – she loved Jon with all the considerable energy pervading her five-foot frame, and developed multi-faceted plans for the future – reform the world for poor people, have a big family, write best-selling anthropological books, and bring the best out of a more sedately-paced Jon, all at the same time. Both stayed on for Masters and PhDs, but true to Catriona's nature and philosophy, fitted it in with getting married and producing two children; Edwina who was born before they had barely completed their doctorate studies, and got jobs with the university's anthropological unit; and Christopher two years later. Financially, it was a hand-to-mouth existence, but they never asked Michael and Kathleen for help, although it was provided, usually in kind.

"I hope these jobs mean you can get yourselves on a firmer footing," Kathleen told them good naturedly as she drooled over the new baby. "I don't suppose you'll be able to stay on the campus for ever. They'll probably want you to go abroad, to somewhere where there's no child care or decent health provision."

"Yes, well, we wanted to talk to you about that," Jonathan said. "They want us to go to Bangladesh for two years." Which was a slight misstatement. He and Catriona, she setting the pace, had volunteered and managed to convince their chiefs, who were reluctant to agree to sending out a couple who had young children.

"Good lord," Michael said. "And what about them?" Meaning the children, three-month-old Christopher and Edwina aged two and a bit.

"We're taking Chris with us. Cat's still feeding him, as you know, and we think it's the only way. We've cleared it with the department."

"And Edwina?"

"We thought perhaps we might leave her here."

"You mean – with us?"

"Yes. We thought with you retiring it might work out rather well – give you something to do and be good for her. You'd start her education off on the right lines."

Michael and Kathleen looked at each other, then at Jonathan. Catriona, who had worked it all out, wisely remained quiet. But of course, they were persuaded, did not really argue. Kathleen privately resolved to wind down her work, and accepted her daughter-in-law's view that no harm would come to Christopher as long as he was breast-fed, with which she meant to carry on as long as she could – for most of their time away, she said.

The potential situation appealed to Michael's sense of humour. "Good lord," he said. "You'll have him asking for it. I can just imagine it. Mummy – titty time." Catriona only laughed. Jonathan blushed and Kathleen said: "Michael!"

Five

The Twins

Josie and Jeanne – Jeannie within the Margerrison family – were always close. They were not identical twins, although born within a few minutes of each other, and they did not look more alike than many non-twin sisters. Nor did they have that telepathic power of unspoken communication common to some twins, although their thoughts often ran on such parallel lines that many people thought they had. But as far back as Angela could remember they spent as much time as possible with each other. They never quarrelled, rarely squabbled even. Once, Angela admitted to her husband, Bill that she found it slightly worrying that they wanted to be together quite so much, even when they were almost grown up. Was it quite natural, she asked – meaning, she had to admit to herself in a mood of critical self-analysis later, was there a lesbian element in it. Bill laughed and reminded her that they had been pretty close when they were cooped up in her tummy for nine months.

The girls shared a bed until they went to university, and even then when they returned for vacations. Years later, Angela would laugh in turn as she recalled an incident when the two were about to go to secondary school. She and Bill thought it was time they had a room each. Theirs was a big house meaning they were able to prepare the rooms in advance, each complete with all new furniture from "three quarter" size beds to work desks ready for the next stage in their lives, and one Saturday night the two were packed off to them, about nine-o'clock. An hour later Bill went to check, found "Josie's room" and bed empty and both of them sound asleep in "Jeannie's". Furniture removal was the order of next day and that was how it stayed for the next seven or eight years. Josie said: "I just couldn't sleep, Mum." She'd gone out to consult Jeannie, met her on the landing!

It must not be made to look however as though they could not bear to be parted at all. Different aptitudes developed, in study and sport, taking them down different routes. Jeannie was especially good at cricket, for which their school was noted throughout London and the South East, while Josie played netball and hockey, captaining teams as their mother had at the same school. At work, both were good at the basic subjects, English and maths, but in the specialisms Jeannie went for the sciences, Josie concentrated on history, world history in particular. They had some individual friends, but as soon as lessons or games were over, it was each other they made the beeline for.

Both won places at Cambridge, at different colleges, which took them apart more than at any previous time in their lives. They enjoyed university life, taking advantage of all it had to offer, working hard, very hard by undergraduate standards, making more friends, but were never happier than when they returned home, reverting to sharing a bed, which Angela had replaced with a larger one. And in the vacations, they tasted the delights of holidays without their parents, climbing in the Cuillins, canoeing in North Wales, walking on Dartmoor and the Cairngorms, almost always just the two of them.

The second year was when the first tragedy of their lives hit them. Bill died from a massive heart attack, at the desk which was then the centre of his laboratory – he was a research scientist. They were devastated. All their lives, they had had a special relationship with their father. He seemed to know what they were feeling and thinking, without being told; had that telepathic understanding they did not quite possess. What that meant for events after he died nobody could say, although Jeannie once asked her mother: "Was he trying to tell me something from beyond the grave?"

When Angela phoned them with the dreadful news, they dashed home and said they were not going back. Their mother and Mrs Davies, their housekeeper of whom all were more than fond, told them not to be so silly. They had to go on and make something of their lives for his sake, if for no other reason.

Jeannie stayed on for an MSc after getting her first class BSc, and in its course met and quickly fell in love with Simon, who was doing a PhD in veterinary science. She got a job in the university's astro-physics department, he in the well-known and sometimes controversial veterinary research laboratories, and they moved in together. In 1985, rather staid and conservative families like theirs had not reached the stage when couples in love, or who thought they were, set up house as almost the first step in the development of their relationship. It was not like that with them, but Jeannie wondered what her mother would say.

"She asked me whether I 'thought it was alright'," Josie told Angela later.

"And what did you tell her?" their mother asked, no doubt a little miffed at being passed over.

"I said it was alright as long as it was for keeps."

Josie took her first class BA into journalism, the field she had always meant to aim for. She had no trouble finding a job, was offered one on a national daily, but opted instead for a big regional, the Birmingham Herald, which she was told had possibly the best training scheme in the country. She stayed there for three years, until she was 24, and decided she must move on. Fleet Street, which was then still the centre of the newspaper world, although about to be ousted by Wapping and Canary Wharf, was the obvious target and she soon had a job with the Daily Courier. But it did not take her long to realise that the Courier was not a paper where she could be happy.

"I won't be there very long," she told Jeannie. "I don't like their approach. The writing looks balanced and moderate but the stories are often slanted to suit their politics."

She told her sister and Simon of one particular item that had upset her, being personally involved in it. An official government report on how the defence industry had performed during the previous year showed that all delivery targets had been met, except one – a specific type of ammunition had been a week late due to a union strike. Not the most significant news item there had ever been. Josie was given the story to write by the deputy news editor, who had ringed round the paragraph about the union action and told her: "That's the intro, kid." She went away, did a quick scan of the report, tried to contact the manufacturer and the union involved, and was told they would call her back within an hour, which was perfectly satisfactory for her, as she would then have plenty of time to write the story before her deadline. Before the hour was up however the news desk man called her over and asked where the story was. She told him what was happening. He said: "For Christ's sake, Margerrison, get your brain into gear. The story's plain enough – the union fucked it up. I want your copy in half an hour." She wrote as her opening paragraph: "Union action which delayed production and delivery of ammuntion marred the defence industry's fine 1985 record in producing arms and equipment for the forces, a Government report has revealed." It was changed to: "Strike action prevented vital ammunition reaching the army by the date it was due, etc etc" and appeared under an inside page lead story headline: "Union action delays vital military equipment."

Simon asked: "And is that how they speak to you?"

"Well, no, not normally. I think Gerry (the deputy news editor) was laying it on a bit to impress a new kid from the sticks. And he wanted to make it clear what sort of line should be taken when a union was involved. If there was a chance of giving them a bashing, we should take it."

Jeannie said: "If anyone spoke to me like that, at work, I'd be through the door. It's disgraceful."

"Yes, well, that's one of the reasons I say I won't be there very long. But it's all good experience. And they're careful not to print anything that's actually untrue. They don't go much for the salacious stuff, either – you know, lurid sex stories and so on. I expect that's why so many people think it's a sober, middle-of-the-road paper, and believe every word they read."

"So what do you think you'll do?"

"Oh, I'll stick it for a year or two. As I said, it's good experience. But I think I'll try to get into broadcasting afterwards."

"Yes, I think you'd be good at that," Simon said.

Josie liked Simon. He was like their father, in many ways. Quiet, and kind. He even resembled Bill physically – tall and thin, wore rather old-fashioned glasses, behind which gleamed quite similar bright blue eyes.

Angela also immediately liked him. But, not yet quite convinced that her daughters could look after themselves without her own guiding hand, and now without Bill's balancing influence, she was worried, when Jeannie and Simon first got together, that the green-eyed monster might rear his head and come between the girls. Because Jeannie was about to be married and Josie still did not have a boyfriend. It was nothing like that. Josie was delighted that her sister was happy. Jeannie was still the person she felt closest to, and she visited often, first in their flat in Cambridge, then in the house they bought in Saffron Walden, just over the county border in Essex.

She stayed with the Courier for three years before taking the plunge of applying to the BBC for one of a number of jobs resulting from a regional expansion programme, and getting it, as a reporter and researcher based at Birmingham. She replied with a neutral smile when Gerry the deputy news editor quipped as he bade her a good-humoured goodbye: "Joining the lefties then, eh, kid." He and her other colleagues genuinely wished her well, however. In her time with them, she had shown herself to be both competent and likeable.

She enjoyed her new work from the start, mostly in radio, but with some television. She rented a cottage in the beautiful little Worcestershire town of Bewdley, on the River Severn, enjoyed furnishing and equipping it, joined a tennis club and played as often as she could. At Cambridge, she had actually made the full university hockey squad, played in the teams a few times; which when it was discovered by one of the girls with whom she played tennis, led to an urgent invitation to join the local club, ready for the coming season. They had not previously had the opportunity of recruiting someone they saw as approaching international standard. All of which opened up a pleasant-enough social scene, which she enjoyed, along with her work. She was however beginning to feel that her life was not quite complete. It was nothing remotely like jealousy. She was truly happy for her sister. But there was a void, which was at least partly the result, she eventually accepted, of seeing Jeannie so happy and fulfilled. And which, although she would never have agreed if someone had suggested it, left her vulnerable to what was about to happen.

*****

Not long after Josie's move to the BBC, and Angela's semi-retirement to take up a part-time consultancy at a Birmingham hospital, she helped her mother find and move into her new house, The Old Mill at Clee Marton in the Clee Hills, in Shropshire, a dozen miles from Bewdley.

Angela enjoyed her new home, even though she was alone in it most of the time. Josie visited regularly, Jeannie and Simon as often as they could, and she quite liked the drive to Birmingham, in her slightly battered old Citroen Dyane, which had always amused the girls. It was however the car's inevitable decline into incurable unreliability, forcing purchase of a new one, that led dramatically to a new phase in Josie's life.

After her clinic, Angela was walking to the garage where her new car was having its first service when she met an old student of hers, Emily Jane Jameson, recently qualified as a doctor and moving towards the same branch of research which had brought her professorship. Emily Jane was on the way, with her brother and his wife, to see their father, who was lying in the hospital in a coma, the result of the road accident in which his wife was killed. Alastair Jameson had been Angela's first love, when she was a sixth-former at the school her daughters eventually went to. And in spite of being married, and very happily, to Bill, a deep feeling for that first love – they only learned later how deep – had never left her. She had actually seen him, and his wife, the day before the fatal accident, although they had not seen her. She knew nothing about the crash, nor that he was in "her" hospital. But from then on she spent as much time as she could with him, with the full approval of his own family after Edward, his younger son, wormed out of her what had happened between them, nearly 40 years before.

Three weeks later, when Alastair was still deep in the coma, Josie, Jeannie and Simon were at The Mill on a Saturday afternoon when the phone rang and Josie answered it. A young man's voice said: "Angela?"

She said "No, I'll get her. Who's calling?"

"It's Edward, Edward Jameson – but it doesn't matter if she's busy."

"No, it's alright. I'll get her," and fetched her mother to the phone. Afterwards Josie teased her: "Whoever is Edward, Mum? He sounds terribly young. You haven't got yourself a toyboy, have you?"

Angela managed to laugh at the idea, although laughter was the last thing entering her emotions when there was a mention of anything involving Alastair.

"You needn't get jealous," she said. "It's Emily Jane Jameson's brother. You know, the girl I told you about. And he's married, quite recently. He's coming round – he's got things to tell me. I've told him you're here. He'll be pleased to meet you. I've asked him to stay for dinner – his wife's out with a girl friend and won't be back until quite late."

"How do you know him, Mum?"

She hesitated.

"His father's in the Royal. He's very badly hurt – in a coma, from an accident. His wife was killed." The girls could see she was upset.

"Oh, Mum, how awful. Do they think he'll get better?"

"There's a good chance, they say. But they don't really know." She hesitated again, then added: "I knew him, a very long time ago, when I was at school."

She went into the kitchen, busied herself there. But she kept watching the gravel road leading to the house, because she wanted to warn Edward that her daughters did not know about her old connection with his father, and when he drew up she went out to meet him, learn gratefully that doctors seemed to think there were signs of improvement in his father, and give him the warning. She ushered him in and introduced him

Josie had always been sceptical about the concept of love at first sight. She'd met many men, often liked them. One or two she'd thought perhaps it might be good to get to know better. But she was too preoccupied with Josie Margerrison, or too busy, or too keen to get back to what she and Jeannie were planning, to allow such possibilities to materialise. Her single sexual experience had left her wondering what it was they all raved about. She always thought of it to herself as dreary, and never told anyone about it, even Jeannie.

So when Edward shook her hand, smiled easily in his ready way, there was no lightning flash, her knees did not buckle, nor the room spin round. But she knew: that this was the man who could make any previous ideas about relationships with the other sex fly out of the window. The scepticism could exist no more.

Angela started to ask him about his wife, and the conversation revealed that he and Stella worked together, and led to questions about their work. He led his firm's development section and she was personal assistant to the managing director. Josie heard it almost in a trance.

It should have stopped there, she knew, should have ended almost before it had begun. He was recently married, not available in any way. Feelings for him should not and could not develop. Perhaps if she had not seen him again, or not for a long time, that is what would have happened. But, the situation being what it was, her mother now in frequent contact with the Jamesons, it was almost inevitable that she would meet him again.

It happened only three days later. She was sent to interview a local mother who with her baby had narrowly escaped death in a railway mishap, an incident that was inspiring concern about some aspects of rail safety. Mother and child were in the hospital where Angela had her clinic, and they met, purely by accident, in the League of Friends teashop after she had completed work, filed her story. They were sitting having tea and in Josie's case a roll, greatly needed for she'd had nothing since breakfast, when he walked along the adjoining open corridor, saw Angela, and joined them.

"Hello, Angela." And to Josie: "Hello."

"Are you going to see Dad?" he asked her mother.

"Yes, I was about to go, when I met Josie. She's been working."

He looked enquiringly at her, and she told him what she had been doing. But it was inevitable. Seeing him again sent the feelings she knew she must not have rocketing round her being.

Although she was anxious to go to Alastair, with whom Edward had already spent an hour, Angela did not want to leave the two of them together, for unknown to either, she and Jeannie had both divined, at The Mill, that "something" was happening.

It was after Josie left. Jeannie and Simon were staying the night. When Edward had also gone, Jeannie went quiet and her mother said to her: "What's the matter, love? Are you not very well?"

"I'm alright."

But after Simon had preceded her to bed, she said: "Did you see?"

"See what?"

"Josie. She was all over him, or she'd have liked to be."

It was Angela's turn to go quiet. But in the end she said: "Yes. I thought perhaps I was wrong. But if you saw it as well ......"

"I think Simon spotted it, too. Oh, Mum, what are we going to do? She mustn't. We've got to 'stop it. The stupid ..... Oh, Mum ...."

Simon told his mother-in-law that she cried, most of the night.

In the hospital tea room, Angela would have liked to take Edward off right away, to see his father. But he had quickly fetched himself a cup of tea, asked them whether they would like another. Josie groped her way through twenty minutes of conversation before Edward and Angela left for the wards. But new damage had been done.

She told herself not to be stupid. This could not be. Even if he was attracted to her – and there had been absolutely no sign of that, how could there be if he was happily married as her mother said – she must not allow herself to become embroiled and wreck their lives. She must put him out of her mind. But that was more easily said then done. He was there. Through succeeding days she found he would not go. She could not sleep – lay awake until three or four o'clock, and then only dropped off fitfully. Colleagues asked what was the matter.

Assignments brought temporary relief. She found she could leave the thoughts of him behind when the job demanded she put her brain, and summon energy, to deal with them. And after a few days things started to improve. He did not invade her consciousness so consistently. She found she was not dreading the evenings so much, felt more normal, slept better.

Then fate, in the person of a producer, Sandy McGrail, intervened to send her back to Square One. He was organising a TV series on important British technical and economic developments and had been told a firm called Protechno, based at Coventry, was one he should feature. They were doing world-leading work in advanced technology. Josie was told to approach them and suss out the prospects, with the help of a technical expert, and to speak first to a Miss Hardy, the managing director's personal assistant. Miss Hardy told her she was sure the firm would like to be featured in a television programme, as long as it could have a proper input into the content. She would put it to her principal, Keith Parkinson and, if he agreed, arrange a meeting. Three days later, she called back.

"I'm sorry I've been so long getting back to you, Miss Margerrison. One of the people we think you ought to talk to, initially, has been out of the country. When do you want to come?"

They made arrangements for the beginning of the next week, and Sandy, Jonathan Paxley who fronted and presented the series, technology specialist Mike Donovan, a cameraman and Josie were at the Protechno premises at 9.30. They were met by Miss Hardy, an attractive, well groomed, coolly assured and, Josie thought, hard-as-nails young woman in her middle twenties. She conducted them to Mr Parkinson's office, where he and two other men greeted them.

This time the knees did threaten to give way. One of the men was Edward Jameson. "Miss Hardy" was his wife.

*****

The fact that she was on a job did little to help, this time. How could it, when one of the subjects of her task was him – and, it soon became clear, even through the fug that now passed for thinking powers, that he was probably the most important single factor in the whole operation.

Miss Hardy, or Mrs Jameson, Stella, introduced them to Keith Parkinson and the others – Edward and the works manager who oversaw any manufacturing that had to be done.

Edward said: "Miss Margerrison and I don't need introductions, actually. I met her, and her sister, through her mother, quite recently. How are you, Josie?"

She managed: "I'm very well, thank you. I didn't realise this was the firm you were talking about when you told us about your work."

After Sandy had outlined the basis of the series and Mr Parkinson told them the history of the firm, Edward explained the direction it was now taking, under his leadership, it appeared. Josie found it impossible to keep her mind on the subject. Not that it was on anything else in particular, even Edward. But she took shorthand notes, which afterwards she found made sense, although at the time she hardly knew what she was writing – must have been on some kind of stenographic auto-pilot, she thought later. She even asked questions, and noted the answers, which again made sense when she deciphered the notes.

Stella had laid on lunch in the canteen, nothing special, just what was available to the staff, presented a little specially, perhaps. She sat Josie next to Edward, who told her he'd seen her mother again, the day before, at the hospital. His father's condition remained the same.

Back at the office, she managed to get her brain into working gear as the team discussed how the programme was to be shaped. Sandy said it was obvious that young Jameson was a key figure and one of Josie's tasks should be to try to bring out what made him tick so he could be central to the programme, help bring a human angle to the science and technology.

That was when she knew that for her the Protechno project had hit the red light. To get closer to Edward, even in the way Sandy meant, was a no go. She was already too emotionally involved to keep a clear head in dealing with him. She should not and probably could not do it. And in any case she must not embark on something that took her into more contact with him. She must tell Sandy and her bosses that she could not handle this project.

She almost decided to do it there and then. But Sandy had to dash off even before their discussions had finished. She made an excuse to go home early, but instead of going straight to Bewdley wandered off into the country, trying to get herself into a state of mind where she could work out the implications. When she found herself within a few miles of home, she left the car and walked along the Severn. The thought even struck her that it would be better if she drowned herself. But a Canadian canoe paddling up stream drove the thought away almost before it was formed. The paddlers were two teenage girls, twins by the look of them, smiling a greeting at her. They made her think of Jeannie, and then of her mother. A decrepit iron seat invited her, and she sat for nearly an hour, but before she made her way back to the car she had reached what she was sure were unavoidable conclusions. Not only about the projected programme, but about staying with the BBC, at least in her present situation, which would inevitably bring her into contact with him. Their third meeting had made her see that however hard she tried, if she saw him again and again she would not be able to stop those feelings, already the most potent emotion she had ever encountered, taking over and bringing disaster, to her life if no-one else's. She had just about arrived at a definite decision, that she must get right away from the Midlands, one way or another; when she reached her house. She desultorily cut herself a slice of bread, spread it with butter and ate it as she flopped into a chair.

She was sitting, smoking – she had started again, out of the office, where it was banned – and trying to decide whether she should ask for a move away from the Midlands, or leave the BBC altogether, when Angela knocked on the door and walked in.

Six

Mother and Daughter: *Angela*

Neither of the girls knew, then, about the depth of my connection with Edward's father. Ed knew – he divined that there was or had been some kind of link between us when I first met him and his sister and they told me about the accident. He got the whole story out of me later when he saw me with Alastair in the hospital. I sometimes found it difficult to hide my emotions.

I suppose the closeness there had always been between my two daughters was why this horrible business with Edward had such an effect on Jeannie. I could certainly understand it, because of what had happened to my own sister Josie when she shacked up, I suppose you would call it, with a reckless and almost amoral ex-RAF pilot, Alastair's supposed friend. I was distressed beyond words, and if Alastair had not come along and "rescued" both me and my sister I don't know what would have happened to either of us. With Jeannie all these years later it was different, but worse in a way. She became angry with her sister. I was afraid it might bring a real rift between them.

My own anguish was just as great, perhaps greater, and with reason. Consider the facts. Edward might well have been, should have been, my own son, mine and Alastair's. He was married, apparently happily, and in the few weeks I'd known him, I'd grown fond of him. He would become my son in fact, almost, if Alastair recovered as I and his family so desperately hoped, and we came together again.

If they had met, by accident or through my link with his father, and fallen in love, when Edward was free, before he knew Stella, it would have been different, wonderful. Nothing could have made me happier. There would have been no reason why they should not have married, and had our grandchildren, mine and his, linked to us by a double bond. But this!

"Hello," I said, trying to sound normal.

"Oh, hello, Mum."

"What's the matter, love? Are you not well?"

"Oh, nothing. I'm alright."

"I don't think you are. Shall I make a cup of tea"

"No, you sit down. I'll do it."

She went into the kitchen. I heard a kettle being filled, cups or mugs being moved. But then I thought I heard sobs, and went to look. She was leaning on the worktop, her head on her arms, her whole body shaking . I put my arms round her, my head against hers.

"Come and sit down, love. Tell me about it. Tell Mum."

Still crying, she allowed me to lead her into the living room, and sit her down on the settee. I said: "I'll make the tea."

I found milk and a tray and took it back to her, putting the tray on a small table. I gave it a few moments, more to allow her a little time than for the brew's sake, before I poured.

Another minute or two of silence, and I asked her: "Won't you drink your tea, Josie? Don't let it go cold."

She started to sip. I did the same, and when she put down the cup, I said: "Please tell me, darling. What is it? What's the matter? Is it – Edward?"

Another outbreak of sobs and tears was the only response, until: "I'm sorry, Mum, I'm sorry .... I can't help it .... I know it's wrong ....."

I let her cry.

"What's happened, darling?"

"Nothing .... It's just that I feel so awful ...."

After a while, I asked: "Does he ..... know you feel like that?"

She was silent, except for the sobs.

"Does he?"

"No .... oh, I don't know. I don't want him to."

"He's very attached to his wife, you know."

"Yes. I've met her. She seems .... she's very attractive...."

"When did you meet her?"

"We're doing a television programme about their firm. I didn't know it was him until we went there today.... oh, Mum.... but I can't do it .... I shall have to tell them I can't ...."

"What's your part in it?"

"Oh, I was just researching it. But Sandy told me he was going to be the main figure in it and he wanted me to see him again and .... I mustn't do it .... I can't .... I think I shall have to leave."

We sat without saying anything. After a while I said: "I don't think you need to do that, Josie. It will pass, you know." As if I did not know better.

"Perhaps it will. But not if I keep on seeing him."

I said nothing. My mind went back 40 years, then leaped to this afternoon, and Alastair.

I said: "I knew, you know. I saw, the other Saturday. And Jeannie did. She's terribly upset. And so would I be, if it ...."

"It won't. I won't let it ...." But she started to cry again.

I thought: "Thank goodness she can talk to me." And I debated quickly with myself whether I ought to tell her how terrible it was for me, and why. I decided I should.

"Darling," I said when the tears subsided somewhat. "I want to tell you something that I hope will help you stick with that. It might make it easier."

She looked at me.

"Is it something about... Edward?"

"It affects him. But it's really more about me. And his father."

She stared.

"When I was a young girl, still at school, I met Alastair, and we fell in love. I loved him more than I can say, Josie, and he loved me. But something terrible happened to him, and he told me I must not have anything more to do with him. I didn't want to go along with that, but he made me, and I never saw him again until I came up here. Forty years, nearly. I saw him by accident the day before the crash when his wife was killed. He's in a coma and they don't know whether he'll recover. But I still love him, Josie. He loved Debra, Edward's mother, and I loved Dad. I'm sure you know that. It brought me my two lovely daughters. But you see, Edward might almost be my son. If you and he had met before he knew Stella, and fallen in love, and married, it would have been wonderful. But the idea of you coming between him and his wife.... do you see.... ?"

The tears flowed again, but more gently now. "Yes, Mum. I see. I really do see. It won't happen, I promise. It wouldn't have happened anyway. But thanks for telling me."

We were both quiet for a moment or two. Then she asked: "What was the terrible thing that happened?"

"He went to prison. He'd helped an old comrade from the RAF smuggle arms and drugs and it was found out. He didn't know about the drugs and not much about the guns, which it turned out were for the IRA, but he was arrested and sent to prison. He was there for nearly four years. He said it would ruin my career if it was known I had a boy friend in prison, and made me promise to go away and forget about him. It was an awful time for me, and worse for him, I expect. But he wasn't bad, Josie. He wasn't. He was just at a loose end, and looking for excitement."

"You didn't think he just wanted to get rid of you because he was fed up with you?"

"Oh, Josie, no, no. And in fact I soon began to see that he was right. And so much of it has worked out for good. I married Dad and had you two, and I think I've done work that has helped a lot of people. And he rescued Debra from an evil gang, and married her – and one of their children is going into my kind of work.

"And there was something else. I don't know whether I should tell you about it, but I will. You mustn't ever mention it to her though – your Aunt Josie, I mean. It's about her.

"She did something silly just before I met him. She was tremendously upset because the boy she was going to marry was killed in the war and she went off with Steve, the man who led him – Alastair – into the smuggling. It was one of those rebound things, I suppose. Your grandparents were both away and I felt terrible about it and I knew it would have been even worse for them. I was only 17. But Alastair managed to get her back home, and they never knew about it. He was so good, Josie."

I'd taken hold of her hand. I kept hold of it and said a little more, that I thought was important indeed. My two girls must never quarrel, not really quarrel, if I could help it.

"Please, Josie, talk to Jeannie about this. If it had gone the way I was afraid of I don't know what would have happened between you. She might never have forgiven you. And I don't know how I could have borne that."

"Does she know about – what you've just told me?"

"No. Edward knows. He got it out of me one day last week. But nobody else, yet. I don't think he'll have told Stella, even. I'll tell Jeannie, before you see her. In fact I might go over there tomorrow."

Which I did, after my clinic in the morning and spending an hour with Alastair in the afternoon. Both she and Simon were at home in the evening. I told both of them all that had happened, about Alastair and me, Aunt Josie, everything, and emphasised how happy their father and I had been.

"You'll be kind to her, won't you," I begged Jeannie. "She's going to have a hard time. She says she's going to leave the BBC, because she feels she's let them down by allowing her own emotions to interfere with the job. I've told her to do nothing of the sort, but I'm not sure that I'm right. Psychologically a change of surroundings, and people, might be the best thing for her."

"I'll see her this weekend," she promised. And Simon said as he showed me to my car: "Don't worry, Angela. It'll be alright."

I was sure it would, between the two girls. But I was a long way from sure it would be alright for Josie herself.

*****

As I have already said, I had become fond of Edward, and my anxieties over Josie extended to him. I wondered how much, if any, he had divined, or guessed, about her feelings. And whether there just a little reciprocation, perhaps? I would like to be sure there was not.

We were both with Alastair one afternoon three or four days after the events I have just described, when Charles, Maria and Emily Jane appeared. After a few minutes I made the excuse that there were rather a lot of us round his bed, said Edward and I had been there for some time, and proposed we go for a cup of tea.

I could not dive straight in with "did you know Josie had fallen for you?" so started to talk about the projected TV programme, and the coincidence of her involvement.

"Yes," he said. "It wasn't as big a surprise to me as it was to her because Stella told me we were meeting Sandy Mac-something and Josie Margerrison from the BBC, and I knew it was her. I don't think Stella had mentioned my name and of course Josie wouldn't connect her and me because she's still called 'Hardy' at work."

"Did it make it awkward, or easier – I mean your knowing her beforehand, or knowing me?"

He looked at me. I think he knew the direction I was taking.

"No. She's very competent, you know. But ours is an extremely technical business, and we were going to have another session or two. And I think they want to make it a bit more personal to me."

"Would that have been embarrassing?"

He looked at me again, with a faint smile.

"You know, don't you, Angela?"

"Know what?"

"That she was thinking thoughts about me she shouldn't have. That's what you're getting at, isn't it?"

"Sorry, Edward. I had to be sure you knew."

"I spotted it almost straight away, you know. In fact I spotted it at your house, that afternoon. I'm sorry, Angela. But I think she knows there couldn't be anything between us."

"Yes, she knows."

"I haven't done anything to.... to .... make her think there could be, you know. At least, I don't think so. I like her, very much, just as I like you, and Jeannie, but not ... like that. There couldn't be ...."

He was quiet for two or three minutes, as we sipped our tea.

"Is she upset?"

"Yes, terribly. But she knows what she's got to do, and she'll do it. I think she's known that, all along. But she kept on coming across you, and it wouldn't go away. She says she's going to leave the BBC and get away from here."

"Oh, no...."

"Don't worry about her, Edward. She'll do well, I'm sure. She's very good at what she does, you know. Many of us have these things to test us, don't we?"

"Yes. But leaving the BBC, because of me..."

"I told her about your father and me. I thought it might make it easier for her. And I think it will, if realising how impossible anything is can take away the pain of something like this. But apart from that, I couldn't stand by while my daughter wrecked your marriage, or tried to, Edward, could I? Not your marriage. Not anyone's. But yours ...."

I couldn't help it. I had not intended to allow myself to become emotional, but good intentions so often "gang agley," don't they? I could not quite hold back the tears. He reached across the table and caught my hand.

"Don't, Angela. It'll be alright. She's your daughter, and she'll behave like your daughter, I'm quite sure."

He leaned over, pulled my hand nearer. I saw people looking at us, wondering no doubt what was going on between a 60-year-old woman and a young man half her age. Was I his mother – I didn't look like him, I could almost hear them conjecturing. But I didn't care. I just found my hankie and dried my eyes. And after a moment he said: "I hope you don't mind my asking this. Do you think she knows how it is between Stella and me?"

"How do you mean?"

"Well, I wondered whether she had the idea that Stella only married me because she thought it was good for her career, or something. That she doesn't really care for me. Some people do think that, you know."

"Edward!"

"They think she's cold and doesn't care for anyone except herself. It's her manner, I suppose. She seems so cool and sophisticated, and hard. But it's just a shell, Angela. She developed it when she was left an orphan and decided she was going to make her way in the world. She came to be fond of me against her better judgement, you might say. She didn't want to become just a housewife. But I won't let her be, if I can help it. I want her to be a success, in her own right." He paused. "We love each other. We love each other more all the time."

"Edward, I'm so glad for you. I can understand it. It was something like that when Bill asked me to marry him."

He seemed to want to tell me something more, but hesitated. Then he said:

"Keep this to yourself, won't you. We've told nobody yet, but I'd like you to know. She thinks she's going to have a baby. It's just a bit too soon to be certain, but she thinks so."

"Edward, that's wonderful." And it turned out Stella was right.

Seven

Bosnia

Josie did not leave the BBC, then, but she pulled out of her role in the TV project about Protechno. She told the producer, Sandy, and her immediate boss, exactly why, and they were both understanding, although disappointed, and assured her it would not affect her prospects. She passed on the results of her work on the project – which resulted in an excellent and informative hour-long programme – and carried on doing worthwhile work for the region, for both radio and television, appearing on screen and behind the microphone herself from time to time.

To her colleagues, friends and even family, except Jeannie and her mother, who had seen the trauma of her encounter with Edward at close hand, she appeared quite normal, cheerful, and enthusiastic about her work, in the weeks following. She even continued to play hockey, with the local club at Bewdley, and a BBC team. But it was a facade. Behind it she was living in that emotional desert she feared she was heading for when she knew that her feeling for him must come to nothing. Her work and play were not much more than oases. The little house at Bewdley, which she had once delighted in furnishing and decorating, became a mere roof over her head.

By Christmas, however, when Alastair had left hospital and he and Angela were spending much time together, and were at Lyndford for the festive season, she was beginning to feel she had to do something to drag herself out of the depths. Pleading the demands of work – she was one of only two reporters covering the region over the holiday period – she did not join the party, which included Jeannie and Simon as well as the Jamesons. Really it was because she could not face meeting Edward and Stella, or even her sister and her husband, in the conglomerate company.

Instead, in the extra week's leave she accumulated by working over Christmas and New Year, she allowed Jeannie to persuade her to join a party of young women in a six-day ski trip to the French Alps. She had never ski-ed before, and found the experience enjoyable, compared with the last few months. Jeannie tried all she knew to get her fully engaged in the apres-ski, talked her into a couple of mountain walks in the hope that she would let it all come out. But Josie would clam up rather than talk freely to her sister, on the subject Jeannie most wanted her to air. Although Jeannie thought their talks, one-sided as they

---

were, were having some beneficial effect. At least they made it clear that their comradeship was still alive.

Halfway through the week, she got into conversation with a gentleman of late middle age who turned out to be a fellow journalist taking a break to do some mountain walking, with his wife, on their way back to Britain from his last assignment before retiring. Alexander Kordic, whose grandfather was a Croat, had been a big news agency's chief correspondent in Yugoslavia for 15 years, before and after the break-up of that always-troubled country, subsequent to the death of Tito. They made up the girls' dining table of six, and he and Josie soon discovered their mutual occupation.

When they gravitated to the lounge, the shop talk that started almost inevitably focussed on the Balkans.

"In a way, I'm sorry to be going at this moment," he told her. "It's going to be the biggest mess you ever saw. God knows how Tito held them together, Serbs, Croats and Muslims, I mean."

"I thought they lived together quite happily under Tito."

"Yes, up to a point, they did. There was a quite a lot of intermarriage. Tito himself was half Slovene and half Croat. But they're at each other's throats now. It was stirred up by a bunch of university eggheads, Serbs, and taken up by this chap Milosevic who fancies himself as the boss of the whole country. He'd like to make it into a kind of greater Serbia. But of course the Croats and the Bosniaks – that's the Bosnian Muslims – don't want any of that.

"Way back, before the war, the country had just about split up, or was on the verge of splitting up. I reckon it was the German invasion stopped it, essentially – made them get themselves together, I mean. When Tito and his partisans fought them, and fought them damned well, he became a hero to most Yugoslavs, although some of the Croats, a mob called the Ustase, who were a pretty nasty Fascist bunch, sided with the Jerries. That was all before my time, of course, but it's been well documented, and my grandfather told me some of it. There were some pretty awful goings on. And not all the atrocities were committed by the Huns. The partisans and another anti-German group, the Chetniks were at daggers drawn, a lot of the time, and neither of them was whiter than white."

"How do you mean?"

"Well, there were cases where they deliberately provoked the Jerries into taking punitive action against the civilians, because they knew that would bring more recruits to them. You perhaps don't know about Hitler's edict that for every German soldier killed a hundred locals were to be shot. I don't know whether that was ever literally carried out, but they went a long way towards it, in some cases.

"Even under Tito, though, ethnic nationalism was there, and it was a potential problem. Tito kept it under by one means or another, but it was only that – keeping it under. It was still there. Then he led the country to a degree of prosperity, although some of it was because of help from outside, after he split with the Soviets. The west wanted to keep him on their side. He was some guy, was Josip Brod – that was his real name. I mean capable. Morally he was a bit of a rotter. He was a womaniser, and he used his power to make himself rich, and he simply rode roughshod over any opposition.

"I don't know whether you know, but Yugoslavia is divided into eight. Six republics, Serbia, Croatia, Slovenia, Bosnia, Macedonia and Montenegro, and two provinces, Vojvodina and Kosovo. Well, Tito kept them together, sort of, by taking oppressive measures against their officials – purges and so on – one at a time, balancing one against the other. It gave the impression of decentralisation, but in fact it was very centrally controlled – by Tito. But it also had the effect of making the lives of ordinary people a lot more relaxed than in Soviet countries."

"So what went wrong?"

"Well, he was wary of appointing a successor president. I don't know why. P'raps he thought no one man could keep it together. So he created a presidency of nine people, most of them heads of the republics. It was a sure road to disaster. Nobody was happy. You see, Tito and his iron rule had only suppressed ethnic feelings, which were strong enough in some of them, especially the Serbs, and grievances. They certainly weren't eliminated. I reckon they never will be, although if they didn't have people like Milosevic stirring it they'd get on okay, perhaps. It's a pretty secular society really. Ethnicity and religion add up to a heritage, that gives 'em values, and traditions, but they're not dogmatic about it – not many, anyway. It was the Serb intellectuals, those eggheads, who started to revive the ethnic nationalism. Last year, no, the year before, a group of them, from the Serbian Academy of Sciences and Arts, issued a statement – a memorandum they called it – that highlighted the Serb grievances, and when it was published it got the country by the ears, or at least the Serbs, and Milosevic has latched on to it. You don't have to be a genius to see what's coming."

"They're going to fight each other?"

"Sure as eggs. And I reckon it'll start in Kosovo. The Serbs are really uptight there."

"Why Kosovo particularly?"

"Well, they reckon it's their spiritual home or something, but they're in quite a small minority there, not much more than ten per cent. So of course they don't get much of a say in running things. Or didn't. Friend Slobodan means to change all that. He set the ball rolling three years ago when he went to Kosovo

Polje. He told 'em it was their land and their ancestors would be defiled if they gave it up or knuckled under. I reckon he was just talking, then, being a politician, but it seemed to set him on fire as well as them and Serbs everywhere in the country."

"Who are the majority?"

"They're nearly all ethnic Albanians – Muslims, mostly."

"So where have they come from? I didn't know that part of the world had ever been conquered, or colonised or anything, by people from the east."

"No, it wasn't, not in the way I think you mean. The Albanian Muslims are Slavs who've converted, or been converted. Up to the fourteenth century, the whole of the Balkans region had been Christianised, by the Roman empire first, then the Byzantines. But from about 1400 – the Battle of Kosovo in 1389, actually – the region was governed by the Ottomans, and there was a high level of conversion to Islam. Under Tito and the Commies, religion took more of a back seat. The Muslim Kosovars are anything but extreme Islamists. But they certainly think of themselves as Muslims."

"How long were you in Yugoslavia?"

"Most of my working life. I ran the agency for 15 years."

"Were you happy there?"

"I loved it. So did Becky – didn't you?" She nodded. "Of course, I had one foot in the soil. My grandfather was Croatian. But we had friends among all of 'em. If we gave a party there'd be people from at least three different ethnic groups there, and they all got on like a house on fire."

"But you're not going to retire there?"

"No. We've got children and grandchildren in England. And to be honest, I don't really want to be in the Balkans when all that I'm positive will happen does happen. Tell you what though – there'll be a hell of a need for good reporting. You should tell your bosses at the Beeb that they should send their best people out. It's going to be the source of some of the most important news stories in the world, before long."

"Who do you think will come out on top?"

"Well, the Serbs are strongest. And they've grabbed hold of the old Yugoslav army, which is mostly Serb, and all its armaments."

Next day, between her ski runs, she thought a great deal about what Kordic had told her. It had almost set her on fire, she confessed later. She waylaid him before dinner so they could talk alone.

"Mr Kordic," she said. "Do you think there would be any chance your agency would employ me?"

"Perhaps," he said. "We haven't got many women. Perhaps we should have. But you've got a job with the BBC. Why on earth would you want to give it up?"

"It's personal, really. I don't want to talk about it. But I want to get out of England."

"Have you any idea where you'd like to work?"

"Yes. In Yugoslavia."

He looked at her in amazement.

"Whatever makes you want to go there? It's no place for a young woman reporter, at present, or won't be."

"Why not? Your wife said she enjoyed it, didn't she?"

"Yes, but she was my wife. I don't think my firm would consider you for minute – not to go there. There are a lot of talented professional women in Yugoslavia, but not in our world. You'd just be laughed at. Nobody'd take you seriously."

"Will you ask them, though? Or tell me who to contact."

Back in the UK, she phoned the number Kordic had given her, and eventually got through to the man she wanted.

"Yes, Miss Margerrison. How can I help you?"

She explained that she wanted to leave the BBC, for personal reasons that she would reveal if necessary, had met Alexander Kordic, and as a result wanted to work in Yugoslavia.

"In Yugoslavia?" He sounded amazed. "Why?"

"Because that's where the big news stories are going to be shortly, and I want to be among them."

There was a silence, before he said: "Miss Margerrison, I must tell you I think you have as much chance of being sent to sell snow to eskimos as going to Yugoslavia for this or any other news agency, or the BBC for that matter. But I'd be happy to see you. Where are you now?"

She told him, and arranged to go to his office on her next free day.

Jeremy Bergstrom was the agency's head of personnel, and a working journalist himself when he had time and opportunity. After asking her for career details to date, he said: "I wanted to see you because of what you said about wanting to go to Yugoslavia. Were you serious?"

"Perfectly."

"Why?"

"It was because of what Mr Kordic told me about it. It's made me want to see it for myself. All the different people have been living together and getting along well for so long, and now they're going to fight each other. It's going to be an awful mess, he says, and the rest of the world doesn't seem to want to know. I want to be in on it."

"Well, if anyone's got their finger on the pulse of the Balkans it's Alex. And he's right, we in the West don't seem interested, at the moment. There are things nearer home that we see as much more important. But I still don't quite see why you 're so keen to go there. You said something about 'personal reasons' for wanting to leave the BBC. Could they be why you want to go to Yugoslavia?"

"Not really. They're why I want to get away from the Midlands, and Britain if possible. I need to move to avoid possible contact with someone. But I knew that before I met Mr Kordic. I've been trying to look up as much as I can about it, but I haven't had time to get very far, yet. That was only just over a week ago."

"Was it a ….. love affair."

"Yes, but not within the BBC, although work was involved. It was more because of family connections. I …. oh, fell in love with someone who can't return it because he's married. And there's more to it. It's very complicated. It won't affect my work, Mr Bergstrom, I can assure you. But I must get away."

"But again – why Yugoslavia?"

"I'm sorry Mr Bergstrom, I don't think I can explain any better. I did know someone who's been there, just for a holiday, and she was absolutely entranced by it. But there are plenty of people who feel like that after they've had a holiday somewhere. It's a lot more than that with me. I've just got this feeling, that it's somewhere I must go to, as a journalist I mean."

He studied her.

"Right, well, look. I think there would be a good chance that we would employ you, Josie – if I may call you that – but I can't see any chance of sending you to the Balkans at the moment. There are no vacancies. But if you will supply me with a formal CV, and give me contact details, I can promise I'll contact you if anything suitable crops up."

*****

Josie continued to avoid Edward, not going to The Mill again because she thought he might be there. She saw her mother quite often, once or twice at Jeannie's where Angela was pleased to note that relations were back to normal, perhaps even closer than before, if that was possible.

Angela was anxious to know whether her wish to get away from the Midlands had been taken any further, and after some hedging was told of her conversations with Alexander Kordic, and that she had already approached his news agency.

"It doesn't look as though there's anything doing with them. But I still want to go there," she said.

When her mother, groping for reasons why getting away from Edward meant going to somewhere like Yugoslavia, asked why that troubled country, she tried to clamp down on any idea that it was because of him.

"It isn't, Mum. I want to get away from .... him. I admit that. But there are plenty of ways I could do that without going to Yugoslavia. I don't really know why it has to be there. But I do know I shan't rest until I've been to see for myself. I'm going to see if there's any chance of the BBC sending me, but I bet there isn't."

Two weeks later, she told Angela of the outcome – much the same as with the agency. She was not experienced enough and anyway there was no vacancy.

"They didn't say 'and you're a girl' but I'm sure that was in their minds," she said. "They're still a bit stuffy that way. But I'm going. I've made up my mind. I'll go as a tourist to start with, and then we'll see."

Angela was quite pre-occupied with caring for Alastair, although by then he was reasonably fit again and did not need too much in the way of care. She stayed at The Mill because it was so much nearer her work at the hospital than was Lyndford, although she also spent as much time as she could with him, and Charles and Maria, at Home Farm. They meant to be married in the autumn, although where they would live had not been decided. His house at Lyndford, an expanded former worker's cottage, was a beautiful home in a delightful spot, but Alastair was concerned that she would find memories of Debra too much in evidence there. Angela was inclined to discount that, and was proved to be right, but for the time being it did not arise. She was also working on plans for finally retiring, giving up the part-time clinic.

"I have to admit I don't really understand why she wants to go to the Balkans so desperately," she told Jeannie. "There doesn't seem to be any prospect of getting official journalistic work there. When I asked her how she meant to manage financially, she told me she was going to use the £20,000 your grandfather left each of you, which she had not touched so far and which had grown by another thousand or so, and her own savings. She'd have about £25,000 altogether, which would keep her for two years at least. I told her I didn't think she should spend it all like that – he meant it to help buy a house, like you have."

"I've been careful not to talk about Edward, unless she raised it first, which she's hardly ever done," Jeannie said. "I can't help thinking that's what's behind it, though."

"Me too. But she insists it isn't. She actually raised it. She guessed that's what I was thinking, and said it was not because of him. There were plenty of ways she could have got away from 'that' as she put it. She could have gone to America, or Australia, or even some other part of this country. Going to Yugoslavia had become the thing she wanted more than anything she'd ever wanted, she said. The more she learned about it, the more she wanted to do it. She said 'If it turns into a success, great. If it doesn't and I have to come back with my tail between my legs, so be it. I'll have done it. If I don't, I'll spend my life thinking I should have.'"

Angela and Jeannie both felt though that however she protested, there was an element of "Edward" in it. Perhaps she had been left with a psychological void that could not be filled by anything else in her life.

She gave the BBC her notice, which was accepted with genuine regret, and in March, with the help of Alexander Kordic who was by then back in Britain and settling down to retirement near Oxford, enrolled for a crash course in Serbo-Croat, the official Yugoslav language. His help was invaluable. They talked in the new language, which he warned her was not universally spoken in Yugoslavia, but would enable her to get by. He also told her there would be no trouble in getting into the country on an ordinary British passport, but if they told her she needed a visa she would easily be able to obtain one.

"You'll have more trouble travelling about than getting into the country as a whole," he warned. "Have you any idea how long you want to stay?"

"Indefinitely," she said. "I don't mean for ever, but …. well, indefinitely."

"What about money?"

She told him, adding: "I want to get to know the country first, so I know the context I'm working in, when I get to the stage of being able to write about it. Even if the things you think will happen don't" …... "They will," Kordic broke in …. "I'm sure I shall want to write about it. And if I run out of cash and can't earn any more, I'll come home."

"Josie, I think you've got what it takes to make out. Whether that means you will, I can't possibly say. It's going to be tough down there, I can tell you. But try to keep in touch. If you need help that I can give, you'll have it."

He also told her he was giving her letters of introduction to some "very good friends" in Belgrade and Sarajevo, who would help her in a number of ways.

"One's a Serb, one's Croatian and one's a Muslim, and there are a couple of Brits," he said. "I shall write to them immediately, but they will only be very short letters, simply asking if you could call on them, and if they'll give you any advice you need. I wouldn't want the longer letters I shall write to fall into the wrong hands. You must take those with you and make sure you keep tight hold of them. And about your money: whatever you do, don't carry more cash that you can help, in fact don't allow it to be known that you have substantial amounts in any form. They're no more dishonest than anywhere else, but there are a few rogues, like everywhere."

A month later, she flew to Sarajevo, and made straight to the friend Kordic had put at the top of his list, Ljiljana Alagic, making the choice also because it was a woman. Dr Alagic, a professor of psychiatry at one of the city's universities, was a Serb, modern in her thinking and indeed in her ways, but fearful of what she thought was going to happen. She greeted Josie warmly and over dinner brought out the elements of what had taken her to Yugoslavia.

"I'm afaid Alex Kordic is right about what's going to happen," she added as they drank their coffee.

"This man Milosevic wants to rule all Yugoslavia. He'd like to make it into a 'greater Serbia.' I'm proud of being a Serb, but the Muslims and Croats have as much right to a place in the world, I mean in this part of the world, as we have. I can't understand why that lot in Belgrade wanted to stir things up with their stupid memorandum, that he thinks he's going to cash in on. They should have put their energy into working out ways of creating a country we can all live in, together."

Dr Alagic had already read the longer letter sent by Alex Kordic. She told Josie: "Alex says he can't quite understand what makes you want to come here, without a job and spending your own money to live. But you're a journalist and want to write about us. How do you think you're going to do it?"

"I don't know, yet. I don't even know, myself, why I want to work here. Like I told my mother, I just know that if I don't try I shall spend my life wishing I had. Perhaps I think I might be able to make my name here. Perhaps I can help make the world take more notice of what's happening. But it isn't just that. I don't know ...."

Dr Alagic looked at her.

"You've had a ..... disappointment, I think?"

"Yes. But that doesn't matter. I've put that behind me."

"I think it does matter, though. I too have had a thing like that, many years ago, and it still matters. But you will get over it. We have to, you know."

"Yes."

"Have you worked out a – what do you call it – a plan of campaign?"

" I thought I should spend a month or two getting to know the country and talking to people like you, Dr Alagic. Getting to know what is behind the thinking of people here – what makes them tick, as we say."

"Please call me Ljiljana, Josie. But I'm afraid I must tell you, if you can find out in a month or two what makes us here 'tick,' you are a better man than I am, Gunga Din, as I think you also say. However, I will do my best.

"First of all, have you anywhere to stay, for the time being?"

"No, I was hoping you could point me towards something."

"If you can put up with my crazy life, you would be welcome to stay with me. I have another bedroom. But I have my meals at strange hours, sometimes. And some of my students come and stay half through the night, often. Sometimes all through the night. They sleep on the floor."

"Oh, doctor – Ljiljana. Are you sure? Wouldn't I be a nuisance?"

"I think I would be the nuisance, to you. No, I would like to have you here. You can tell me about life in England. I was there once, a long time ago."

"I would pay you, of course."

"Oh, my dear, there is no need. You can buy food, sometimes. That would help you find out how we 'tick'. I could teach you how not to be cheated, anyway."

She stayed with Ljiljana Algic for a month, initially. The lifestyle was not as hectic as her hostess had implied, but a few students did come, and she learned quite a lot from contact with them, although they were not so different from students everywhere.

While there, she walked about the city, noting the contrasts between its modern development and some of the beautiful and historic parts. One of Ljiljana's students tacked himself on to her and helped a great deal with the language although she soon found that many people either spoke English or could understand the Serbo-Croat she tried to use. She bought food from the shops and market stalls, telling Dr Alagic what she had paid and, usually, being congratulated on her judgement.

She made copious notes about what she saw and the impressions gained. Chief among them was an apparent cosmopolitan atmosphere, with little or no sign of tensions between people of different ethnic origins. Not that ethnic origins were easy to spot. She saw less of what people in Britain thought of as Muslim dress – headscarves, burkas, long beards for example – than she would have seen in Birmingham.

Two weeks after her arrival, she made contact with another of the people to whom she had been referred by Alex Kordic. Milan Terzic was ethnically an Albanian and a Muslim, like many Bosnians, and had been born in that country during its German occupation in the Hitler war. Now he worked as news head for a minor radio network and had his finger firmly on the local pulse. He lived less than a mile from Dr Alagic, who knew him well and walked with Josie to his home, an apartment quite like Ljiljana's only rather bigger.

His wife, Hatidza, opened the door. "Ah, Lili, how nice to see you. And this must be Miss Margerrison, from England – Milan's had a letter about you from Alex Kordic. Please come in and sit down. He's in his office. Milan!"

He also greeted her warmly, and while his wife produced tea and cakes, asked her and Lili into his office, where Josie produced the longer letter from Kordic and submitted to another version of Dr Alagic's mild inquisition. But the outcome was the same – she was assured of all the help he could give, although he too could not quite understand why she was in Sarajevo and what she was going to do in the way of work.

Towards the end of her stay with Lili, she decided she would keep Alex Kordic's other contacts in reserve and go to Belgrade to visit his successor as chief of the news agency. She set off in the morning, by train, and by mid-afternoon was in the Yugoslav capital. She had the agency's address and soon found her way there.

The new chief, James Meredith, was expecting her, having also been contacted by Alex Kordic. But just like Alex, Dr Alagic and Milan Terzic he found it difficult to understand why she was there, without a job or any indication that she could get paid work. He agreed however that the region was on the threshold of a chaotic time, although the rest of the world hardly seemed to want to know about it.

"We send story after story about it," he said "but they get hardly a mention on TV or radio, in Europe or America. And even in the quality dailies, it's usually tucked away well down an inside page.

"I suppose they think 'oh it's only the Balkans, at their squabbling again' and I know they're pre-occupied with what's happening in the communist countries. But my view's the same as Alex's – there's going to be a huge bust-up that they'll not be able to ignore. This man Milosevic will see to that."

Josie asked: "Can you see any opening for me at all? For example, if I came up with a good story, would you handle it for me?"

"I couldn't pay you for it directly. But if I thought it was good enough I could let you send it through us. What sort of stuff are you aiming at – political, human interest?"

"I don't know, until I find it. Either, or both."

He said nothing for a few moments. Then: "Look, I tell you what. The balloon's about to go up in Slovenia. As I expect you know, that's the most industrialised part of the country. About a tenth of the population produces a fifth of the GDP, and they're pretty pissed off about it because they think they're carrying a top-heavy and inefficient administration. And they're right. The locals are pressing hard for reforms and I reckon it's going to end with Slovenia breaking away. There's talk of a referendum on independence later on this year.

"We've got our eye on it, but only from here. We haven't the scope to send somebody there long term and anyway the interest in it round the world seems to be just about zilch.

"I know it's not much to offer, in fact I'm not really offering anything, because you'd be doing it all off your own bat and paying for everything yourself. But if you were to go to Ljubljana and look at the situation on the ground it might come to something. I'd give you contacts and a letter of introduction telling them who you are and that I've suggested you go there. I don't think you'll be unwelcome, especially if they think you're going to try to tell the world a bit more about them. What do you think?"

"Mr Meredith, I think that would be great. It's more than I expected."

"Call me Jim, Josie. I hope something comes of it."

She was elated. As she told Meredith, something as positive as this was way beyond her expectations. The most she had hoped for was that he would point her towards one or two people worth talking to. But Jim was impressed by the girl, both personally and by what he could see, and hear from Alex Kordic and contacts at the BBC, of her journalistic abilities and drive.

She arrived in the Slovene capital just in time to see the forthcoming spring elections opened up to non-communists. As Meredith forecast, the politicians, even the communists who were themselves at odds with the central party command, welcomed her as the first western reporter to wish, apparently, to take a real interest in what was going on. Jim's introductory letter opened many doors. And on her part, Josie warmed to them, and to other people she met, the hotel staff, waiters, shopkeepers. Between her arrival in January – after squeezing in a return to Sarajevo to spend Christmas with Ljiljana Alagic – and the elections in April, she travelled round the little country to see the progress of the various campaigns, and to delight in its beautiful mountains, forests, farms and villages. When all this is over, I'm going to spend time here, she told herself. Even though it has to be alone, alone, alone, another voice reminded her.

She sent regular reports to Meredith, and was delighted when he told her that some of them had resulted in stories in British and American papers, and she would be paid for them. Not very much, because the stories had not been displayed with any prominence, and they could not carry her by-line. And as he had told her, western interest in Slovenia, at that time, was almost nil. But she was encouraged.

By the time of the elections, foreign press representation had increased, but it was mostly from neighbouring countries, and from radio and television. So that when the polls brought victory for the DEMOS coalition – a seven party grouping including the Christian Democrats (essentially strong Catholics, the Farmers Alliance and the Greens – Josie's reporting was still a substantial part of the print media coverage, although even then it did not add up to much in the way of column inches.

With Jim Meredith's encouragement, and such small financial support as he could come up with, she stayed on in Slovenia, watching and reporting on the pressure mounting towards secession from Yugoslavia, amidst the complicated and usually unsavoury series of political manouevres there which were to result in the bloody conflicts of the next few years.

The big development in Slovenia was the referendum in December which brought a massive vote in favour of independence, duly enacted by the government in the following June and which, the Slovenes knew, would bring the weight of the JNA – the Yugoslav People's Army – down on them. They had been making military preparations, very cleverly, but so had the JNA - which however was wrong-footed by the Slovene government bringing forward the date of the independence declaration by a day. This brought another minor scoop for Josie, although it was, once again, ignored by huge sections of the western media. But it started the ten-day war that finally saw Slovenia's two million people break free with eventual recognition as an independent country by the European Union, America, and the United Nations.

Josie covered the war from start to finish and, partly through the confidence she had established with the Slovene leaders, was able to reveal aspects of it missed even by many of the locals. It was a very minor affair in terms of the conflicts that were to follow in Bosnia, and over much of the world since; less than fifty JNA soldiers were killed, and fewer than twenty Slovenes. Slobodan Milosevic, the Serb and Yugoslav leader, was not very interested in Slovenia – he had bigger fish to catch and fry. But Josie reported it as accurately as she could, often getting closer to the action than she ought. So close to it on the ground, she thought, as the shells and bullets flew, that it did not merit the label of "phoney war" attached to it by much of the rest of the world. She saw it through, and stayed on to note the eventual result.

"You've done a good job, girl," Meredith told her, back in Belgrade. "I wish the rest of the world was a bit more interested. And I wish I could offer you something permanent. What are you going to do now?"

"I almost think I could stay in Slovenia. It's lovely and the people are great. But that would be nothing but self-indulgence. I want to see other parts of the country. I'm going back to Sarajevo first."

"Will you let me know how things are there? On the ground, I mean. We have contacts, of course, but I'd like to know your version. I know it'd be accurate and objective. I can let you have a card saying you're an associate of ours. I know you won't abuse it."

"Oh, thanks, Jim. Of course I won't abuse it. And I'll let you know how I see things."

"Good luck, Josie. Take care of yourself."

Eight

Bangladesh

Michael, nearly 70, proved to have no difficulty in becoming a housefather or taking the lead in looking after Edwina, especially as the little girl showed great intelligence, making her a delight to teach. She was already toilet-trained which made his task easier, and was anything but a fussy eater.

She was tiny – Kathleen thought she would have delighted her own mother, who got her name of Dolly by being equally small – with Catriona's flaming hair and blue eyes, but athletic from an early age. The athleticism and the love of adventure she inherited from her mother showed one day, not too long after her third birthday, when she gave the slip to Mrs Jellicoe, the household's long-standing help who still went in mornings to clean and look after her while Michael had his weekly thrash round the golf course, and undertook missions where he could not take the little girl. The good lady found her well up the garden's twenty-foot cherry tree, holding a lively conversation with a boy next door.

"How'd you get up there?" she heard the boy ask. "It's awful high."

"I got my likel ladder so I could reach the branches. It's easy. Why don't you do it, up that tree there?"

The boy made a half-hearted attempt to scale a small tree a few feet away, much easier to climb than the cherry, but soon gave up.

"Won't your mummy be angry? he asked.

"She's not here. Nor Daddy. Gone to Bangerdesh."

"Where's that?"

"Don't know. But the people there are awful poor and Mummy and Daddy have gone to help 'em."

Mrs J. waddled down the garden and made sure she was under the tree where she could at least break the miscreant's fall if that was what it came to.

"Edwina! What on earth are you doin' up there. Come down this minute." Then a moment later: "No, it's too dangerous. Stop where you are but keep still. I'll 'ave to get the fire brigade."

"Why? Is there a fire?"

"Just stop where you are. Don't move. Do you hear? Keep still." And she hastened back to the house to carry out her intention. It took a few minutes, to tell the operator what it was about and where to come. She set off to mount guard under the tree – only to meet Edwina at the back door. She managed to halt the fire brigade before too much embarrassment was caused. When he was told about it, Michael stuck his tongue in his cheek and gave the little girl a good telling off, further showing his disapproval by building her a tree house!

Kathleen kept to her intention of winding down her work, stopping the television appearances altogether, agreeing to fewer radio interviews, and cutting out her Sunday paper column. And she told her daily paper that she would be giving that one up at the end of the year. She was after all well past normal retirement age and she wanted, once Jonathan and Catriona returned to reclaim Edwina, to have more time to spend with Michael, and their grandchildren. Also, she had some books to write. Michael was less sanguine that it would all work out as she planned. He sensed the constant itch in Catriona's feet, if not in Jonathan's.

They went to Alastair and Angela's wedding, of course. If it had been a church ceremony, Edwina would have been a bridesmaid, as Alastair's great-niece. Instead, she was asked, or perhaps permitted would be the better word, for as soon as it was mentioned she was all agog, to join cousin Dorothy in presenting posies. It was the first time most of the family had seen her, and she was an instant hit. She got on well with Dorothy, and Charles's other two, and even better with such of the farm animals as she was allowed contact with. It was the first time she had come close to four-legged creatures.

The Housmans could only stay one further day at Lyndford, because of Kathleen's commitments. Back in London, they settled to a routine which saw her spending longer at home, and as the year neared its end they were looking forward to the return of Jonathan, Catriona and Christopher. They had received frequent if irregular letters, and one photograph, of the three of them looking incredibly healthy, Chris with a mop of hair the same colour as his mother's and Edwina's. The letters were mainly about their work, and some of them alarmed Kathleen, for example when Jon spoke about water in country wells being affected by the high level of arsenic in the soil. But he also emphasised how healthy and well Christopher seemed to be.

In the letter with the photo enclosed, he wrote: "As I hope you can see, Chris is doing very well. He has hardly had a day's sickness since we got here, apart from a spell of tummy trouble that had us worried, because that kind of thing is endemic among Bangladeshi children. It arises from the poor sanitary conditions, I'm sure. The latrines are usually some distance away from the houses and they do their best to make sure the waste is properly channelled away and disposed of, but sometimes they don't succeed very well. This is one of the things we are surveying in the hope that we can encourage better arrangements.

"Whenever we can, we take Chris with us when we are working, He's always a big hit with the ladies. They've never seen red hair like his and Cat's. But occasionally we have to be away overnight, or perhaps for two nights. Where we are now we have a lovely lady who looks after him in those cases, and in fact in other daytimes when it's impractical to take him with us. In spite of the tummy trouble I mentioned, which was soon after we got here, we are not too worried about infections, because we have a good supply of preventative medicine. I think Cat's breast feeding is the best preventative of all, though."

Just after Christmas, Jon wrote to say they expected to be home by May.

"We're being moved to Chittagong for the rest of our spell here," he told them. "Life in the cities is quite different, and Chittagong is a busy port as well as an industrial centre. There is a sizeable textile industry, and factories where they process jute. I expect we shall be based in the city and travel out to do our surveys."

His next letter arrived on April 20th, and told them they would be flying home on May 10th.

He added: "We're all fine, but we won't be sorry to get away, now. Since we've been in Chittagong, the arrangements for Chris have not been quite the same. Most of the time he's had to stay at home because we've been travelling out by boat to do our work. He's being well looked after, by a really good young woman who's got two children of her own, and he's spending some time in a nursery, with other children, which I think is good for him. But it's not the same as having him with us most of the time. Tamana – that's the girl he's with – speaks good English but her children talk mostly in Bengali and Chris is picking up quite a lot of that. It will probably be a funny mixture for a while."

He added that he would confirm details of their return home in another few days, as soon as he knew flight numbers.

On the last day of the month, news channels told of the massive cyclone that started in the Bay of Bengal and devastated the southern coast of Bangladesh, and its islands, causing much damage, flooding large areas of the country and bringing many hundreds of deaths. The total was eventually put at nearly 140,000.

Kathleen and Michael were sitting together, giving Edwina her supper when the disaster was reported on BBC TV's early evening news.

"Oh, my god" she said. "Oh, Michael ...."

"I'm sure they'll be alright," he comforted. "They're capable. They'll have coped." But he was on the phone early next morning, to the anthropology unit at the university. They had no information at all about personnel, at that stage.

Telephones appeared to be completely out of action and radio communication was severely disrupted by the storm.

It was another two days before they could learn anything about Jonathan and Catriona, and then all the unit could tell them was that the two had gone north, by boat, three days before the storm broke. Nothing had been heard from them since, although that did not mean a great deal, in the circumstances.

Michael was speaking to the unit's head of research. He asked: "What about …. Christopher …. the boy?"

The man said: "Christopher?"

"Yes. Their son. My grandson."

After a silence: "I'm sorry, Mr Housman. I have no information about that. I didn't know they had any family with them. I've only been in this post for six months. How old is your grandson?"

"He'll be nearly two-and-a-half, now. He was only three months old when they went out."

"I'll see what I can find out and call you back."

They heard nothing that day. Kathleen called her paper and told them they would have to suspend her column. The editor asked if he could do anything to help and wondered whether he might include a brief item explaining why. She agreed, reluctantly but appreciating that it would be unfair on the paper and its readers to say nothing.

Next day the research chief, Paul Wykeham, rang: "I have at least some news, Mr Housman.

Your grandson is in the city, in the care of a Bangladeshi lady, Mrs Tamana Saha, who lives in a part not as seriously affected by the storm or the flooding as other areas. One of our people in Chittagong has been to see her, and she says Christopher seems perfectly well and happy. It appears he's been spending quite a lot of time with her recently."

Kathleen was listening on the extension phone. She said: "Oh, thank god. Have you heard anything about Jon and Catriona?"

"No, I'm terribly sorry. We only have two other people in Chittagong and their office has been badly affected by the storm. I understand the ground floor is three feet under water right now. We can only reach them through the UN office in Dhaka. But of course trying to establish contact with your son and daughter-in-law is very much their priority. At the moment though I can tell you no more than that they went up the coast and then up the delta on April 26th to survey some villages.

"I can only promise you that the instant we have any news we will contact you, Mrs Housman. The instant."

He kept his promise, an interminably long four days later. To tell them that the bodies of Jonathan and Catriona had been found. It seemed they had been trying to help a family get their small children to safety as the flood threatened, when the storm struck at the height of its devastating ferocity. They and the family they were trying to help were discovered, barely recognisable, under tons of fallen timber and debris that had also been several days under water.

*****

Having to deal with the return of Christopher while continuing to care for Edwina kept Kathleen sane, she would say later. For a few days after the dreadful news she was in a state of depression such as Michael, himself brought lower than at any time in his life, had thought never possible for her. It made him worry about her long-term stability.

He need not have. Kathleen, hard as she was hit by the loss of her only child, possessed an inner strength that eventually must come out on top.

Her own work had brought national and even international recognition; her marriage tranquillity, peace and a sense of comradeship which helped make light of threatening deadlines and occasional brushes with the high priests of male superiority and privilege. Michael's parliamentary career had flourished in a way she admired. There were no headlines when he "slammed" his party leaders or even the opposition; he was never a slammer. Plenty though in their local weekly when campaigns to which he gave support saved a community hall from extinction or a lollipop lady from the axe. Apart from her vigorous, relentless and sometimes bruising demands for female equality, mostly in print, that was the way Kathleen was, too. Quiet, middle of the road, supporter of the underdog, even when she knew that same animal could reward the support by turning round and taking a bite out of her. People who only knew her through her writing were amazed, when she spoke at their conferences or gatherings, by her modest, almost self-effacing, personality. Everyone liked her, even those high priests.

All this, Michael came to realise, must surely mean that she would eventually return to an even keel, as her father had after suffering dreadfully when his father, Squire Jameson, killed himself because his son married a servant girl. It was all reflected, also, in the outpouring of sympathy and concern that erupted as soon as the public learned of the loss of Jonathan and Catriona. But at first, it passed over her almost unseen and unheard as she retreated into the shell of a personal hideaway that even little Edwina could hardly penetrate.

"Whatsa matter, Granny?" she asked more than once. She had not been told – they could not bring themselves to the terrible task.

Michael started to apply his mind to what must be done about Christopher. He had been assured that the little boy was being well cared for and that the NGO the university unit was attached to would make sure this continued, but of course he must come home as soon as possible. He could not leave Kathleen in her present state, and wondered whether there was anyone in the Jameson family who could be asked to fly out to Bangladesh and bring him back. His sister-in-law Angela, perhaps, maybe with Alastair. But before he could progress beyond preliminary thoughts and the merest of mentions to Kathleen, she said: "I'm going. I want to see where .... where they are." He was grateful, that she was at least back on the track of taking action.

"Darling, we'll both go. I want to, as well."

"What about Edwina?"

"I'll work something out."

In fact he had already glimpsed a possibility. Could she go to Lyndford, to stay with Charles and Maria for a few days? She had loved being there at the time of the wedding.

Kathleen continued to pick up as their plans were made, and she led the way in telling Edwina the dreadful truth.

"Would you like to go and stay with Alastair and Dorothy, and Douglas, for a few days?" she asked her.

"Ooh, yes. An' Mima, an' Jack."

"And there'll be some little lambs, I expect."

"Ooh Granny. When are we goin'?"

"Tomorrow or the next day, I think. But Grandad and I won't be staying. We've got to go somewhere else. But you'll be alright with Auntie Maria, and Eva, won't you?"

"Where are you goin'?"

Kathleen hesitated. Should she tell her? She'd have to know sooner or later. She hedged.

"We're going to Bangladesh to fetch Christopher."

"An' Mummy, an' Daddy?"

"No .... they .... can't come ...."

"Whatsa matter, Granny?"

Michael had to take over, and decided quickly that she must be told..

"Sweetheart, Mummy and Daddy won't be coming back."

"Why?"

"Something's happened, you see. There was a terrible storm in Bangladesh.

Mummy and Daddy were trying to help some boys and girls, like you, and there was an accident."

"In a car?"

"No, love. It was trees, and houses, blown down by the wind. It was a terribly strong wind."

She stood away from him, pondering, trying to picture it.

"Were they killed, Grandad?"

He was almost in tears himself. He hugged her to him.

"Yes, my darling."

She was thinking.

"But Kistopher wasn't killed?"

"No. Christopher wasn't with them."

Edwina stood, silent and solemn. Then turned to look at the photo from Bangladesh, of Jonathan and Catriona, with baby Christopher, enlarged and framed.

"Do Mummy an' Daddy still look like that?" she asked.

*****

Charles and Maria were more than ready to take Edwina into the Home Farm brood for as long as necessary. Michael and Kathleen did not even stay the night, and back in London, at once began to make arrangements for the trip to Chittagong. Michael, telling Paul Wykeham of their intentions, asked if it was known what had happened to Jonathan and Catriona after they were found. He was told they had been buried immediately.

"I'm sorry, Mr Housman. It had to be immediate. They.... the bodies.... were already.... starting to ...."

"It's alright. I understand. You know of course where they were buried?"

"Oh, yes. It was in the nearest cemetery that wasn't flooded. We shall be making arrangements for permanent memorials. You and Mrs Housman would like to be involved in that, I'm sure?"

"Yes, please."

Wykeham seemed to want to say a little more. He asked: "Mr Housman, could I come to see you before you go?"

"Yes, but we're going the day after tomorrow. The flight's booked."

"I'll come this afternoon, if that's alright?"

When he arrived, a pleasant, bearded man in his forties, was offered and accepted tea, Edwina sent to play in the garden, he told them: "For one thing, I wanted to see you face to face to tell you how deeply sorry we all are that your son and daughter-in-law should come to such an end by doing work for us."

"They were doing something they felt passionate about," Michael said. "They wanted to do it more than anything else. Not too many people are able to earn their living by working in the passion that drives them."

"Thank you. But I also want to tell you that they were doing quite outstanding work. Their reports and the information they included were of a very high standard. But more than that. The local people, in all four areas where they worked, came to think highly of them. You can imagine that under the present state of the country, paying tribute to foreigners gathering information wouldn't be a top priority. But we've already had a number of messages saying how very much more they did.

"It seems they never missed an opportunity of helping people. They gave them food, and went without themselves to do it; and ferried children to hospital; and helped build houses; even I gather worked in one woman's field when her husband was ill, to make sure the crop was planted. Our people are never backward at helping where they can, but your son and daughter-in-law were exceptional."

Kathleen could not keep back her tears. Michael had to work hard to prevent himself joining her. He asked Wykeham about one aspect of the tragedy that had been worrying him.

"You've been in touch with Catriona's father, of course?"

"We haven't spoken to him. We've tried, several times. He's on the phone, and we found the number but it's constantly engaged. BT have checked it and they say there's nothing wrong – he must have the receiver off. So we've asked the local police to see him, and I believe they have. And I've written to him, and told him everything I've told you. It's worrying me, Mr Housman."

"Yes, it's worrying us. I don't think he's seen Catriona since her mother's funeral, before she went to university. And of course he can't have seen the children."

He thought for a few moments.

"As soon as we get back, we must work out something. We must take them up there. Look, give me his address – believe it or not, we haven't got it – and I'll write. And if he contacts you, will you tell him please what's happening and what we intend to do?"

Two days later, they landed at Chittagong, made straight for the survey unit's office, and one of the two staff took them to the home of Tamana Saha and her husband. Christopher did not of course know them. He had been a tiny baby when they last saw him. Kathleen thought the best approach to uprooting him from a family with whom he had now been for more than a fortnight, apart from previous shorter periods, would be to spend as much time as possible with him in his familiar surroundings, for two or three days. Their flight home was booked for a week later. But the little boy, happy as he was with his foster-family, took to his granny and grandad immediately, gabbling away to them in the mixed language he used with Tamana's own two.

Reassured, they left him with her and set off, in a twenty-foot boat piloted by a local employee of the unit. The devastation was plain to see, although soldiers including some Americans and Indians were hard at work trying to sort through it; as far as could be seen was water, more like a sea than a lake. As they chugged slowly along, they were treated to the ghastly sight of animal and even human bodies – it was often impossible to tell which – tangled in the floating islands of debris and vegetation.

They took most of the day to reach the slightly higher area of land where Jonathan and Catriona had been working.

Kathleen asked their guide: "Can you tell us where.... where they were when...."

"Yes. Just there," he said, pointing to a spot not more than a hundred yards away, still under water.

Neither of them asked any more questions. There was no point – nothing to be seen. They went a mile or two further up what they assumed was the river until the boat pulled in to another piece of land.

"Here is the burying place," the guide said. They left the boat and shortly came to an area of a few acres with perhaps a hundred gravestones, or in some cases wooden pillars. The ruins of houses and what could have been a small church or mosque were nearby. The guide stopped at a group of six, four wooden posts, each with a small plaque attached, and two wooden crosses, with the names of Jonathan and Catriona inscribed.

He said: "We have given them crosses because they were Christians. But I expect you will like stones to be put there as soon as possible. Yes?"

"Yes. As soon as possible," Michael said.

The guide said: "I will leave you now. I will be at the boat."

"Thank you," both said.

They stood for ten minutes, Kathleen weeping quietly, her hand clasped in his. Then she said: "Take a photograph, please, darling." Which he did, of the crosses and the whole graveyard.

They placed the flowers they had brought at the foot of the crosses and walked among the graves, pleased to see how well they seemed to be kept.

Accommodation had been arranged for them not far away, in a hastily constructed hostel for relief workers. They enjoyed a meal of rice and fish curry, slept well on the temporary charpoys and after a breakfast of fruit were back in Chittagong by mid afternoon, going immediately to see Christopher and his foster family.

Next day they discussed arrangements for the eventual memorials to the point of deciding on the inscriptions, went back to Tamana's and took her, the younger of her children and Christopher for a restaurant meal, in line with their plan of allowing their grandson to get used to them while still in familiar surroundings. They told him they would shortly be going to England, on an aeroplane.

"Engaland. See amma, babba?"he asked in his odd little mixture of tongues. Michael had to tell him they would not be there, but he would see his sister, Edwina.

"Ha. Dwina," he responded.

His English, once away from Tamana's children, was quite good, for a child not yet three, and Michael and Kathleen had little trouble getting through to him. They spent the rest of the week finalising arrangements for the memorial stones, seeing as much of the devastated country as they could, and upgrading their flight from economy class to first, to make it easier to keep Chris happy and able to sleep.

Back in England they faced the inevitable questions as to why three were returning when two had left, a week before, but fortunately the British Embassy in Dhaka had co-operated fully in providing the necessary documentation, including a fast-tracked passport for the little boy, who had travelled out on his parents'.

At home in London, they lost no time in contacting Alastair, Charles and Maria who told them that Edwina was well and enjoying herself, and looking forward to seeing "Kistopher." Kathleen and Michael spent two nights at home before driving to Shropshire and returning next day with both their grandchildren. Michael also quickly spoke to Paul Wykeham to ask if he had heard anything from the children's other grandparent, Angus McArthur.

"Yes, we've had a letter from him. It was rather odd, it simply thanked us for letting him know what had happened and asked if there was anything he had to do. We had already told him that you were fetching the little boy from Bangladesh and that Edwina was staying with her cousins in Shropshire, and we gave him their address and phone number."

"Have you said anything about our taking the children to see him?"

"Yes, we said we thought you intended to do that. He didn't refer to it in his reply, though."

"We shall try to get in touch with him. But we shall certainly take them up there."

Michael was a little worried. The letter from Mr McArthur had been rather brusque, certainly very short.

"You don't suppose there was something between him and Catriona?" he asked Kathleen. "I mean, we know he didn't want her to go to London. Did he perhaps dislike the idea of her marrying Jon?"

"She didn't talk about him much. But on the other hand I never got any impression that they had quarrelled, or were estranged. They just hadn't seen much of each other, for twelve or fifteen years, had they?"

"What about the aunt she lived with while she was at school? Do you think we ought to try to contact her? I mean, we don't want to go to him and have an unpleasant scene that would upset the children, do we?"

"We don't even know her name, except Auntie Mary and she lives somewhere near Edinburgh. Or did. I think we should write to Mr McArthur and tell him what we plan to do. Give him some dates and ask him when it would be alright for him, to visit. Make sure we don't make it look as though we want to dump the children on him, but on the other hand we certainly don't want to freeze him out.

"Oh, Michael. I haven't the faintest idea what he's like, but just think. He lost his wife, now his only child. What a state he might be in. You and I have got each other, and the children ...."

Michael wrote: "Dear Mr McArthur: Please forgive me for taking so long to get in touch with you. We did not have your address and then we have been away, fetching Christopher, our grandson and yours, from Bangladesh. But we found a lovely little boy, and Edwina is an equally delightful little girl, and very bright, like her mother.

"We did not see very much of Catriona, but it was enough to know that we liked her a great deal, loved her indeed. She and Jonathan could not have been happier together. What happened to them was tragic. But at least they were doing what they both wanted to do so much, and were doing it exceptionally well, we have been told. Indeed going well beyond even the extremes of duty, in helping people about whom they were only paid to gather facts.

"We saw where they are buried. It is in a little cemetery not far from where they died and near a village. At the moment their resting places are marked only by wooden crosses, but we have left instructions for permanent memorials. We took photographs but they have not yet been processed. I will send them to you as soon as they are, or we will bring them. Which brings me to the next point.

"I am sure you would like to see your grandchildren. We would like you to, and discuss their futures with us. They are as much yours as ours. Could I therefore ask if you will give me dates when it would be alright to come to you, with them. Or perhaps tell us when it would NOT be convenient, and we can go from there. Also, perhaps point us in the direction of accommodation, for us all.

"Yours most sincerely, and looking forward to meeting you ...."

The reply when it came was somewhat longer than Mr McArthur's to Paul Wykeham, but still very brief, and giving little hint of his feelings towards the children. It read: "Dear Mr Housman, Thank you for your letter and what you have done for the bairns. I would like to see them, and yourselves. Any time would be fine, if you would give me notice of one or two weeks. You will have to take the ferry boat from Oban to Castlebay, on Barra island. You can drive from there now, over the causeway, if you are bringing a car. If not, there are taxis. When you get to the first houses, ask where I live. Anybody will tell you."

They decided to go in July. But before that they had to settle on a school for Edwina, and went first to the nearest their home in Lambeth, and told the headmistress that it was their granddaughter they were concerned with, and she was now an orphan.

The head told them: "Of course we'll be able to take her. Bring her along on the second of September, Tuesday. That's when term starts."

Kathleen said: "Don't you want to know anything about her?"

"Yes, but that will all be dealt with when she comes," the head said. Kathleen thought she seemed completely uninterested. She was not – just had a hundred and one problems demanding more immediate attention than one new pupil, whose advent was weeks ahead. But it had not been like that when Jonathan started, she thought, and said so to Michael.

"Do you think we should take her somewhere private?" he asked.

"And go against one of the principles you've believed in and argued for, most of your life?"

Their soul-searching ended in a decision to send her first to the local school, and if they did not think it was working out, to switch to an independent option. A few days later they left for the Western Isles.

Nine

Vatersay

Driving in Michael's Rover, Edwina and Christopher strapped snugly and happily in their child seats, they set off for Oban via Lyndford, spending a day and two nights there, the children at Home Farm, Michael and Kathleen with Alastair and Angela at Jasmine Cottage. The youngsters would happily have stayed with their Jameson counterparts while Granny and Grandad went north, but that would have defeated the object of the exercise.

After an overnight stay in the busy little port, they all enjoyed the five-hour ferry trip through the Sound of Mull and across a wide expanse of sea to Castlebay, on Barra, from where they drove the few miles south to the new causeway linking the island with the tiny isle of Vatersay.

Michael and Kathleen were by then encountering a few butterflies as they wondered what kind of reception they were heading for at the hands of Catriona's father, who from such contacts as had been made gave the impression of being a somewhat unusual character.

On Vatersay, there were rather more houses than they expected, but only one road, on which they took Angus McArthur's advice and stopped at the first dwelling with a visible human presence.

"Excuse me," Michael said to a man cutting grass verges to a path leading to a front door. "Could you tell me which is Mr McArthur's house?"

"Now which McArthur would that be?" the gentleman asked in the lilting Hebridean tone which is as different from Glaswegian or indeed most mainland Scots accents as is Wrexham Welsh from Machynlleth. "The maist of us are McArthur."

"Mr Angus McArthur is the one we're looking for," said Michael.

"Ach, weel, ye're not far away. It's that hoose yonder," and he pointed to a sizeable cottage about two hundred yards away from the road, with one or two outbuildings attached or close by, and a track leading to it. "And you'll be Catriona's father-in-law, I wouldna min' guessin?"

Michael admitted he was.

"Ach, weel, he'll be glad tae see ye. He's been talking o' ye. An' I know they're hame. I saw the truck drive up just now."

"Thank you very much," Michael said. But he was taken aback by being told "they" were at home.

"Did you hear that?" he asked Kathleen as he got back into the car.

"I did," she said. "Well, well. Quiet waters run deep, perhaps."

They drove up to the house, a comfortable-looking bungalow showing signs of recent extension. Both got out, leaving the children in their seats, went to the door and knocked.

Prepared by the neighbour, they were not quite as surprised as they might have been when it was opened by a youngish – and apparently pregnant – woman.

Michael took the initiative.

"I hope we have the right house. Mr McArthur – Angus McArthur?"

"Aye, that's right. He's away with the sheep, but he willna be long. And you're Mr and Mrs Housman, are ye no? Come in, will ye. We've been expecting ye."

"The children are in the car. Can we bring them?"

"Ach, aye. The puir bairns. Bring them in. Let me see them."

They unloaded the two, took them indoors, where they stood shyly surveying the new lady and her surroundings.

Michael had to know. He said: "I'm sorry – we didn't know – are you Mrs McArthur?"

"Aye, Jennie. He should have told you." She smiled. "He's like that with his letters, though. An' then, with what happened …. he wouldna like ….

"But sit ye down, please. Ye'll have a cup of the tea, will ye no? It's a wee bit early for much else.... although – ye've had ye're dinners, I hope?"

"Yes, thank you," Kathleen said, almost the first words she had spoken. "We had something at Castlebay."

Jennie went through a door and there was the sound of a kettle being filled from a tap, and cups rattling. She came back.

"Now, you must be Edwina," she said to that young lady. "And ye're Christopher." Both smiled shyly. "Would ye like something else to drink?"

Kathleen answered for them. "They're very fond of Ribena – you know, blackcurrant. But if you haven't got that, orange squash , lemonade, anything."

"I have them all. We keep them for the visitors." She went back to her kitchen, returning with full glasses, four cups and saucers, teapot, milk, sugar and a plate of scones, all on a huge wooden tray.

"I've brought a cup for Angus. I've just seen him coming over the brae," she said. And she had hardly finished filling the cups when the door opened.

"Weel, ye've come. And the bairns," Angus said. "Guid day to ye, Mr Housman. And Mrs Housman." He held out his hand to each.

Both were surprised by the man they saw. For some reason, they had expected someone of their own age. Angus was barely fifty, Michael thought, and although his face was as weatherbeaten as could be expected from an outdoor life, some of it on the sea, he appeared anything but aged. His hair was relatively short, but abundant, and dark. Catriona's flaming mop had obviously not come from him. Also, in spite of expecting to find some dour, uncommunicative character with whom they would find it difficult to make meaningful contact, they liked him immediately,

"Michael, please," as he shook hands. "And Kathleen," she added.

"Ach, verra guid. Angus, and Jennie." He turned to the children. "You must be Edwina. And Christopher."

Michael interposed: "This is Mummy's daddy, you know, don't you. Your other grandad."

Edwina looked at Angus solemnly for a few seconds in the contemplative manner she often adopted when she was faced with a new situation.

"Hello, other grandad," she said. "Mummy's dead, you know. She was trying to help children like me an' a big wind came an' she was killed. An' Daddy."

They could see Angus struggling with his emotions. But he managed to say: "Yes, ma bairn, I know. Ye must be verra proud o' your mummy and daddy."

"Please take ye're tea," Jennie said after a short pause.

Angus, cup, saucer and scone in hand, said: "Ye asked me to arrange some accommodation for ye. But ye don't need it, ye know. There are two spare bedrooms here, and a separate bathroom. We've no visitors until next week so ye'll be most welcome if it will do for ye."

Kathleen said: "Are you sure? We really didn't want to impose on you."

"Have you kept your rooms vacant because we were coming. Because if you have, we must pay you," Michael added.

"Ach, dinna talk so," Angus said. "We didna have any booking, anyway."

Michael said: "Well, can we take you somewhere for dinner tonight? Castlebay's not far – I'm sure there's somewhere we could take the children as well."

"No, you cannot. Jennie is all ready tae cook for us all just now. And there's a lot tae talk about after the bairns are in bed. Is there no?"

After the meal, Michael and Kathleen put the children to bed, together, and they sat down with tea and coffee in a comfortable sitting room.

Kathleen asked: "I'm sorry to be so inquisitive, Mr ….. Angus …. Jennie …. have you been married long?"

She said: "Nearly two years. But I knew Angus for a long time before. I was the nurse here when Morag took ill.

Catriona was a wee slip of a thing when I first came to Barra. I was born on Harris."

"She used to come over to Vatersay on the ferry boat, with her bicycle. There was no causeway then," Angus said. "She was awfu' guid tae Morag."

"It was ma job," Jennie said. She and Angus looked at each other. It was as though she was trying to encourage him. And after a while he spoke.

"I tellt ye there was a lot tae talk about," he said. "It isnae good. But I'd like ye to know it all. Ye must ha' been wonderin .... An' mebbe the bairns will ask questions, someday, and they'll hae tae be tellt. Some of it, anyway."

Michael said: "You don't have to tell us anything you don't want to, Angus. Only what you want to. Or leave it, and tell us some other time."

"Nae, I have tae tell ye. I've been preparin' tae."

He leaned forward, looked away as though he was still finding it hard to start. At last, he said: "Ye know, dinna ye, that Morag died. The puir lassie. She was verra young."

He looked at his feet. They could see he was finding it hard to talk.

"We were verra happy at first," he continued at last. "She was awfu' guid-lookin', and a hard worker, inside the house and out. We were both verra young, an' puir. She didna ha' much, the lassie, but that didna worry her. And when the bairn came along she took it all in her stride, ye know. We wanted another, but it didna happen. I thought afterwards that mebbe ....."

"I've told ye, love, it wasna that," Jennie broke in.

"Ach, weel, mebbe no. Anyway, she was fine until Catriona was about eight or nine. Then she seemed tae change. Started to get very short-tempered, wi' her as weel as me. Not all the time, ye understand, but every now and then. It seemed for no reason. She just seemed to want to snap at ye, for nothing, a'most. And the bairn would snap back. I couldna make it out. They'd been sae guid wi' each other. Morag always helped her wi' her school work, and they used tae talk and read taegether."

He went quiet again.

"She was always clever – bright – the bairn I mean. And when the time came to go to a high school the teacher here said she must go to a guid one, not stay on Barra. Ye see, the school there was not thocht much of, at that time. She said she'd never 'fulfill her potential' there, was how she put it. She should go somewhere where she could be sure o' good 'highers' and go on to university. She said she ought tae go to a boarding school. Weel, that was out o' the question, o' course. It would tak more than everything we make. I said she could mebbe go to ma sister near Edinburgh. She's always said how good the school is where her own bairns went and indeed they've done awfu' weel."

"Ye'd hae thocht I was suggesting she should be sent to the other end o' the airth. She carried on for days. I didna know what tae do. In the end I thocht the bairn's future was the most important thing, and I arranged wi' Mary – ma sister – and the school, through Mary, for her to go. We had the telephone put in so I so I could talk to her. It was the first on the island. Morag would never use it, or even answer it.

"Anyway, it was all fixed up for her tae go. I took her to the ferry, and Mary came all the way frae Edinburgh to meet her at Oban. Morag wouldna even go to the ferry wi' us.

"Funny enough though she seemed better after that. Least, she didna shout and snap so. And she read the letters the bairn wrote, at first, although she didna talk about her much. Weel, not at a' really. An' then she started tae be puirly. She had a lot o' headaches and she was sick. She saw the doctor, but he couldna find anything wrong. An' her temper got worse again. It seemed to be against the bairn, though. I hardly dared mention her but she'd fly up. She even hit me. It was when a letter came frae Mary. It was only asking for a wee bit more money for somethin' the lassie needed but it set Morag off."

He stopped, his head went down, but after a minute or two he rose, went towards the window and stood gazing out over the sea. After a while he returned to his chair.

"I tried to get her to see the doctor again but she wouldna go. So I asked him to come here. She answered him staightforward enough, told him about her headaches and the sickness. He said she needed tae see a specialist, but he couldna persuade her tae go. I went with him to his car and told him how she was about the bairn. He asked me what had happened, an' where she was, but he didna say anythin' more. But it was after that Jennie started tae come."

She broke in: "What Angus told him made him very concairned. He really did think she should see a specialist – a brain specialist. But he couldna make her, so he asked me to visit her regularly and note down what I found – how often was she sick and so on. I was usually on Vatersay once a week but I tried to make an extra visit to see Morag."

"Ye did a lot o' guid for her. After ye'd been she was always quieter. Still, it became verra clear tae me that she wasna really gettin' any better. The worst part though was her temper was getting even worse. It seemed tae be against the bairn, mostly. I hardly dared mention her – she could fly up in a minute. She'd say awfu' things about her."

He stopped, got up again, said to Jennie: "Ye tell it," and went out through the door."

Kathleen asked: "Is he .... alright?"

Jennie went out herself, but was back in a moment.

"He's alright. He'll be back in a wee while. It's just.... he doesnae want you tae see him greet."

She went on: "We'd got her to see the doctor two or three times but every time he wanted her to go over the water to a specialist she refused," Jennie said. "Dr McFadden knew better than I did there was something seriously wrong, and he was worried about it, but he couldna make her go. So one day I had a real go at him. I told him Angus was going to be driven to something terrible if it went on. I could see the man getting' lower and lower, in himsel'. It was me suggested what we should do. I got him tae give her something that would calm her down, or rather tae let me give it her. It was only a sedative, a powerful one mind. Only a doctor is allowed to give it a patient, really, but by then he was as worried about her as I was. I shouldna tell ye about it but the man's dead now and it doesna matter who knows I did it. My idea was to get her to agree to go to the hospital while she was under it. I gave it her in a drink, an' asked if she'd come wi' me to the doctor and she said she would, an' before she could change her mind we had her on the ferry. I went with her. They'd got a scanner at the hospital and they found the tumour. But they couldna do anythin' about it. They couldna operate.

"Angus thought it had come because he'd sent Catriona away to school. I knew it wasna, of course, and the doctor, and we tried to tell him. The thing in her brain was the cause, not the result. But he wouldna have it. He was in a terrible state. He wouldna write to the bairn to tell her, and in the end I did it, through Mary. But Catriona never replied.

"She hung on for another two years. I tried to look after her as weel as I could. She had her good days when she was quite normal, but towards the end it was pretty bad. Dr McFadden gave me more sedatives for her, and late on she was under them almost a' the while."

Angus had come back while she was speaking. He seemed recovered. He said: "Jennie was wonderful. Morag gave her a hard time but I never saw her anythin' but patient an' calm. She had tae make special arrangements wi' the ferry boat man so he could bring her over at different times. I didna know at the time but I've been told since she paid him herself because the health folk wouldna let her go over the quota.

" Ye mecht think it was awfu', wi' ma wife so bad, but that was when I started to get.... fond .... o' her."

"There was nothing, ye know, improper or anything," Jennie said quickly. "We never said anything, even, tae each other. An' I dinna think there was any talk about it. After all I was the nurse and he's near twenty year older. But it was just as much me as Angus. Even before she … died…. I think we knew…. we'd …. like tae be together."

Angus resumed: "The bairn – hech – she was a young woman – came back for the funeral, an' I wanted to tell her everything then, but somehow I never did. An' ye know, I'd come to be a bit at odds wi' her ma sel. I daresay these psychiatrists would talk about it bein' somethin' tae do wi' ma subconscious or somethin' blamin' her for Morag dying. Then when she went to London I thought she was desertin' me. She didna help. She didna write, only to her aunt. An' Mary was a bit loath to pass it on to me, it seems. I suppose it was because it would have been admitting there was something wrong between us. She didna even write to tell me she was getting married, although she did tell Mary and asked her to tell me. Mary tellt me how she was gettin' on after that – how she'd got her degree and was doing another one. Then about the first bairn."

They could see he was again finding it hard to continue.

"I knew I should write to her. But I didna." His head went down again, almost masking his muttered: "Ach, may God forgive me."

Jennie moved closer, put both arms round him. Michael caught Kathleen's hand.

After a minute or so, Angus picked his head up and spoke again. "I didna even know about the wee laddie. Or that she'd finished her studies and had a job wi' the university's research department, along wi' Jonathan. Or that they'd gone to Bangladesh.

"The first I knew about a' that was when the policeman came," he finally managed. And after another silence: "I didna see how I could live wi' masel. An' the bairn on the way…. I wasna fit tae be a father…."

Jennie said, as Angus again went silent: "Ye see, up to then he'd thocht they'd come together again, one day. I told him so, an' I meant to make sure they did."

She too was finding it difficult to continue. But finally she said: "It was ye're letter made the difference, Mr Housman," she said. "He's been a deal better since…"

All four sat silently, mourning with Angus, embarrassed but coming as near as they could to feeling his grief and shame. Michael and Kathleen had lost their son, but he had left them with their words of love and encouragement in his ears. Angus, they now saw, hardly knew his daughter, the instincts that drove her. They were worse than strangers, for they both knew their blood tie should have made them cling to each other. Morag's illness ought to have brought them closer together, not driven them apart. Later that evening, as they went to bed, Kathleen soliloquised. Should the child have been sent so far away, hardly ever to return? But then Angus, out of love, had thought he was doing what was best for her. And if she had not gone to the Edinburgh school, she would almost certainly never have made the university where she met Jonathan, and fulfilled her destiny, short-lived as it turned out to be. She and Michael could see that Catriona, full of energy and talent as she was, was a quirky little character, but they never had the opportunity of getting through to the flaws in her family relationships which Angus and Jennie were now exposing.

Before that, it had been she who broke the silence: "Angus, you must put it behind you. You've got Jennie, and you're going to have a son or daughter. And these other two. Won't you help us bring them up? Share them with us? They're as much yours as ours, aren't they?"

Angus was still silent. But Jennie said: "Of course he will, Mrs Housman. Of course he will."

*****

Next morning, Angus seemed in better spirits, and after he had seen to the few cattle and sheep needing attention, and they had breakfasted in the kitchen where, Jennie told them, their visitor guests usually ate, he offered to take Michael, Kathleen and the children round the island, and his own land.

They all piled in to his elderly Toyota four by four, the child seats transferred from the Rover and secured by various unconventional fastenings. First they travelled south to the actual village of Vatersay, a scattered township of a dozen houses plus a church and the big house built by the island's former owner, via the narrow isthmus linking the isle's two halves.

"In really bad weather the water can blow right across here, frae one side tae the other," he said as they crossed the 600-yard wide strip of machair with the road in the middle. The road ended at the township, and they went back to the northern end. He showed them the memorial pillar to the tragic deaths of more than 300 passengers and crew of a ship which had hit rocks just off the island in 1853. They also saw scattered wreckage from a Catalina flying boat which crashed almost on the sea shore in 1944, killing three of the crew. They too were commemorated on a memorial, put up comparatively recently.

Angus told them of other stories from the island's history, or folklore, like how servants of Vatersay's one farmer at the time stole rings from the fingers of the drowned emigrants from the wrecked ship, and cut off fingers to do it; centuries further back, how the chieftainess, "Marion of the Heads," imprisoned people in a cave where the water came up and drowned them; and had others decapitated, which was how she came by her soubriquet.

Eventually they got back to his own croft of about 100 acres, the biggest on the island, and his 70-strong flock of sheep, and a dozen beef cows, mostly with suckling calves, which looked in excellent shape.

"Prices are going up a bit lately," he told them "but we'd be hard pushed to live if we didna get a bit from the visitors. There used tae be the fishin, an' I had a bit share in a boat, but that's a'most gone now."

"Have you never thought of leaving and going to the mainland?" Michael asked.

"Ach, no," he said. "I couldna. Nor Jennie. It'd ha' tae be the city, tae get a job, an' we couldna take that. We'll get by, an' I hope we'll get mair visitors now the road across is built."

"You just had to use the ferry before, I suppose. Did you get visitors then?"

"Aye, we had a few. But a lot o' folk used tae bide in Castlebay and come over here for the day. There were more coming tae stay longer, though. That's why we built the new bedrooms. There was only one and a wee bit box room when Morag an' me came here in 1960. And no water, nor the electric. I did maist o' the buildin' work masel, wi' a bit help frae Jennie. She was still nursin', then."

"You did a very good job," Michael said. "How did you get the materials, before the causeway was built?"

"Ach, the merchant would take it to the ferry, and I'd fetch it frae there wi' the tractor or the jeep. It's awfu' dear, though. Concrete blocks cost half as much again as ye'd pay in Glasgow. An' cement. Sand's alright through. Costs us nothing.

"You've always lived on Vatersay, Angus?"

"Aye, an' my father, an' mother. My grandfather came frae Barra, before the first war. He was one one o' the folk they called the Vatersay raiders. Ye'll have heard o' them, mebbe."

"Yes, a little. When I was first in Parliament there was an old Scottish member who remembered the case. Didn't they come over and build houses which turned out to be illegal?"

"Aye, an' went to gaol for it. My grandfather was one o' them. But they were desperate for land, and Vatersay was owned by a lady who let it all out as that one farm, an' never came near hersel'. It helped make her rich an' kept less than a dozen folk in a livin' when it could ha' kept three times as many. But there was a big fuss about it, in Parliament, and the government bought it and split it up into crofts."

"What happened to your grandfather?"

"Oh, he spent a few weeks in gaol and came back tae the new croft, where he'd built a little house. He made it a bit bigger, an' better, I suppose. My father was born there, an' he came here, eventually, an I was born here. I moved away tae Barra, when I was 14 an' left school, an' worked on a fishin' boat."

"But you came back?"

"Aye. My mother died an' my father became ill. I don't think any of us knew what it was, really. We just knew he wasna going tae be with us much longer. I'd met Morag, an' we wanted tae be wed. I was 19 an' she was 18. My father wasna really fit tae do it, but he gave his consent. Morag's father was dead but her mother gave hers and we were wed an' came tae live here. We couldna move my father so we had to sleep in the little box room I told ye about. That was where we spent our weddin' night. An' I've been here ever since."

"Is the farm the same as it was then?"

"Well, we still make a livin' frae the sheep, an' cattle, mostly. But two o' the folk next to us didna want to keep their crofts an' we were allowed tae take the land. It nearly doubled the size of ours, an' we were able to build up our stock. It can get a bit bigger yet. We havena got full security of tenure for this extra land, but it canna be used for anything but crofting, so I think it's pretty safe."

"And do you think you might get more?" Michael asked.

"I've no idea, Michael. I canna see any that's likely at this moment. But I'm no' concerned, ower much. I dinna want tae be rich. Least, I'm not worried if I never am. However puir we are, we've a guid life here."

They had all left the Toyota and Kathleen, some distance away, was telling the children how the sheep had been sheared and the wool used to make coats and jumpers, but was now growing again so they would be warm for the winter. Michael and Angus leaned on the vehicle and Angus started to talk again.

"Ye havena seen much o' her yet, but I can tell ye – Jennie's a fine lassie. She'll never let me an' the bairn that's comin' get at odds like it was wi' Catriona. She'll keep us on a level keel. But I've learned a lot, Michael. It willna happen again."

Michael took his hand, and shook it.

"No, I'm quite sure it won't."

That afternoon, Kathleen persuaded Angus and Jennie to go with them, and the children, to Castlebay for a meal in the unpretentious hotel where Jennie had worked as a young girl. Next day Michael, Kathleen and the youngsters toured Barra, following an itinerary suggested by their young hostess. And in the evening, they talked about the children's future.

Ten

Primeval

Stella's menstrual calendar had never been terribly regular, which was why Edward could only tell Angela, that day in the hospital, that they thought she was pregnant. But in another month, when she still did not have a period, and she was beginning to experience bouts of morning sickness, there could be no doubt about it. And it was quickly confirmed by a visit to her doctor.

The decision to go for a baby had been hers. He was resigned to putting off having a family, perhaps for years, even maybe for ever. It was all part of the contract he had made with her when she agreed to marry him. But strange things were happening to Stella, inside the polished exterior she presented to the world. She had struggled against the love that invaded her life when Edward came into it. She must never be tied down by domestic strings. She actually told him that she herself was the most important person in her life, and she must fulfill her potential, even if it took her away from him from time to time.

But after they were married, as the months went by, she found the need for personal success in the world of work, the impelling demand to get away from the poverty of her youth, were no longer quite such overiding dictates in her life. The leisure hours spent with Edward, at home and elsewhere, stepped up in importance. She found pleasure in searching for and eventually buying a home together, a detached three-bed house, modest enough in itself but in a quiet, pleasant, slightly up-market village a few miles from Protechno's headquarters. She could not quite help an inward purr of pleasure as she indulged in a comparison between her new home and her childhood on the Salford council estate. Then in taking her driving test, something that had slipped by, passing it with ease, first time, after only a handful of lessons, and being congratulated by the examiner; and buying her first car so she could be fully mobile when Ed was away, or working late.

And then there started to creep in that other urge, the primeval need encountered by nine out of ten women, however they may try to convince themselves that it's not like that, for them, and keep it subservient to the demands of a good time, or career, or buying a house. First, she started to realise that leaving Edward for days or weeks at a time, which another job of the kind she had been thinking of as her next step would almost certainly entail, was anything but attractive. When his work took him away from the factory, only for one or two days, she found herself fretting and longing for his return. Her friend Pauline tried to fill the gap with theatre visits and the like, and while she was grateful and rarely refused, the diversions came nowhere near to making up for Edward's absence.

It was Pauline however who finally brought her to admit, to herself, that there was something else she wanted, and needed. Her friend told her she was having a baby.

"Are you going to leave us, then?" Stella asked after the usual congratulations.

"Oh, no, not if I can help it. I don't think they'll want me to go."

"Did you – was it – planned?"

"Not exactly. I mean, we always meant to have children, but not just yet. I miscalculated. But it's alright. We're both pleased. And really, it's about time. I'll be thirty next year. I don't want to be dragging a toddler around when I'm 50."

Stella lay awake most of that night. And this time it was not just through wishing for Edward's hand cradling her breast.

He was home in time for dinner next evening, after paying a brief visit to his father as he left the airport. Over the meal, he reported briefly on Alastair, and afterwards, as they drank their coffee in front of the fire, she asked how his trip – to Sweden – had gone, and he told her, going into the detail she now increasingly comprehended and appreciated.

At the end, she said, after a few moments of silence: "Darling, there's something I want to tell you. I hope you won't be angry."

His stomach jarred. "Oh, god, she's been offered a job. She's going away." He'd said, when he asked her to marry him, that she must fulfill her career potential, and if that meant periods away from him, so be it. And he meant it. But now it was here ....

"My sweetheart, you know I've always said you're your own person. Of course I won't be angry, if it's something you want."

"I want us to have a baby."

He looked at her, incredulous. That was the last thing he expected, at this stage. He was almost in tears. It took time to find words, and when they came, they were almost incoherent.

"Darling .... do you mean it .... ?"

"Of course I mean it. I wouldn't say it if I didn't ...."

"I mean.... now ...."

"Not this instant, Edward. The age of miracles may not be past, but that would be asking a bit too much, wouldn't it?"

He laughed. "You know what I mean. I mean don't you want to wait a bit, until you've...."

"Until I've what? Made myself into a superwoman or something?"

"You are a superwoman, darling. Of course I don't mean that. But fulfilling one's potential is important, isn't it? And you've got a great deal of potential."

"Perhaps. And I want to fulfill it. But right now I want to have a baby – our baby, my darling. While we're still young. The other can wait a while."

"Are you sure? Don't you think if you were tied down looking after a baby you'd become what you told me you were determined not to be – just a housewife?"

"And don't you think .... ?" But she could not easily find the words she wanted. She wanted to tell him that was a year ago, and things had changed. She was no longer Stella Hardy, the back street girl determined to hoist herself out of poverty and into a good position in the world of business. At least, not that alone. But success would no longer be enough. The heights she had been set on scaling once the poverty was left behind might have satisfied her if the other things had not come along. She had actually fought, or tried to fight, against falling in love. But she lost the battle, with the inevitable result. Love changed everything, as real love so often does.

She was sitting on a low chair, in front of Edward on the settee. She left it, knelt againt him, her arms clasping his hips, finally finding the words she wanted, which would have been impossible for her, not so long before, even through the vocabulary she had so carefully nurtured.

"Don't you know, my darling, that love can change everything, everyone, even someone like me? I didn't want to love you. I tried to stop myself. But I couldn't, and now loving you, and you loving me, is the most important thing in the world. And that means I want our baby. Babies. Perhaps the other will happen, someday. But I'll never stop loving you."

And that was it. But a question mark over how satisfied she would be as domesticity took over a larger part of her life persisted in Edward's mind, and he asked more than once through the next days, whether she was sure. Before she knew him, she had spent ten years relentlessly responding to an urge to "get on," ignoring almost all the calls of social life that lured her contemporaries. The result was a young woman who would be able to hold her own in any business atmosphere in the world, he was convinced. How soon before that urge again became the most important thing in her life? He was not afraid that she would stop loving him, or the children she was now determined to have. But what turmoil, practical and psychological, might it involve for her? But those questions stayed within his own mind. She was quite sure, she said.

The confirmation of the pregnancy came just before that other milestone in their lives – his father's first steps towards recovery. The two events were almost euphoric. But there was one other factor in his life that prevented Edward living permanently on Cloud Nine. He could not rid himself of a feeling of guilt over Josie's passion for him. He had done nothing to promote it, and time after time he told himself so. But it was there.

Before his father left the hospital he saw Angela frequently. She was the person he found it easiest of anyone to talk to; in this case, easier than Stella, to whom the affair had never so far been mentioned.

He said to her: "I feel terrible about it."

"You shouldn't. You couldn't help it. You did nothing wrong. It was just one of those things."

"I know, but I can't help feeling .... responsible, I suppose. The trouble is, I like her very much, just as I like Jeannie, and you. It's awful, having to deliberately steer clear of her, or her steer clear of me."

"Edward, please try to stop feeling guilty about it. There really is no need."

He knew Angela was right. But still he could not help it. If he heard her name mentioned, there came that nagging little doubt. Had he really done nothing to encourage her? Had there been a too-welcoming smile, some flash of recognition beyond the norm of family connection that now existed between him and her mother?

He asked Angela, regularly, for news of her. He felt she would not misinterpret the inquiries. And she did not. She knew that far from inflaming any feelings of passion, any news of Josie progressing through a normal life would ease his unfounded feelings of guilt. But as Josie was beginning to make something of a mark in the Balkans, in Slovenia, he and Stella encountered the first tragedy of their married life. She lost the baby.

Eleven

Revelations

Angus and Jennie McArthur became parents of a little girl three months after the Housmans' visit. Angus was not and never became a fluent correspondent, and the letter in which he told Kathleen and Michael the good news, while friendly and warm in tone, did not amount to much more than a note in length. But they were delighted when it concluded with asking them to tell Edwina and Christopher the good news and hoping they would come to see "the new bairn" as soon as possible. It was then September, however and Edwina had just started school. They were not keen on travelling to the Outer Hebrides during the Christmas holidays, when there was not time enough to make it to Oban in daylight, in comfort, even from Lyndford. The trip would have to wait until Easter.

A Pickwickian Christmas was spent at Home Farm and Jasmine Cottage, with the big farmhouse kitchen well filled for the Yuletide dinner. A trestle table was brought in from the old dairy and laid at right angles to the Jacobean oak board that had once graced the dining room at the manor. Round the T-shape were Alastair and Angela, Kathleen and Michael, Peter and Aelwen, although not their children and grandchildren because they had conflicting calls on their presence; the five little ones, of course; Edward and Stella, taking almost a whole week from their work in Germany; Emily Jane, of whom more shortly; Angela's daughter Jeannie, her husband Simon and either a son or a daughter, they did not know which because he or she still resided in Jeannie's tummy; and of course the hosts, Charles and Maria, and Evinka, the au pair who had stayed to become almost one of the family.

They were 19 in all, stretching the sleeping accommodation as well as the culinary. It should have been 20, Angela – and Jeannie – could not help thinking. But of course if Josie had still been around, she would not have joined a party which included Edward, they realised almost in the same breath. Neither had received more than three letters from her in more than two years.

The children all occupied one bedroom – "more like a school dormitory," said Kathleen, who took on the duty of persuading them to go to sleep – eventually – by reading stories. Edwina and Dorothy shared a bed, Christopher took Dorothy's old cot, Douglas another cot dug out of the attic, and Alastair had a sleeping bag on the floor.

As it had been made clear they would on previous visits, the children got along like a house on fire. Edwina and Christopher's flaming hair did not seem to indicate flaming tempers, in fact Edwina's apparent chief characteristic was a quiet thoughtfulness. Sometimes, she appeared almost withdrawn, making Kathleen wonder whether the loss of her mother and father might be behind it. But the little girl slept well, ate well, encountered no traumas like bed-wetting, and happily recounted stories from her first term at school to the junior Alastair, who reciprocated with his own experiences, only taking care to emphasise that of course his tales were about boys; and Dorothy, a quiet but intelligent little girl, who was about to start her education.

On Boxing Day, Charles and his father delighted children and adults by revealing that they had dusted off Uncle Giles' old horse buggy, and given it a thorough overhaul, and for those prepared to wrap up warmly they could offer trips round the farm and the lanes. The buggy had not been used on more than a dozen occasions since Alastair and his mother had taken the recuperating Debra for a spin, more than 40 years before, although Giles had always kept a "trotting pony" stabled and Alastair and Charles continued the practice.

Almost everyone jumped at the offer, and Whitefoot the pony had more exercise in one day than in most months of the previous year. But Edward engineered things to give him an opportunity of a conversation he had wanted to have for some time.

Making sure he and Stella were not on the same buggy trip, while she was gone he suggested to Emily Jane that they should take a walk together. He did not realise that the walk was almost an echo of one taken seventy years before by his grandfather and his sister, but with a somewhat different objective. Charles had wanted to bring his, and Billie's, secret loves to each other's knowledge. Edward was resolved to try to discover if his own and the others' concerns about Em's personal life had any foundation.

"It's so good to see you, you know," he opened. "We seem to have grown apart – you in London, us at Coventry and Charles here."

"It's inevitable, isn't it, in the modern world. I'd bet half the families in Britain are in something like the same situation."

"Yes, I suppose so. But at least we know what Charles and his family are up to, don't we? And Dad. And we know this is where our roots are. I don't even know where you live, except Chelsea. Or much about your work. Are you doctoring, or researching, nowadays?"

"It's a bit like it was with Angela. I'm essentially a researcher, but it involves treating patients, and spending quite a lot of time in the hospital with them, just as she did in her younger days. I think I've been able to move sooner into more research that she could. And my field is developing more widely. She started out by being concerned mostly with cystic fibrosis, and it led to genetics. I rather start from the genetical angle. But in practical terms I don't suppose there's much difference. I don't think I'll ever be as good as she was, though. I keep coming across people all the time who can't stop saying how she inspired them. Not just by her personality, which was important, of course, as we know, don't we; but how very good she was in her actual work."

Edward felt he was in danger of being sidetracked. He wanted to know about her research, but not as much as he wanted to find out about her personal life. Angela had told him she had boyfriends, at least one who she lived with, but there had also been a woman, an older woman, and there was some talk about them. He realised however that he must not frighten her off, above all by seeming to be critical. And he was not critical. People, even his own family, were entitled to their sexual orientation, even if it was a kind he thought unnatural. But he needed to know. She was his sister.

"You're happy in what you're doing, though?"

"Good heavens, boy, of course I am. You have your frustrations, of course. You're following a line of research that looks as though it's going to lead somewhere worthwhile, and it peters out. That's happened twice to me and my colleagues, already. It made one of them pack it all up. He said he was going for general practice – at least you could see that you were doing some good, to some people, he said."

She paused a moment. "Have you ever known anyone with cystic fibrosis, or muscular dystrophy, Ed?"

"No, I don't think so."

"Well, apart from my work, I've known two. One was my best friend at school, you may remember her, Lydia. She knew she was likely to die, before she was 30, and she did. The one with MD is still alive, wishing he could die, because he can't do a damn thing with any of his limbs. The proff – Angela – will tell you, perhaps she already has, about the little kids with cystic fibrosis she had to watch die when she was a young doctor. I couldn't give up trying to help find cures, or preventions, Ed, could I?"

Edward felt almost ashamed as he saw the intensity in her face, and heard it in her voice. What on earth did it matter whether she was lesbian or what, compared with the passion engendered by this need to help conquer these misery-creating diseases? But he must find out more, if only to let his father, Angela, Charles and Stella know what the facts were. Hopefully to reassure them. His approach still had to be indirect, though.

"Tell me about where you live, Em. We know the address, but that's all. Is it a house, or a flat, or what?"

"Good heavens, I couldn't afford a house in Chelsea. It's a flat – two bedrooms, and a living room, a bathroom and a kitchenette you can only get in one person at a time. It's ridiculously expensive but it's only walking distance from the hospital. I can't keep a car because garaging or parking would cost almost as much as the flat."

"Do you get about London much?"

"Not much."

"No theatres, or concerts, or art galleries? You were keen on music once."

"No."

"The social life isn't over full, then."

"No."

"Is that alright? Don't you need a bit of company and so on?"

She said nothing. Nor did he. They had stopped at a roadside gate; the gateway where, although they did not know it, Angela had pulled in her elderly Citroen and seen their father and mother walking across the same field; the day before the accident which took Debra from them all, two-and-a-half years before.

Edward made to open the gate, with the intention of walking back to Home Farm, or Jasmine Cottage, by the road. But before he could disengage the hook from its staple, she said: "You're quizzing me, aren't you, Edward? You think I've got secrets."

Edward left the hasp alone. "We do wonder about you a bit. You're one of the family, you know, and it's important to know you're happy. Or unhappy, if you were. But I know Dad worries about you, and so do Charles and I. We're all proud of the work you're doing, but we'd like to know more about the rest."

She leaned on the gate. It was a beautiful winter's day, and she could see the magnificent vista even more clearly than Angela had.

"Do you think you'll ever come back to live round here?" she asked.

"I don't know. Impossible to say. But I hope so. What about you?"

"Oh, yes. Someday."

"Shall we walk on?"

"Just now .... I'm going to tell you all you want to know, first. And you can tell the others if you want to.

Another short pause.

"I know you've all been wondering whether I've had boyfriends. Or girlfriends. Well, I have, both. One I've still got, although I hardly think you'd call her a girl. But never mind that. We'll come to her in a while." She leaned on the gate, looked across the fields and hills.

"When I was in my first year at St Thomas's, I met a boy, a student. Barry. He was doing electronics at London University and lived with a bunch of friends in a house near where I was then, in Notting Hill. We spent a lot of time together."

She hesitated.

"Yes, we lived together, eventually. It wasn't because we wanted to sleep together, Ed. We'd already done that. He loved me and would like us to be married, when we could, he said. I don't know whether you'd say I was in love with him but I certainly liked being with him.

"I was in halls for two years, but then I had to find somewhere outside to live. Barry suggested we should get somewhere together, and we settled for a tiny furnished flat in Lambeth. And I mean tiny. The living room was about ten by ten, the double bed almost filled the bedroom entirely, the bath and washbasin left a space 18 inches wide in the bathroom, and the toilet was shared with the other ground floor flat. Oh, and the kitchenette was even smaller that the one I've got now. We managed though, and stayed there for two years. Dad paid the rent, but I never told him or Mum about Barry."

"Why?"

"I don't really know. I suppose I was ashamed of living with him without being married. Mum once told me about a girl who'd done that – Angela's sister, I believe – and all the upset it caused. And you know how Mum was about that kind of thing. Anyway, I didn't tell them."

"I think it would have been better if you had. They'd have got over it."

"Yes, I think so now. But I didn't."

"So what happened then?"

"Well, Barry got his degree and found a job, quite a good one for a young graduate, and we were better off financially, so we found a better flat. I still let Dad send me a rent cheque because if I'd said I didn't want it he'd have wanted to know why." She went quiet, continued to lean on the gate.

"We were quite happy. My work was going well and they said they'd accept me on the genetics courses, which was what I always wanted to specialise in. That's when I met Angela. But it's when it started to go wrong for Barry. He started to have trouble walking and lifting things of any weight. He went to his doctor who sent him off for tests. They found he'd got muscular dystrophy.

"I expect you know its a wasting disease of the muscles, and it's progressive. A few people live with it until middle age or even beyond, but they're the exceptions. The worst damage is done when the muscles of internal organs are affected. That hasn't happened with Barry, so far, but he soon began to lose use of his arms and legs. He carried on working, but it became increasingly difficult and eventually he could only walk with a frame. I used to go with him to work and he would wait there in the evening until I arrived to help him get back to the flat.

"But he could still work?"

"Yes. And he and his colleagues modified an electric wheelchair so he could work from that, and get about the labs."

"And is he still doing that?"

"No. He can't do anything now. He's in a nursing home. He has to have everything done for him. He can't move his legs at all and his arms only very little. He can't even read because he can't handle a book – can't even turn pages. He listens to the radio a lot, and watches television, but that's just about the total of his activities, unless someone reads to him, or he can get hold of an audio book. And he seems to be losing the urge for that. When I went in just before I came up here he was sitting there with his eyes closed, and the nurse said he'd been like that for hours."

"He can talk, though?"

"Yes, but it seems to make him tired, quite quickly."

Another pause.

"I think he's wishing he could die. He's very low, Ed."

Edward opened the gate and they started to walk down the road.

"You're on your own, now, then?"

"No. And that's the other part of my life. Perhaps it's the part you think I may be hiding. I have a friend, who lives with me. I wouldn't call her a girlfriend, because she's 20 years older. And we're not lovers, Edward. We're not lesbians. We're very fond of each other, but we don't have any kind of sexual relationship. I suppose you could say she's like a mother to me, only she's not a replacement for Mum. She isn't a replacement for Barry, either. We were close friends when he was still living with me."

Edward sensed some kind of triangular relationship, which his father might find it hard to comprehend.

"What's her name? Is she married, or has she been?"

"Her name's Lisbeth. Not Elizabeth, Lisbeth. Yes, she's been married, no children, she can't have any. Her husband left her for another woman, she thinks that was why. He wanted children. She was very fond of him, they were happy together, but she understood that, and she let him go. She works in admin at the hospital and we talked about Barry, and the work I was involved in. She was very interested in that, still is. We just seemed to get closer and closer, Edward.

Hardly anyone else knew about Barry, but they could see how close Lisbeth and I were, I suppose, and they put two and two together and made five. I think even the Proff got a wrong impression. It was not long before she retired.

"Lisbeth was a tower of strength as Barry went downhill. Her hours at work were more regular than mine and she was able to help him get home and so on. Often she would stay with us. I didn't sleep with Barry, because he needed all the bed to be comfortable, so she slept with me in the other room. I don't know whether anyone outside actually knew about that, but of course if they knew, or guessed, the old two and two maths would come into operation again. Then when he went into hospital and after that the home, and it was obvious he would never come out again, we decided to go for the flat in Chelsea.

"That's about it, Edward. I wish now I'd told Mum and Dad about it as it all happened. I think I'd rather you told Dad now, and Charles, and Stella, if you will. But if you don't want to, I'll tell Dad, or Angela. I can talk to her."

"How long do you think Barry.... ?"

"I really can't say. Dystrophy isn't my field. It could be years. I hope not, for his sake."

"Did – do you love him very much, Em?"

"You may think this is awful. But I didn't, I don't love him the way you love Stella, Ed, or Charles and Maria love each other. I liked him, quite a lot, and he loved me, I know. But I wasn't passionate about him.

"You know, I think I'm under-sexed or something. Not completely asexual, and I'm certainly not homosexual or bisexual, but I just can't get excited about it. Barry stopped wanting that kind of thing quite soon after we discovered his illness, but before that I always went along with it in a way that I hope made him happy. But I prefer the kind of relationship I have with Lisbeth. It's warm, and loving, and undemanding. She's always there when I need someone to lean on, and confide in, and I hope I'm the same for her. We don't sleep together, but she always comes in to say goodnight. I'm usually the first to go to bed."

They walked another hundred yards, before Edward said: "If it's alright with you, Sis, I'll tell Angela. I don't know why, but I've always been able to talk to her, ever since I've known her. She'll take it from there. And of course I'll tell Stella."

Dr Emily Jane caught his hand, and they walked on. It was good to be "Sis," still.

Twelve

Vukovar

Angela's third letter from Josie came from Slovenia, while she was following the election campaign. It was a real letter, four foolscap pages, and gave her reassurance that her daughter was coping with her situation. When she then heard nothing for nearly a year, by when she and Alastair were married, she called Jim Meredith in Belgrade, who told her Josie was still in Slovenia and had done a particularly good job there, including covering the ten days of war that had recently ended with the acceptance of the little country's independence. There was still little in the British news media about the political situation in Yugoslavia, but Meredith told her how things were becoming increasingly tense. All he could tell her about Josie, at that point, apart from her Slovenian efforts, was that she had gone back to Sarajevo from where she had sent him various items of worthwhile information. However, he was now able to give her Ljiljana Alagic's address, where he thought Josie was staying. Angela wrote to her there, but it was only Dr Alagic who replied, greeting her warmly but able to tell her no more than that Josie had gone to Kosovo.

Josie's next letter did indeed come from Kosovo, the disturbed little province at the centre of the Serbian nationalist urge. It was semi-independent from Serbia, within the Yugoslav federation, but the Serb activists wanted to end that formula, and bring it wholly under their rule, although they were only a small proportion of the province's population. A big majority of the people were Muslims of Albanian ethnicity.

"It is very difficult to forecast what is going to happen," she wrote. "I am trying to keep my finger on it, and I keep sending stuff to the papers and the broadcast media. But of course, although with everything I send I restate my previous connections with the BBC and the Courier, and Jim Meredith has given me a card saying I am an associate of the agency, I don't really have any official status. And everything has to go as written material, typed on a little portable. I have no other means of transmitting it, at present, which means it's days old by the time it reaches them. I'm trying to make contact with papers, and radio, by phone, but it's horribly expensive, especially to America, and apart from the weekly, News Mag, which carried my stories about Slovenia, they don't want to know a freelance trying to tell them about things they're not interested in. I ask them to call me back but none of them have, up to now, except that one. They ask for my cellphone number but there are no networks here yet, at least in areas where I've been. Jim Meredith tries to be helpful and I know he's told people that I could be very useful and I'm getting my finger on things. Perhaps that will pay off when the balloon really does go up as Alex Kordic says it will, and I think he's right."

In fact the balloon had already gone up, in effect, with the secession of Slovenia, tacitly accepted by Milosevic because it fitted in with his nationalist scheming. Croatia, which emerged by the end of the century as the strongest part of the former Yugoslavia, saw the war as part of a pact between the Slovenes and Serbs.

The war which then started in Croatia – although it was never officially declared as such – was a result of the republic declaring itself independent at the same time as its Slovenian neighbour. Some areas with a predominantly Serb population refused to accept the declaration and the Serb-dominated Yugoslav People's Army, the JNA, moved in to support them. The result was the Croatian War which brought the first instances of the ethnic cleansing which was to feature the worst outbreak of mass crimes against humanity since the Nazi holocaust.

By the time Angela received the letter from Kosovo, Josie was 200 miles away, in the east Croatia border town of Vukovar, besieged by a section of the JNA, and Serb paramilitaries. By now more journalists were on the spot, but she was surprised and pleased to get a message from Jim Meredith telling her he had been authorised to recruit her on to his agency's strength. Satellite phones were in operation by then, in that area.

She joined the thousands of Vukovar citizens, not all of them Croats, living in common shelters, and wrote a vivid and well-received story about a Serb woman and her cries from the heart because she had been separated from her Croatian husband and their children. There was at one time a single escape route from the city, a footpath dangerously exposed to the fire of Serb snipers, believed to have killed a total of 30 people using it to flee. Josie, against the advice of such officialdom as there was, herself used the path, twice, for she returned, and was fired on both ways. One bullet from a sniper's rifle thudded into a fence post no more than a yard behind her. She was very frightened, but again she was able to write vividly about it in an article that made headlines in the American news magazine – and brought a tongue-in-cheek telling off by Meredith.

During the siege, she got to know a reporter from Croatian Radio, Milan Halilovic. It was after her return via the dangerous path, and he interviewed her for his channel, which was still going out and helping keep up the spirits of the Vukovar citizens remaining after thousands had left.

Off air, he asked her: "Whatever made you come to this hell-hole, Josie?"

She told him how her conversations with Alex Kordic had fired her, and he went on to ask about her work with the BBC, and her background. They struck up a close working relationship, and Josie had the feeling that he wanted it to be more, even while, perhaps partly because, they were under such high-level tension. Her feeling for Edward was still there, and she could not see herself becoming deeply involved with any other man. But, away from her mother and sister, the emotional desert was beginning to seem even vaster and more dreary, and the stress of living in constant danger was having an effect. Milan was not only a serious person and a good reporter, he was warm and likeable and she found herself responding, looking forward to being with him whenever their situation made it possible.

One evening, after she had again been exposed to the besiegers' shells and bullets, he invited her to his flatlet.

"I have some food and good wine. Come and share it with me, Josie," he suggested. She well knew where the wine and food was likely to lead, and it did.

It was the second sexual experience of her life. The first had been when she was at the Courier. A young sports sub-editor who "fancied" her – even he would not have put it stronger - persuaded her to go out with him and she accepted, as a deliberate experiment on her part aimed at finding out whether the game half her colleagues seemed to play all the time was worth the candle. She found it was not. For her, it was just a wooden, joyless experience that simply left her puzzled, wondering like Mary Webb's Gillian Lovekin what it was they all made such a fuss of, and the matrons so determinedly kept from young ears and behind locked doors. By now, via the completely unfulfilled experience with Edward, she knew, as Gillian had found out, what had been missing. It was love.

She did not love Milan in that way but when he asked her, after they had eaten and watched a harrowing television report from his own station: "Will you stay with me tonight, Josie?" she simply said: "Yes, Milan, I'll stay."

He kissed her, very gently, and said: "I will not let you be hurt – I mean, I will take .... measures ...."

She answered: "There's no need. It's alright, this week."

This time, it was not wooden or completely joyless. Both knew it was not the start of a lifelong love, but neither was it simply an act of animal lust.

Milan, unlike the Courier man, knew what girls needed to find pleasure. Josie found a chemist able to supply her with the necessary pills, and stayed with him for most of her time in the city..

During a respite at the agency offices in Belgrade, a few weeks later, after Vukovar surrendered, she wrote to Jeannie: "Don't tell Mum about this, although I think she'd understand. I lived with someone in Vukovar, a radio reporter and presenter, Milan. I don't, or didn't love him the way you love Simon, but we slept together and I found that good. I don't know why, because I think you know I don't go along with that kind of thing, really. But it's like that, in this kind of situation. It's as though you have to grab at anything to relieve the tension. I see it all the time. He's a really good guy, but I don't intend to start it up again. If I went along that road again, it would have to be because I'd found someone I just couldn't live without, and that's not likely to happen, I think you know why ...."

She never knew that she could not have found Milan Halilovic, if she had looked. He was one of dozens of Croat men killed by the victorous Serb militia after the surrender, and thrown into a mass grave.

She spent the next few months reporting on different parts of the war in Croatia, trying for herself to make sense of the confused picture that baffled everyone except the zealots who pursued their megalomanic aims. Then in April another balloon went up, the one that was to see much of the murder and persecution which at last awakened America and Europe to what was happening, although the action they took was for a long time as misguided and ineffectual as the nationalism of some of the Serbs and Croats was xenophobic and bloody minded. The war in Bosnia, which up to then had been conducted mostly between the politicians, moved on to the ground, in Sarajevo. As hundreds of city residents, of all backgrounds, demonstrated against the very idea of ethnic conflict, Serb paramilitaries opened fire.

Meredith sent Josie to join his small team of reporters in the Bosnian capital. She went straight to Ljiljana Alagic, confident of a friendly reception although Dr Alagic was a Serb, and was proved right.

"Oh, my dear, whatever must you think of us?" Ljiljana almost sobbed. "We here don't hate each other. We've lived together for hundreds of years. We like living together. It's how people everywhere should live. I'm a Serb and proud of it but some of my best friends are Muslims, and I'm happy that they're proud of being Muslims. The idea that all this is a result of old ethnic feuds is wrong, so terribly wrong."

"Do other people think that way?" Josie asked.

"I don't know anyone who doesn't. They might not say it as strongly as that, but it's behind the way they live, the way we all live here, in Sarajevo. And in most of Bosnia, I believe."

"Could I put it in a story?"

"Yes, of course you can. It needs to be said."

"And quote you, Lili?"

"Yes, although I think perhaps you should ask some others about it as well as me. Let us go to Milan."

Milan Terzic, a local radio man, and a Muslim, who Josie had met when she first came to Sarajevo, was as firm about ethnic relationships as Dr Alagic, and he and his wife readily agreed to his opinions being included in Josie's story.

"We're not worried about our names appearing," he said. "If things go badly it won't make any difference. They'll kill us anyway. Well, they'll kill me. And Fikret." Fikret was the Terzics' 12 year old son.

Josie wrote her story, in the context of the Serb attack and siege of the city which was to last for nearly four years. It made no difference, of course. Nothing, journalistic reports, diplomatic efforts by top people like Cyrus Vance and David Owen, appeals from the suffering people, could make any difference until the blood lust had been sated.

Thirteen

Stroke

Towards the end of Edwina's first term at school, before the Pickwickian Christmas at Lyndford, Kathleen and Michael had a letter from Jennie McArthur, expanding on Angus's brief communication. She and the baby were well, the infant was to be called Ailsa, and Angus was over the moon. There was also good news on their crofting. They had been offered another twenty acres, almost adjoining their existing land, because its holder had died and his widow did not want to carry on with it.

"We are doing fine all round," she wrote. "The extra land will mean we can keep more ewes, probably about 30 more. Angus has ideas about pedigree breeding, because he has been told there is a good demand for our island rams, in the South. We have more visitors booked through the winter than usual, too, and many already confirmed for next summer.

"Which brings me to something I must ask you. You said you were coming here again at Easter. Could you let us know whether that is still your plan, and if so, when exactly so we can make sure we have no visitors then. Please come if you can. I do want you to see the bairn.

"Angus has been ever so much better these last months. I think seeing you, and the little ones, and talking about it all, did him a deal of good. He says he will write, but he finds writing letters very hard work, and he says he is sure that anyone reading them will think he is a miserable old something or other. But he sends his very best wishes to all of you and is looking forward to seeing you again."

They checked on dates of holidays and term times and wrote back to Angus and Jennie saying when they would like to go and congratulating them on the baby; and emphasising that they must not put off any potential paying customers to accommodate them.

"We can easily stay in Castlebay or anywhere you like to suggest," Kathleen wrote.

Kathleen and Michael spent the last months of 1991 and, after the Christmas break at Lyndford, the first part of the following year, keeping a careful eye on Edwina's progress at her first school. Somewhat contrary to the impression they had gained before their trip to Vatersay, the little girl's background, history and potential was carefully noted and acted upon. By Easter she was reading all the infant books that came her way, and could tackle basic arithmetic, and although her grandparents were at first knocked back by the bustle and apparent chaos of a school for several hundred small children, they saw no reason for switching to a private establishment.

As Michael said: "As long as she's doing well, we'll do better to put the money on one side for her."

They decided to go to Vatersay for five days in April, and Jennie replied that she and Angus would not hear of their staying anywhere else.

"We will not turn anyone away," she wrote "but if necessary you and the bairns can have our room for those four nights and we will have a bed in the byre."

As it turned out, the cow-house did not have to be brought into use. The McArthurs accepted bookings from two visiting couples that week but one of them cancelled at a late stage. The weather was delightful and allowed Edwina and Christopher to spend time on the beach. One day was occupied in taking a trip to Eriskay, and an evening watching and listening to a local ceilidh band in Castlebay.

They could see, as Jennie had written, that Angus was in a much better frame of mind than when they had first met him seven or eight months before. He was tackling his farming with vigour, enthusiastically taking visitors who wanted a guide round the island, telling them facts of its history as well as the myths and folklore in which it was so rich. For this purpose and for his own interest, he had borrowed all the books he could find on the subject from the visiting library van. He was currently learning songs from the 600-item repertoire of the legendary Nan Mackinnon, who had come to the island with the "Vatersay invaders" early in the century and spent her life preserving the folklore, before her death in 1982. Jennie described him as "not the greatest singer in the world" but said he was now being asked to play his part at the island's ceilidhs by rendering them.

"Ach, I am nothing of a singer, and I would never dream of trying to imitate the Mackinnon," he told them. "I dinna think they're in any danger o' dyin' out. They were all recorded before she died – that's where I'm learning them from. But I think they should be sung again, even as badly as I sing them."

Kathleen and Michael listened to his singing, and thought it was much better than he implied. They could even detect something of Nan Mackinnon's own unique style and tone when he played them some of the taped recordings.

They spent four happy days on the island and on Barra before again embarking upon the five-hour ferry trip to Oban.

"We'll have to do this at least once a year, won't we?" Kathleen said as they and the children watched the islands recede into the distance. "I can't see any prospect of Angus and Jennie coming south. They're just too tied, quite apart from whether they can afford it."

They would have liked to go to Edinburgh, where neither of them had ever been, but thought Edwina and Christopher would be bored by art galleries and the like, and would be much happier spending a day or two at Lyndford. They headed east, prior to turning south, and were driving along the northern shore of Loch Awe when Michael suddenly swerved, luckily into a layby. His foot was hard on the brake, the car turned half round and stopped. The engine, still with top gear engaged, stalled. Kathleen stifled a scream as Michael slumped over the steering wheel. The children started to cry.

"Darling, darling, whatever's the matter?" she cried. He did not answer. His eyes were wide open, and he seemed to be trying to say something, but no words came. A car had come up behind, could not get past because the Rover was blocking the layby. The children cried louder. After a few moments the driver of the other car, a youngish man who looked Indian or Pakistani got out and went to Michael's window. It took him only seconds to assess the problems and he ran round to Kathleen's side. She opened her window.

"I think my husband's had a heart attack," she gasped. "Can you help? Could you find a phone and send for an ambulance."

The man ran back to his car and spoke to his woman passenger. He came back to Kathleen and said: "We have a mobile phone. My wife is calling the ambulance. I'm a paramedic. Can I have a look at your husband now? We may be able to do something."

He opened the driver's door, switched off the ignition and started to ease Michael back from the wheel. The children were crying louder. The man said: "I think it would be better if you got them out of the car, ma'am. My wife will help me. She's a nurse." Kathleen obeyed, gratefully, took the youngsters from their seats. Edwina was crying "What's the matter, Granny?" just as she had when they all learned of Jonathan and Catriona's death in Bangladesh, only by now her words were perfectly formed.

"Grandad's been taken ill, darling. These people are looking after him. We've got to wait for an ambulance to take him to hospital."

"He's not going to die, is he, Granny? I don't want him to die."

Kathleen tried to reassure her, doing her best to put the conviction she could not feel into her words. She took the children to a seat against a low stone wall.

After a few minutes, the paramedic came to her. "I think it's a stroke," he said. "That is why he cannot speak. One side of his face is affected, and I think his left arm. We got through to the ambulance and they are on their way. I do not think they will be more than ten minutes and I have told them what I think." He spoke with little trace of accent but his words were carefully enunciated.

"Oh, thank you. You're very kind."

"It is good that we are able to help," he said. "I do not think I can do any more for your husband until the ambulance arrives. They will have equipment. I will go to stay with him now. Perhaps my wife could help you with the children?"

"Thank you. Perhaps she will watch and see if she thinks I need help."

He went back to the car. A moment or two later his wife came over to Kathleen and said: "Your husband would like you with him. He seems to be trying to say something." She did not appear to be Asian and spoke with a slight Welsh accent. "I will stay with them"

"You will stay with this lady while I go to Grandad, won't you, Edwina?" The red mop nodded.

Kathleen eased into the Rover's passenger seat and caught Michael's hand. There was no response from the limb but she thought there was an appreciative flicker in his eye. The paramedic said: "Yes, I thought so. He wanted you near." He was squatting inside the car door, re-arranging Michael's clothes after the perfunctory examination he had been able to carry out.

He asked: "Have you far to travel, Mrs ….. Perhaps you could tell me your name? Mine is Ashok Berinda. My wife is Megan."

"Ours is Housman. Michael and Kathleen. Edwina and Christopher are our grandchildren. We live in London but first we're going to Shropshire, to visit some family connections. We've been at Vatersay, in the outer islands, seeing the children's other grandfather."

"Ah, Mrs Housman, we are going by Shrewsbury. We live at Brecon, in Wales. Megan is from Wales.

After another few moments, he asked: "Do you drive, Mrs Housman?"

"Oh, yes."

"I am thinking. I do not know where they will take Mr Housman, because I do not know the hospitals here. Almost certainly back to Oban, I should think. You will want to drive your car to wherever they go, will you not. The best would be for Megan to come with you to help with the children and I will come in my own car. Yes?"

"Oh, Mr Berinda, I couldn't possibly ask you to that. I shall be alright. You've already been so good, helping us like this. You must get on your way."

"Mrs Housman, we are pleased to be able to help."

"Thank you so much. It's really very kind," she said as they heard a siren and saw flashing blue lights – the ambulance and a police car."

Berinda spoke briefly to the ambulance men, the two police officers standing by. Michael was extracted from the car and laid gently on the ambulance bed. Mrs Berinda helped load the children into the car as the policemen started to ask Kathleen questions. She said: "Can't it wait? I need to go after the ambulance, to stay with my husband."

"That'll be alright," one of the officers told her. "We'll lead ye to the hospital and ye can give us the information there. There's naebody else involved, is there?"

"Only Mr Berinda there He stopped to help us. He says he's coming to the hospital so his wife can help with the children. They're our grandchildren."

The ambulance had not long unloaded Michael when Kathleen, Megan Berinda sitting in the back between Edwina and Christopher, and Ashok coming behind, followed the police car to the hospital at Oban.

*****

The hospital's emergency stops were pulled out and within an hour a doctor told Kathleen that Michael had indeed suffered a stroke but because it had been caught quickly there was every hope that the damage could be minimised.

"We are transferring him to the special stroke unit at Glasgow," he added. "The helicopter will be here any minute and he'll be there in not much more than half an hour."

"Will I be able to see him there?"

"Yes, but it will take you a great deal longer to get there – two and a half hours at least. I understand you are on your way south and you have two small children with you. I would suggest you stay somewhere local for tonight. Our administration staff will help you find somewhere."

"Can I just see him on to the air ambulance?"

"Yes, of course you can. Have you got someone looking after the children – your grandchildren, are they?"

"Yes, a lady who stopped to help us, with her husband. He's a paramedic and she's a nurse."

"Oh, good. Come along and stay with him, then you can go out to the helicopter with him. I'll be with you. You can't go to Glasgow, I'm afraid, the regulations don't allow it, and anyway there isn't room, but you can see him off."

A few minutes later, Michael was in the air. Kathleen returned to the

Berindas and the children. Ashok suggested they go to the tea room where they could discuss what was to be done next.

"Mr Berinda, you've done too much already. You must look after yourselves. I can manage. The hospital will find me somewhere to stay, the doctor says, and I'll go to Glasgow tomorrow."

"Let us have a cup of tea, anyway. I'm sure you need it."

Seated in the cafe, tea and muffins in front of them, Kathleen found herself starting to flag. After the initial shock of Michael's collapse, and the near accident, the energetic resolve that had always been part of her character took over but now the immensity of her fears for her husband was taking its toll.

"Have they said how long they are likely to keep him at Glasgow?" Ashok Berinda asked.

"No. Have you any idea?"

"I think it will be at least a week. Probably more."

"I shall have to find somewhere to stay there."

"You do not have any friends or relatives in Glasgow?"

"No.... Mr McArthur – that's the children's other grandfather – has a sister near Edinburgh and our daughter-in-law lived with her for years, but we've never met her or even spoken to her. I don't even know where she lives."

"I should not pry, Mrs Housman, but may I ask – where are the children's parents? Are they in Shropshire?"

She looked down, hesitated. "They died. A year ago. They were killed in a big storm in Bangladesh. They were working there."

He looked at her. "I am terribly sorry, Mrs Housman. I should not have asked. But the people in Shropshire are relatives?"

"Yes, my brother's family. I've never lived there, but it's our old family home."

Ashok said he would chase up the accommodation for Kathleen and the children. Megan Berinda stayed behind, sitting by the children, smiling at them but saying nothing.

Kathleen asked: "Do you work at a hospital in Brecon?"

"Yes, but I'm leaving soon."

"Oh? Don't you like it?

"I'll be leaving to have my baby."

"Well, I would never have guessed. It doesn't show."

"No."

"And does your husband work at the same hospital?"

"No, he's a motorcycle paramedic. He'd like to be a doctor."

Berinda returned with a secretary who had been sorting out possible accommodation for the night. She had found an hotel with a family room and asked if she should book it. Kathleen agreed, and asked for directions.

Ashok said: "Could you see if they have a room for me and my wife as well, please? I do not think we can get home tonight."

"Mr Berinda, we are putting you out too much."

"It is alright, Mrs Housman. We have three days before we must be back at work. There is only the cat at home, and a neighbour is looking after her."

"I must at least pay for your stay here tonight."

"Please, Mrs Housman, no. It is very kind, but there really is no need. We were thinking we would have to stay in Scotland for another night anyway. That is why were stopping at that layby, to make a decision. It is a long way to South Wales."

The secretary returned with confirmation of both bookings. "And they do evening meals if you want them," she added.

They finished their tea and buns, much appreciated by the children, and made their way to the hotel. Kathleen's first move was to call the hospital at Glasgow to ask about Michael. She was told the doctor was with him, he was in a stable condition and there may be more to tell her later. It was by then six o'clock. The Berindas had asked if she and the youngsters would eat with them but she thought it would be better if Edwina and Christopher were got to bed sooner. The hotel staff said they would bring them some supper and she asked to be included. That over, she bathed them and was pleased to find they were ready for bed, on two little divans in the same room as herself.

Christopher was asleep almost before his head touched the pillow. Edwina, thoughtful as ever, lay with her eyes open, her hand in Kathleen's, sitting by her bedside.

"Grandad will get better, won't he, Granny?"

"Oh, my darling, I'm sure he will. The hospital he's been taken to is a very good one. They know what to do to make him better."

Another few minutes, her eyes still open: "Megan's a nice lady, isn't she, Granny? Do you like her? I do."

"Yes, my love, I'm sure she's a nice lady. It's very good of her and Mr Berinda to help us, isn't it?"

More minutes, and she had still not gone to sleep. "I'm going to ask God to make Grandad better, Granny." And she closed her eyes. After a few minutes, Kathleen could see she was asleep.

A light tap on the door sent her to it to find Ashok Berinda. "Are they alright, Mrs Housman?" he asked.

"Yes, they're both asleep."

"We'll be having our dinner shortly. Would you like us to watch them while you have yours?"

"I had something with them. Perhaps you will join me here, for a cup of coffee."

They went away and she phoned the hospital. She was put through to the sister in charge and was told Michael was having treatment, but he was comfortable, a stock answer but all that could be expected at that time. She asked if she would be able to see him in the morning and was told: "Of course." She told the Berindas when they came for the suggested coffee, which she ordered for the lobby outside to avoid disturbing the children.

Ashok said: "Megan and I would like to stay up here and help you with the children. But I'm afraid it's impossible, because of our work. We must start our journey home tomorrow."

She broke in: "Oh, please, don't worry about me. I'll manage."

"I am afraid you will find it very difficult. You will want to spend as much time as you can with Mr Housman, and he will need you. But not with the children."

"Perhaps I can find a creche for them, or something. The hospital may be able to help – perhaps they have one there."

"Yes, it is possible. But Megan and I have an idea. The children like being with your family in Shropshire, do they not?"

"They love it. I think they'd live there if they could."

He said: "You would be able to manage much better without the children, Mrs Housman. We could take them back to Shrewsbury, to your relatives. It is on our way."

Strangely, Kathleen thought many months later, she was tempted to accept. She was in no doubt that the Beringas were honest and trustworthy. But she knew that consigning the children to the care of any outsider would leave her feeling she was deserting them.

She said: "Thank you very much indeed. But I don't think I could. It's not that I don't think they'd be fine with you, but I'd feel as though I was abandoning them. You see, when their mother and father were killed, they were left with nobody but us. I'd feel terrible if I let them go."

"Are you sure? I really do think you would be more able to help look after Mr Housman if you did not have the children to care for."

"I'm sure you're right. But I really would feel terrible if they did not stay with me."

"How would it be if we stayed here for another few days? Our employers at Brecon would allow it, I am sure, under the circumstances."

"Oh, no, I couldn't possibly allow you to do that. I shall be alright."

He started to say something else, but stopped, and said only: "Good night then, Mrs Housman." She thought he seemed put out.

Upstairs, she checked on the children, found them sound asleep, and was glad to find that the lead on the room's phone enabled her to take it into the bathroom, so that she could make a call without disturbing them. She rang Alastair and Angela, told Angela all that had happened, including the help given by the Berindas, and their offer.

At the end, Angela said: "I think you've done the right thing. I'm sure this couple are everything you think they are, but you couldn't let the children go with almost perfect strangers. But don't worry. Some of us here will be up there with you by tomorrow night. I'll call you back when I've spoken to Alastair."

A few minutes later, she did. She was coming, to Glasgow, with Charles who would do most of the driving.

Next morning, Kathleen tried to see the Berindas, but was told they had already checked out. She drove with the children to the city and the hospital, to find Michael already starting to make progress. Angela and Charles were there by late afternoon, and stayed at the same hotel the hospital had arranged for Kathleen and the children. Next day they drove directly back to Lyndford, the two little ones in the child seats which lived permanently in his car.

*****

Kathleen stayed at Glasgow for nearly three weeks, helping take Michael's rehabilitation as far as it could go in that time. His speech was still uncertain, and he could do little with his left arm, but he could walk quite well and did not appear to have suffered permanent brain damage. They spread the journey back to Lyndford over two days. Edwina's joy at seeing her grandad almost well again was unbounded.

Alastair and Angela, Charles and Maria urged them not to return to London, for the time being, and they agreed. Edwina and Christopher were re-absorbed into the Home Farm family and their grandparents stayed with Alastair and Angela at Jasmine Cottage. It enabled Kathleen to concentrate on helping Michael, taking him to hospital for physiotherapy and other treatment every day.

He made good progress and in another three weeks was able to use his left hand and arm to a limited extent. His left leg could bear his weight, although it tended to collapse under him from time to time. With the help of a stick he walked over to Home Farm, on "good" days. His speech was somewhat slurred, but coherent, and he could read for half an hour at a time. His mental capacity seemed unimpaired, but of course he could not drive – in fact he never drove again.

He worried however about getting back to London, re-installing Edwina at school, and being a burden to them all at Lyndford. Kathleen too was concerned that they could not stay indefinitely. On top of which, the effort of caring for Michael, including driving to and from the hospital most days, was beginning to have its effect on her. She tried to work out how they were going to manage in London, concluded that she would have to have a permanent nanny as well as a replacement for Mrs Jellicoe, who had given up work, and was glad they had decided against sending Edwina to a private school, which might have stretched even their relatively comfortable finances.

They did not know that Charles and Maria were discussing the situation and had come up with their own ideas.

"You know, darling, I don't know how they're going to manage with those two children," she said. "I can't see Michael getting very much better. Can you? He's what, 74, and Aunt Kathleen's almost the same. They'll be 80 or so before Edwina goes to another school."

"Yes, I've been thinking much the same. So what can be done?"

It was Evinka's day off, they had just put the children to bed, and were sitting at the kitchen table having a much-needed cup of tea. They looked at each other.

"Are you thinking what I'm thinking, Mr Jameson?"

"Mrs Jameson, I probably am. I usually am."

"It would work for the children."

"Yes. They'd be more than happy."

"What about Aunt Kathleen and Michael?"

"They'd need persuading. They're their own flesh and blood. They'd feel they were abandoning or deserting them."

"How about if ...."

"If?"

"They could live here, somewhere. Very close to the children."

"Yes, that might be the answer. But where?"

They were quiet for a few moments.

"Let's talk to Dad and Angela." He picked up the phone.

"Dad. Have you had your dinner? Can you come over for a few minutes. We want to talk to you."

"Should Kathleen and Michael come with us?"

"No, not tonight. You'll know why in a few minutes."

"Is something wrong?" Alastair asked as he came through the door.

"No, not really," Charles said as he poured his father a whisky and soda, and Maria made more tea. "We want to know what you think about an idea we've had. Maria'll tell you."

"I wouldn't mind betting I know what it is," Angela said "but go on." Maria returned with the teapot.

"We're worried about Aunt Kathleen, and Michael, and the children," she began. "We think they won't be able to cope, as time goes on. He's doing very well, but he's always going to need some looking after, and Aunt Kathleen's not getting any younger, is she?"

"None of us are, but we manage. And she would," Alastair said.

"Yes, I'm sure she would, for a time. But I don't think she should have to."

Charles broke in: "Look, I'll tell you what we're thinking. We think Edwina and Christopher should stay with us."

"What, permanently?"

"Yes. Well, for the foreseeable future."

Angela said: "Yes, I thought that's what you were going to say. But quite apart from anything else, do you want two extra children on your hands? They're two lovely kids, and we all know they love it here, but five children ....?"

Maria answered, looking at Charles: "We were intending to have another one, but we'd drop that idea, wouldn't we, darling?"

"Yes," said Charles, who might have added: "It's the first I've heard of it, but I'll go along."

"They won't like being two hundred miles away from the children," Alastair said. "I don't think they'd agree to it."

There was pause. They all had to agree.

"Unless...." Angela said thoughtfully.

"Unless?" Charles asked.

"Unless they could live here, or somewhere near, in a house of their own."

"But where?"

"Perhaps we could go to my house at Clee Marton and they could have Jasmine Cottage."

"It's a possibility. But your house is let, isn't it? It might be ages before it comes vacant."

Alastair came in: "I think I might have an answer. The school house. Now they've closed the school it'll be on the market. It probably wants quite a bit of work, but I'm sure it could be bought and all the improvements done for a lot less than they'd get for their house in London. Or the school itself. That'll be for sale too, and it would make a good house. But of course that would need more work."

"That's another point, too," Angela said. "Edwina will have to get back to school soon."

"No problem there," Charles said. "She can go with Alastair to the new school at Buryton."

Buryton had been built two years before as an area school to replace four others where pupil numbers had fallen below the twenty mark. It was about four miles away but transport was provided.

"Are you quite happy with Buryton, then?" Angela asked.

Maria said: "It seems fine." And Alastair added: "It should be. The headmistress is almost a relative of ours. In fact she is a relative, although the connection is a little tenuous, after all the years. My mother and her grandmother were sisters. My Aunt Kate was cook at the manor when Mum was the kitchen maid."

"Shropshire's a very small world," Charles said.

The outcome was unanimous agreement. Alastair would check with the county education authority about sale of the school house. And Angela would put it all to Kathleen and Michael, which was made easier for her when she came on Kathleen looking very low, almost in tears, she thought.

"What's the matter, dear," Angela asked.

"Oh, Michael's very down today," she said. "He's worried that we're being such a burden to everyone. And so am I, up to a point. We must get back to London, from under your feet. And Maria's got enough to do without two extra children."

"But however would you be able to manage, with Michael and the children?"

"We can get someone in to help look after them," Kathleen replied, slightly miffed that her capabilities were apparently in doubt.

"Yes, I'm quite sure you could do that," said Angela "but I don't think you should have to. You don't have to."

"Angela, we mustn't stay here indefinitely. Apart from anything else, we must get Edwina back to school. And you've already done too much for us."

"We have ideas," Angela said. "Alastair and I, and Maria and Charles."

Kathleen looked at her. Angela quickly marshalled her thoughts.

She asked: "If it was possible for the children to live with people who want them, but close to you, as close, say as we are to little Alastair, and Dorothy, and Douglas, would not that be an ideal solution?"

Kathleen saw immediately where she was heading.

Francis John Simcock

"Do you mean they should stay with Charles and Maria? But that's impossible. They have three little ones already."

"It was Maria suggested it. They were going to have another themselves, she said. They just wouldn't, in that case. And Edwina and Christopher love it here, don't they?"

"But what about us? Have you got ideas for us, too? We don't want to be far from them."

"Well, there's my house at Clee Marton. That's only 15 miles away. But we think we know something better. The old school house in the village is on the market. It wants work, but even with what you'd have to spend it would cost you much less than you'd get for your house in London, I'm sure. And it's probably nearer to Home Farm than this, even. Five minutes walk."

Kathleen said nothing.

"I know you've never lived here, Kathleen, but it is your family's home, isn't it? Wouldn't you like to come back, as it were?"

"It isn't Michael's ancestral home, though, is it?" Kathleen said after a time. "Has he got one?"

"Not like this. I mean no. He was born in Hampshire, but his father and mother moved to somewhere near High Wycombe, when he was quite small. He was a parson, you know."

After another pause, she said: "I don't know, Angela. I don't like the idea of letting the children go. They're Jonathan's. Wouldn't it almost be like saying we don't want them?"

It was Angela's turn to wait before she spoke. Then: "What about their losing you, Kathleen? It's bound to happen, sooner or later."

Kathleen thought again: "I must talk to Michael about it. And Charles and Maria."

Not really to her surprise, Michael was not averse to the Jamesons' ideas. In fact he was relieved to think that it would mean Kathleen was not going to be saddled with an extra burden which must become heavier as time went on. He was concerned about Edwina's education, but his worry was allayed when he was given assurances about the quality of the local school. Although he was a southerner born and bred, and had lived most of his life in London, he did not want to be 200 miles from the children and was pleased by the prospect of spending the rest of his life at or near Lyndford.

Alastair pursued the possible purchase of the old school house with the county council's estates manager who grabbed at the prospect of a sale with a minimum of effort or cost. Michael and Kathleen were able to buy the property outright without waiting for their London home to be sold, and within six months the most essential work – adding on a downstairs bedroom with attached bathroom – was completed and they moved in.

The arrangements proved completely satisfactory, Angela told Jeannie and Josie, although she could never be quite sure that the information reached Josie. Edwina and Christopher slotted in to the Home Farm family, playing and occasionally fighting like siblings everywhere. They were no more than 300 yards from the old school house, and rarely went more than a day without seeing Granny and Grandad. And Edwina loved her new school, and did well.

*****

Kathleen wondered a little what happened to the Berindas, and why they had left the Oban hotel very early, without saying goodbye and without breakfast, having paid their bill overnight. But just before Christmas she found out, in an agonisingly unpleasant footnote to the Scottish chapter in their story. A couple she instantly recognised were all over the newspapers and the television screens. They had stolen twin baby girls from a supermarket car park in Cardiff. Both pleaded guilty to the charge of abduction. Ashok told the judge his wife could not have children, and it was preying on her mind. She had already had a nervous breakdown. He was sentenced to three years in prison, his wife ordered to stay in a mental hospital and have supervised psychiatric treatment.

Kathleen recalled the young woman's rather strange quietness, and how she had said she was leaving her job to have her baby. Immediately after the trial, her old paper, The Monitor, which she still read regularly, carried a full-page article about childlessness and its effects, featuring the Berindas' case among others and written by the woman who had succeeded to her columnist's spot. Part of it, obviously researched before the trial but published immediately afterwards, told how Megan's deteriorating mental condition had built up to her husband's decision to steal a child or children, and related some of their abandoned or aborted efforts. One instance described how they had stopped to help a man who had had a heart attack or stroke, and his wife, and their two grandchildren.

"At first, I had no idea of taking the two children. I was just trying to help. But when I found out how ill the man was, and his wife obviously had confidence in us, I offered to take them back to their relatives. I almost thought we would be doing her a favour, taking the kids off her hands. Their parents were both dead."

Kathleen read it all with a mixture of relief and sorrow. The reason for the relief was obvious. Her emotions behind the sorrow were harder to pin down. There was anguish at the thought of a woman so desperate for a child that it could bring her to mental breakdown and to stooping to such awful measures; and of a husband, who had seemed such an intelligent, decent and caring individual but who could delude himself into action that must cause the most desperate distress and agony to a mother. She wondered how such people, any couple, could bring themselves to the conclusion that the remedy was theft of two little human beings from the mother who had borne and nurtured them. What kind of conversation must there be in such a marital home? she asked herself, and Michael. And she was hit by even more anguish when she thought of the mother whose babies had been stolen.

Fourteen

The Chief Executive

At first, Stella appeared to shake off the disappointment of losing her baby quite easily. She was back at work within a few days, tackling the job with all her old, apparently effortless vigour, in fact, to the eye of the casual observer, bringing new energy to it as she waded into catching up on matters that had been shelved during her week's absence. She spent two days in London organising Protechno's end of an engineering conference at which Keith Parkinson was the main speaker, and made a major impression on the industry bigwigs.

"My word," one said to him. "That's a remarkable young woman you've got there. She runs rings round most of us."

"Yes, I know. They're a remarkable couple. I reckon Edward's got one of the best technological brains in the world – well, in Europe or America, anyway. And Stella seems to see the pros and cons of any business situation while I'm reading the introduction. But hands off – they're ours."

As the weeks went by, however Edward, Parkinson, her friend Pauline and Angela all began to see some changes. First they were marginal, in her dress and appearance . The poise did not seem quite so effortless or complete. Her hair was not so perfectly arranged. Once Edward had to tell her as they left for work at 8am that her lipstick, usually so unobtrusive and perfectly applied, was smudged. He was normally an hour later getting home than she was, and their evening meal was invariably on the table. They had a daily help, but only up to midday, and Stella did all the cooking, unless Edward was free to take his turn. But one evening, about three months after the miscarriage, he found the food only half prepared and Stella slumped on a kitchen chair, her head in her hands and on the table. He dropped his briefcase and wrapped his arms round her.

"What's the matter, darling? What's the matter?"

She lifted her head and he saw she had been crying. He had never known Stella shed tears.

"It's alright. I'll be alright. I was just feeling a bit .... oh, I don't know, a bit down."

It was soon passed off. Edward made her drink a glass of wine while he carried on cooking the meal. Afterwards she told him: "I'm terribly sorry. I don't know what came over me. I won't let it happen again." But that night, after she had clung to him even more closely than usual, he woke to find her sitting on the edge of the bed, not crying, but shaking from head to foot. Again she insisted there was nothing the matter, got back into bed and appeared to sleep.

Through the next weeks there were more incidents of a similar kind. And at work, although her actual tasks, which now often involved advising Parkinson on business matters, were carried out as efficiently as ever, he, and Edward, noted little hesitations, an apparent slight loss of the confidence that had always marked everything she did or said.

Her depressed state continued, even became worse, all through that spring and summer. Edward could never persuade her to go out with him, or with anyone else. She had been a regular if not avid reader. Now the only printed items he saw her with were papers connected with her work. Their sex life, which had been so happy and fulfilled, became almost non-existent. His natural urges were still there, but hers seemed to have disappeared.

Edward, as he became seriously worried, confided in Angela who told him what she thought the problem was – post-natal depression made worse by loss of the child. They eventually persuaded her to see her GP, and that was indeed the diagnosis. But the treatment prescribed seemed to have no beneficial effect, although between incidents like these she appeared to be, and she insisted she was, quite well.

Gynaecology, psychiatry and psychology were not far from being closed books to Angela as a doctor. It was no doubt the result of being deeply involved for so many years in an unrelated specialism, she told Edward in one of their many discussions.

"You know the definition of an expert: someone who knows more and more about less and less," she smiled.

"But as a non-expert, I've worked out what I think has happened to Stella. She's really far from the hard nut she's appeared to be, as you well know, don't you? You've said so yourself. The kernel inside is anything but hard. She suffered a terrible blow when her mother died, when she was just a child, really. She dealt with it by enclosing the soft core in a shell and developing an overriding urge to "get on" in the world. And she's done that already because she's highly intelligent and has a great capacity for hard work. She's already in a job that most young women would look on as the pinnacle of ambition. But she knows now that she's capable of more – probably a lot more. She started out just wanting to leave poverty behind but before you came along ambition had taken over.

"This may all sound far-fetched, as though it's coming from the remote corners of psychiatric philosophy, Edward, but I've thought about it a great deal. You see, I think that when you came along she couldn't help falling in love with you, and her ambition had to give way. Then she was hit by that other need, a primeval one that most women encounter. Motherhood, I mean.

"What I'm trying to say, my dear, is that I believe it is the complicated, cumulative effect of it all, not only losing the baby, that resulted in all this."

Seriously worried, Angela talked privately to psychiatric consultants at her hospital and from her previous working life. But neither they nor the lay views of Alastair, Charles and Maria, Emily Jane, Jeannie and Simon offered any solution, although none of them thought her diagnosis implausible. The move that brought the important action came from Keith Parkinson.

He, Edward and the other director had been discussing the possible setting up of a branch of the firm in Germany, by then their biggest export outlet. One of the problems was who was to head it. The MD thought it perhaps had to be offered to Edward, but that would leave a gap in the development work that was Protechno's lifeblood. And anyway, management was not Ed's forte, Parkinson knew.

He had developed an affection for Stella, as well as respect for her abilities and, it had to be admitted, a knowledge of her value to the enterprise. Years of working together had enabled him to see far enough beyond the polished exterior to know there was material of real human worth there. He would have hated to see her potential, either human or commercial, wasted because she herself had somehow got her emotional priorities mixed up, which he, like Angela, believed was essentially what had happened. Neither of them thought she was clinically depressed in medical terms. If that had been the case, her GP's treatment would surely have had some beneficial effect. But Keith, applying business pragmatism, and need, to personal knowledge of Stella, thought he could see the way forward. It amounted to something of a gamble, he knew, and hard-headed businessman Parkinson was not a betting man. First however he consulted Angela, spending an afternoon with her and Alastair at their new home at Lyndford. Afterwards he got together with Edward to discuss the German project, not for the first time.

"Ed, this may seem crazy to you, and perhaps you'll think I'm interfering in your private life. Which I am, I suppose. But I've got some ideas I want you to think about," he said.

"I'd been moving towards thinking we were going to have to bring in someone from outside. Perhaps a German. It would have advantages, but there'd be snags." And they went on to again discuss the pros and cons.

"So I think we're agreed, aren't we, that we can't see any obvious solution. We'd prefer it to be someone from here, but we can't see who," Parkinson concluded.

"Now take a firm grip on yourself, and don't jump more than two feet in the air, when I tell you what I've come up with. I think it should be Stella."

Edward stayed attached to his chair, but stared incredulously at his boss, who said nothing more until the suggestion had been taken in.

"I can hardly believe you're serious," Edward said finally. "Especially under all the circumstances. For a start, she's had no executive experience. But more than that, she's still suffering from this depression. And I can't agree to her going to live hundreds of miles away for perhaps weeks at a time. It would surely have a terrible effect on her, mentally I mean. Not to mention what the stress and strain of a job like that would do to her." He sounded almost angry. If anyone else had made the suggestion he would have exploded.

Parkinson started again. "I'm quite serious," he said. "I've thought about it a lot. And before we go any further, I'd like to tell you that I've discussed my ideas with someone I know you think a great deal of." Edward stared again.

"Your step-mother. She agrees with me."

It was a master stroke in terms of persuading Edward. But it had also confirmed his own view. He had found Angela's ideas about the cause of Stella's trouble surprisingly similar to his own, to the extent that she had agreed that his plan was a good one. Certainly more likely to work, in terms of reversing Stella's obvious downward slide, than anything else she could think of, including doing nothing. Especially doing nothing. How good it would be for Protechno, she was not qualified to judge. But if Parkinson was happy with it ....

"Let me tell you my thinking, Edward," Keith said. "For a start, let me say that I believe, and Angela agrees, that what I propose would be good for Stella. I also believe it would be good for Protechno. Your wife, you know, is something pretty special in the way of businesswomen. She has a brain in that respect as good as yours in the technical field, and that's saying something." Edward shook his head, but Parkinson went on: "She has, you know. You say she's had no executive experience, but that's not really true. Some of the most important decisions we've made during the last year or two have been at least partly down to her. I'm getting to the stage of not wanting to make a decision without consulting her. Now I think she vitally needs something to get her back to that, hoist her out of the state she's in. Something to bring the spark back. Something that would work for her like a good idea does for you. I wouldn't suggest anything that wouldn't work for us, as well, however much I wanted to help you and Stella, but I'm as sure as I can be that it would be a sound move for this firm. When I came up with this idea at first I thought it must be a gamble. But the more I think about it, and after talking to Angela, I've come to believe the element of gamble is very small."

Edward was still too stunned to say anything. But Parkinson continued: "Now let me tell you the details of my idea. I suggest you move to Germany with her. In fact more than suggest – I'd stipulate it. You know you can work anywhere, don't you, Edward, with all these new computer set-ups. Your position in the company would stay just the same. You could tell people what you wanted them to do just as easily from Germany as from here. And of course you could come back here just as often as you needed. And don't think for one minute that it would stop you and Stella going for a family again. Whatever arrangements were needed in that case would be made. I promise you.

"Now, I don't expect you to say yes or no right now. Think about it. Talk to Angela about it. If Stella turns it down, we'll say no more about it. But I'll make a bet with you now. She won't."

Edward had remained silent through Parkinson's exposition. Now he said: "Of course I have to think about it. What you've said is very persuasive, but it wouldn't be right to make a snap decision. Although of course the decisions are really for you, and Stella. Just one point, though. Do you think you can replace her here? Apart from what you've just said, I do have some idea of how valuable she is, to you."

"No, Edward, I don't think I can replace her. Not like for like. I'll have to go back to just having a secretary. Perhaps I'll poach your young lady – no, don't worry" – as alarm showed in Edward's eyes. "Young Rosemary has become quite efficient. Perhaps I'll promote her. But don't worry about that. And I'll still be in touch with Stella, won't I? We'll cope."

Next day, Edward went to see Angela and his father. She did not find it difficult to persuade him to accept Keith's proposals. And she agreed with Parkinson's idea that he should move to Germany with her.

"You must do what you think's best, of course. But shall I tell you something Mr Parkinson said, that I don't suppose he said to you, and you certainly mustn't tell her about? Or mention to anyone else. Especially don't mention to anyone else."

"Go on."

"He said Stella will be his successor as managing director of Protechno, if she can resist the other temptations he's certain will come her way."

*****

Edward told Keith Parkinson that he accepted his plan but wanted to be the one to talk first to Stella about it, which his chief immediately accepted.

That evening, she seemed in a depressed state again. He was not certain it was the best time, but he decided to go ahead. For once, he drove home with her, leaving her own car at the office, and told her he was cooking the dinner. It was smoked salmon, which she especially liked, with a bottle of wine that was also her favourite. Although she was so low, she divined there was something special about the evening.

"Have you got something awful to tell me?" she asked. "Are you going away or something?"

"No, darling, I'm not going away. I have something to tell you, but it's not awful, at least I hope you won't think so. I don't think you will."

She looked at him.

"You know this German thing we've been talking about. Well, Keith's decided it must go ahead."

"Yes, I thought he would."

Edward was silent for a few seconds. Then he said: "He wants you to head it."

Edward did not quite know what reaction he expected. Certainly not for Stella to burst into violent sobs and tears. It was so untypical of her, no doubt a result of the state she had been in for months. He folded her in his arms and let the emotional outburst run its course.

"But what about you?" she said, still sobbing. "It should be you. It was something like that I thought you were going to tell me."

"I shall stay exactly the same. Except that I shall come with you to Germany and work from there. As he says, I can work from anywhere. I'm not a business person, sweetheart, not in that way. That's you."

Two-and-a-half years before, when the love for Edward, that had changed her life so much, had barely begun to dawn, Stella would have taken the proposal now being offered with the calm assurance and poise that everyone thought of as the essential Miss Hardy. It was the kind of thing she was heading for, although perhaps coming quicker and in a bigger single leap than expected, she would have said to herself. No way would it have brought sobs and tears and a collapse into the arms of a man. But it was a shock of the best kind, and it did not take long for some of the old Stella to re-assert itself. The gloom that had been descending on her again lifted. She knew a great deal of what was being proposed for Protechno's German offshoot, but not what "heading" it meant. Her mind started to range round the possibilities. Edward was delighted when she started to ask questions.

"I don't think I can tell you very much," he said. "Mainly because I don't know. But what do you think about it? Are you pleased?"

"Of course I am. But what about you? Are you happy with it?"

"I wasn't when he first told me. I thought it would be too much for you. But I am now. Keith went to talk to Angela about it and found she thought almost exactly the same as he did. They've been terribly worried about you, you know. But he says he wants you to do it because it will be good for the company, as well as you. And he says he'll insist that I come to Germany as well. He didn't put it like this but I know it's so you and I will stay together. He's very fond of you, you know."

She was quiet for a while, before she said: "There are things to think about, aren't there?"

"Yes, but they can be sorted out." He knew what she meant, although she said nothing for minutes. Then: "I mean, I still want to have our babies."

"Yes, my darling. And I want to. But that's one of the things Keith's promised. He says that when the time comes, whatever arrangements need to be made will be."

Stella thought she ought to feel ashamed of suddenly feeling so happy when hours before she had been so miserable, and she said so. But Edward told her: "My darling, you don't need to feel like that. It's the essential you. It's part of what makes you the girl I love."

That night, they made love in a way they had not since the tragedy of the lost baby. Stella clung to him, kissed him passionately, again and again. And in the morning, Parkinson had them all together to discuss his plans.

It was some months before they actually moved to Germany. But Stella's appointment as chief executive of the new company was announced immediately, and she spent most of her time getting it off the ground. Nobody who knew her, in or out of the company, was surprised. She looked and was exactly like the old Miss Hardy, not that hardly anyone apart from Edward, Angela, Parkinson and one or two immediate colleagues had noticed any decline. But they could all see her regaining some of the bubble that had emerged after her marriage and when she was expecting the baby. She relaxed, and Edward with her, by visiting Charles and Maria, Kathleen and Michael, Peter and Aelwen and of course Angela and his father.

*****

The German project went well, and grew from half a dozen employees to half a hundred inside two years. One of Edward's new developments spearheaded the expansion, and both he and Stella became well known in Odenthal, a town near Cologne, which they had made their base because of the help they were given, by the municipal council, in finding suitable premises and initially somewhere for them to live. Stella, showing no hint of the depressive attacks from the day she took on her new role, did an intensive course in German before they left England, not that it mattered too much because all the younger people in the Ruhr spoke English, often quite well. They found a ready and enthusiastic pool of technicians eager to follow Edward's lead, and soon engineering concerns all over the country were demanding and paying well for the innovations, usually the products of his brain, that his teams installed. He worked mostly in an office attached to the house they rented, aided by the middle-aged and widowed secretary, Rita, who had been with him in England and agreed to move until he could recruit someone locally. Edward, unable to abandon his work to learn the language, tackled it at a more leisurely pace than Stella. He spent little time in the Odenthal factory and even less in travelling to England, usually flying.

For Stella, the time in Germany was as happy as any in her life to date, she told Angela and Alastair when they visited her and Edward and took trips down the Rhine and into the Black Forest.

The driving urge for advancement had gone, replaced by an apparent delight in tackling and almost always conquering the problems of establishing and running the business. She saw less of Edward, at work, than she had in England when he had inhabited the office next door and she took in his morning coffee and afternoon tea. But they felt "together" and when they were able to put the psychological closeness into physical practice they found happiness indeed.

They took no holiday of more than a long weekend, which usually amounted to leaving Odenthal on Friday evening and returning 48 hours later. They too explored the Schwarzwald and the Rhine's castles; imagined the sirens luring their victims on to the rocks of Loreley and wondered where the myth had come from; watched the huge barges on their way from Switzerland to the North Sea ports. At first, Edward worried that she might find it difficult to leave her work behind, and indeed she did not want to do it too often. But when she did, she became a Stella even he had never seen before: vivacious yet relaxed, alert and interested in everything she saw, while ready to sigh with pleasure when his arm stole round her.

They had been in Germany for two years when she made her big decision. She stopped taking the pill, without even telling Edward, and hoping he would not spot her slight change of habit. And sure enough, a few weeks later, she was able to ask him: "Darling, have you not noticed anything?" But he had.

"You haven't had your monthly visitor. Is everything alright?"

"Perfectly alright." She smiled.

"You don't mean.... ?"

"Yes, darling. I do mean. It's time."

"But what about.... ?"

"What about nothing, Edward. I can take care of 'what about.' I'm a superwoman, remember?"

He took her almost roughly in his arms, kissed her.

Later, he asked: "How do you propose to deal with it? I mean, being away from the job and so on?"

"I don't propose to be away, not for any length of time. I might have to rest up, I suppose, afterwards, and perhaps before, but I'm not going to hand over to anyone. Gretchen (her secretary) is getting very good and I'm sure I'll be able to work through her."

Keith Parkinson told her she must not do anything silly.

"You're too important to this company to be allowed to become seriously ill. I told Edward two years ago that we would make any arrangements necessary, and we will."

"Yes, but please let me decide when 'necessary' arrives. I promise I will not allow the company to suffer."

"No, my dear, I know that very well."

As the parallel date to the loss of the first baby approached, Edward became edgy, although he tried not to show it. Stella showed no signs of such worry. She had left the morning sickness stage well behind, and been plagued with no other complaints, in fact seemed to be in even ruder health than before. During the last months of her pregnancy, visiting customers and other businessmen goggled when the imposing young woman rose from behind her desk and edged a swollen tummy round its corner to shake hands. Her doctor told her she ought to take things more easily; go into work only in the mornings, he said. She asked why. She was happier working, would only sit around and worry about it if she stayed at home. Through the last couple of weeks, she did go home early in the afternoon because, she told Gretchen, she was feeling "a bit tired," which really meant "absolutely shattered." But as it turned out, she did not miss a single day at work, before David Alastair Edward made his entrance one day in late January. It had been something like that when Edward's mother was born, years before in Jamaica, Debra often told the family. Her mother was cutting sugar cane when the pains began.

Stella was not cutting sugar cane, but she had gone to work that day, only to realise by coffee time that this was it. A call to Edward, a few final instructions to Gretchen, and she was on the way to the maternity hospital; and by evening it was all over, with Edward sitting beside her bed and congratulating her.

"Efficient as ever, superwoman."

She was back behind her desk in little more than a fortnight, David – the name chosen because they liked it and it meant beloved, and swift – installed in a cradle on wheels that could be moved to Gretchen next door if she had to deal with important visitors, pending the enrolment of a nanny. Alastair and Angela, Keith Parkinson and his wife, Aunt Rhoda and Uncle Joe were early travellers from England to see them, while she was still at home, although running things through Edward and Gretchen. Rhoda, who has not had too many mentions in these pages but had been instrumental in enabling her to progress, beamed.

"I always knew you'd do well," she said. "Chief executive! Eeh, your mum would have been proud."

"We were going to call her Margaret if it had been a girl." She did not say that Edward had suggested calling him after her father, but backed off when reminded that his name was Jud. And in any case Jud was not her father, which even Edward did not know, nor ever would, she thought then. She did not herself know the name of her real father, the young greengrocer. That Jud was not her parent had only been revealed after his death, as her mother was dying. No doubt it had become another rowel in the spur.

Fifteen

Sighted

If only she could know that Josie was safe instead of being often, if not constantly under threat in the war-torn Balkans, Angela's cup of happiness would have been full when she and Alastair were married. And it would have overflowed when she received Jeannie's wonderful news – she was having a baby.

She had no more worries about Alastair. He was almost completely recovered from both his bodily injuries and the brain damage which had left him unconscious for many weeks. But the anxiety about her other daughter could not go away, even under the influence of Alastair's gentle concern and the joy of their re-union.

He could not do more in Josie's case than continue to be there, for Angela. He had no more knowledge of what was happening in Yugoslavia than ninety-nine percent of people in Britain or any other western country, although both scanned the papers keenly, listened to radio and watched every TV programme that might offer relevant information. His own dislike of sectarianism and racialism had if anything increased, as he grew older and it was occasionally fuelled by incidents involving his own children and grandchildren. He had never understood the divide in Northern Ireland, and did not want to. It was senseless and without reason, in Alastair's eyes, and the war in the Balkans was the same.

He was truly delighted by Jeannie's news. Angela had been so well received in his own family, latched on to the Lyndford brood as though they were her grandchildren by blood. Now it was good to know that through her daughter she was making a physical contribution to the pool. He was driving again – he had been off the road for nearly two years, and Angela had wondered whether he would ever want to get back to it – and they spent two days at Saffron Walden, getting to know Jeannie and Simon, who he had met only when he and Angela were married. Jeannie was five months into her pregnancy but still working in her astro-physics laboratory.

Neither Angela nor Jeannie received letters from Josie after Vukovar, when they learned she was going to Sarajevo and was now on the strength of the news agency of which Jim Meredith was the chief. A few months later however the city was prominent on the pages, screens and radio bands of a world media which had almost ignored the build-up to the Yugoslav tragedy.

It soon became nearly impossible for ordinary people to contact Sarajevo as hundreds, sometimes thousands of shells a day rained down on the beautiful city of half a million people, which had last been in the international public eye when it hosted the winter Olympics ten years before. But Belgrade and the agency's headquarters was a different matter and when they had still heard nothing, after nearly a year, Angela called Meredith.

"We're getting regular copy from her, Mrs Jameson, and it's up to her usual standard," he said. "Although with half the world's Press there now it's much harder to get exclusives. About the only other thing I know is that she's staying with her friend Ljiljana Aligic, or was a week or two ago.

"She's a great lass, and she's become a real acquisition to us. I sometimes have to tell her off a bit for taking too many risks, but you can't expect anything else from someone like her.

"You could try writing to Dr Alagic, if you've got her address, although what chance you'd have of it getting through I wouldn't like to say."

She took up the suggestion, but heard nothing. And in the meantime she and Alastair had the small matter of her grandson James's birth to occupy them. They again went off to Essex for ten days, Angela fussing like a mother hen – Jeannie said – and finally, after a distressing encounter with Simon's estranged father, being more or less ordered to go home, where she continued to scan the papers for any mention of Josie, although she was unlikely to find one as her daughter's stories if carried would be under the agency's by-line. Until one evening in the spring of the next year she had an excited call from Jeannie.

"Mum," she almost shouted. "Did you see her? Just now? Josie. On television, from Bosnia!"

"Oh my god. Was she alright? What was she doing?"

"She was talking to some women who'd been beaten and.... and raped. Their husbands and some of their children had been killed. Oh, Mum it was horrible. They showed a bit of them being beaten. It was at Srebrenica."

"Oh, Jeannie. How awful. But what about her? How did she seem?"

"Not bad. Her hair looked a bit of a mess. A bit straggly, and long. And she looked older, Mum. But okay, I think, considering. But you said you thought she was in Sarajevo."

"Yes, that's what the agency told me. She must have moved."

Angela was reluctant to call Jim Meredith again, but from that point she and Alastair, and the whole Lyndford family watched and listened as often as they could. But they neither saw nor heard anything more of her until July when Angela received a letter from Ljiljana Alagic.

She wrote: "My dear Mrs Jameson: I hope this reaches you. Yours to me took five weeks. Things here are terrible. Postal services are hardly operating at all. I only got your letter because I went to the post office, what is left of it, to see if there was any mail for me.

"Yes, Josie was staying with me, but in May, soon after the shelling started here, she was asked to get to Srebrenica, if she could. I do not know how she did it, or why she was asked to go, but I know she got there, because we have seen her on television, which amazingly we can still receive. She was interviewing a woman whose husband had been killed, and her son, and she had been raped and beaten. It was awful. I do not know how people can do such things to each other. We have lived so well together, here. It is worse for me in a way because it is my people, Serbs, who are doing the worst things at present, although some of the others are not blameless. Josie has told me a lot about you and your husband's family and how he married a girl from Jamaica. If it can be like that in Britain, why do we have to beat and kill each other? Although I suppose your Northern Ireland troubles did not make sense, either.

"I will try to let you know if Josie comes back to me, or if I hear anything about her. She must have some means of communicating with her office in Belgrade. Perhaps she has a cell phone for that."

Angela could no longer put off a call to Belgrade. Meredith told her after she made her apologies: "Don't apologise, Mrs Jameson. I appreciate you must be very worried.

"The situation is terrible in Srebrenica. The incident your daughter saw on television was pretty horrible, but incidents like that are happening all the time. They've almost become non-newsworthy. That one was particularly grisly though because some of the Serbs videoed the rapes and the beatings, and gave it to the TV people, who actually showed clips of the beatings. Josie was dragged in to do some of the interviews because the TV channel's front man had been injured. She did a very good job."

"She's still in Srebrenica, Mr Meredith?"

"Yes, but we've asked her to get out if she can and go back to Sarajevo. It's not easy, but the militaries and paramilitaries do seem to be honouring Press passes, at least. I'm sending someone else to Srebrenica but I'd like Josie to be in Sarajevo because, frankly, she's the best, and she knows the place well by now.

"When I speak to her I'll tell her you've called. I don't suppose she'll ring you because landline phones are almost non-existent there and she won't want to use her mobile because it takes an enormous amount of power to call the UK and keeping them charged up can be difficult."

Angela, Alastair and everyone at Lyndford and Saffron Walden watched, read and listened. But they heard no more of Josie as the siege of Sarajevo ran into its third year.

Sixteen

Back to the islands

Kathleen did not immediately tell the McArthurs about Michael's stroke. She had a feeling that it might have an adverse effect on Angus, now so much improved from the low mental state in which he had obviously been when they first knew him. Michael himself continued to progress after they moved into Old School House. Walking became no problem for distances such as the 300 yards to Home Farm or Jasmine Cottage, his speech sounded almost normal, and he developed some use in the left arm that had been worst affected. But there was one thing worrying him. A year after the incident, he had still not been given the go-ahead to drive, and he feared he never would. And it was time to take Edwina and Christopher to see "Other Grandad" and Jennie again, not to mention the Vatersay baby. Kathleen insisted it was no problem. She was perfectly capable of doing all the driving, she said, but Michael did not want her to. They resolved the issue by going by train, in the Easter holidays, just a year after their previous visit. They did not even tell Angus and Jennie that they were going, stopped in Oban overnight from where they booked in at Castlebay the next evening and called Vatersay to let them know what was happening. Jennie gave them a good telling-off for staying at Castlebay. They told her they were not travelling by car and would arrive by taxi, which brought another reproof. "Angus will fetch ye," she said. "The taxi's already booked," Kathleen countered.

The children, Edwina especially, enjoyed the whole varied experience. She had never been on a train before, and revelled in everything about it. At six and a half, she could read almost anything, hardly seemed to tire but slept like a log in whatever bed she had to occupy, and between periods of being apparently lost in thought, engaged Michael in conversations about subjects as diverse as the workings of Parliament and why she and Christopher had red hair. Kathleen sometimes had to ask her to stop talking and asking questions because Grandad was tired and too much of it, even with her, was not good for him after his illness. She would immediately obey, but a short time later when he was asleep, or next day, would ask Kathleen what a stroke was, that had made him ill. Or some other question over which she had clearly been pondering during her thinking times, as she herself called them. Both her grandparents, and her foster parents at Lyndford, thought she was a remarkable child.

At Castlebay, Kathleen wondered whether she had been right to keep

Michael's illness from Jennie, if not from Angus. She telephoned from their hotel before the taxi picked them up.

"Jennie," she said. "There's something I think I ought to tell you, before we see you. Michael's not as well as he was."

"Ach, no. What is the matter?"

"He's had a stroke." And as Jennie gasped she added quickly: "Don't worry. He's a lot better than he was, almost normal, and he's still improving. But he can't drive. That's why we've come by train."

"Oh, Mrs Housman, I'm so sorry. When did it happen?"

"Jennie, please stop calling me Mrs Housman. You know my name. Actually, it was a year ago, on our way home from you. I'm sorry I haven't told you before, but I thought it might upset Angus. When he sees him now I think he'll realise there's nothing to worry about. We'll tell you all about it when we see you. We'll be there inside an hour."

Angus, slightly misjudging their time of arrival, was out with the sheep when they rolled up at the croft. The ewes had not quite finished lambing and he had to give them a great deal of attention. But Jennie's apprehensions were quieted when she saw Michael lift Christopher out of the taxi. She had told Angus about the stroke when he had come in for a late breakfast, but he could not put off attending to one particular ewe. Michael, now in on Kathleen's thinking, thought he would help further by walking out to Angus, following Jennie's directions. He found him as he dried the lamb he had helped the ewe deliver.

"Michael. Man, it's good tae see ye. I canna shake hands, as ye can see. Have ye had a good journey?"

"Yes, excellent, thank you. The children have enjoyed it – and so have we. It's much less arduous than driving."

"Aye, I'm sure. Well, man, ye look well. I didna quite know what tae expect when Jennie tellt me about ye're trouble just now. An' it was on the way back from here, an' we didna know. Ye should ha' phoned us. We could ha' helped, mebbe."

Michael smiled: "I was in no state to do anything, Angus. I hardly knew what was happening, myself. But never mind that now. Kathleen will tell you and Jennie all about it. There's quite a lot to tell."

"I must just mak' sure this wee lassie is suckling, then I'll be with you. Do you go back to the house – I'll no' be long. I don't suppose ye ought to get cold."

"Oh, no, I'll wait for you. I'm not at all cold." He watched as Angus expertly brought mother's nipple and baby's gums together.

"Ye know, I've done this hundreds o' times. But I still canna help thinking how marvellous it is. This lamb isna half an hour old, but look at her. Standin' there on her own four legs and goin' for it as though she'd been starvin' for a week. I don't think I need have bothered tae help this one. It's a fine wee lamb."

"Have you many more to lamb?"

"No, only about half a dozen. I like ma sheep, but I shallna be sorry to finish the lambin'. Ye get a wee bit tired when ye have tae be up and down all night, sometimes. Jennie helped a lot last year but I couldna let her do sae much now she's got the bairn. Eh, she's a grand lassie, Michael. I dinna know what I'd do without her."

Michael – and Kathleen – thought Angus, in spite of being "a wee bit tired," looked years younger than two years before, when he had been relating the trauma of Morag's illness and his strained relations with Catriona. Jennie was blooming, in spite of still breast feeding baby Ailsa, who up to now had encountered no infant problems to speak of, apart from teething which was now in full swing.

It was the Housmans' turn to be the story tellers, including what they had come to think of as a near miss at the hands of the Berindas. Jennie was horrified when she saw the report and feature in the Monitor, which Kathleen had brought along.

"Ach, the poor creature," she said. She did not say which woman she meant, the robber or the robbed. Probably both, like Kathleen, who however felt that more explanation was needed, particularly as to why they had not told their Scottish counterparts all that had gone on over the year, as it happened.

"You must be wondering why I didn't tell you about it at the time," she said. "And talking to you now I think I should have. Of course, during the first few weeks I was so preoccupied with Michael that my brain didn't want to move in any other direction. Then when we could see he was going to make a good recovery, and I thought I must phone or write, I thought 'whatever will they think, that I haven't told them sooner.' Then there was little Ailsa and I didn't want to worry you both with our troubles."

"Ach, ye dinna need to fear about me, Kathleen. I'm fine, now. But how did you manage, havin' to look after Michael, when he was ill, as well as yon two. Ye must have your hands full, even now."

"Oh, not now," she said, but wondered, not for the first time, what he would think about their having given up most of the care of the children – his daughter's children. She decided she must tell them everything, in detail. How they had stayed at Lyndford with Alastair and Angela, the children at Home Farm, and Charles and Maria had come up with the idea of having them permanently.

"We didn't want that," she said."Not and live in London. I thought I could manage, if I took on a permanent nanny. But they found us a house at Lyndford, so we'd be close to them. I think they thought we'd be under their wing, as well. Anyway, this house, the old school house was on the market, and we bought it, for much less than we got for our London house, as it happened."

"So is it near – Home Farm?" Jennie asked.

"About 300 yards – five minutes walk. I wondered whether Michael would want to leave London. You see, it's my family's home village, although I've never lived there. But I think he's every bit as happy there as I am. Aren't you, darling?"

He nodded, and added: "Yes. I was a bit worried about school, for Edwina, because she seemed to be doing well at Lambeth. But she's forging ahead at Buryton, which is what they call an area school. It's about four miles away. The one where our house is had become just too small, in terms of pupil numbers."

"Aye, like here," Angus said. "It was down to four when they closed it two years sine. Ailsa will have tae go to Castlebay when her time comes."

"Buryton's only between 60 and 70 pupils – it's a real country school. And the headmistress is almost a relative. Her grandmother and Kathleen's mother were sisters. And as I said, Edwina's doing really well there, and Alastair, Charles's eldest."

"But tell us, are you happy with them going to live with Charles and Maria?" Kathleen asked. "They're your grandchildren, as much as ours. Really, we should have talked to you about it first."

Angus thought before he answered. "I hardly know what tae say. I dinna know your nephew, or how they live. I canna say something like 'whatever you like' as though I don't care where they are and I've no responsibility for them. But what I can say, Michael, and Kathleen, is that I dinna believe ye two will do anything but what's best for the bairns. Ye've looked after them so well since they lost their mother and father. I'd like tae meet Charles, an' Maria. I canna see any prospect o' us comin' down there, but perhaps if they ever tak a holiday, they mecht come here."

"Oh, Angus, I think that would be wonderful. It's time they had a holiday. They've not had one since they took over the farm. I shall work on them. They've got some very good people who would take care of it all while they were away. Yes, I shall work hard on them," Kathleen said.

"Michael and I are very happy to see the children there, though. We think it's much better for them to be in a normal family than with a couple of increasingly elderly grandparents, don't we, darling? As much as we love them." Angus and Jennie signified agreement.

They had done the right thing in their eyes, she saw. But the prospect of a visit by Charles and the family brought another thought. Would they feel the same when they found that he, like his brother and sister, was half West Indian? Coloured people were almost unknown to an Outer Hebridean people who had known no racial change for hundreds of years. The southern islands in the chain were strongly Roman Catholic. Further north they were even more firmly Scottish Presbyterian, Calvinistic, with shops, pubs and places of entertainment closed on Sundays. There must be a question mark, against such a background, over what degree of ethnic tolerance was to be found, Kathleen thought, somewhat fearfully. She would talk it through with Michael, when they went to bed.

She found the same question had been raised in his mind.

"I think it'll be alright," he said "but they'll need time to get used to it. I think we should tell them the whole story now, as far as we know it. Everything: Alastair's past, Debra, Angela, even your mother and father, everything we know. We know Angus's story, and that's got its sordid side, but we have no qualms about him. I think he'll appreciate it."

Next day, Michael went out round the animals with Angus, saw three more lambs born to two ewes and told his host the story of how his brother-in-law Alastair had fallen asleep through sheer exhaustion and Debra, unable to wake him, had taken over the role of midwife-shepherd.

"She was only 18 or so, then. It was before they were married and she was staying with his mother. But he always says she became the best shepherd in Shropshire and the Welsh Marches," Michael told him. Quite deliberately, he did not say anything about Debra's origins.

Angus also told him about his pedigree breeding plans. Much research and thought had brought the conclusion that it would be better to concentrate on a producing a type of ram which would improve the performance of the islands' ewes rather than think of selling them further afield. He now knew exactly what he wanted and was planning a trip "over the water" to buy animals. And he showed Michael his 20-year-old "new" tractor, and implements he had renovated after buying them for a song and with which he would shortly be ploughing some of his fields suitable for cultivation and sowing improved grass for silage-making.

"Ye canna stand still, can ye," he said. "It's a good life we have here, but ye have tae look tae the future."

That evening, Kathleen prepared the way for telling Angus and Jennie all that had led to the appearance of African blood in the family.

She said: "When we were here a year ago it was you who had a lot to tell us. Now it's our turn. We want to tell you the story of my family, mostly, and I think some of it will surprise you. But we think it's important that you know it."

Helped from time to time by Michael, she went, briefly, 300-odd years into the past, and the Jamesons' Scottish origins; in more detail into her father and mother's romance and her grandfather's suicide; and on to Alastair's life history, sparing nothing; especially how he had redeemed himself with interest; rescued the little West Indian girl he had found, apparently dying, on the roadside, and eventually married her; the accident in which she lost her life and he was left in a coma; been re-united with the sweetheart of 40 years before; and how their great concern now was for Josie, away in the bloody maelstrom of the Balkans.

Angus and Jennie listened, asked a few questions. Jennie could not keep back her tears from time to time. And at the end Angus said: "Thank ye very much, Kathleen. They sound like a very fine family. I hope we can meet them soon."

Seventeen

"Make her come home"

Jim Meredith may have told Angela that he had sent Josie to Sarajevo because she was "the best" but Josie herself was not happy that she was doing a good job. Her dispatches were not much more than dreary chronicles of day by day shellings and mortar attacks, food and water shortages and electricity blackouts, she thought dismally. She faithfully recorded heart-rending stories of rape and murder – group rapes and multi-murders, often – filtered back through survivors of parties who had tried to escape through the forests, only to fall into the hands of the besieging armies and paramilitaries. But as time went on and the Serbs tried to split the city into two, murder of Muslim men and boys, and the rape and beating of their wives, daughters and sisters became so frequent that it was almost commonplace. She herself was almost an eyewitness of one such incident when twenty-odd men and boys, some not even into their teens, were deliberately rounded up and shot as the Serbs pounded the old Turkish quarter, Bascarsija, peopled almost exclusively by Muslims, the only part of the city where the population did not consist of families of all ethnic backgrounds and religions, living happily side by side.

It was the tiniest microcosm of what was happening all over Bosnia, sometimes even without any fighting. Muslims were either simply ordered out of their homes and villages, the possessions they left behind destroyed or commandeered; or, just as often, the men and boys were rounded up and either shot or dumped into makeshift camps. The women and girls were also herded together and made free with by the soldiers, with the full approval and encouragement of their officers. It was all part of the deliberate ethnic cleansing.

At Bascarsija it became personal for Josie. Her Muslim friends the Terzics lived on the edge of the quarter. In the course of trying to get as close to the action as she could she spent a night with the family. As dawn broke there were crashes and bangs, some shots, and paramilitaries burst into the house.

"Out, down there," their apparent leader bellowed in his own language at the Terzics, still in their night clothes. Some of them broke into the room where Josie had been sleeping with the 14 year old Elmina.

"Come on, quick," they were ordered. Outside, Milan Terzic said: "Where are you taking us?" "You'll see," said the leader. He prodded Josie with his

Kalashnikov. "Go on, you Turkish bitch, get going." Terzic protested: "She's not one of us. She's British. Press. Leave her alone."

The Serb leader dealt him a vicious blow to the head with the barrel of his weapon. "Don't tell me what to do, pig." But to Josie he said, in English: "British, eh? You'd make a good fuck. But there are many more waiting. Get back to where you come from, quick, before I change my mind."

She asked, aggressively: "Where are you taking them? I shall report this in my paper, you know."

He laughed: "Who cares? Just go, or I'll have those jeans, and your pants off you. Go." And he followed his men who kicked, pushed and prodded the Terzics towards a larger group of people, forty or fifty of them, she thought, a hundred yards away.

Josie started to follow, but the soldier turned back, confronted her and pushed his rifle's barrel into her crotch.

"I told you to go, English bitch. I will not tell you again." He prodded her in the same place, with the rifle. "You would not want a bullet there, would you? That is what you will get, if you step one more metre this way." She thought he meant it.

She had no option but to leave the scene and make her way through the city to Ljiljana Aligic's, nearly a mile distant. Professor Lili was only just getting up.

"Oh, my god, Josie, what's the matter? Where've you been?"

"Milan Terzic, and Hatidza, and Elmina, and Fikret .... they've been taken away .... soldiers. They were taking me until Milan told them who I was. It was awful, Lili."

"Where were they taking them?"

"I don't know. They drove them towards some more people they'd taken. I bet they were going to kill the men and...."

Lili insisted she had something to eat while she told the story. Immediately afterwards she had a bath in the tiny amount of tepid water that was all the system would yield, and felt better, at least not so horribly unclean, and set about trying to find out what had happened to the Terzics. It meant going back across the city, risking the shells, and the bullets of the snipers. She found her flak jacket with "PRESS" displayed prominently on front and back and hoped, not too confidently, that it would protect her from the sharpshooters. But she made it and found the local radio station where Milan was the chief still in operation, although it had suffered some damage, and she asked the man she found there, his second in command, Adil, whether he knew anything of his boss and the family.

"They killed about 25 of them. I know because Bakir saw it. They beat them then they made them lie down, or knocked them down, and shot them in the head. Some of them were little boys, Bakir said. He was too far away to see who they were, but it was the people they rounded up near Milan's house, he was sure." Bakir was Adil's brother, one of the radio station's "leg men."

"Did he see anything of what happened to the women?"

"No, they were not there. But we know what will happen to them, don't we – if it has not happened already."

Josie had already told him she had been with the Terzics when they were taken away. Now she told him of her treatment at the hands of the Serb soldiers' leader.

"I'm sure you're right about what will happen to them," she said.

Back at Ljiljana's she set about composing an article relating in detail what had happened , holding back nothing including her own treatment. Generalised or even specific reports of murder and rape were by now so common as to arouse little interest, she reasoned. A British reporter physically assaulted with a rifle in the sickening way she had been might make more people realise what was happening every day.

The piece, phoned via her mobile to the Belgrade office, opened: "Today I was involved in a horror story of the kind that is going on every day in the rubble heap this beautiful city is fast becoming. A family of four, my personal friends, were snatched away and a father and son, only 12 years old, were beaten to the ground and shot in the head, along with a score of other men and boys. Their crime was that they were Muslims.

"The two women of the family – if you call a girl of 14 a woman – were taken away, by the same Serb paramilitary squad, at the same time. I do not yet know what happened to them, but if their fate followed the usual pattern of such incidents they were beaten, raped and thrown into an internment camp where they would be raped again and again.

"I had stayed the night with Milan and Hatidza and their children because I needed to get close to the fighting in this part of the city. We were awakened at dawn by the soldiers smashing in the door and ordering us all out into the street, the family still in their nightclothes. I was fully dressed because I had no other clothes with me.

"I was being treated the same as the other women, but Milan, who is the head of a local radio station told them I was Press, and British. I told them I should report it all in my paper but their leader laughed and said: 'Who cares?'

"When I tried to follow them he pushed the muzzle of his Kaleshnikov into me, between my legs and said if I did not go as he had ordered he would put a bullet there, and called me an English bitch."

She went on to say how she had learned of the fate of Milan, Fikret and the others; and that the incident mirrored many more she had learned of at second hand through survivors of bands trying to escape the city. And continued with the latest information she had of the general situation in the city. Next day, she had a call from Jim Meredith.

"Josie, I hope this is alright with you, but anyway I've done it. I put your piece out all over, under your own by-line. And I've had the Courier on, and the Monitor. The Courier want to know whether it's OK to use a picture of you with your story. They've got one on file, of course. The Monitor are asking whether they can get one from your family. They say they won't do it without your agreement because it might put you at risk.

"Thanks, Jim. Tell them it's OK. I don't think it'll put me at more risk than everyone here is in all the time."

"I'm sure. You can probably guess that some of the others won't bother to ask your permission, anyway. I shudder to think what the Globe'll make of it."

Immediately after talking to Josie, Meredith called Angela to warn her that she would probably be contacted by the Monitor, adding that Josie had no objection to a picture being used.

"Thank you, Mr Meredith. But when you speak to her, will you ask her to please get in touch if she can. It's more than a year since I heard from her."

He explained the difficulties, but said he would try to get her to call, if possible, and sure enough, next day Josie came through.

"This is going to be very short, Mum. I've got almost no time left on my phone. How are you all?"

"We're fine, darling. But what about you? It must be horrible for you."

"Oh, it's no holiday camp. But I'm doing OK. I'm staying mostly with Ljiljana, and we seem to have escaped most of the shelling. Food's a bit scarce, but we get by. We've got it easy compared with a great many people here. But there's something I must tell you. You're probably going to be ...." But the phone cut off abruptly.

Angela realised that Josie was probably going to warn her about the picture request and the stories that would follow. Indeed, the Monitor came on very soon after. Angela did not have a recent photo but, knowing the paper's reputation, gave the go-ahead for use of a picture if they could find one.

Two days later, when lurid headlines including: "British girl threatened with rape by bullet" appeared, everyone in the family was horrified. Aunt Josie said: "Angela, it must be driving you out of your mind. Can't you get her to come back?"

Jeannie almost screamed at her mother: "Mum, Mum, make her come home! Please, Mum, make her come home."

Eighteen

More revelations

Edward read the report in a German newspaper, where it was given more sober treatment than in the home tabloids and even the "qualities." But the distress mounted all the same, almost as sharply as in the breasts of her mother and sister. It was because of him that she was in Bosnia at all, was it not? And this time Angela was not on his doorstep to tell him not to be so foolish; that he had no reason to feel any reponsibility, nothing to blame himself for.

He had been in a state of near euphoria since the birth of their son, three months before. Everything in his life was good. His work was going as well as ever, the ideas and their development flowing, if not always smoothly, at least without serious hindrance. The German operation had proved an almost unqualified success.

Most of all, there was Stella. She seemed unbelievably happy, her love for him and David exuding from her almost visibly, at the same time as revelling in running the new company with confidence and apparent ease. They had a full time nanny, but she was under orders to take the baby to Stella's office at feeding times. Occasionally, at this time and over the next months, a visiting businessman or representative would be told by secretary Gretchen: "Mrs Jameson is sorry to keep you waiting, but she has to finish feeding the baby. She will be free in five minutes." And five minutes later the astonished or amused engineer, business whizz-kid or hopeful employee would be ushered in to the chief executive's office to find Stella, cool, groomed and confident as ever, rising from behind her desk to greet him, the only sign of little David a faint odeur d'enfant and perhaps Nanny disappearing through a door behind her.

Edward had never told Stella about Josie. Around the time she developed the unfortunate attachment to him, he had more than once felt he should. Embarrassment more than anything else had prevented him. Now, when Stella again began to wonder aloud what had taken her to Bosnia, under her own steam when her career at home looked to be burgeoning, he could not stop his distress showing, even after another lecture from Angela, who he had called earlier in the day after reading the horror story.

"Darling, I should have told you about this before," he said. "It was because of me."

She looked at him in apparent disbelief.

"Don't say you had an affair with her."

"No, darling. I've never thought of another woman that way, since I've known you. And I never will."

"What then? Did you do something that damaged her career, or something?"

"No. At least, not knowingly. Although in a way it did amount to that."

"Please explain, darling. How come she went to Bosnia because of you?"

Edward took a breath. "It started just before we did that TV programme. I met her at Angela's – I told you about that, didn't I? It seems she …. oh, fell for me. In a big way. I don't know why, darling. I don't think I did anything. I didn't feel anything …. you know, like that. I don't think I was any different with her than with her sister. I thought she was attractive, but I thought Jeannie was, as well. They're both very pretty girls. But she and Angela, and Simon, all saw it, apparently. Then there was that day at the office, when they came to start work towards the programme – "

"Yes, I remember. She did seem a bit – oh, I don't know – not quite with it, for a time. But it seemed to pass, and she got on with the job. I thought she was just starting a period, or something – you know, I sometimes feel a bit off at that time – "

"And then I met her at the hospital, when I was seeing Dad. That was the last time I saw her, but Angela's told me what happened. She decided she couldn't stay around the Midlands, where she was likely to meet me …. oh God, it sounds awful. Angela said she was in a terrible state. She'd already decided she …. wouldn't do anything about it ….. I mean she'd keep away from me …. and then Angela told her about her and Dad and it …. strengthened her resolve, I suppose you'd say. But she still felt she must not allow herself to be in a position where she would run into me, Angela said.

"She seems a real toughie, doesn't she? But this was something she couldn't deal with emotionally, obviously. She didn't come to Lyndford that Christmas, did she, and it was apparently because you and I were there. She went ski-ing instead, and that was when she met a chap who'd been a news agency chief in Yugoslavia and she got fired up about what was happening there, or about to. At least that's what she's told Angela. But she – Angela I mean – thinks it was mostly because of her emotional state.

"I don't know. But I do know I can't get away from the fact that it all happened because of me. If I hadn't been around it wouldn't have happened." And he sat with his hands clasped together, his elbows on his knees, staring at where the fire would have been if there'd been one. Stella left her chair and sat beside him, her arm round him.

"But you didn't do anything to encourage her, did you? So you shouldn't blame yourself."

"That's what Angela told me. But I can't help wondering whether I could have done something to discourage her, or even whether I was bit too nice to her. And then there's you. I should have told you about it long ago."

"It doesn't matter, darling. But you mustn't let it get you down. I know you love me, and I love you. You're the most wonderful husband anyone could have. I don't think there's another man in the world would put up with a wife like me, who can only be happy when she's fulfilling her stupid ambitions."

"Sweetheart, many women, perhaps most, are driven into depression by losing a baby, like we did. It didn't make me feel on top of the world, and I'm only a male. I can only be grateful that you're the kind of woman who has the other side to her, that pulls her out of such a state. It's one of the things that makes me love you. You're so special. Many women have good business heads, I know, but not many are such terrific wives and mothers as well."

She hugged him closer, and they sat, clasped together, for minutes, before she said: "Darling, there's something I haven't told you. I thought I never would tell you, or anyone, but I've decided I want to."

"If it's in the past, it doesn't matter. But if you want to, tell me. It won't make any difference to us, I promise."

"It's in the past alright. So far in the past that I don't even know about it. Before I was born."

"Are you going to tell me your father was a bank robber or something. Like I said, it won't make any difference."

"No, it isn't that. It's about my father though. It's ….. I don't know who he was. I don't even know his name."

Edward stared: "You mean your – your mother's husband – Jud – wasn't your father?"

"Yes. My mother told me, just before she died." And she went on to tell him of her mother's death-bed confession.

"But she didn't say who it was?"

"Not his name. She only said he was the son of a greengrocer she worked for, a few years after she left school. And I didn't ask. I suppose I was too shocked. I was only 16. And I didn't want to upset her any more. It was only three days before she died. She could hardly speak. I'm sorry, darling. I should have told you before."

"It still doesn't matter. It doesn't change you."

"I want to know, though. And I'm going to try to find out, some day. It isn't that I want to know him. I'm sure he was not a nice man, or he wouldn't have treated my mother like that. But I just want to know. There's a gap there and I want to fill it, in my own mind."

"He's not Clive's father, though?"

"Oh, no. He's my – Jud's – son."

"Does Clive know about it?"

"No. Mother told me not to tell him. But she thought I ought to know. She never told me his name, though, only that he was the son of the greengrocer."

She went quiet for a few moments, before she continued: "It's been on my mind for some time. Since you told me about your mother, before we were married. It didn't seem to matter at first.

I suppose I was too concerned with my own affairs. But I think it'll become more important as time goes on." Edward thought.

"Yes, I think you're right. It will. And I can understand your wanting to know, although it won't have any practical effect on us. Have you any idea about how to find out? If you don't know his name, there's nothing to go on."

"I think we'd have to employ enquiry agents or something, if we wanted to do it from here. But I've got a different idea. I think we should leave it until we're able to take a holiday, and do it ourselves, through some old fashioned detective work on the ground. We'd be able to see Clive, and your family. You've only met Clive once, at our wedding, and that's the only time I've seen him since I left Salford. It might not be for a year or two, but I don't mind that, now I've told you about it."

"That's a very good idea – although I hope we can snatch a few days in England before that."

Stella was quiet again, but only for a very short while, before she said: "I haven't finished yet."

"Not more skeletons?"

"Not skeletons. Flesh and blood. I want to have another baby, just as soon as it's practical – for me, physically, I mean."

"Sweetheart – are you sure? You must be worn out, now."

"No, I'm not. I may get a bit tired sometimes. But when I think of how my mother had to work, at a miserable, uninspiring job, when she had two small babies, and how your grandmother was cutting sugar cane when the labour pains started, I think I have it incredibly easy. All I have to do is take a few minutes every few hours away from work that hardly seems like work.

"You make it sound so easy, but I still think it must be taking a lot out of you."

"I don't think it is, and anyway I've got my whole life to recover. I'm only 32, darling. We're not going to take any anti-baby precautions. I don't think I'm likely to get pregnant while I'm still feeding David, and after that it'll be the right time. Just one more. P'raps it'll be a girl. Would you like that?"

"If she's like you. But whichever – it won't matter." He hugged her again.

Nineteen

The Bigot

The entrance of James Simon Levison into the world brought much pleasure to Angela and the Jameson family. But it also highlighted a situation, and sparked an incident, that was to echo through the lives of Jeannie and her husband for years.

Strictly speaking, they were not related, but James was almost seen as an addition to the Lyndford family. He was Angela's first blood-related grandchild, although she hardly thought of Alastair, Dorothy and Douglas as anything else; nor indeed Edwina and Christopher, by now so much a part of the Home Farm brood that they usually addressed Charles and Maria as Mum and Dad.

James was a healthy baby from the start, but Jeannie had a tough time of it, through her pregnancy when the sickness that often disappears after the first months persisted much longer; and especially at the end when she was in labour for more than 24 hours, refusing a caesarean delivery because, she said, "it isn't natural." Angela and Simon were with her throughout, in turns, at the Cambridge hospital. She did not know what she would have done without them, she said afterwards. But in moments of near delirium the name that came through her agony was Josie's.

"I thought I saw her, Mum," she said afterwards. "She was being dragged away by some men, and there was shooting, and shells bursting. Do you know where she is now? I hope all that wasn't actually happening to her."

"Oh, I don't suppose so," Angela soothed. "I think you were just connecting her with what you've seen and read about all that." But she hoped so, too. The two girls had always been so very close. Although they had never shown any sign of a power of telepathic communication, it might just happen at times of extreme stress. She had been in touch with Jim Meredith, first at the time of the market square bomb in Sarajevo, the Serb mortar missile that killed nearly 80 people and wounded more than 200 more, and been assured that Josie was not among them. Now she contacted him again but was told Josie had sent copy as recently as that morning.

Jeannie was comforted, but was still in a highly emotional state when Simon's father appeared, almost out of the blue, less than a week after James's birth. Simon was taking three weeks holiday, but Angela was still with them. She had always liked Simon. He reminded her of her first husband, Bill, in looks and ways. But when his father appeared, just before she planned to leave, she was made to wonder where her son-in-law's mild and gentle nature came from.

Simeon Levison was an orthodox Jew who had no time for any other creed or religion, and even less for people with no religion at all. A city banker, he had tried to stop Simon marrying outside his own faith, and warned him that he could expect nothing in the way of financial help, or inheritance, if he did. Simon would have been happy enough to continue to live within the tenets of Judaism, although he had little in the way of religious conviction himself, if he had not met and fallen in love with Jeannie. But although it seemed gentle and placid, his love for her was far stronger than respect for a father who showed up as little more than a bigot. It was almost an echo, in a very different setting, of what had happened in Alastair's father's family, Angela thought afterwards.

Simon had seen nothing of his parents after the confrontation over Jeannie. His mother was a mild and gentle woman, no doubt where his own character came from, but utterly subservient to his father. Dutifully however he wrote once a year telling them of the important facts in their life. He never received a reply until he sent a brief note on the birth of James. Almost by return of post there came an even briefer response.

"Simeon," it opened. (Simon had dropped the "e" from his name years before.) "I shall come to your house on Friday October 21st, to discuss the future of my grandson. Yours sincerely, Simeon G. Levison."

Simon did not quite know what to make of the note. Did his father want to take James away or something? Surely not. But it looked as though there was going to be some kind of unpleasant encounter.

Angela opened the door when Mr Levison knocked. He was not quite as tall as Simon and rather heavier built, although by no means fat, but she at once saw the facial resemblance.

"Good morning," he said. "I'm Simeon Levison. And you are?"

"Oh, hello, Mr Levison. I'm Angela Jameson, Jeannie's mother. Please come in."

He stepped into the hallway and immediately asked: "Is Simeon at home?"

Angela did not need to answer as Simon came down the stairs.

"Hello, father," he said.

His father looked at him as though inquiring whether this was still the same son who had defied and broken faith with him ten years before.

He said only: "I want to see my grandson." No hug, or even handclasp.

Simon looked at him, the old distress still there, and silently thinking: "It's still the same, then." But he said only: "Yes, sir, of course. They're upstairs." He turned round to lead the way, leaving Angela speechless.

Jeannie was fully dressed. She had been nursing the baby but Simon had seen his father arrive through the bedroom window and she had laid him in his cot.

Simon said: "This is my father, darling." To him: "Sir, this is my wife, Jeannie."

The older man barely glanced at her. He said: "I came to discuss the future of my grandson, not for any other reason."

Jeannie could see Simon was trembling, but he said only, very quietly: "Yes, father, of course."

"You put yourself in a position I could not accept for a son of mine when you married against my wishes and broke vows I had made for you," Simeon said. "That cannot be changed. But now it is possible for a new start to be made in the case of my grandson. Do you understand?"

Simon understood perfectly well where his father was heading. But he said: "No, sir, I don't think I do. Please explain what you mean."

"I mean that he will be counted as one of my family in terms of financial support and inheritance if I can have an assurance that he will be brought up in our faith, as he should be, until he is ten years old. At that age he will come to live with me."

It was not far from what Simon had expected. He started to tell his father, firmly but respectfully, that he could not agree to any such suggestion. But before he could get out half a dozen words Jeannie, who had listened in open-mouthed disbelief, took over. Always the more fiery of the Margerrison twins, and still emotionally worked up, she waded in with verbal fists flying.

"Mr Levison, if someone had told me that any parent had made this suggestion, I would not have believed them. It sounds like something out of a Victorian novel. Simon will not tell you what he thinks of it, out of respect. But I'll tell you what I think. I think it is utterly disgraceful. To suggest taking a child from his mother .... do you know what I went through, only a week ago, bringing him into the world? And his religion .... neither Simon nor I will presume to dictate what it should be, or if he should have any religion at all .... he will make up his own mind as he grows old enough...."

"I hope that's not your answer, Simeon?"

"I'm afraid it is, father."

"You're no son of mine. I wish you good-day." And he went out of the room, almost sending flying a tray of coffee cups in the hands of Angela as she reached the top of the stairs. He had not been ten minutes in the house.

Jeannie sank on the bed, her head in her hands.

"Oh, darling, I'm sorry.... I shouldn't have spoken to your father like that...."

Simon was trembling, but he put his arms round her. "It doesn't matter," he said. "You were quite right. I would have said the same, one way or another."

Angela asked: "What happened?"

Simon, although struggling to get out the words, told her, and she listened almost in disbelief. But then she recalled what had happened when Alastair's father married the maidservant. What she had just witnessed was akin to the immoveable obduracy that had brought tragedy to the Lyndford family. Poor Squire Jameson, driven to suicide because his son loved the so-loveable Dolly, she had often thought. Now she wondered what kind of grief Simeon was causing himself.

"You are right, of course, absolutely," she said "but I feel terribly sorry for him. It must be terrible to be so ….. like that ….."

Simon transferred his embrace to his mother-in-law. "Thanks, Angela," he said.

The new confrontation with his father brought deeper distress than he had suffered when he and Jeannie were married, when the anger of a father he knew to be bitter and bigoted weighed comparatively lightly against his love for her. This new anguish stayed with him for years, now he was a father himself, although he did his best to keep it from Jeannie, and usually succeeded. She soon returned to normal, although she could not do a Stella and get back to her work within a fortnight. In fact she and Simon debated whether she should go back at all, for the time being. She was keen on her job, and was making good progress in it, but there had also crept in a desire to be just a mum, at least for a time. Financially it was feasible. Simon was now earning enough to cope with their needs including mortgage, food, clothes and transport. And if she decided to stay at home, they would not have to employ a nanny or household help, they reasoned. She discussed it with her astrophysics boss at the university who assured her there would be no difficulty in finding a job, full or part time, if and when she wanted to return. Halfway though her maternity leave she made the decision. She would not go back. Simon backed her decision wholeheartedly. He loved having her there to greet him, with James and hopefully, in another year or two, a little brother or sister when he returned from his laboratory. And no doubt it helped stave off the worst effects of that awful encounter with his parent.

But while she happily made that decision, Jeannie and her mother became increasingly anxious about Josie. After Angela was assured by Jim Meredith that she was still sending copy from Sarajevo, shortly after James was born, they heard nothing, read nothing they could be sure originated from her, through the rest of the year.

Christmas came, with the usual gathering at Lyndford. This year Emily Jane brought her friend Lisbeth. Barry's suffering had ended with his death in November. Neither could be anything but relieved for him. Edward, Stella and David came from Germany; Jeannie, Simon and James from Essex.

They had all left by New Year. Angela, as she had promised Jeannie she would, called Belgrade. Meredith responded cagily when she asked about Josie, if she was still at Sarajevo, still sending copy.

"No, I don't think she's there now," he said after a pause.

"Do you mean you don't know?"

"She was planning to get out of the city. She was intending to go to one of the eastern enclaves because she thought she could do more good there, in terms of news. I didn't want her to go but I didn't actually say she mustn't."

"So did she go?"

"I must assume she did."

"You don't know?"

He was silent.

She asked again.

"I'm terribly sorry, Mrs Jameson. No, I don't know. We haven't heard anything from her, or of her, for nearly three months."

*****

Alastair had not seen Angela so distressed since the time 40-odd years before when the other Josie, her sister, had become entangled with Steve Parrimore. Her nights were almost sleepless, and she put off calling Jeannie. She was terrified of the effect the news from Belgrade would have. Alastair spent all his time with her, forgoing the golf he played with Peter and even the walks he and Michael regularly took round the Home Farm acres and sometimes further afield. But of course when Michael asked why, he and Kathleen had to be told. For them, it brought back the time they had spent after Jonathan and Catriona went missing, in Bangladesh. But it was only a few days before Jeannie herself rang, and had to hear.

"I'm coming over," she said. Angela, thinking of Simon who would be almost equally worried, wished she would not, but could not think of actively dissuading her, and Jeannie arrived that same day.

Left to herself, Jeannie would have called Jim Meredith every day. But

Angela, who had been promised by Meredith that she would be told the instant he had any news, convinced her that it was pointless. She also persuaded her daughter to take herself and their son back to her husband. They were young and must get on with their lives, for all their sakes.

Both of them scanned the papers for anything that might give a clue to what was happening to Josie. Angela had always read the Monitor but started to also take other dailies as well as the American news magazine which she knew had contained articles by her daughter. Jeannie rang her mother almost every day to ask if she had heard anything. But the days turned into weeks, the weeks into months, and still nothing, except for one call from Meredith, in March, to say he had heard from a fellow journalist in Sarajevo who believed Josie had gone out through the tunnel dug from the city's Dobrinja area to enable arms and supplies to be brought in, and a limited number of citizens to attempt escape.

"I think she might have been making for Srebrenica," he had told her. "An awful situation has developed there and Josie always wants to be in the thick of things. I'll let you know immediately if I hear any more."

Three months later, the world media was awash with the ghastly happenings in and around the town in eastern Bosnia. There were reports of thousands of Bosnian Muslims being driven from their homes, the men and many of the boys summarily executed, women and young girls raped, many of them also murdered, in the worst single act of ethnic cleansing of a war that was all about ethnic cleansing, or genocide; of Muslims by Serbs, Serbs by Croats, Croats by Serbs and even Serbs and Croats by Muslims, who were most often the innocent, injured parties. But the Lyndford watchers, and Jeannie, did not hear, read or see anything of Josie.

In August Angela, unable any longer to bear the agony of not knowing, without doing anything, again called Jim Meredith. His response was even more negative than four months before. He had heard absolutely nothing of her, either from Sarajevo where he now had another main correspondent, or from Srebrenica.

Although she rightly guessed it would yield nothing, she contacted the British embassy in Belgrade; the same with the Courier, Josie's former newspaper employer; and the BBC. Whenever anyone spoke to her, from inside the family or without, the first question was invariably: "Have you heard anything?"

After a time, the questions ceased. Everyone was afraid to mention her, to Angela. The year wore on, the wars were brought to a halt as America, at last spurred into action by the horrors of Srebrenica and frustration over the rest of the West's inability to get to grips with the situation, took a firmer hand, although the "solution" that emerged proved only that might rather than right had prevailed.

The guns had gone silent by the time the Jamesons, Housmans and Levisons gathered for another Lyndford Christmas.

Twenty

The Quintet

While boys no older than young Alastair were being shot in cold blood in Bosnia, babies snatched from their mothers' arms and their throats cut while the mothers themselves were savagely raped, the Home Farm quintet grew and thrived.

Taking the Housman children into the household had gone well, all along. Charles' and Maria's three had been delighted when Edwina and Christopher came to visit, before Michael's stroke, and the pleasure continued when it turned into a permanent stay. The set-up became the nearest thing to an extended family likely to be found among English people near the end of the twentieth century. Two sets of grandparents, in effect, although Michael and Angela were not blood relations to Edwina and Christopher, lived only a few minutes walk away, and there were not many days when one or other of the five did not put in some time at Jasmine Cottage or Old School House.

As in any family, there were disagreements, sometimes mildly violent, and as the years went by five children developed into five young people with five distinct characters. Alastair, his namesake grandfather said, was for all the world like his father Charles at ten or eleven years old; quiet and studious – most of the time – but physically active and competent and on his way to being good at sport; in looks, he was more like his Uncle Edward and great-great Uncle Giles than his father, with grey eyes and a tight crop of brown curls.

Edwina, now turned ten and with her flaming mop trimmed to shorter proportions, was almost a carbon copy of her mother, Catriona. The fair skin inclined to freckles, so often found with red hair, housed blue eyes that seemed to be able to penetrate a shield of steel. One characteristic that had shown up as a four-year-old was still there. She would lapse into silence, for minutes on end, sometimes in the middle of conversation or play, and just as suddenly "return to the world." As it had puzzled her grandparents back then, it worried her teachers, who suggested the doctor ought to be consulted. He sent her off to a child psychiatrist who carried out tests but said there was nothing to be concerned about. Edwina told him it was her "thinking time." And the teachers had to admit there seemed nothing wrong with her comprehension and work. In class she still appeared to have taken in the entire content of the subject in hand, even though she had apparently gone mental walkabout for minutes at a time. She also kept up the agility and athleticism she had shown when she climbed the cherry tree in the London garden, joined in all the Home Farm activities, and generally played the part of what she was, a charming and intelligent little girl.

Edwina and Dorothy, within a couple of months of the same age, were good friends, rarely quarrelling or even at odds. There was little passion about it, just an amicable acceptance of the other and her needs. The notable closeness in the family – as they and their elders increasingly thought of the five – was between Alastair and Edwina. They were the two most likely to be embroiled in the occasional spats, yet most likely to be found together. It was always Edwina who Alastair sought to join him when he came across something interesting, in school work, garden or woods. "Dwina, come and look at this," he would say.

As the years went on, they would often disappear for hours on end, usually with Blinda, an alsatian-poodle cross of strange appearance but with almost human intelligence who, Charles said, never bit anyone in her life but who frightened more than one person, notably those in uniform, like the postmen until they got to know her, almost to death. Maria would say she never worried about the children if Blinda was with them. Not quite true, although it might have been, because the dog was the nearest thing to a guardian angel they could possibly have. Her name came from her former owner, an old lady who lived in the village and who dumped the year-old bitch in one of the farm buildings while she went shopping, sometimes without even asking. Her driver would not allow the animal in his taxi and Linda could not leave her at home because she was still in the stage of wanting to tear everything to pieces.

"Bloody Linda, she's left that dog here again," Henry the stockman muttered on the last occasion, when he found her in a loosebox in which he wanted to accommodate a new-born calf and its mother.

"What did you call her?" asked Edwina, who, as always interested in events like the arrival of a new calf, happened to be following close behind

"Bee Linda" Henry hurriedly improvised. Hence Blinda, dubbed on the dog, whose original name they did not know and never found out because Linda did not return. The old lady had collapsed in the supermarket and been taken to hospital.

All the children went to the "area" primary school at Buryton and in due course to Ludstone, where Charles, Emily Jane and Edward had all been, as a grammar, but which was now an 800-pupil comprehensive. Parents and grandparents had all been happy with Buryton, but question marks were raised in some of their minds as to whether the all-in establishments were up to scratch.

It was Alastair's brother Peter who set them thinking. He asked his nephew, when young Alastair was starting his last year at Buryton: "Aren't you a bit worried about sending him there, Charles? I've heard some of the staff who've come from the modern aren't up to much, and the boys and girls will be a very mixed bunch."

Charles, as ever, consulted first Maria then his father, and Angela, who had both, many years before, been educated at fee-paying schools, Alastair at Shrewsbury. Maria hit the consensus when she said: "We must do what's best for the children. I wouldn't mind sending them to private schools if that was the only way to make sure they had a good education, and I know that's why Uncle Peter is in favour of it. But I hate the thought of copying the likes of the Sydnams who are doing it because they're snobs.

"And what about Edwina and Christopher? I can't see how we could afford to send five of them to boarding school, and it would be awful for them if they were left out."

"I expect Michael and Aunty Kathleen would foot the bill for them," said Charles "but we must talk to them before we take it any further."

Michael and Kathleen were quite clear about it, however. They recalled how they had pondered in the same way when Edwina started school, had adopted a wait and see approach and been pleased with the result.

"I know it's a different situation," Michael said. "They're at a really good primary school now and Ludstone's a bit of an unknown quantity. He's your boy, Maria, and it's up to you and Charles. But I will say that if it was Edwina I had to make a decision about for next year I'd be inclined to go the way we did at Lambeth – send her to Ludstone and see how it worked out. Certainly go and talk to them and see how they come over. I bet you could get Alastair in at Shrewsbury later, with your family connections with the school, if you felt Ludstone was no good. And if that didn't prove to be the case, the money you wouldn't spend on school fees could go into a fund for them later. And of course, we'd pay for Edwina and Chris if it became necessary."

Which was how it was left, by unanimous agreement. Alastair started at Ludstone and Edwina followed a year later.

Edwina and Christopher spent time with Michael and Kathleen, Edwina more than her brother. Not worried about the "thinking time" phases, her grandparents watched her develop from toddler to ten-year-old with almost unallayed satisfaction. Even while she was still at the Buryton school, they were pleased to see that she emulated her great grandmother Dolly in wanting to read everything she could get her hands on. Black Beauty, Little Women, What Katy Did – and did at school, and did next – Malcolm Saville and even Roald Dahl were read and to some extent digested before she achieved double figures in age. They made no attempt to guide her reading, simply turning her loose among their well-stocked shelves. One book which took her eye just after her tenth birthday bore her mother's name, Catriona, and led into a conversation with Michael which helped confirm his opinion of her as a child with an exceptional power of thought.

"Is that where my mummy's name came from, Grandad ?" she asked.

"I really don't know, sweetheart," he replied. "I think it's quite a well-known Scottish name, or at least it was."

"Can I read it?"

"Of course you can. But before you read Catriona I suggest you read Kidnapped, because the two books are one story, really. They should be together on the shelf because they're both by Robert Louis Stevenson." He stood up to search the shelves. "Yes, there's Kidnapped. Shall I get it down for you ?"

"Thank you, Grandad."

She took it and started to flick through the leaves, not at all put off by the small print.

Michael asked: "Do you talk about the books you read with the others?"

"I do with Ally, a lot. And with Dot."

She closed the book and sat looking at the photograph of her mother and father, and Christopher as not much more than a baby, taken in Bangladesh not long before the fatal storm. She was clearly thinking, although not in the trance-like manner of her "thinking time."

"Do you think I'll see Mummy and Daddy again when I die, Grandad?"

He did not know what to say, how to answer such a question from a ten-year-old, even this one.

"Why do you ask, darling? Don't you think you will?"

"Ally an' me were talking. It was in the churchyard and we were looking at the graves and working out who they all were. Some of them had got words on them like 'until we meet again' and 'safe in heaven' and things. We didn't see how you could put people in the ground and then expect to see them again. He said people just rot away. Do you think that's what'll happen to Mummy and Daddy, Grandad? And some people are cremated when they die. That's burnt, isn't it? How can you ever see them again if they're burnt up?"

He took her in his arms, and on to his knee. "My sweetheart, you are asking some of the biggest questions there are. I can't be sure I know the answers. You'll have to make up your own mind about these things, when you're a bit older.

"You're absolutely right though that one way or another, our bodies disappear when we die. They disappear slowly when we're buried in the ground – Alastair's quite right, they rot away – and very quickly when we're cremated. But a lot of people believe there's more to it than that. They believe we all have a soul, or spirit, that doesn't die."

"What happens to it, Grandad? Does it go to heaven?"

"Many people believe so. Most people, I should think."

"And does it stay there, for ever?"

"That's what the Christian church teaches."

"Is that where God is? And Jesus?"

"That's what we're taught."

She went quiet, then asked:

"You don't believe that, do you, Grandad?"

He had to think hard before he could reply. He must give her an honest answer. Edwina would never accept platitudes or evasions. But before he could quite get his thoughts together, she came up with the biggest question of all.

"Do you believe there's a God? Ally doesn't."

"I don't think Alastair's quite old enough to make up his mind. It's something you have to think and think about and then you might never be sure. I can't be sure I know the answer, and I'm seventy-six years old."

"But what do you think, Grandad?"

Should he tell her, or should he repeat that she must work out her beliefs for herself? No, he must say what he thought, he decided. Then it must be up to her.

"I'll tell you what I think, but I beg you, Edwina my darling, please don't think that you have to accept it, just because it comes from your Grandad. Make your own mind up.

"I think there may be a God, a being of some kind, but I don't have the faintest idea what form he, or she, or it, takes. Some people see him as like a human being. The Bible talks about God creating man in his own image. But I don't think I can believe that. He may be a spirit, permeating the universe – you know what permeating means, it means spread everywhere, doesn't it? - or not even a spirit. Just a force, perhaps – one who created life and the universe.

"I certainly don't believe that we all go to Heaven, and live for ever in a beautiful place where there are no tears, or pain, or work, or play, or any other things we all know and live through. I believe immortality – everlasting life – comes through the things you have done, or made, and your children, and their children. You and Christopher make me and Granny immortal."

She still sat on his knee, the one he always made sure she exercised because the other still suffered somewhat from the effects of the stroke, looking thoughtfully across the room to the photo of her mother and father.

"But I don't criticise other people for believing in God. As long as they don't try to force their beliefs on other people, or fight wars over the way they believe, or put people to death because they believe in a different god, or in the same god in a different way. There have been some terrible things done in the name of religion, you know. A few hundred years ago they put people to death, in this country, and in Spain and France, and other countries, by burning them alive because they would not change from one church to another."

He hoped he had not gone too far, said more than she could take in, or understand.

"I hope that helps you, sweetheart. But please don't think I'm trying to make you think the way I do. It's up to you. Listen, and read, and think about it. But don't worry about it."

He paused again, wondering whether to put to her the essence of the creed by which he, and Kathleen, tried to live. The creed of decent humanity, tolerance, honesty, hatred of cruelty, dislike of greed. Or to hold up the example of Debra, who was a strong believer all her life, but lived it always by that same creed, rather than by religious dogma. But he decided he had said enough already, perhaps more than enough; and anyway there was no need. This child would never live any other way.

"Thank you, Grandad," she said, squeezed his hand and snuggled a little closer. But she had not quite finished.

"Can cousins be married?" she asked.

"Yes. Why? Have you got one you want to marry?"

"I'm going to marry Ally."

"Oh. Does he know?"

"I asked him whether he wanted to marry me when we're grown up."

"And what did he say?"

"He just said: 'Suppose so.'"

"Well, we shall see, shan't we. It can't be for a long time. But you're not cousins, you know. Not first cousins, anyway."

"What are we then, Grandad?"

"That takes a bit of working out. Let me see: Granny and Alastair's grandad are brother and sister; that makes your Daddy and Uncle Charles cousins. I don't know what number cousins you are, but it can't be less than second. Probably third, or fourth." He thought she looked pleased.

Twenty-One

Awful truth

Kathleen and Michael had kept up their yearly trips to the McArthurs, on Vatersay, in the Easter holidays, and Jennie and Kathleen maintained the correspondence. The Hebrideans pressed for a visit from the Jamesons, and at Easter 1996, most of the spring arable work having been done in an open early season, Charles at last decided he could spare the time to go. They had still heard nothing of Josie, and Angela's anxiety continued. Not knowing anything at all was the worst part. But she and Alastair agreed to join the trip.

They hired a large people-carrier, more like a mini-bus, rather than take two cars, and planned to stay at Castlebay on Barra, for accommodation for nine would have been too many for even the flexible Jennie to cope with. Neither Charles nor Maria had ever been to Scotland and they proposed to incorporate some travel on the mainland, perhaps see the area from where the distant Jameson ancestors had sprung, nearly three hundred and fifty years before.

They found the McArthurs thriving, in Western Isles terms. Ailsa was now nearly three, and was quickly adopted by Edwina and Dorothy; Charles and Alastair, once they had taken in the basic nature of Angus's 150-acre croft, admired his developing flock of sheep, and his ram-breeding project. Alastair, harking back to the struggle of his early days at Forest Farm, was particularly appreciative of his host's adaptations of elderly machinery, and his efforts to improve such of the grassland as was improveable. And he entertained both Angus and Jennie, who already knew Debra's story, with anecdotes of her shepherding prowess.

Angus took them round the island, showing them the crashed Catalina, the cave of rocks where "Marion of the Heads" was supposed to have drowned her victims; and they heard him sing some of the songs from the Nan Mackinnon collection, for which he was now becoming known, at a music evening on Barra.

He was completely transformed from the depressed individual Michael and Kathleen had found when they first met him. He was especially delighted with the obvious progress Edwina and Christopher were making as they grew. "She's the image, the spittin' image," he told Angela.

"I never knew Catriona," she said "but I know, from all I've heard, that she was an exceptional young woman. And I can assure you, from all we know of her from school, and from Kathleen and Michael, and what we see ourselves, that Edwina is on her way to becoming just as exceptional. And she often talks about you, you know."

"She says she's going to marry young Alastair. D'ye think she will?"

"Oh, I don't know, Angus. A great deal can happen before that time comes. But if it did work out that way, none of us would worry. They're two fine children. And the blood link is very thin. There couldn't be any fear from that point of view."

"No, there certainly could not. Not like here on the islands. There's been a deal tae much inbreedin', for sure, here."

He paused, seemed to want to say something else. "Angela, I think Michael and Kathleen were a wee bit worried that we mecht no like the idea o' Edwina and Christopher going tae a family, with, ye know, different blood in the veins ...."

She smiled. "You mean, Angus, Charles' mother being West Indian."

"Aye. Well, Angela, there's a lot here wad tak exception, I can tell ye. But not me an' Jennie. An' now I've met them, or some of them, I can tell ye I think they're a grand family. I think they've a deal to be proud of."

"Thank you, Angus. So do I."

She added: "They told you all about Alastair and me, didn't they?"

"Aye. Two years ago. I dinna think there's much they didna tell us. Ye havena many secrets."

"Do you know about Josie – my daughter?"

"Aye, Kathleen tellt us, in her letter. I'm awfu' sorry, Angela. Ye havena heard anything?"

"No. But you know, don't you .... ?"

"Aye, I know. But I think mebbe it's worse for you. Wondering, I mean."

"I can only think the worst. It's been so long. But even if.... something terrible's happened .... I think I'd rather know. And there's Jeannie – you know, don't you, my other daughter, her twin .... they've always been so very close. She's going through the same as I am."

"She's just had a bairn, has she no? Kathleen told us."

"Yes. He's a year old, now."

"Ach, well, perhaps it'll help stop her feeling so bad."

He was quiet for a while.

"D'ye know if Kathleen and Michael think about going back to Bangladesh at all? Ye know, to see where Catriona and Jonathan .... ?"

"They have mentioned it. But Kathleen is a bit reluctant for Michael to go. He seems quite fit and well now, but he did have quite a severe stroke, and he's 77. I'll tell you what, though. Edwina will go as soon as she's old enough. What happened hasn't got her down – after all, she was only two when they went – but I know they're still in her mind. Kathleen has told us she sometimes sits looking at that photo for half an hour at a time, and she's asked us to get her a copy. As I said just now, she's a quite exceptional child, Angus. You can be very proud of her. And I'm certain she will always stay close to you, as well as to Michael and Kathleen."

"Ach, ye know the things a man wants tae hear, Angela. No wonder ye were a professor."

"Nothing to do with that. I've known one or two professors who were as thick as two short planks, as they say in Shropshire, when it came to understanding people. But thank you, Angus."

After three days with the McArthurs, they drove up the Outer Hebridean island chain, enjoyed the two ferry crossings, before returning to the mainland via Skye and another ferry, staying at Portree, doing a half day's walk in the Cuillins, crossing over the bridge to Kyle of Lochalsh. They stayed two nights at Perth, using part of the intervening day in searching the city archives for traces of the Jamesons in the 16th and 17th centuries, before Douglas Campbell Jameson was recruited by Oliver Cromwell to look after seized land in the Welsh Marches. The microfiches yielded mentions of a number of Jamesons, but none they could positively identify as ancestors. Both old and young Alastairs, Charles, Edwina and Angela however took great pleasure in the search, while Kathleen and Maria took the others to less taxing pursuits, in the city. But they all enjoyed seeking out the wynds and other features of the town and conjecturing how they fitted into Scott's tale of the ancient city.

They were cruising down the M6 in Lancashire when Angela's mobile phone trilled. It was Jeannie.

"Mum, Michael Housman's just called .... he's had a message from Belgrade .... Josie.... oh, Mum ...."

The phone cut out. Angela said: "Pull in, Charles.... reception's gone .... Josie .... oh, Alastair ...."

Alastair said: "We're coming to services in about two minutes. The signal might be alright there. And there'll be payphones if isn't. Go in there, Charles. Who was it, darling?"

Angela could hardly speak. "Jeannie – she'd had a call from Michael. He's heard from Belgrade .... she sounded terrible .... Alastair ...."

"Give me the phone, love. I'll try her. Keep going, Charles, and go into the services."

The phone worked, Jeannie answered. He passed the instrument back to Angela.

"Mum? Where are you? Please come, Mum. Josie's .... oh, Mum .... Mr Housman says they've found her ...."

"You mean .... she's alright.... ?"

"No, Mum, no. I can't tell you .... please come ...."

"Please tell me what's happened ...."

The younger children started to cry, as they felt the desperation in Angela's voice, the anxiety flooding the car.

"I can't tell you, Mum.... you've got to come ...."

"We're on the motorway, about two hours from home. We'll come as soon as we get there."

They were pulling into the Charnock Richard services. Alastair took the phone from Angela.

"Jeannie, love, we can't hear you. The children are crying. Mum'll call you."

They parked up. Charles and Maria made all five children get out, three of them still sobbing, and went with them towards the building.

"We'll get them something to eat," said the ever-practical Maria.

Alastair called Jeannie, as Angela sat, trembling.

"Jeannie, my dear, you've got to try to tell us something. Your mum can't wait to hear until we get to you. She'll go out of her mind."

"Oh, Alastair, I'm sorry. Yes, I'll have to tell her, what I've been told."

"Just tell me, first. Is she .... alive?"

Jeannie did not answer.

"Jeannie?"

"No."

"Will you speak to her now?"

"Can I tell you first?"

"Of course."

"It sounds awful, Alastair. They found her.... buried. And she'd been mutilated.... oh, I can't tell you any more ...."

"Try, please. If I know it all I can tell your mother better, I think." There was a long pause. Alastair could almost see Jeannie trying to gather herself together.

"Simon's just come," she said at last. "I must talk to him."

"Yes, of course. Look, I'll ring Michael."

"Yes, please."

He switched off the phone, took Angela's hand.

"Darling...."

"She's dead, isn't she?"

"Yes, my love," he almost whispered.

"But there's something else."

"Yes. But look, it's all very second hand. Michael had it straight from Belgrade – from Jim Meredith, I expect. I'm going to call him. Will you stay here? I'll tell you if I get him." She said nothing, just shuddered, and he got out of the car. It was pouring with rain. He reached back inside for an umbrella.

Michael and Kathleen's number at Old School House was engaged. He kept trying it, and after half a dozen attempts Michael answered.

"Michael, it's Alastair. Jeannie's rung us."

"Oh my god. Does Angela know?"

"Some of it. We know she isn't alive. But there's more, isn't there?"

"Bloody hell, Alastair, that's the good bit."

"Tell me all you know, please. I'll handle it."

"Well, I've only got it from Meredith, and he'd been told by somebody else, but there doesn't seem any doubt about it. They found her in a shallow grave. They think she'd been dead for several months, so she was pretty .... And she'd been mutilated, horribly. It seems she was pregnant, and they'd cut her open, and taken it .... the baby .... out."

"Oh, my god, Michael. Are they sure it was her?"

"Yes. The lady she'd stayed with in Sarajevo was certain it was her, in spite of .... you know, decomposition .... and there were other things, her clothes, and some photographs and things. And the baby.... it was nearly full time, and it was with her .... they'd killed it after they ...."

"Alastair?"

"Yes, I'm still here. I'm switching off. I'll call you again."

He folded the umbrella, got back into the car. Angela was still sitting, but with her eyes closed.

She said: "Tell me, please, darling."

"They found her buried. In a shallow grave."

"Where?"

"I didn't ask. Near Srebrenica, I think."

"Was she .... alright? I mean, had she been.... ?"

"Do you want me to tell you now, darling?"

"Yes, please. I want to know before I talk to Jeannie."

She seemed to have become quite calm. He told her.

*****

Family members were amazed by Angela's apparent ability to cope. At Lyndford, only Alastair knew the full truth of her distress, and even he continued to be surprised that she did not break down, only coming near to it in the privacy of their own home. Charles and Maria commented on how brave she was, how well she was bearing up, although Maria secretly wondered how much of it was a charade. Kathleen and Michael were not easily taken in, either. They knew, through their own experience, what her calmness was masking.

Perhaps helping Jeannie face it all was a contributing factor. Not much more than an hour after arriving back at Lyndford, she and Alastair set off for Saffron Walden as she had told Jeannie she would, despite having already travelled more than two hundred miles that day. Arriving there late at night, they found her in a state of near-collapse, Simon tending to baby James' needs. As even very small children will, he seemed to know that something terrible was happening, would not settle down in bed, pushed his food away almost angrily.

Angela could only try to comfort her. She could not lie about the facts, or play down their worst features, because Jeannie had been the first to learn them, apart from Michael.

"She never saw him," she sobbed hysterically – meaning James. "Oh, Mum, why did they have to do .... that .... to her? Make them bring them here, Mum. Give them to me. I'll cut them to pieces ...."

After being persuaded to take a soporific she eventually dropped off to sleep, for about five hours. Next day she was quite different, quiet but deeply withdrawn, would not eat and seemed hardly to recognise James. They called the doctor who thought she was suffering from traumatic shock and came daily for nearly a week. She improved slowly, however, and Simon went back to work. Jeannie and her mother talked a great deal about Josie, increasingly naturally and normally, and after another week she insisted that she was perfectly able to look after herself, James and Simon.

"Go home, Mum. I'm sure they want you back at Lyndford. I'll be alright now."

"You won't do anything .... silly."

"Oh, Mum, don't be ridiculous. I've got this" – she was feeding James – "to look after. What would happen to him? And Simon. No, Mum, you don't have to worry that way. It was just .... something like that happening to Josie ...."

Angela also had to worry about Edward as she remembered how he had reacted when Josie's assault in Sarajevo was revealed. She did not tell him of the culmination of the tragic story while she was in Essex, for fear of further disturbing Jeannie, but as soon as she was back home she wrote to him and Stella, choosing to communicate that way rather than telephone. It probably made no difference.

Stella wrote back: "He's in a terrible state. He seems to think it's somehow all his fault, as he did before. Of course, I try to tell him it's nothing of the sort. He could not help Josie getting a fixation on him, as we both told him then, and he knows that's right, really. In any case, we don't know that it was because of what happened with him that she went to Bosnia. But it seems to make no difference. He goes to the office every day but I don't think he's doing any work to speak of. Please call him, Angela, and try to persuade him, as you did before. I won't say try to talk some sense into him, rather talk some of the nonsense out of him, perhaps."

Angela called him at his office. His secretary told her: "Mr Jameson is not taking any calls, for the moment."

"Please tell him it's Angela. I think he'll talk to me."

She could only repeat what she had said to him two years before, and hope it was working. It was difficult to know, on the phone. She called Stella.

"Let me know how he gets on, won't you," she concluded, and offered to go over to see them if Stella thought it necessary. Two days later Stella replied, said he seemed to be back to something like normal.

In the meantime, there was the question of whether Josie's remains should be brought back to Britain. Angela started to think about it immediately, and almost the last thing Jeannie said to her before she left for Lyndford was: "Can't we bring her home, Mum? I know it doesn't make any difference to her, but I'd like her to be somewhere we can put flowers and things. Wouldn't you?" Angela said of course she would, and she'd talk over ways and means with Alastair.

Unknown to them both, Jim Meredith had already broached the subject, through Michael.

He said his agency would pay the transport costs. Actually, most of it would come in personal donations from himself, other staff, and Alex Kordic, but he kept that to himself. Michael thanked him, said he thought Angela and Jeannie would want her brought home, and he would talk to them about it.

They decided that of course she should return, but were not sure where she ought to be buried. Angela's elder sister, Josie's namesake, still lived in London, but their brother Stewart had been in America for many years; there were no close relatives on her father Bill Margerrison's side; Jeannie lived at Saffron Walden with no immediate prospect of moving. It was however she who made the suggestion finally decided upon.

"I think she should come to Shropshire, Mum. She loved it at The Mill – she'd have lived there if she could."

Angela was pleased. She and Alastair were advocates of cremation, but she could not tolerate the thought of her daughter's body being subjected to that or any other further abuse. Josie was laid to rest in the Lyndford churchyard, alongside Debra, and near all the Jamesons, of whom, spiritually, she had been one. Only four people outside the extended family were present: they were Alex Kordic and his wife, and Erbie and Connie Johnson.

Twenty-Two

How to find a Father

Stella did not waver in her determination to have another baby, and by the time David was two years old, if possible. She found herself expecting his sister, or brother, by the midsummer of 1997. As usual, they swelled the Lyndford numbers for Christmas, this time taking nanny Magda and staying until after New Year when the firms' workforces returned to their desks and benches. Magda had been offered a holiday but she had never been to England and was pleased by the opportunity offered.

Before they left Germany, Stella decided she would implement her plan for finding out what she could about her real father. She said nothing to Edward then, but sprang it on him on Boxing Day. He was not happy, for the new baby was due in rather less than three months, but Stella pooh-poohed his doubts. She called her brother Clive, with whom she had kept up a regular if infrequent correspondence, and received an invitation to stay with him and his wife Alison. They were both teachers at a big comprehensive at Sale, where they also lived. Magda, happy in the company of the five youngsters, and their parents and grandparents, would stay at Lyndford, with David.

Clive did not know about the different parentage, and now they told him only that Stella wanted to look round the area where they had been brought up. He was not terribly interested in Salford because he had been adopted as a fourteen-year-old and regarded Bolton as his home.

It was twelve years since she had been to Salford, and she found it changed. She clearly remembered the street where she had been born and brought up, and they were able to drive down and spot Number 74. That too had changed almost beyond recognition, for it had been bought under the right to buy legislation and boasted a smart new front door and porch, plastic windows, a tarmac drive and an Audi standing on it. But the primary school two streets away, where she had been a star pupil, had disappeared.

Her mother's deathbed revelation had not even included the name of the greengrocer's where she had worked, or its location. They found no greengrocery in the immediate locality, but an old lady who still kept a newsagent's remembered one.

"It were Robbisons, i' Galton Street. That were t' name. An' I remember they 'ad a lad, Gerald. But they give it up, oh, 10 'ear ago, I should think," she said. Which would have been soon after Stella left the town.

"It were t' supermarkets killed shops like that. But they've done alright sin', from what I've heard. They went to a stall in t' market i' Manchester and worked it up into a wholesale business. Somebody told me t'other day as Percy Robbison died and t' lad, Gerald, carried it on. Not as he'll be much of a lad, now. Must be ower 50."

Back at the car, Edward asked: "Well, what do we do now? What do you want to do?"

"Oh, I'm going to try to find him. I haven't come this far without getting to know what he looks like, at least, if I can. It looks as though Robbison's the name, doesn't it?"

In the city, they parked up and went to the information centre, to be told, without anyone going to a great deal of trouble: "Oh, yes, Robbisons. They're in the market but they've got a depot in Green Street, just down there. Turn right out of that door, and Green Street's second on the left. They're about halfway down, on the left. You'll probably see one of their vans in the street. The traffic wardens are always on at 'em about it."

Less than ten minutes walk took them to two vans, marked P. Robbison and Son, Wholesale Fruiterers and Greengrocers. They walked into what was obviously the depot, with two more vans being loaded or unloaded, and saw a row of office cubicles. A young man came out and Edward asked: "Could you tell us where we can find Mr Robbison, please?"

The man, dressed in a light-coloured warehouse coat over a smart shirt and tie, said: "I'm Frank Robbison. What can I do for you?"

Edward said: "It's Mr Gerald Robbison we'd like to see."

"He's me father. But you can talk to me, if it's about business," he said, glancing at her swollen abdomen.

"It's not business, Mr Robbison."

Stella came in. "It's a personal matter." And seeing concern in his face, she quickly added: "Don't worry, Mr Robbison. It's nothing to be worried about. We – I – would just like to see him."

"What about?"

"I'd like to tell your father that."

"You can tell me first, and I'll ask him if he'll see you."

"Then we shall have to take steps to see him elsewhere, Mr Robbison. I repeat, it's nothing to be concerned about, but now I know where to find him, I am going to see him."

Before the young man could say any more, the door of the office he had emerged from opened and an older man stepped out.

"Have you told 'em, Frank?"

"No, I was on me way and these people stopped me. They want to see you."

Robbison, a pleasant looking man, apparently in good humour, smiled and said: "Oh, I am flattered. I don't get beautiful young ladies wanting to see me every day. What's it about?"

Edward said: "It's a personal matter, Mr Robbison. But as my wife told your son, it's nothing to be worried about. Could we perhaps go into your office?"

Robbison had been looking at Stella. His face changed, the cheerful but faintly sceptical smile sobered. He said: "Come in."

Seated, the older man behind his desk, he asked, quite quietly: "Well, why do you want to see me?"

Stella said: "I think you know, don't you?"

"You're .... Margaret's girl."

"Yes. And yours. How did you know?"

"You look like her. And you said it was personal."

They sat, silent, all three wondering where they went from there, how to bridge a 30-year gap, or back off from attempting. Robbison made the first move.

"Is your name Stella?"

"Yes. Stella Jameson. This is my husband, Edward. We've got a little boy, David, and as you can no doubt see, another quite soon."

"What's made you find me out? Are you after money?"

"No, we're not after money." Another silence.

"I just wanted to see what you looked like. I wanted to see what kind of a man it was who would deny what he had done to my mother. You see, she told me about it, when she was dying. She never told anyone else, and I've never told anyone else, except Edward. And I'm not going to."

He was looking down at his desk, covered with documents, invoices, cheques, bills, in labelled trays.

"I'm not proud of it," he said eventually. His accent was distinctly Lancashire, but not coarse or untutored. "I never did anything like that again, before I was married. Nor since."

More silence.

"You've hit me very sudden," he said. "It's no good pretending I didn't think but what this might happen, some day. But I didn't expect you just to walk in on me like this. I thought it'd come through lawyers or something."

"You needn't be afraid of that kind of thing," Stella answered. "I just wanted to know."

"I'd like to talk about it, though. Like I said, I'm not proud of what happened. But there's a bit more to it. I'd like to tell you some of it. And I'd like to know about you. It's a bit difficult, though, here ...."

"Could we meet somewhere else?" Edward asked. "This evening, perhaps."

Robbison thought.

"Are you stopping at an hotel?"

"No, we're staying with my brother, Clive, at Sale. We must go back – they're expecting us."

"Could you get away for a time later on? Or tomorrow?"

"Yes."

"I often go to the Rotary club on a Wednesday night. Could you meet me there? Say half-past seven?"

They agreed, and Robbison told them where it was, and that they should tell the club staff they were meeting him.

Back at Clive's by mid-afternoon, Stella thought she ought to tell her brother what it was all about, starting with their mother's death-bed confession. He and Alison listened, amazed. It was a complete surprise to them.

"What's he like, Stella?" Clive asked. "Is he anything like our – my – dad?"

"No, very different," she said. "Mum gave me the impression that he and his mother and father were not up to much and just wanted rid of her. But he says it wasn't quite like that and he wants to tell me about it. And he wants to know about me, and Edward. I think he was a bit worried that we were after money, but I told him we certainly were not."

"Well, I hope it works out. It's a bit of a shock. But you're still my sister. Mum was the important one, wasn't she?"

After dinner they left for Gerald Robbison's club. He took them into a quiet corner and ordered drinks, a fruit juice for Edward who was driving.

"I take it you've had your tea – dinner I expect you'd call it," he said. "They'd do you something here if you haven't."

"Yes, thank you, we had dinner at Clive's," Edward said.

Robbison seemed, not at ease exactly, but faintly eager, or excited. In spite of his taking the initiative in wanting to talk, Edward had expected Stella's parent to be embarrassed and edgy. It was as though he was pleased it was all coming into the open.

"Will you tell me a bit about yourselves? Where do you live, for a start."

"We live in Germany," Stella told him. "Not far from Cologne."

"Oh. Work there, I suppose?" he asked, directing the question at Edward.

"Yes, both of us, for the same firm. Protechno. It's based in England, near Coventry, but we have a branch in Germany."

"And what do you do? What sort of a firm is it?"

"We develop technology – advanced technology, applied mostly to engineering, especially the motor industry. Stella's the chief executive of the German firm. I'm technical director of the whole concern."

Rollison's eyes opened wide.

"Chief executive, eh? That means you're the boss .... ?"

"I'm head of the German branch."

"It sounds a very important job."

Stella said nothing, but Edward, always ready to air his wife's talents, said: "Stella's an exceptional woman, Mr Robbison. I'm very proud of her. And she's done it all by her own efforts. A lot of talent, and a great deal of hard work and determination."

"It sounds to me as though I ought to be asking you for money, not the other way about. No, I don't mean that. Won't you tell me a bit about it? How've you got on, like that?"

"Stella doesn't talk about it, but I will," Edward said, and he ran, more or less accurately, through her career to date, including how she had gained her qualifications through night school, progressed at Protechno and in Germany and taken the birth of their son in her stride, hardly taking any time off. Her newly discovered father listened in silence, and did not speak for a little time. Then he said, quietly, his eyes on some object in the far corner of the room: "I know I've no right, but you make me proud, you know. I don't mean of what happened. I'm not proud of that, like I said this afternoon. But I can't help being proud that a daughter of mine is doing so well." He paused again.

"It wasn't quite like you thought, Stella – I can call you that, can I? "

She said: "Yes, of course."

"I can't really expect you to believe this, but it's true. You see, I was getting fond of her, before.... what happened .... and they didn't like it. My mum, especially. She thought Margaret – your mum – wasn't good enough for us, I mean where she came from. She said they were nothin' but a lot of Irish gippoes. Then I told 'em she was goin' to have a baby and it was mine, and I wanted to marry her. She told me not to be silly, I was only 19. She wasn't going to have one of that sort in the family, she said. I was to say I knew nothin' about it.

He paused, looked down at his glass.

"I'd have married her, you know. I liked her and I think she liked me. What happened wouldn't have if we didn't. It wasn't quite all me. But they told me to think about which side my bread was buttered and I gave in.

"I was a bit worried about her being in the family way, and for a week or two I thought I'd have to keep tabs on her and try to make sure she was alright. But then I heard she'd married Jud Hardy, and I was pleased I'd got away with it so easy. I thought there was plenty more fish in the sea."

Stella had been looking at him as he spoke, and could see he was telling the truth. But she said nothing.

"When I heard she'd had the baby – you – I was pretty sure it was mine. I remember working out the dates. Then I got to know who you were, one way or another. There was a gang of you used to knock about together, and got into bits of mischief – oh, nothing terrible, just what kids do. I remember one day, you'd be eight or nine, you were all standing outside the shop and Dad was worried you might start pinching the fruit. He asked the girl who worked for us if she knew any of you. There was one seemed to be the leader and she said she was Margaret Hardy's girl, Stella. My ears pricked up and I could see you were very like her – your mum, I mean. Then a year or two later I saw you in your high school uniform and you looked even more like her, and I heard the girl you were with call you Stella."

"Did you never think of trying to find out where I was, what happened to me?" Stella asked.

"Eh, lass, I was too busy getting on with everything else. First there was the shop going bottom-up, or being on the way to it, then starting this business, with my dad. And there was getting married, and the family. We've got another lad beside Frank who you saw, and a girl. But every now and then I'd think about you. I never saw you though after that time when you were at school."

He seemed to have finished, and sat silent for a few moments.

Stella asked: "What's your wife's name, and the other children?"

"She's got a posh name – Dorothea. The other boy's Richard, and the girl's Barbara. She works with us, in the office, does the accounts and acts as a sort of secretary. Richard's in Australia, married an Aussie girl who he met over here. Frank's the youngest. They're good kids."

"Dorothea's a nice name – it was my great grandmother's," Edward said.

All through the conversation, he had been watching Stella, wondering what her thoughts were. For himself, he rather liked Gerald Robbison. He hoped she could bring herself to like him, too. After all, it was a long time ago, more than 30 years.

He said: "You seem to have a good business here, Mr Robbison."

"It's alright. My dad started it. The shop at Salford were gettin' hammered by the supermarkets just round the corner and he thought a stall in the market here was a better bet. Then he found one or two others were having difficulty

Francis John Simcock

getting good supplies, he'd always had good contacts with growers and it went from there. We supply half a dozen supermarkets now as well as the smaller shops and stalls. We've always concentrated on quality and I reckon that's why we're still here. The margins are very small but we get by."

He went quiet, Edward and Stella also saying nothing.

"Is this it, then, Stella? Do you mean to take it any further? Edward knows it all. Is there anyone else you're going to tell about it?"

Her reply answered Edward's questions.

"I'd like to keep in touch," she said."We're very close to Edward's father and his wife – his second wife. I think I'd like to tell her. And perhaps others in the family, sometime. Not just yet though."

"I could tell the missus," he said. "She'd take it. She comes from a bit of an upper-crust family but she's got her feet well on the ground. But the kids – I don't know. I'd like to see what she says."

Neither of them need have worried. Both families took it almost in their stride, as the kind of thing that happened in so many. They waited until David's sister, Marianne was born before telling Angela about it and leaving it to her to take it from there. Stella and her father never established an intimate relationship but as she said she wanted, they kept in touch. He was always "Mr Robbison" when she wrote to him, and Christmas cards were always addressed to Mr and Mrs Robbison and their children by name, and the card would contain as much information about what was happening to them as it was possible to squeeze in. A gap in their lives was filled, and nothing but good was done to anyone.

Marianne was born in March, just before the Lyndford contingent took their trip to Scotland. Again it was an easy, no-fuss birth, she taking time away from her office for rather longer than when David was born because, she told Edward, things could take care of themselves now. The German enterprise was continuing to grow, and there was talk of setting up another in Turkey, where the automotive industry, with which much of their business was connected, was growing. The main reason for some hesitation, Parkinson slightly jokingly told Edward, was that he could not immediately put his finger on another Stella, to run it.

Twenty-Three

Why Lisbeth married Tom

By the time she was 40, Emily Jane had made quite a mark in genealogical research, although without her name becoming known to the general public. Before the end of the century she had become well-enough off financially to buy a terrace house in Marylebone, to which she and Lisbeth moved from the cramped flat.

Her work involved collaboration with similar research teams in America, and brought more than one approach from the other side the Atlantic, but she turned them down because she did not want to leave her long time companion.

"I don't know whether I'd like living in America, anyway," she told Edward, always her first family confidant. "Perhaps I could do more in my work there because there's more money for research. But I couldn't leave Lisbeth."

"Wouldn't she like to go with you? She's retired now, isn't she, and she's got no family ties here."

Em did not think Lisbeth would like to move. But in the end the question never arose. Their lives took an unexpected turn on her next visit to the States.

Working in the Massachusetts research group to which she was connected was a scientist from Wyoming, Randall Goodrich. They were thrown together by the necessities of their work, but she found him an agreeable companion with ideas, in and out of the research, that often gelled with her own. At first they were Dr Goodrich and Dr Jameson, but he was as unstuffy as Em, and first names quickly became the norm. Sessions in the laboratory, on the computer, or in the hospital to which they were attached naturally led to feeling hungry at the same time, and to taking lunch together, usually coffee and a sandwich in the hospital staff diner. And just as naturally, to talking about matters outside genetics.

The conversations at first were on the conventional lines: did she live in London, and was his home base in the Rockies? More questions from him revealed that she did indeed live in London but came from Shropshire, where her father's family were farmers.

"Oh, so are mine – ranchers, at least. You couldn't call them farmers. The nearest they've ever come to growing what you might call a crop is improving the hay meadows."

She soon noticed that there was no mention of wife or children in his conversation. They were about the same age, Em thought, and at first she wondered whether he was leading up to making a pass at her. He was medium height, strongly built but not overweight, with thinning brown hair, grey eyes and a clean-shaven face she would have described as "ordinary." Ordinary, but nice. The idea of being the target of a pass from him was good for her ego, despite her avowal of ultra-low-key sexual orientation. But she soon decided he was doing nothing of the sort. He almost studiously avoided physical contact, and her next thought was to wonder whether he might be gay. There was no mention of "partner," either, however, through four or five lunch breaks at which their conversations probed beyond the original near-banalities.

"Whereabouts in Wyoming, Randall?" was an inevitable question.

"It's under the Big Horns, on the Western side – pretty remote," he said. "The nearest town is Shell, about ten miles away, and you'd hardly call that a town. I don't think there's a couple of hundred people there. Sheridan's about 50 miles, over the mountains. That's officially a city, about 17,000 people."

"You didn't want to stay there, though?"

"There was no work for a science graduate. I enjoyed working on the ranch, but they couldn't possibly afford to keep me on. And then ….." He hesitated, but continued: "Dad works it on his own, with help from Mom. She's as good as any cowboy. They breed horses for the dude ranches, and run a few cattle. They just about make a decent living."

"We always think of ranchers in America as rich people. Cattle barons and all that."

"Well, they're not. Oh, don't get it wrong. They're not on their uppers or anything. They own the land, but their income is certainly not as much as – mine, say."

"But they stay there. It sounds a bit like my family. Roots and so on."

"Dad's the fourth generation. His great-grandfather worked as a cowboy on the same land when it was part of a huge ranch, and bought it when his boss died."

Em wondered what the "and then" meant, but that particular lunch was over, and next time it was Randall asking the questions.

"Do you like living in London?"

"It's alright. I've never lived anywhere else since I left school. I always think of Lyndford as home, though."

"Lyndford?"

"It's a little village where my brother's farm is. In the South Shropshire hills, not far from the Welsh border."

"Tell me a bit more about it."

"Well, it's got a church, and oh, I should think about 30 houses, and a manor house, that belongs to our family but it's rented out to a university for their field centre. It used to be the centre of a big estate, about 20 farms I think, that had been in the family for 300 years. But most of it had gone, through taxation – death duties – by the start of the war. My father's uncle was the last Jameson to live at the manor, and he moved out to Home Farm when he got married, late in life. Estates usually had a farm they called Home Farm and that's where my brother Charles is now. Our father retired ten years ago and lives in a house near to."

She almost carried on to tell him more, about her father and Angela, her ex-professor, but thought she would only bore him. He wanted to know, though.

"Have you only the one brother?"

"No, there's Edward. He's an engineer – something quite grand in advanced technology. He's the technical director of a firm that his wife's the boss of. Managing director – I expect you'd call her the president, here."

"So his wife's his boss?"

"Technically, I suppose. But really they're partners. He's the technical brain, she has the business head. She's a girl and a half. American dream stuff. She dragged herself up from being orphaned at 15, on a council estate near Manchester. We all thought she was hard as nails, but she's not, really. She's very nice. They've two children."

Em was only in America for three weeks, this trip, and the second week was coming to an end. But she was enjoying his company, and when he asked, on Saturday after they had again done a morning's work, whether she might fancy a trip into New Hampshire, where she had never been, she was ready to accept.

He said: "I know a good little hotel in a town called Bristol, where I've stayed a couple of times. Can I call them and ask if they've got rooms, for tonight? Then we could go a bit further north, tomorrow, and into Vermont."

She knew she'd heard correctly, but to make sure, and emphasise the basis for the trip, she asked: "You did say rooms, Randall, didn't you?"

The look on his face made her cringe, inwardly.

"Of course," he said. "You didn't think, did you .... ?"

"I'm sorry, Randall. I'm terribly sorry. Thank you very much. I'd love to come."

*****

She enjoyed the weekend greatly, despite rain on Sunday morning. They were a little too early in the year to catch the full golden glory of the New

England fall, but still it was mind-numbingly beautiful, she thought. The hotel was small by American standards, but they were made very welcome and served with a delightful dinner. Afterwards they strolled by the lake.

"Won't you tell me a bit more about yourself, Emily?" he asked.

"Either Emily Jane or Em, please," she smiled.

"Which, then?"

"Emily Jane, I think. That's what Lisbeth calls me. My brothers call me Em sometimes."

She felt an awkwardness emanating, no doubt at the mention of Lisbeth. Did he think they were lesbians?

"Please don't get the wrong idea, Randall," she said. "Lisbeth and I aren't lovers. Just very good friends. She's a bit like a mother to me, although no-one can replace my real mother. I did have a lover, and she helped me look after him when he became ill. He had muscular dystrophy."

"Oh, I'm terribly sorry."

"It's alright. It's years ago."

"Would you like to tell me a bit more? If you want to."

"His name was Barry. I met him when I was at medical school and he was at university, and eventually we lived together. He became ill soon after I'd got to know Lisbeth. She was wonderful. Used to pick him up from work, and cook a meal for him if I hadn't got back. Eventually though he had to go into a home, and he stayed there until he died, five years ago now. I was so glad when he went. He was almost completely immobile. He wanted to die."

"Was that anything to do with your wanting to do this kind of research?"

"No, not with going into it. One of the reasons for that was a girl friend I had, at school. She had cystic fibrosis. She always said she'd die before she was 30, and she did."

She wanted to ask about his own life, but first she felt a need to say more about herself, or rather about Angela, and her father.

"I was inspired as well by someone else, my tutor at St Thomas's. She was a wonderful teacher and a beautiful person. And do you know, she's my stepmother now. She married my father."

"It sounds a wonderful story."

"Yes, it was – is." And she told him, all forty-plus years of it. It was going dark by the time she finished.

They returned to the hotel, had a nightcap, and went to bed. She thought of calling Lisbeth, but realised that the time difference ruled it out.

Next morning, despite the rain, they set off northwards, turned west, then south and stopped for lunch in a small town off the beaten track called Chelsea, deliberately chosen by her for obvious reasons. The rain which had started about eleven was still falling. As they drank their coffee after lunch the owner of the little diner asked where they were heading and said: "Oh, you got plenty of time. Stop as long as you like, folks. It's no day for starting out before you gotta."

They sat down on two easy chairs and Em said: "Randall, you started to say something the other day when you were telling me about your father's ranch, and why you couldn't stay there. You said it was after – something – but you didn't say after what. Did something awful happen?"

He seemed to hesitate, and she said: "Please don't tell me if you'd rather not. I shouldn't be so nosy."

"Yes, something awful did happen," he said. "I got married."

He seemed to be gathering himself together to continue, and she said: "Please, Randall, don't. I can see it distresses you."

"No, it's alright. I'd like to tell you. There's not so much of it, and it was a long time ago."

He folded his hand round his coffee mug and started to speak, in his usual manner, slowly and quietly, not looking at her.

"When I was at college I met this girl, Eugenie, and I fell for her like a ton of bricks. I was totally besotted. We got married as soon as I'd finished and I took her off to Wyoming to see Mom and Dad. I'd not told her much about home. All I wanted to do was make love to her, and she never asked much. I was sure they'd love her and she'd love the ranch. But it was awful. I didn't know then whether it was the place, or being so far from what she called civilisation, or my folks, or what. She seemed to change completely. I've thought since that she'd conned herself into thinking she was marrying into some rich ranching family and couldn't take it when she found they were quite ordinary. I still can't understand it. It started when we came to where we had the first sight of the house. She seemed to take a dislike to it even from half a mile away. I know the house is nothing marvellous. When my great-great-grandpa bought the land in 1890 there was no building on it, and I've been told the house he built and he and his wife and kids lived in for years was not much more than a shack. But they built another, and added to it until my grandpa built the present one. There was good money in cattle in those days. My folks didn't do any more building but they made improvements inside, like bathrooms and kitchen things. They preferred, quite rightly I think, to spend any money they could find on some extra stabling because the money had gone out of ranch beef and he was switching to breeding horses. But I think Eugenie expected it to be one of those mansions like you see in Gone with the Wind. I thought she'd be bowled over by the mountains, and the forest, but obviously they meant nothing to her. The house might as well have been in the middle of a desert. She made her feelings known to me that very night. Said I'd deceived her and brought her to 'this God-forsaken hole in the middle of nowhere' and my Mom heard her. I caught her crying, and told Eugenie, but it made no difference. She was plain rude to both of them, as well as to me. I realised what a fool I'd been. I'd just fallen for a pretty face. I saw there was nothing more, and I fell out of love with her as quickly as I'd fallen in, and a lot harder. Gosh, I must have been an idiot."

He paused, glanced at her shamefacedly. She said: "You were very young, weren't you? These things happen. But what did did you do? You didn't quarrel with your parents, did you?"

"No, I didn't. But right then I couldn't say what I should have. I just said we'd got to get back to Chicago where I had a job waiting, and we left straight away, didn't even stay another night. When we started to look for somewhere to live she scoffed at everything we could afford and went back east to her mother. I found a little apartment and got on with my job. It was only a month later I had a letter from a lawyer saying she was divorcing me on the grounds of failing to provide a home for her. I just didn't argue. There was no property or any other complication and I was glad to be rid of her. I agreed to pay the legal costs but no more, and she didn't press it. I guess she'd found some other guy she thought was a ticket to riches, by then.

"I haven't seen her or heard of her since, in twenty years. And you're the first person I've told all this to, except Mom and Dad."

Emily Jane had been looking at him all the time he was speaking. "I'm terribly sorry, Randall," she said. "I'm terribly sorry. But have you never met anyone else you wanted to marry?"

He did not answer, but rose, took her waterproof jacket from a peg on the wall, and |ushered her out to the car.

Through the following week, the daily pattern continued. At work, they talked research; over lunch, a variety of topics, none of them personal. She thought their conversation was not quite so easy, there was an element of constraint. She was due to fly back to Britain on Sunday, early, and would not be going in to work on Saturday. On Friday evening, as he left the office where she still had a task to complete, he said: "Could we go for lunch or something tomorrow?" It was a slightly odd way of asking, she thought, almost peremptory. But she said: "Yes, sure – when and where?"

He picked her up from her hotel, in a cab, and they went to the smartest restaurant in town.

"Pushing the boat out, aren't we, Randall?" she protested mildly.

"I want to talk to you. And I don't know when I'll see you again."

She thought the constraint of the last week was more marked, but they had a pleasant if expensive lunch, for which Randall insisted on paying, and took their coffee in the otherwise empty lounge, sitting on two leather easy chairs, at right angles to each other.

He said, without preamble, taking her hand, or any other opening gambit: "You asked me the other day whether I'd met anyone else I wanted to marry. I hadn't, until now. Would you consider marrying me?"

The abruptness was quite unlike the gentle western politeness she was used to from him, and took her aback. She looked straight at him, and said: "Randall, are you serious? We haven't known each other a month."

He looked her up and down, then away.

"I feel as though I've known you for years – decades. I've never met anyone I enjoy being with like I enjoy being with you. I remember what I felt like with Eugenie, more than twenty years ago. I was on and off cloud nine . It isn't like that with you. Being with you just feels good, and right. I'm not much of a sex merchant, but I've been to bed with one or two women, Emily Jane. But I'd marry you if you said you didn't want that, because I know it'd make me happy just to have you in my life. Across the table, other side the fireplace. I just want you around."

She wanted to say yes, she would marry him. The comradely companionship they clearly enjoyed; his readiness to unburden himself to her; her own readiness, no, more, desire, to tell him about her self; if these were not love, they were the nearest thing to it she had known; it was how it was with Lisbeth, only more so. The thought of going to bed with him was pleasurable. But she knew what her answer must be.

She said: "Randall, my dear. I would like to say I'll marry you. I think we'd be happy. In fact I'm sure we would. A short time or not, I've found I like you very much. But I cannot marry you. I can't possibly leave Lisbeth. She relies on me as much as I do on her. I'd be deserting her. She's lost too much from her life already. I mustn't do it."

Randall took her hand to his lips. He said: "I thought you'd say that. I knew you'd be loyal. Will you say you'll see me as often as you can, though?"

"Yes, dear Randall. Of course." She leaned over and kissed him, gently, on the lips. She debated whether she should ask him to come to her hotel, that night, but decided against it. It would spoil it. Sometime, though.

*****

She flew home next day, called Lisbeth from Heath Row, told her she would be home in time for their meal. She thought the older woman seemed a little out of her usual calm sorts.

Lisbeth said nothing of import when she arrived, simply greeted her lovingly as always, hoped she'd had a good trip and a good two weeks at work. But Em knew something was the matter, and said so, after they had eaten.

"What's the matter, Lisbeth? There is something, I can tell. Are you not well?"

"I'm fine," she said "but there is something. Something's happened." She put the dishes she was carrying on the kitchen top, and looked at Em.

"Tom's come back. She's left him. He wants me to marry him again."

"Oh, Lisbeth .... Are you going to?

"I've told him I won't."

"Why? Don't you think it would work? I thought you'd never stopped .... caring for him."

"No, but it doesn't matter. I'm not going to."

Em sat down on a kitchen chair. She knew why. It was for the same reason she had said no to Randall. But now it wasn't a reason, was it? Lisbeth had never stopped loving her husband. They had parted only because he was desperate for the children she could not have, and he had gone to Australia to rediscover someone who could.

"Are there any children?" Em asked.

"Yes, one. But she's staying with her mother. They've gone to Western Australia."

"Do you think Tom still cares for you?"

"He says so. And I think he does. I believe he does."

"Then you should marry him. Really. And I'll tell you why."

*****

So, Lisbeth married her Tom; and Emily Jane decided she would marry Randall, if he still wanted her. First though there was an assurance she needed.

She had told him about her West Indian mother, how she had been brought to Britain, in the course of relating her family history as far as she knew it. Randall had not even referred to it at the time, and it was shortly afterwards that he asked her to marry him. It was obvious it was not an issue as far as he was concerned, right then, and she did not for one instant think it would become one. But what about his parents? From all he had told her about them, she knew they were from long-established, pioneering western stock. Was that the kind of family background that countenanced mixed marriages, she wondered. It was unlikely, at her age, that she would have children. If she did however, they could well be quite dark-skinned, like her brother Charles. She wanted to dash off a letter, or call – she hated the thought of an e-mail – to tell him about Lisbeth and how it changed her situation. She trembled with pleasure at the thought of telling him she would marry him. She knew there would be no problem about finding work in the U.S. But then the potential problem hit her.

"My dear Randall," she started to write, and stopped. That looked as though she was going to say something he would not like to hear. Perhaps she was, though. She let it be, and continued: "I have something important to tell you. Lisbeth's former husband, Tom has returned from Australia. His wife has left him and he wants them to be married again. She said she wouldn't but I told her she must, and she's going to. I thought 'how marvellous, now I'm free, I can marry Randall if he still wants me.'

"But then something else hit me. Do your parents know about me? I know we're both middle-aged, or nearly, and rather beyond having to ask their permission. But from what you've told me about your people I think they care a great deal about you. What I'm trying to say is, do they know that my mother was Jamaican and would it matter to them? I would hate to hurt them.

"I soon came to realise that I love you, and I know we would be happy together. But I believe I would have to think hard about marrying you if I thought that either your folks or mine would not be happy for us. I am quite sure of my family. If they met you they would welcome you with the widest of open arms. Are you able to assure me that it would be alright with yours? If you are, my dearest man, and if you still want me to, I will marry you, and in the meantime long for the day."

His reply came within a week.

"My darling Emily Jane, You have made me the happiest man in the world. I tried to call you as soon as I got your letter but your lines were busy so I sat right down to write this. When you told me you could not marry me, and why, I knew even more than before that I had found a woman in a million, one who put loyalty and honor before her own desires, because I could see that without your care for your friend Lisbeth you would have said yes.

"My dear, I am as sure as I can be without your name ever having been mentioned to my folks that they would love you from the moment they set eyes on you. I have never discussed color or its associations in any depth with them, but I have never detected any racial bias in them. It won't be an issue.

"I would like us to be married immediately, if not before (!) But as we will have the rest of our lives together, I don't think a month or two delay will matter so much. So I'd like to make these suggestions, so that little question mark in your mind can be quite rubbed out. I would like to take you to Wyoming to meet Mom and Dad; and I would like to come to your Lyndford and get to know your family. Perhaps we could be married there.

"Please either write or call, e-mail if you have to, to let me know what you think. And by the way, if you decided you would like a job here, I can assure you our unit would snap you up."

Not a blade of grass was allowed to grow under their feet. Emily Jane, wondering at herself after her declaration of ultra-low sexuality, found excitement growing. She could see that her declared intention of returning to Lyndford "someday" was going to go by the board. Her Lyndford someday was going to be Big Horn County, Wyoming. She called Randall as soon as she got home, knowing he would still be at work.

"It's me, Emily Jane. No, Em. Oh, anything. I got your letter."

"It didn't make you change your mind?"

"Oh, Randall, of course not. But I'm sorry...."

"What for, my dear?"

"Saying things that might make you think I had doubts. I haven't, you know. I've never had less doubts about anything."

"My darling, it only showed me, again, what you're like. You hate to hurt people. But what do you think about my ideas?"

"I think they're wonderful. But I'll be worried until your mother and father have seen me."

"So we'd better make it quick. But I can promise you, faithfully, that your worries are completely without foundation."

"I love you, Randall."

"Sure?"

"I love you. As sure as – as there's a wy in Wyoming."

After one or two further exchanges of a similar nature, which would have left people who knew them pondering an apparent personality change in two such level-headed, middle-aged individuals, they got down to discussing arrangements, first of all for telling the families. Then Randall was to consult his hospital and research set-up about taking on Emily Jane. It all came together smoothly. Because she had been working with the American unit, she could join it almost immediately, she found. Arrears of leave added up to being able to take several weeks holiday.

Almost inevitably, it was Edward, still in Germany, that she told first. Then Angela and her father. They were all delighted. Even the prospect of losing her to America did not worry them greatly, for it was more than twenty years since she had lived in Shropshire. Her happiness was what really mattered. "I think it's wonderful," Ed told Stella. "And Lisbeth and her husband. Great."

Two months after she had met him, Randall carried her off to Wyoming to meet his parents, who had spent years intermittently worrying about their son after the tragedy – it could not be called anything else, in their eyes – of his first brief marriage. They had spotted more of the girl Eugenie's nature than Randall had realised, and were secretly glad when she took her fortune-hunt for a husband elsewhere. Their old-fashioned Western natures had been concerned for him as the years went by and he remained alone, and they were pleased when he called to say he planned to be married, to a lady he worked with, slightly apprehensive when he told them she was English, but somewhat reassured when they learned that she came from a farming family. It would have been difficult for anyone to work out who was more pleased with whom, when he took her over the Big Horn mountains and she first saw the house and its barns and stables against the beauty of the western forests, slopes and pastures. Randall stopped the car as they approached the ranch.

"This was where .... she .... saw it first," he said. "What do you think?"

"Oh, Randall! It's beautiful. Like a big version of Lyndford. It's wonderful. She must have been crazy."

"She had a different agenda. But it was a long time ago. It doesn't matter, now, to me. I hope it doesn't to you."

"You know it doesn't. But I can't understand anyone like that."

His parents greeted her warmly. Ann Goodrich, a wiry five-foot four, still good-looking in spite of weathered features showing the evidence of an outdoor life, had never met more than a handful of British people in her 62 years, and was obviously anxious, Randall could see, to make it clear that her nationality would be no bar to accepting and welcoming her into the family. Randall soon spotted also, however, that his mother detected something other than "English" in Em's features, and Ann's early questions the first time they were alone together led to an opportunity to talk about it. It was on the afternoon of their arrival and Emily Jane was being shown round the ranch buildings, and some of the horses, by Randall senior, and a down-to-earth but slightly embarrassed Mrs Goodrich needed to sort out the accommodation arrangements, to avoid the chance of worse embarassment.

"I didn't like to ask you on the phone," she said "but – do you need one room, or two?"

Randall, also somewhat confused, said: "This is 1997, Mom. We sleep together, if that's okay by you."

But he took advantage of the situation to broach the subject worrying Em.

"Mom, while I've got you alone, I'm going to mention something that Em's a bit concerned about. I've told her she needn't be, and I know she accepts that, but it'd be good if you could somehow get it over to her yourself."

"I know what it is. She's – part coloured, isn't she?"

"Her mother was Jamaican. There's a helluva story behind it and I'll tell you sometime, or Em will."

"Yes, please, son. But of course it makes no difference. If she's as nice a girl as I've already come to think, it makes no difference at all. In fact …."

She did not go further, because Emily Jane and Randall Snr appeared. But Ann knew what she was going to do to make sure this English woman knew how welcome she was in Wyoming, and to her and her husband.

*****

They did not have many days, on that occasion, to spend there. But, although she had never been on a horse before, except for a childhood essay or two on the small, fat pony at Forest Farm, Emily Jane rode out with Ann on a tour of inspection.

"We won't go far, since it's your first time on a horse. We could go in the jeep, but I hate the cussed thing. It's not right, somehow. This country's for horses, not autos," said Mrs Goodrich as she helped Emily Jane onto the gentle old pony kept for the occasional eastern guest."Not far" meant "only" nine or ten miles, most of them at an ambling walk. Em was stiff, and a little sore for days afterwards but it did nothing to stop her falling further in love with the mountains, and forests, the ranch, and Wyoming.

When they had ridden for an hour or so, and Ann had shown her a bunch of brood mares with their foals, and thirty cattle almost ready for market, they stopped for a drink of the coffee brought with them in a thermos. The horses were hitched and they sat on a fallen tree trunk.

"Randall's told me there's what he calls a helluva story about your mother," Ann said.

"Yes, it was awful. It started awfully and it ended awfully, although in between it was good, and happy." She paused.

"I'd surely like to know," Ann said. And Em told her, trying but not completely succeeding in keeping her professional cool through the worst parts of Debra's ordeal, but delighting in telling of her mother in the lambing shed and becoming what her father called "the best shepherd in Shropshire and the Welsh Marches." The telling took most of an hour, and long before the end, Ann's work-stained hand was cradling hers.

She said: "Randall told me you were worried that we wouldn't accept you because your mother was .... coloured."

Em smiled. "I needn't have been, need I?"

"My dear, I hate racism, and so does Randall. It sometimes does us no good with one or two of our neighbours. Western country folk are good folk. They're generous, and ready to help one another, and open-hearted. But they've got one or two faults, and not liking black folk and Indians is one of them – among some." They remounted, and rode on.

In a few minutes Em saw a small house, with a smoking chimney, inside a fenced garden of half an acre or so, on the edge of a piece of forest, and a track leading away to the west and the north-south ridge Ann had just pointed out as the boundary of their property.

"Who lives there?" she asked.

Ann said nothing but rode towards the house, stopped at the fence, dismounted and tethered her horse, and signalled to Em to do the same. A woman came to meet them as they opened the gate and walked towards the house.

"Hello, Delilah," Ann greeted her. "On your own?"

"Yes, Mis' Goodrich. Pete's workin' in Shell, helpin' build that new hotel. He took Rosebud to school an' he'll bring her back."

"I've told you Lord know how many times my name's Ann. 'Lilah, this is Emily Jane, from England. Emily Jane Jameson. She's going to marry Randall."

The young woman held out her hand. "Welcome to Wyomin', Mis' Jameson. Good to see you. Have a cup of coffee?"

Ann said: "Thank you very much, 'Lilah, but we gotta get back. And we just had a coffee – brought a flask. Horses alright?"

"Yes, they're with that bunch in the north pasture. Have to come in soon, though, Pete says."

A few moments later, they said goodbye and started back towards the ranch, still at an ambling walk. Ann said: "I expect you're wondering who that is, Emily Jane."

"I was a bit surprised to see a house out here."

"They're Arapaho. Their name's Runniman – comes from Pete's grandfather's Indian name, Running Man. Randall met Pete when he took some colts down to the reservation at Wind River to sell to the big Arapaho ranch there. They raise organic beef. The little girl's only five, and she's got cancer - Leukaemia. There's a lot of it down there, comes from an old Uranium waste dump, they think, and from contaminated water because of gas and oil working. You wouldn't think that sort of thing could happen in country like this, would you? But that's America for you, Emily Jane.

"Randall and I have a lot of feeling for the Indians. They've had a raw deal, and a lot of them are still having it. Anyway, Pete helped him with a few things down there and Randall got to like him and realised he was an all round good guy. End result was he told them they could come up here, with their horses which was how they made a living. They owned a house on the reservation and if they sold that and built something here they could run their horses with ours and help with the ranch work, for pay. And that's what happened. They've been here two years now. Pete has found quite a lot of work and with what he does for us they get by a lot better than down at Riverton."

"What about the little girl – Rosebud did I hear her mother call her?"

"She goes to Sheridan for chemotherapy and it seems to be working. And they're going to have another."

"Wasn't there a problem about building a house out here. I mean, aren't there planning laws or something?"

"We've said nothing about it. Pete and Delilah built the house themselves and lived in a tent while they did it. They dug the sewage pit by hand. They burn wood out of the forest, and plant two trees for every one they cut down. That was Pete's own idea. If anyone kicks up a fuss about it we'll convert one of our barns for them to live. But the fuss if it ever happens will be because they're Indians, not because of the house. We're very happy to have them here. Pete's a top class guy. He's a good cowboy and stockman, and a handiman, and we're not getting any younger."

She reined in her horse, and Em did the same.

"I reckon we owe the Indians, anyway. We stole their land, and crippled their way of life, didn't we? At least, our folks did, not all that long ago. The guy my Randall's great-grandpa bought this land from was one of 'em, I guess. One of the pioneers that most here think of as the salt of the earth – and they were, in many ways. But they were still stealing the native Americans' birthright, weren't they? Expecting them to just move over and make way for white folk. Manifest destiny – our right to inhabit the earth just because there were more of us and we thought our ways and beliefs were the only right ways and beliefs. P'raps it was inevitable. P'raps they had to turn into farmers and tradesfolk rather than hunters – some of them were, anyway. But that didn't make it right, not the way it was done, anyway. Not many see it like we do, though. Most see the Indians as a lot of drunken bums. Some are – but I'd like to ask who turned them into drunken bums? Before we came, they were fine independent people who lived in harmony with the land. You'd never have found them polluting the creeks and rivers with oil and chemicals."

Ann's tone had become acerbic, almost bitter, and as she finished speaking she looked at Emily Jane with a glance of apology. She said: "Sorry, Emily Jane. Riding my old hobby horse again, I'm afraid. But I do get a bit worked up about it."

Emily Jane, sensing echoes of her own ancestry in Lyndford squirarchy and West Indian slavery, replied: "I couldn't think of judging people here, or the Indians, or you, Ann. But I can't help thinking you've got it about right." She knew that if ever she came to live at Little Fork Ranch, it would almost be like going home to Lyndford. And although Ann never mentioned it, she guessed that her mother-in-law-to-be had deliberately introduced her to the Arapaho couple as part of an emphasis on how unimportant to her was Em's own proportion of non-white in her make-up. Perhaps not so unimportant. Perhaps she was pleased to have the chance to make another statement of her beliefs.

The next move was to introduce Randall to the Jamesons and associated families. They flew directly from Sheridan, via the USA's east coast, and he was received as enthusiastically as she had been in Wyoming. Before the year's end they were married, at Lyndford Church with all the trimmings, and Randall Snr and Ann in attendance, the ranch left in the charge of Pete and Delilah.

Twenty-Four

"Burn in the hottest corner of Hell"

The rest of the year went by without Angela or Jeannie learning anything more about how Josie met her death. Angela thought at one time that she ought to go to Bosnia herself, to try to find out, but was dissuaded by Jim Meredith. She would only be frustrated by running up against brick walls, he said, and promised he would tell her immediately he got to know anything. As the situation in Sarajevo improved after the end of hostilities, she also made contact with Ljiljana Alagic, and established a warm if long-distant relationship with her.

But in the spring, light was at last shed. It came, indirectly, from a most unexpected source – Josie herself.

Angela took a call from Jim Meredith. "Something's happened I think you'll want to know about, Mrs Jameson," he said. "Two of Josie's notebooks have come into our hands. They cover part of the time from when she left Sarajevo until she .... died."

After a few moments, she was able to ask: "Are they important – significant?"

"Both," he said. "They're going to help send some people to prison for a long time, I should think."

"What's happened, Mr Meredith?"

"A man who was a colonel in the Bosnian Serb army when they were carrying out the Srebrenica massacres has been arrested by the SAS and indicted by the international tribunal. They found the notebooks among his belongings. Our man on the ground learned about them and offered to help interpret them – they were almost all shorthand, of course. He found he couldn't, because his shorthand was what they call tee-line and Josie's was Pitmans. But I told him to let me have them and I would transcribe them, or try to. Technically they're our property anyway, because she was our employee. But of course the lawyers are very interested in them. They haven't put a subpoena or whatever they call the order on them but they know we've got them and I'm sure they will. They'll want to use them in evidence when this man Pavelic and perhaps some others come to trial."

"Will you be able to let me know what's in them?" Angela asked.

"Legally, I don't know. Possibly not, until after the trials, and that could be many months, probably years. But if you'll give an assurance that you'll not let it go anywhere else, and you won't tell anyone else what's in it, I'll give you a copy when I've completed it. That's if you want it, Mrs Jameson. There's some pretty awful stuff in it. I should think she'd been intending it as the basis for a major article, or perhaps even a book."

"I've got to know," she said. "And I couldn't possibly keep it from my other daughter, or my husband. But I could certainly promise that none of it will go any further, or that the document wouldn't go out of my hands."

"That's good enough for me. We don't of course want to do anything that will prevent these people being brought to justice, and legally we'd be in trouble if it was thought we had, but I can't see how letting you have a sight of your daughter's notes can do that."

A month later, Jim Meredith came to Lyndford, bringing his transcript of Josie's notes.

"I didn't think I could risk any other method of getting it to you," he told Angela. "And I must admit I wanted to see you all – her family. We all thought of Josie as a remarkable young woman."

He also offered to tell her more of what he had been able to find out about when and how Josie came to be found.

"It won't make very pleasant hearing," he said "but I'll tell you if you wish."

"Yes, please. I want to know as much as I can."

He said: "The UN people were excavating a mass grave, where they found several dozen bodies. They found that the grave had previously been disturbed by the Bosnian Serb forces, and many bodies removed, apparently by bulldozers or mechanical diggers, presumably in an attempt to hide evidence of the massacres. But there were three separate mounds nearby which they also decided to investigate. They turned out to be individual graves, with one woman in each, in a makeshift coffin. The bodies in the mass grave were not in coffins, of course.

"Our reporter there knew Josie was missing. He told me about the graves and said the three were not Muslim women, as far as he and the UN people could tell. He also thought they were probably identifiable. I knew Ljiljana Alegic quite well and she agreed to go to Srebrenica. She was quite positive – it was definitely Josie. And other items about her confirmed it"

"Where was ….. the baby?"

"It was inside the coffin, with her."

"Why do you think these three were buried separately? Was it because they were women?"

"No, I don't think so. There were women in the mass grave. They can't be certain, but they think it was probably because they weren't Muslims, although how they came to that conclusion, in Josie's case, it's difficult to say. They didn't treat her any differently from the Muslim women when they were in the prison sheds."

"You haven't learned anything about about how she ....died?"

He hesitated, looked away, then back again.

"She'd been shot. The baby's brains had been beaten in. It was almost certainly alive when they took it from her, they said. It was a boy."

*****

The transciption was still in diary or note form, and there was the odd space where Meredith had not been able to accurately decipher Josie's shorthand. But Angela was easily able to follow it, and Jim stayed long enough to help her if necessary, and meet other members of the family.

The first entry was dated mid-February 1995, and revealed how she planned to make her escape from Sarajevo, with a family of three, Tijo and Fahriza Milovic and their sixteen year old son Alija.

"Have persuaded Tijo to let me go with him, Fahriza and Alija. Must go. Not doing anything worthwhile here. Utter misery here but cannot go on reporting same thing day after day."

Meredith explained, to Angela and Alastair, some of what she meant by "doing nothing worthwhile" and more of the background to that brief note. He said that since her story about the fate of the Terzics, especially her own experience of it, which had been given much prominence, she had found nothing to hit the headlines, make people in the wider world sit up. The siege itself, the suffering, deaths, hunger and all kinds of privations were no longer newsworthy. The news was mostly about the feeble attempts of the west to get the warring parties to see sense, as most politicians in Washington, London, Paris and every other capital still saw it.

"We felt that her presence in Sarajevo was still important, from a news point of view, but she was such a go-getter that she couldn't stand not being able to get up and go with some important hard news," he said. "She'd established such good contacts that she knew almost everything that was going on in the city, and in the end that was going to be important to us and the world. But even if we had known what she planned, we wouldn't have forbidden her to do it, although we advised against it, strongly. But I'd grown to have such respect for her abilities and instincts that I couldn't come the heavy-handed boss with her."

He paused, looked away. When he turned to them again, Angela thought she could almost see damp spots below his eyes.

He said: "God, I wish I had. I wish I'd clamped down. I should have."

After a few minutes, he continued his explanation of the background. One of the important things of which she had intimate knowledge was the building and development, in 1993, of the tunnel linking the Dobrinja area with the so-called neutral zone of the city's almost defunct airfield, which enabled some arms, ammunition and food to be brought in. In fact, he said, the tunnel probably saved her life on the fifth of February the following year when the market square mortar bomb killed sixty-nine people and wounded more than 200. It was a Saturday and thought to be a quiet day, so that people went out to try to buy food and supplies, and Josie might well have been one of them but for being shown, at the time, the latest work in the tunnel.

Later that year she started to develop an idea that followed from reports she had done on survivors of parties who had managed to escape from the city but been caught by the besieging Serb forces. Heart rending as they usually were, such stories were no longer top news, unless there was some kind of special feature attached to them, like her own experience.

"She filed some of these stories, and we put them out." Meredith added "But they never made any great impact - there were too many of them around."

He also told what he had been able to gather, through a visit to Sarajevo after the hostilities there ended, and conversations with a number of people, notably Ljiljana Aligic, about how she had come to join the Milovic trio. Tijo and his brother Bakir had already been included in a larger party attempting escape, and although it had failed and a number of their companions had been captured, and no doubt killed, they thought it had shown them a way of avoiding the Serb army. They formed a plan for trying again, in two smaller parties, each led by one of the brothers.

"Lili said their idea was that a small group of fit and agile people stood a much better chance of getting through," he said. "Many of the previous attempts were by large parties which often included old people and children."

Josie had got to know the family quite well, and eventually persuaded Tijo to let her go with them. He accepted her assurance that she could run, and climb, and carry as much as anyone else. And four was a pretty good number, he concluded, as long as all four were strong and active. He knew they would take at least three days to get through the Serb lines, by the route he and Bakir thought they had worked out, then several more to make the relative safety of Bosniak-held territory, or a UN so-called safe area.

Josie's first note added "Have been warned will be tough. Tijo says will take three days to get through Serb lines. If we are caught they will kill him and Alija. They might not kill me and Fahriza but it might be better if they did, for us. He does not think my press pass will help. We are all wearing warm, dark-coloured clothes, with no changes. Shall take two pairs of knickers and socks."

Two weeks later: "Have persuaded people manning tunnel to let us through. They ration numbers using it because its main purpose is to bring supplies in, not people out. And we must pay, they say. Terrible to think some of these people are profiteering. Ready to go now."

The next note, dated March 10, told how before daylight the three emerged from the tunnel, only half a kilometre from the nearest Serb positions. The first part of Tijo's plan was to stop in a tumbledown shepherd's hut he and Bakir had found when they were getting back to the city after the previous escape attempt. It was almost under the noses of the soldiers but was so decrepit, two of the woven walls almost gone and part of the roof sagging nearly to the floor, that he thought it could never be seen as a shelter for fugitives.

They reached it safely, before dawn, put their small rucksacks on the floor and sat on them, awaiting daylight. There was an unpleasant smell, but they had no torch – such luxuries, or batteries for them, were almost non-existent in Sarajevo – and although Tijo had matches he dare not strike one, meaning the source of the odour could not be investigated until daylight.

When it became light enough to see, they had an unpleasant shock. There were twin causes of the stench; one Josie had exacerbated by dumping her pack on the half-rotted carcase of a small goat; the other was the excremental evidence that the hut had been used, in the not-too-distant past, as a privy, no doubt by a soldier or soldiers.

Unpleasant as the smell was, they dared do nothing about getting rid of its sources. But Tijo was immediately worried that the same thing might happen again – one of the soldiers would decide to make use of it. They were only about 300 yards from the nearest Serbs, the crew of a gun emplacement.

"He said we must have a plan if one of them did come," she noted. "He must be killed. He would hit him on the head with his pistol then kill him with his knife, and Alija must help. I have never conspired to kill or even hurt anyone before but now I just accept it. So does Fahriza, who is a really kind and gentle girl. What is this war doing to us!"

No soldier came, but they spent an increasingly uncomfortable day in their miserable hiding place. They became very hungry, but stuck to their agreed determination not to raid their sparse food supply until just before they left, which must not be until it was properly dark. They became used to the smell, but as the day wore on they needed a toilet themselves. It was too close-quartered to simply ask people to turn their backs, and darkness when it came brought great relief.

The next stage in Tijo's plan was to get to the top of the forested escarpment via a route he and Bakir had spotted. A small stream ran down, deep in a steep gully which almost became a tunnel in places. Noise made by anyone trying to climb up it would be masked by the water. But the climb, almost all of it in the stream itself, was extremely difficult. There were two sheer waterfalls, one nearly eight feet high, with no possibility of going round it without getting out of the gully, which they dared not attempt because they knew there were soldiers near.

"Alija, tallest, stood with his back to the rock. The water was pouring on to him, wetting him through, but he stood there while Tijo helped Fahriza and me on to his shoulders. Then Alija took off his belt and hung it round his neck to make a step for Tijo. To get Alija up Fahriza lay down with her head at the top of the waterfall and caught hold of Alija's hands, Tijo and I pulled her by her feet and we hauled Alija up. All very cold and wet."

The near-impassable route had the virtue however of taking them past the main Serb positions, and thence they walked north eastwards, in daylight much of the time but sticking to the dense forest and with one person, usually Tijo, scouting ahead on the basis that one individual was least likely to be spotted.

By the time they were about 30 miles from Sarajevo they walked openly on tracks and roads, because they had seen others doing the same. The weather, although still cold, was dry. They came on a column of civilians who had joined forces to leave a village they felt was about to be "cleansed."

"They are in better shape than us. They lit cooking fires, and offered us food," Josie noted.

Three further days on, in a supposedly UN safe area, and by then rounding the besieged town of Srebrenica, they were confronted by a squadron of soldiers in four-wheel drive vehicles, an armoured troop carrier and a high-sided lorry.

An officer, who turned out to be Colonel Pavelic, spoke to the leaders of the column, among whom was now Tijo Milovic. He asked who they were and where they were going.

"Tijo told him and said I was a British reporter with an agency based in Belgrade. I showed him my agency card and press pass. Made me give them to him and he tore both of them into several pieces. Said, in English: 'That is what we think of your British press.' Made us all get into lorry.

"Tijo asked where we were being taken. He said:'You will see.' One man said he and his wife and children, two girls, were not going. Officer told two soldiers to hold man and he took out his pistol and shot him in the head, in front of wife and daughters. Soldiers threw body into bushes on roadside.Wife ran to him, but they caught her and threw her into the lorry, and the girls.

"Vehicles all drove off. Came to big village. There are some industrial and agricultural buildings. They separated us from the men and put us into a big barn where there were already about fifty other women. Tried to speak to the officer, think he is a colonel. Only laughed and made some kind of joke to the other soldiers. Did not see what they did with the men.

"The other women told us they had been there for two days. There was no food, only what they had brought with them, and the only water was in a cattle trough. They were keeping one corner of the barn as a toilet area. Said the previous evening soldiers had come in and taken some of them out and raped them. One said she had been raped four times."

The next note was dated two days later, March 15th. It said she and some of the other women had been taken out of the barn, two or three at a time, and raped by soldiers.

"Three men came for me and took me behind a wall. One of them spun a coin, twice. I think to decide who should have first turn. There was a wooden platform about the height of a table. I suppose it was some kind of a loading platform. There was a ramp at one end. They dumped me on it and took my jeans and knickers off. Knew was no use trying to fight them. Tied my arms out wide to the platform supports. Two took my legs and held them out wide while the other one raped me. He went all the way. They wiped me with my own knickers and one of the others did the same. And the same with the third. They were laughing and encouraging each other all the time. Afterwards they told me to put my clothes back on and took me back to the barn.

"Some of the women who had been raped were in a bad way. They were crying and writhing on the floor. Two daughters of one of them, about 14 years old, I think they were twins, had been taken out at the same time as their mother. One, Zineta, was raped twice, she told me. Then she was made to watch while it happened to her mother. She said the officer, the colonel, had stood watching it all.

"Another woman, Hatidza told me she was taken out but the soldiers had rejected her because she was too old. She was seventy, she said. But she had also been made to watch. She also told me she had seen men taken out of another building, two or three at once, and taken round the back. Then she heard shots and the soldiers came back, but not the prisoners. This happened twice while she was watching. One of the groups taken out included a young boy, no more than 12 years old, she thought. I never saw anyone shot but heard shooting."

Josie did not appear to have made any notes for the next three days. Then she wrote: "March 18: They seem to be going through us and taking fresh women for raping, in turn. Fahriza taken today. Obvious it is part of a deliberate policy of humiliating muslim women, not just a means of satisfying soldiers' sexual appetites. Fahriza said she saw some soldiers who were being laughed at by their comrades. She thinks it was because they did not want to take part.

"They are bringing us some food now. It is only bread, and water, and some potatoes which we are able to cook by making a fire with some of the wood we rip off the old stalls in the barn. They have also brought us some buckets to use as toilets. We found one or two old shovels and cleaned up the excrement that had had to lie on the floor before.

"It looks as though they are systematically killing the men and boys. We keep hearing shooting and some more women have seen men taken round the back of the other building. Fahriza seems to accept it philosophically. They knew it would happen if we were caught, she said. Perhaps they will shoot us. That would be best. We can have no life under these beasts.'"

On March 21 she recorded an incident that made the rapings seem mild by comparison.

"The day before yesterday one of the women, Elmina Pilav, who had not escaped being raped although she was heavily pregnant, went into labour, which went on through the night. Yesterday morning I asked the soldiers who brought our food, who seemed more reasonable sort of men, if they could take me to see their officer to ask for help for Elmina. They took me to the officer, who they said was Colonel Pavelic. He was in an office in another building and there was another officer with him, who I immediately recognised. It was General Malevic, a top commander in the Bosnian Serb army. Pavelic is a terrifying man who you feel is capable of everything bad but he is an angel compared with Malevic who seems to breathe evil and hatred. I do not think I have ever been frightened by the mere presence of any single person, but I was terrified of him. But I managed to hold myself together and ask Colonel Pavelic if a doctor could see Elmina, who had been in labour for twenty four hours.

"He said: 'Our doctors have more important work to do than bother with Turkish trash.' They took me back to the barn. Elmina's agony continued all day but everyone did their best to help and in the evening she gave birth to a baby boy. This morning two soldiers came in and snatched the child from her, and took it away, holding it upside down by its legs. She begged and pleaded with them but it made no difference. I asked where they were taking it and one laughed and drew his fingers across his own throat."

"March 22: Soldiers came in and told us all to get outside. They loaded us into two high-sided lorries, all except Elmina. I do not know what happened to her. We never saw any of our men but we saw a bulldozer digging a big hole near where we knew at least some had been shot.

"The lorry drove for about an hour and stopped outside what looked like a factory building.

We were disembarked and taken into it where we found probably two hundred women and children.

Two of the women told me they had been there for about three months, but others for a shorter time. They said they were given food and could use the toilet and washbasins in the building, but really the place was a brothel for the use of the soldiers. One told me: 'Most days, they come and take three or four of us out and make use of us. It is usually different ones they take. They do not seem to want just the young ones. One day they took two young girls, their mother and their grandmother at the same time. Two women asked to be let alone because they were pregnant, with big bellies. They took them just the same but they never came back,' she said. I asked how they came to be there. They said the soldiers had just marched into their village and rounded up almost everyone, and set fire to some of the houses. Most of the men and boys had been shot, in front of them.

"March 23: Fahriza and I taken out today, just we two. Had to endure two men each, but it was not so bad as first time. We were not tied down or held. Suppose they knew we had learned resistance useless."

On March 31 she recorded that three lorry loads of the women, including herself, were taken to a large village she recognised as Potocari, and put into a factory warehouse type building where there were already a large number of others. Food was brought but there were no washing or toilet facilities and they had to sleep on the bare concrete floor. The same pattern of rape and ill-treatment followed, but this time they also heard and occasionally saw men being shot in larger numbers than at their previous location.

On April 10 she wrote: "I asked a soldier who was in charge here. He said it was General Krstevic (think that is correct spelling). I asked if I could see him. He said he would ask Captain something or other (did not quite catch name). This captain came and asked why I wanted to see the general. I said I was a British reporter based in Belgrade and I wanted to know why I was being treated as I was. I told him how I had been assaulted. He said he would see. He came back and said the general would see me.

"General Krstevic did not seem as brutal as Malevic and Pavelic. He asked why if I was a British reporter I had been with the people from Sarajevo and if I had documents to prove my identity. I told him Colonel Pavelic had taken them from me and destroyed them, torn them up. He said he did not believe me – Colonel Pavelic would not do that. He ordered soldiers to take me back to what he called 'the detention centre.'"

Her notes, and the transcript, ended there.

*****

Meredith told Angela and Alastair: "I have no idea what happened to her after that. There was plenty of room left in one of the notebooks. I can only assume they were taken from her at that point, about the middle of April. She did not die then, because when she was found in the February following, the pathologists thought she had been dead for three or four months. That would fit in with the advanced state of pregnancy, which we must assume, I'm afraid, was the result of the assaults, the rapes."

He said he had no information on how the notebooks came to be among Colonel Pavelic's possessions. Perhaps it was part of a conspiracy of silence among the Bosnian Serb officers, although one had to wonder why they were not simply destroyed.

"There's a lot we don't know, and probably never will," he said. "It was a truly terrible business. You just cannot understand what must have been going through their minds.

"Nobody, not even the Muslims, the Bosniaks, who suffered most, can be said to be completely blameless. They committed more than one atrocity. The Croats boxed clever and came best off in the end, but there should be a lot of guilty consciences among them, I can tell you. The Serbs – well, I know a lot of very nice and good Serbs, like Lili Alagic, but there are others who should take note of what Larry Hollingworth said about them – he hoped they burned in the hottest corner of hell."

Alastair and Angela listened in silence. He was holding her hand. After a while, he asked: "Do you think anything sensible and workable is coming out of it, Jim? Have any lessons been learned?"

"Good heavens, no," he said. "It'll all happen again, when the international troops are pulled out. And do you know what I think was the worst part. It was the attitude of us in the West. We treated it as some kind of family squabble and all we had to do was pat them on the head and tell them to behave like good boys, and it would all work out. It took Srebrenica to stir us into any real action, and then we had to leave it to the Americans. And what was the solution they came up with anyway? In effect, it was to accept that might was right. The strongest got the spoils."

Twenty-Five

Darkness and light

Alastair and Michael were quite different personalities, but always got on well. As soon as Michael was able, after his stroke, he rejoined Alastair and Peter in their weekly game of golf – Peter was a low-handicap player but the other two always described themselves as "very ordinary", although they usually took part in the club competitions, normally using a ride-on buggy, for the five miles of hilly walking involved was too much for Michael. He and Alastair also walked regularly round the Home Farm land, and Kathleen and Angela or some of the children joined them from time to time. Occasionally they would go further afield for a picnic at one or other of the beauty spots abounding in the Marches.

He became well-liked in the village, both among the decreasing number of "natives" and the newcomers who bought up the cottages and smallholdings. "My grandfather must be turning in his grave," Alastair said as he and Michael watched another Wolverhampton or Lancashire couple supervising the unloading of a furniture van. But it was part of the penalty of living among all the Marches beauty, and farming nearly 1,000 acres with a workforce of half a dozen when Squire Jameson had employed nearly half a hundred. Most of the incomers were pleasant enough people, however, often happy to take part in whatever was going on.

As the century rolled to its end, the village was putting on its own millenium party, in the Manor gardens, Michael leading the way in the organisation. Kathleen and Angela had gone to Shrewsbury to collect party goodies and would not be back until mid-afternoon. Alastair was at the Manor, helping Charles and some neighbours get the place into final shape for the occasion, and Michael had stayed home to make last-minute phone calls.

They had arranged to pick up him up and go for a lunchtime sandwich and pint at the Hare and Hounds at Buryton. Charles stopped the Land Rover outside Old School House, expecting Michael to appear immediately. When he did not, after five minutes, Alastair said: "I'll see where he is." He went to the front door, found it locked, continued round the back but moments later emerged from the front, shouting to Charles: "Come in here, quickly. I think he's had an accident."

He had found him at the bottom of the stairs, apparently unconscious.

"Oh, Christ, he must have fallen," Charles said. "Can you find something to cover him with, Dad, and I'll ring for an ambulance."

The ambulance was there within quarter of an hour. The paramedic asked: "How long has he been like this? It looks like a stroke."

He was in hospital inside half an hour, but this time little could be done. Michael was more or less completely paralysed. They thought he had probably had the stroke as he climbed the stairs, hours before. Charles could not contact either Kathleen or Angela – both had mobile phones but they were switched off – and they did not learn what had happened until they arrived back at Lyndford and were told by Maria. Angela drove Kathleen and Edwina to the hospital.

The party, much subdued, went ahead, but without Kathleen and Edwina, watching over him at the hospital. They were told he could hear what was said to him although he could not himself speak.

Edwina kissed the distorted face and said, softly: "Grandad, I don't want you to die but I know you're going to. You once told me it was through Christopher and me that you can live forever. I'll try and do good things for you, Grandad, and I'll try and make Chris do them, as well. I do love you."

Kathleen's tears could not be held back. But she thought her husband's eyes flickered, and his lips moved, as though he was trying to say something.

They were both with him two days later when he died, very peacefully, and glad to go, she thought. He was cremated and his ashes buried at Lyndford Church, which was what he had told her he wanted. Most of the village and a dozen of his old political colleagues, including a former cabinet minister, came to the burial service.

*****

Kathleen bore the loss of Michael with fortitude. Despite the tragedy of Jonathan and Catriona, they had had a full and satisfying life and she did not resent coming to the end of it, even when it was her beloved Michael who had to go first. It was the people who had done little with their lives who she felt sorry for, when they died.

She continued to make her annual trip to Vatersay, with Edwina and Christopher, and, usually, Alastair and Angela and one or two of the other Home Farm children. They bought themselves a people-carrier vehicle when they found the hire firm would not accept them as drivers, being over 70, and in her case, and Alastair's, more than 80.

Angus's two grandchildren were always keen to go, especially Edwina, and he delighted in seeing their progress and Edwina's continuing strong resemblance to her mother. But as the years went on they found another of the brood anxious to be included in the party and reluctant to come away.

It was Douglas, the youngest of Charles' and Maria's three. He was like his older brother, Alastair in many ways, although not very interested in sport, despite being athletic, always ready to climb a tree, or a cliff, walk and run long distances, ride and jump horses, handle farm animals with ease and confidence. Contrary to the ways of many farmers and farm children, who have tended, in the past especially, not to be great nature lovers, although often good naturalists, Douglas always loved all animals and birds for their own sake.

From the first time he went to Vatersay, when at six years old he was the youngest of the party, he seemed to discover an affinity with the place. And not only with the place, but with the people, Angus, Jennie and Ailsa, two years his junior. He always liked being with Ailsa. He would spend a large part of the few days they were there being shown her books, and helping her to read, and write. And she was usually with him in the hours he spent watching the sea for signs of seals, otters, porpoises and basking sharks after he learned that they frequented those waters. Over the years, the boy's attachment to the isles, and to the McArthur family, grew steadily. Even before the Jamesons' ancestral links with Scotland could mean much to him, he seemed to be thinking of himself as Scottish. He loved pipe and ceilidh music when other youngsters were turned on only by electric guitars. On a brief visit to Bannockburn after one of the Vatersay trips, when he was no more then nine, and was told what it was all about, he asked: "What were the English doing in our country anyway, Grandad?"

When he was 12 he told Charles and Maria he wanted to spend his summer holiday on Vatersay. They told him they could not spare the time to take him.

"I could go on the train, like Auntie Kathleen did, and Edwina and Christopher," he pleaded. A year later, provided with a mobile phone and strict instructions to call home at specified intervals, he had his way.

"Do you think this is alright?" Charles asked Angela as they put him on the train for the third time, by when he was nearly 16 . "He's a bright boy. Shouldn't he be thinking of something a bit more than otters and seals, and sheep on a croft in the islands?"

"Leave him be," she said. "You're right, he is a bright boy. But that doesn't mean he has to go in for something that makes a lot of money. He might be like you, Charles, care more for the land, and the place, than how much you can make out of it. My guess is he'll marry Ailsa and take over from Angus. I don't think Christopher will want to go there, even now .... But he might be another Gavin Maxwell, as well, and write something like *Ring of Bright Water*. Wouldn't that be wonderful?"

*****

With her mention of Christopher, Angela was putting her finger on one of the few dark passages in the story of the young Home Farm quintet.

Like Edwina, Chris slotted in easily and comfortably when he joined them as not much more than a toddler. He appeared to love all their activities, including the trips to Vatersay. At their primary school, he more than held his own in classroom and outside, and was described by his teachers as "hard-working and intelligent." But at Ludstone things started to go wrong. He shunned Douglas, his junior by a year – not that there was anything so unusual in that – and by the time he started his GCSE courses, the standard of his work had gone down noticeably and teachers were complaining of unco-operative behaviour. They warned, reluctant as ever to write off any pupil but forced into it by the concern of his "parents" and grandparent who were almost asking what they, the teachers, were doing wrong, that the poorest of results were likely unless there was a change in his approach. Nobody could understand how a boy from such a family, whose attitudes and enthusiasms made them beacons in the school, could be so lackadaisical and unresponsive.

At home, Kathleen wondered whether the loss of Michael was anything to do with it, but Chris had never seemed as close to his grandfather, or to her, as Edwina had. She, Charles and Maria tried every approach they could think of, from logical persuasion to warning that he was going to end up with no exam grades and no worthwhile role in life.

Charles tried to get him to show interest in the farm, but there was a complete lack of positive response. Kathleen tried to have heart-to-heart talks with him, and at first thought she was having some success, but there was no practical result. Alastair, his own past in mind, perhaps, thought "the boy will come out alright in the end" – the implication being "blood will tell," or "children with parents and grandparents like his cannot really go wrong." Which was all very well, Angela said, but what would happen to him in the meantime if he came out of the GCSEs with results making him unemployable or not even able to stay on at school. Not that he wanted to either work or learn, it appeared. And from his response to Charles, it looked as though staying at home on the farm was a non-starter. It was a situation that had never before shown up in any of the Lyndford families.

Two terms below the point at which the GCSE's were due to reach their climax, he started to stay away from home, telling Charles and Maria that he had been invited to a sleep-over, which was usually true. His work at school continued to go downhill, and all that was elicited by more consultations was that Chris was consistently unresponsive and appeared to associate with a bunch of boys of a similar nature, most of whom however did not start from such an advantageous background.

As a last resort, because using one member of the family against another was anathema to them, they asked Dorothy what she knew, especially who he associated with.

Dorothy, almost a mirror image of her mother in looks and character, had always been ready to "look after" the year-younger Chris, in earlier days. Childhood and schoolgirl loyalty brought a struggle with her conscience but eventually she realised what she ought to do, and it was she who came up with the information, gleaned from her friends in the sixth form to which she had recently graduated.

"They're a pretty awful lot, Mum," she said. "And I think they're into drugs. I don't mean heroin and stuff, but they're smoking pot and taking pills. Now I know about it, I can see it. And you can smell it."

They tackled him over the issue, but all they got out of him was a surly: "You can't tell me who I can have for friends. And what's wrong with a bit of weed, anyway."

They threatened to take away his pocket money, ostensibly given for doing jobs about the farm, but really completely unearned. He responded only with: "I don't care." which worried them. Where else was he going to get his money? Through harvest, when Alastair, Dorothy and Edwina all helped, driving grain trailers, doing chores round the buildings, running errands, Christopher lounged in bed until lunchtime, when he would disappear, only coming back late at night. They discovered later that he had been joining his friends, in Cravenbury. Maria, perhaps rather more au fait with the possibilities than Charles, or even Kathleen, went to bed every night for weeks dreading a phone call or heavy knock on the door.

It did not happen, but something as bad, or worse, did. One morning as she prepared to go shopping, she checked her handbag and found her purse missing. It contained nearly three hundred pounds, drawn from the bank the day before. She knew immediately where it had gone. Christopher was also missing – his bed had not been slept in.

She dashed out to the field into which Charles was about to set the combine.

"What shall we do?" she asked after she had told him what had happened. "Ought we to tell the police? It's not the money, is it, but we've got find out where he is."

Charles said: "We'll go to Cravenbury and see if we can find out anything. You go back and ask Dorothy if she has any ideas, and send Alastair up here. I'll put young Wayne on the combine and Alastair can take his place on the baler. But I don't think I'd say anything to Auntie Kathleen for the moment."

Dorothy could only suggest they try the home of one of the boys with whom she knew Christopher was friendly. He was home, although he had to be dragged out of bed, knew nothing of Chris's whereabouts, but suggested they try another acquaintance, in Ludstone.

"What's the matter, Mr Jameson?" the boy's mother asked. They said nothing of the money, only that he had not come home the night before.

A visit to the other aquaintance's home brought an even more negative result. He had not seen Christopher since the end of term, he said. They decided they had no option but to go to the police.

"Do we say anything about the money?" Charles asked.

"Not if we can help it."

Charles knew the inspector in charge at Ludstone, to whose office he was shown when he told the woman officer on the desk what it was about, and had given her the basic details.

"Good morning, Charles, Mrs Jameson," he said.

They told him about Chris's disappearance, and he asked a few questions.

"I appreciate you're anxious. But I don't think you should be too worried, at this stage. These youngsters are always doing this kind of thing, you know. We'll probably find he's having a night out with a girlfriend. It happens at their age.

Do you know whether he's got one?

"Not that we know of," Charles said. "He's got some friends we don't like, and we've spoken to two of them, but they say they've no idea where he's gone, and we think they're telling the truth."

"Has he got money with him, do you know?"

"Yes, we think he has," Charles said.

"Much?"

"Some hundreds of pounds, we think."

"That's a lot of money for a fifteen-year-old youngster. How come he has so much? Is it missing from the house?"

Charles and Maria looked at each other. They realised they had little option but to admit it.

"You think he's taken it, in fact?"

"He has pocket money, for doing jobs round the farm. But Maria's purse is missing."

"Containing how much?"

Maria said: "About three hundred pounds, or a bit more. I drew it from the bank yesterday, to go shopping."

The inspector looked grave.

"Mmmm," he said. "Look, this is just an informal chat. You have not yet said the money has been stolen. But I would urge you to think carefully about it. Of course you don't want to label your son as a thief. But it may well be that the kind of rap over the knuckles he'd get, if we find him and he's charged, would make all the difference to him in the future. In the meantime we'll treat it as a missing person case. It will be given priority, of course, because of his age. You'll let us know immediately if he turns up, I'm sure."

"Thank you, Bob," Charles said. "We will think hard about the other aspect." And they did, as they, a distraught Kathleen and the rest of the family tried to get on with their lives at an exceptionally busy time. But they were not given long to think.

Three days later Inspector Armstrong phoned to say Chris had been found, beaten and with stab wounds, in London, and was recovering in hospital. He had of course no money, watch, or mobile phone, and was lucky to be alive.

Charles and Maria once again left Lyndford in the care of the older and younger generations, and with Kathleen went immediately to the hospital where they found Chris out of any danger but looking bruised, battered and woebegone. He turned his face away when they approached his bedside.

Maria bent over and kissed his forehead. Kathleen took one of his hands. Maria asked: "How do you feel, love?"

Chris started to cry.

Maria took her hankie and dried his eyes. "Don't cry, Chris. You're going to be alright. We'll soon have you home."

He looked at them through his swollen eyes.

"Can I come home, Mum?" he sobbed." Will you let me come home?"

"Oh, Christopher .... Christopher .... we want you home. It's awful without you ...."

The tears started again. "I'm sorry, I'm sorry ...."

He was in the London hospital for a month. Charles and Maria stayed in the city overnight and spent as much of the next day as they could with him. Kathleen went home on the train and brought Edwina to see him the following day, Maria and Dorothy immediately afterwards, and there were few days throughout the period when no-one from Lyndford spent time at his bedside or with him in the day rooms.

Two weeks before he was discharged, he asked for some of his schoolbooks and a laptop computer. He was not fit to return to school at the start of the new term, and when he did go back, after Christmas, it was to the year group prior to the one he should have been in, at his own request and with the school's reluctant agreement. They wanted him to go to another school, and it was with difficulty that Charles and Kathleen persuaded them that the boy should be allowed to work out his own rehabilitation and salvation, as he desperately wanted and as they were now sure he would. Alastair had by then left the school to go to Harper Adams Agricultural College, but Dorothy was still there, for another year, to keep a careful eye on him.

Bob Armstrong told them the Metropolitan Police had not been able to find out anything about Chris's assault. Obviously though it was at the instigation of someone who knew him or of him, and that he would have an amount of money worth stealing. Months later he revealed to Maria what had happened. He had been prompted by one of his school gang to steal the money and join him in the capital. The boy in question simply disappeared.

But by then Chris was working hard and again earning the approbation of his teachers. The dark chapter was on its way to being obliterated.

Twenty-Six

Revolution

Keith Parkinson retired as Protechno's managing director soon after the millennium and Stella took over as chief of the thriving and expanding concern. They had already added a Swedish string to the firm's bow, which she played a major part in launching, usually taking her two children and nanny Magda with her on the Scandinavian trips.

As Parkinson called it a day, they completed another expansion, by acquiring a controlling interest in an American concern. And before the 21st Century was five years old they had opened two more branches, in Turkey and France. Stella was always the driving force from the business angle, but Edward remained the technical brain, although as more eager young technocrats came under his wing, his role consisted increasingly in vetting and supervising their ideas and their work.

At Lyndford, he came in for a certain amount of banter from his brother and even his father, who asked which he liked best – being a tycoon, or husband to one.

He and Stella could indeed have been seen as approaching tycoon status, although Edward would sometimes swear that they never quite knew where their next day-to-day pound was coming from. It was a Protechno success story that was due to his scientific and technical flair and drive as well as to Stella's remarkable business ability. Angela, as she told Alastair and Kathleen, was pleased to see that success seemed to do little to change him from the caring young man she first knew and became attached to. With Stella it was quite different, as the three sometimes mused. She still kept herself beautifully groomed; experience had made her even more competent as a businesswoman; but the family now had to search for the hard edge that once seemed to hit them in the face.

"And if they're tycoons, we need more like them," Angela said once. "They couldn't have worked harder and none of it's been done at the expense of other people, or driving their staff into the ground. All their employees share in the success, it seems to me. That's a wonderful bonus scheme they have. Paying it in shares means most of the staff have a stake in the company."

When they returned to live in England, they bought a modest house near

Coventry and, partly because Magda wanted to return to Germany, sent the children to a co-educational boarding school, which neither liked.

"Wish I could go to a school like Douglas, and come home every day, Auntie Maria," David told her on one of his frequent visits to Lyndford.

A feeling that they would like to have the children near them, more of the time, had much to do with what happened next in the Jameson saga, when the Lyndford wheel completed another revolution, something like the one which brought grandmother Dolly back to the Manor as its mistress rather than its kitchen maid.

When Alastair's Uncle Giles married in his sixties, and left the Manor for Home Farm, it was let to a university as a field centre, at a low rent on the basis that the tenants must keep it in good repair. They managed it well, alterations carried out were done with a minimum of structural change, and the arrangement worked satisfactorily for more than 20 years until the college decided it no longer needed a field centre.

Alastair was nominally the Manor's owner, but he always said that was a technicality. It belonged to the family, having been the Jameson home ever since it had been built by the then Squire Jameson halfway through the eighteenth century. He consulted the other senior members, Peter, Kathleen and Angela, and decided there should be a meeting of the whole adult tribe, in-laws included. Everyone turned up, except Emily Jane who was by then in America, and sat round Home Farm's big oak dining table, slightly battered through the attentions of generations of children, and which had once done the same duty in the Manor itself.

The consensus was that it would be a great pity if the house went out of the family, meaning there was little alternative to trying to find another tenant. Charles said: "I'm sure we could sell it, but we can't stipulate who would buy. I don't think we'd be happy if it turned out to be some pop star or even a city banker. It's always been a working house, even when it was 'The Squire' living there."

Heads nodded and Peter, who had been an estate agent, said: "Shall we get things under way on those lines, then? We want to let it?"

He started to talk rents and conditions, before Edward interrupted.

"Could you hang on a minute, Uncle Peter," he said. "Stella and I are wondering – how would everyone feel if we said we'd like to live here?"

"Everyone" felt fine about it. The idea of a Jameson family back in the old home delighted them. And it was another rags to riches story that appealed particularly to Alastair and Angela; even more rags to riches than in Dolly's case, two generations before, for Stella had come from a spot lower in the social scale, by the relative standards of different times.

As soon as he learned that the manor was coming vacant, Edward had been fired with the idea of living there and bringing it back to Jameson family use. He and Stella had already been thinking that it might be an idea to create a Protechno nerve centre, because their Coventry offices, already twice extended, were fully occupied with administrative staff and further extension was physically impossible. First they thought it might be located at the manor, which was certainly big enough, but soon rejected the idea; firstly because they did not want to live on the job; and secondly they did not fancy bringing any kind of industrial activity to Lyndford. The field centre had been different. It was agriculturally orientated and only occasionally brought numbers of people there. They knew they ought to have no problem finding somewhere on the Shropshire side of the Midlands for their nerve centre, and started looking. It did not take long to locate – a new business estate at Southbridge, on the Severn, a comfortable drive from Lyndford on a pleasant country road. Preliminary inquiries among key staff indicated that there were enough people ready to move to the country. There would be no problem about the work, in the burgeoning computer age. And the developers of the new estate almost snatched their hands off, at the prospect of the kudos a firm like Protechno would bring. Edward, with Stella, would have discussed the possibilities with his father before the day of the meeting, but time overtook them.

Edward and Stella did not really want a house as big as the Manor, but all agreed that the wing which did most of the housing of convalescing soldiers in the first war, and land army girls in the second, could make a substantial, attractive separate home.

The Lyndford wheel completed its revolution.

Twenty-Seven

Autumn idyll: *Angela*

This is going to be a long chapter, for I have been entrusted with the task of finally bringing the story of Lyndford and its people into the twenty-first century. I know many of the facts have already been related, in a book that rambles all round the families and much of the world, and I hope I'll be forgiven if my own narrative sometimes reads like the ramblings of an old woman.

Perhaps I should begin by concluding the story of Josie. I nearly said the sad story, but that would have been the wrong word. Horrific, indeed, part of it was. So horrific that I had to think hard about whether it should be revealed here, at least in such terrible detail. Hard-hitting journalist though she was, I'm sure she would not have told it so graphically if she had written it for public consumption.

We learned, as much as we could ever learn, about how she finally met her death a year after the discovery of the notebooks. Jim Meredith wrote to me, Alastair and Jeannie.

"We have found out what we think happened," he wrote. "It seems that just after the date of the last entry in Josie's notebook all the women, about 50, who were held in the barn at Potocari, were taken out and lined up for execution. They all had their hands tied behind their backs and their ankles hobbled so that they could not run. But for some reason one girl, Almeira Haladic, missed being tied, and when the shooting started she threw herself on the ground so that it looked as though she had been hit. It seems there must have been a panic on the part of the Serbs to get the thing done quickly, because they don't appear to have made sure that all the women had been killed, as they usually did. While they were gathering up the bodies for burial in the mass grave Almeira spotted a chance to get away, and did so. She was discovered later by UN people, hiding in the forest with a small group of others who had escaped from Srebrenica. She was in a terrible state, as you can imagine, but eventually their questioning brought out what I have just told you. It was verified, as far as it could be bearing in mind all the other women had died, by people who knew she was with a party which had been in that locality at that time.

"There are still a lot of questions that are not fully answered, I'm afraid.

For example why were Josie's notes never destroyed? These officers, vile characters as they obviously were, were intelligent men. They must surely have seen they would count heavily against them if things went wrong for them. Being in shorthand, Pavelic could not read them, and perhaps he would think that no woman would reveal things that happened in the way Josie set them down. Also, why were Josie and the other two buried in separate graves. We think it was probably because they were not Muslims, as I think I told you, but we cannot be sure. The other two have never been identified. Much of it does not quite fit in with it all being done in a hurry, or a panic. The same with the fact that the mass grave was later disturbed. But I think there can be no doubt about the basic fact of the mass execution."

Jim's postscript to Josie's story of course jolted our lives once again. But it had nothing like the effect of the discovery of her horribly mutilated body in the first place. The modern talk about "closure" cuts no ice with me. It is nothing more than a media invention. Josie had been missing for many months when we learned of that awful find. But the idea that either that event or this last one means I should or could close the chapter in my life headed "Josie" is unacceptable, unreal. And I'm sure Jeannie feels the same.

But I still refuse to think of her life story as "sad." Sad stories are those of people who have done nothing with their lives, or devoted them to realising greed or pursuing chimeras like wealth and material success. Even in the Balkans, grim as those final months were, Josie, I am sure, found fulfillment in striving to understand the people in that troubled region, interpreting what was happening there and helping convey it to the wider world, when it could be persuaded to listen. Jeannie and I were delighted when her news agency employer instituted an annual award, bearing her name, for outstanding foreign news reporting by a British journalist. The judges included my very dear sister-in-law Kathleen, and Alex Kordic, and I was asked to present it to the first winner, a young print reporter, for his penetrating and discerning coverage of the Congo War.

*****

Because she played such an important part in my first days with Alastair, all those years ago, I must tell what happened to the other Josie, my elder sister. Readers of *Angie and Debra* will know that she was in an emotional trough because of the death of her fiance in the war; that she was "rescued" by Alastair when she "shacked up" with his neer-do-well and reckless friend Steve, when I was still in medical training; and that she married Martin, a research scientist and colleague of my first husband, Bill, a few years later. But at that point she seems to have disappeared from these pages.

Well, they were very happy, and had two fine sons. They continued to live in London, and I kept in contact regularly if not always frequently, and saw them at the same kind of interval. Martin succeeded Bill as head of the department in which they both worked, but Josie gave up her job with a firm of stockbrokers when the first of their boys was born. She kept most closely in touch with me when I, Alastair and the rest of the family were agonising over my daughter Josie and what had happened to her. Martin died of a heart disease, five years ago. Josie is still alive, but in a care home, suffering I'm afraid from that curse of the modern world, Altzheimer's Disease. She did not know me last time I visited. Happily, her sons and grandchildren are able to see her quite often.

My brother, Stewart, who has been only sketchily mentioned, is still in America, with his wife and family.

*****

Jeannie and Simon had another son, Justin, two years after James was born. She has comparatively recently gone back to work, in the university's astro-physics department, both the boys now being at secondary school.

"I think I ought to start to earn some money again, bearing in mind the uncertainty about Simon's health," she told me.

There are blots on my pages, and Simon's health is the origin of one. Three years after Justin appeared, he suffered the first of a series of bouts of depression. The doctors said they were probably caused by stress. But I believe that they were the result of his quarrel with his father, which at the time he apparently rode through without any serious psychological ill-effect. Mr Levison Snr has never spoken to him since that day just after James came into the world, even to tell him of the death of his mother. Simon only learned of it through his sister Miriam. He went to the funeral but even there his father ignored him, Jeannie told me. Religious bigotry that can lead to such an attitude, towards one's own child, and be carried to such terrible lengths, is surely beyond human comprehension. It was soon after the funeral that the first fit of depression hit him. The consultant's treatment restored him to apparent normality but he has had two more since, the third only last year – that's 2010 as I write. I am beginning to wonder whether the estrangement from his father should be brought into the open, the doctors told about it at least. Simon is too good a man, and husband, to be allowed to sink into intellectual or any other kind of oblivion. And James and Justin are both bright boys, although like him not terribly athletic or interested in sport, and need a father who can play his full part in their lives.

They are both a long way from retirement, but Jeannie has asked whether The Mill could be available for them when the time comes, or even before if things go seriously wrong with Simon. I have told her it will go to her anyway "when anything happens to me." And before that, if they need it.

****

Edwina and Alastair junior still seem joined at the hip. At the ripe old age of 23, and in the middle of a PhD in philosophy, she does not now talk of an intention to marry him, but when they are at home they spend almost all their time together. I am convinced they will end up married, or partnered as now seems increasingly the norm. Probably they already are, in effect. She is fulfilling the potential she showed as a child: highly intelligent, and a deep thinker, which is by no means always the same thing; and a loving, caring person.

Alastair has followed his father's course almost exactly, going to Harper Adams College and joining Charles at Home Farm. They have bought another 200 acres, adjoining the existing land, and originally part of the old estate, but with only half a dozen people on the staff of a farm adding up to 1,200 acres, including Forest Farm, they have to work hard. Charles though seems almost to have taken on the mantle of the Jameson squires. He cherishes the land and everything about it, and revels in the work. Those journalists who seized disparagingly on his West Indian parentage when he became, they said, probably inaccurately, Britain's first "black" farmer, implying that nothing but disaster must follow if families who put the great in Great Britain allowed themselves to be invaded by alien blacks; have they any idea how Charles feels for the land? Feels for it just as deeply as his great-grandfather. Could it be that the African blood brought into the family by his mother has had something of the effect forecast by his great-aunt Billie when she told her father the squire that his landed gentry family needed the new blood of Dolly the maidservant, seventy years before? Or is it just Charles' reaction to learning how his Jamaican grandparents had to struggle to feed and clothe their family from a patch of land no bigger than the smallest of the Lyndford fields? See what I mean about rambling!

Dorothy is so like her mother. Not as intellectually bright as the others, perhaps, but expecting a good degree from her health and nutrition studies at

Aberystwyth University. I have no idea what she will do with it, except that she will apply it to caring for other people, in some form.

Douglas has never relinquished his urge to spend all the time he can in the Western Isles and with the McArthur family, Ailsa in particular. When he was near leaving school, with the prospect of good A-levels, he said he did not want to go to university. "I'd rather go and live up there and help Angus," he said. Charles and Maria pointed out that Angus and Jennie could not afford to pay him, or even keep him, which he accepted. Studying prospectuses, he discovered that he could do a degree in sustainable development at the new University of the Highlands and Islands, a college with many campuses, one at Stornaway on Lewis, an easy and inexpensive flight to that wonderful beach airport on Barra. He's in his second year there now, and Ailsa has started her first. I still believe they'll be married and eventually live on Vatersay. Everyone's happy about it, including Angus and Jennie who have thrived within the limits of the Hebridean economy. They were able to further add to their acreage on Vatersay as crofters grew older and did not want the burden of caring for livestock. The ram-breeding enterprise was moderately successful, there was a good demand for lambs and cattle for the meat market, and a steady flow of summer visitors who, after the causeway link made communication with Barra a matter of a few minutes drive, seemed to like staying with them as a jumping-off point for a tour of the Outer Hebrides.

And Christopher: he is still the new boy who emerged from the terrible episode when he was fifteen or so, although he has had one or two spells of gloomy introspection when things have gone marginally wrong in his life. He worked hard, at school and at home, brushing off the would-be attentions of the remnants of the bunch of no-hopers who tried to get him involved with them again, and amazed us all by winning a place at Oxford on the strength of a full house of top grades in his A-levels; and, obviously by suitably impressing the interviewing panel, despite having only gone to a state school. (Some of the Oxbridge top brass still do not seem to have their priorities in order.)

There, he met and fell for a girl who threatened to undo his own good work; not by leading him back into bad ways, but by her sheer brilliance. Chris had begun to think he was himself something special, intellectually, and when he found that Corinne left him behind in that respect, he lost his self-belief and came home after his second term in a mood of wondering whether he should carry on. Maria, terribly worried that history was repeating itself, asked Kathleen and I to talk to him, and I think we made some headway. But what started to bring him back, more than anything I said, was a phone call from the girl, asking whether she could come to Lyndford. Chris had told her so much about it, she told Maria, that she felt she must see it for herself. And she thought he needed "cheering up a bit." Brilliant she may have been, but, far more important, she proved to possess a wealth of common sense, and employed it in restoring him to an even keel. They are still together, and I hope will remain so. They're a bit like his mother and father – Catriona was the brilliant one, but she loved Jonathan passionately.

******

At Forest Farm, Erbie and Connie were at last persuaded to retire. We further improved the cottage where they first lived and more or less gave it to them – sold it to them for £100 so they would have something to pass on to their children. It was in lieu of the pension they had so thoroughly earned, Alastair told Erbie. He said they had been able to make provision for themselves, but Alastair brushed that aside. They are a lovely couple and still my very good friends.

The farmhouse is let, with a ten-acre paddock and one or two buildings, to a family with horses. They want to buy it but we are keeping it in hand until we are sure none of the family need it.

******

Emily Jane, of course, married her Randall, went to live with him in Massachusetts, and amazed her family and friends by producing a Goodrich heir, at the age of 43. Before that, as related earlier, she had met, delighted and been delighted with, his parents, who had spent many years worrying about their son after the tragedy, you could not call it anything else, of his first brief marriage.

She won't return to Britain, to live, obviously, although she and Randall, and now young Randall have come for several visits. Edward – usually her first point of family contact, and still "Sis" to him – helps keep us in touch. They have sold their house in the east, built a retirement home for Randall's parents in the little village of Shell and moved to the ranch themselves. Randall thinks they will carry on working in research for a time, at long range, and he is taking his parents' Arapaho Indian friends, Pete and Delilah, into business partnership. They still breed horses as the main enterprise but they are developing the raising of organic beef cattle as another string, inspired by the success of the Arapaho Ranch on the Wind River reservation. Pete and

Delilah's little girl, Rosebud, has made a good recovery from her leukaemia and they have another daughter. Alastair and I went with Em and Randall to Little Fork, soon after they were married. Ed and Stella have also been, and Charles and Maria are planning a trip, now they can leave the farm in the hands of young Alastair. We all think it's wonderful there – as near a big-scale version of Lyndford as could be. And Emily Jane, now nearing retirement herself, is truly happy.

*****

And now, at last, I must try to get over the essence of what has been the most marvellous part of an often wonderful and happy life. Alastair and I were married in the September of 1990, a year after he left hospital. When I was making notes for an earlier part of this book, I remember thinking I would not say too much about our life together. I was so happy and grateful to have found him again, but it was not something I wanted to babble about. Now he's gone, and it's different. I can best serve his memory by trying to get across how fulfilling and exciting life and love can be long after the primal urges of youth have faded. Not that many, many people of my age need telling that. You only have to see the way their hands seek each others, their eyes light up when they meet to know that their love is still the most important thing in their lives. And not that those urges faded, completely, for us, for many years and somewhat to my surprise and delight in Alastair's case, after those weeks in an apparent brain-dead coma. Even when my supposed quota of three score years and ten was nothing more than a memory, and the breasts drooped, the tummy bulged, he would look at me and say: "God, you look good, girl." With a result, sometimes, about which I shall not babble.

Our wedding was a quiet affair, at the register office and afterwards at Home Farm, with all the families as they then were there, except Josie, and Kathleen's son and daughter-in-law who had just started their stint in Bangladesh. Alastair's first wedding had been at Lyndford Church, because Debra was very much a Christian, but although I am perhaps not, or was not then, quite such a defined agnostic as he was, I did not want a church wedding. We went to the church afterwards, just Alastair and I, to put some of the flowers they had given us on the graves, of Debra, his parents, and grandparents. Helping care for those graves, and Josie's, has been one of our sacred duties, and I use the word deliberately because you don't have to be religious to hold things sacred.

We, or rather I, decided to live at Jasmine Cottage. Alastair was sceptical at first because he thought its associations with Debra might prevent my being happy there. Why they have not I don't know, because new surroundings are so often vital to a second marriage. Perhaps it was because of all that happened in the hospital, where I had helped him grieve for her. The only way I ever felt concerned about Debra's former presence, either as mistress of the house or as Alastair's wife, was in wondering if she would approve of some alteration I was making. But if her ghost ever did visit Jasmine Cottage, it was obviously a friendly spirit, pleased that I was looking after the man who had been her saviour and beloved guardian.

Anyway, he was insistent that the house should be as I wanted it, and I made one or two changes, more to convince him than because I really wanted them. They did though bring the benefit of helping accommodate the family when we had largish gatherings later on.

I knew I was going to love Alastair the first time I saw him, in the company of those ghastly good time girls and his devil-may-care RAF friend Steve, when I was only 17. It took a little longer for Alastair to realise he loved me, he has told me since. He just thought I was a pleasant, friendly little girl with a bit more to me, as he put it, than the others. He did not realise I was already well on the way to falling for him in the biggest of ways. I won't attempt to claim that it was the greatest love there ever was. Many young and not so young couples have experienced passion as great, that has lasted a lifetime, I'm sure. What has been so wonderful for us is the way it never went away through forty years of separation. Four decades when we never set eyes on each other. When we both married and yes, loved someone else; parented our children, lived full and happy lives. Neither of my marriages fitted Alan Bennett's description, via that sad Mrs Donaldson in *Smut*, of a typical marital union: happy at first, then satisfactory, and finally dull. My married years were happy, and indeed satisfactory, from start to finish. Never, never dull.

I believe now that it was that one action of Alastair's, back then, that contained the seed from which grew the great tree of my seven decades of love for him. I knew he had goodness in him, from the way he rescued my sister from a situation that would have ruined her life if it had continued. But it was the way he made me cast myself off from him, the hardest and most painful decision he ever made, and made at a time of the most abject misery, because he believed that having a convicted criminal for a lover would be an impossible millstone round my neck, that instilled the knowledge that there was more than goodness. There was a shard, at least a shard, of greatness. And nothing that has happened since, including his rescue of Debra and his marriage to her

– especially his marriage to her, and the reasons behind it – can change my mind about that.

He became involved with Steve and his associates because he did not feel he could settle down to any ordinary job. He has always said it was I who was instrumental in bringing about the change. I may have been the trigger, but I know that decency, readiness to help other people and a capacity for hard work made up the innate basis of his character, as they had of his father and mother who sadly I met only once.

Despite the injuries sustained in the accident when Debra died, and the weeks in the coma, Alastair recovered to enjoy quite robust health. Even well into his eighties, he never liked a day to pass without having done some kind of productive work, although it became tempered by a need for relaxation in the form of reading, doing a crossword or two, listening to the radio and occasionally watching television. He was always ready to lend a hand on the farm, not that physical work is much in demand on large farms nowadays. And he played his golf, and walked, with me, Michael and other members of the family.

The darkest years in my life with Alastair came after Josie's hopeless passion for Edward blasted her life – and I am still convinced her desperate search for a substitute fulfillment was what sent her to Yugoslavia and the horrors that followed. Unlike the "rescue" of my sister, half a century before, there was nothing he could do about it, only be there, with me and for me. Yet I do not know, I cannot imagine, how I would have coped without him. He said very little about it. He knew better than to try to heal my anxiety and grief with torrents of words. He seemed to know that no balm could soothe like his presence. But no-one who has ever lost a child needs telling how the chasm that appears can never be completely filled, even by the love of someone who cared for me as Alastair did.

So I must not pretend that our life together was one long idyll. There were far too many ups and downs in family affairs. Josie most of all. Simon and his father, Jonathan and Catriona, early fears about Stella, young Christopher. Also the periods, happily brief and becoming less frequent with time, of what he said his father and his Uncle Giles used to call "the black dog" - sessions of depression connected with incidents in their past lives. With Giles it was the death of his sweetheart Meri after he left her; his father Charles when his father, Squire Alastair, killed himself after Charles married the servant maid Dolly. In my Alastair's case it was when something reminded him of the RAF incendiary operations over German cities which could only, Alastair said, be called terror raids. He recalled how he had sometimes awakened, when he was in prison, to nightmare visions of women and children fleeing into cellars only to suffocate because the intense heat had sucked out all the air. I would remind him of the evil regime their bombs had been fighting, undoubtedly speeding its end. I hope I helped. I don't know. There may be some things nobody can help with – they have to work themselves out. But as with him and my agony over Josie, I think my presence was what helped most: the feeling that flowed without words being spoken. I hope so, my darling Alastair.

Then we had our own differences of opinion, which would occasionally bring quite fierce arguments, always though on minor matters. I remember Edward appearing in the middle of one, and saying: "Scrapping, you two?" We were actually discussing the identity of a stranger bird we had just seen on our feeding table. He said it was a long-tailed tit, I knew it was a coal tit. Edward got out the bird book to prove that – his father was right! But that illustrates the level of our disagreements. On any point of importance, philosophical, political, family, our minds ran almost completely in parallel. We often found ourselves arriving at the same point in our inner thoughts, at the same time, without a word having been said. He would start to raise some matter or other, with: "Darling, do you think we should etc etc" and I would burst into laughter, because I was thinking exactly the same, and was about to ask the same question. And it could be a matter great or small.

There were many idyllic moments, though. It could not be otherwise when you were as happy and fulfilled as I was with Alastair, and lived in a place as beautiful as Lyndford. We would be walking in the woods or fields and see something so beautiful it made us gasp. A fawn, almost invisibly nestled in a ring of bracken, its mother, no doubt a fugitive from the deer park not far away, nowhere to be seen, of course, although no doubt watching us; a mother – or was it father – thrush feeding a fledgling almost as big as her or him self, who had obviously just been persuaded to leave the nest; from the farm's high points, the almost heavenly view of hills and valleys in whichever directed we turned. All these wonders, and many more would make me grasp his hand, and wonder whether I was right in rejecting the idea of the existence of heaven – surely this was it, here before us. Idyllic is not perhaps the right word, perhaps magic moments, or magic hours would better describe the Christmastime afternoon spent side by side on the settee watching a TV pantomime with one grandchild draped across our knees and another on the rug at our feet. The first time we walked up the road to the gateway where I had parked to see him and Debra, the day before their terrible accident, was as moving to both of us as it had been to me a year or two before. In my usual sloppy way, I could not hold back a few tears. His arm went round me, he kissed my hair. You could not call it happiness, the feeling that came over us. It came in spite of our happiness, yet in some strange way added to it. The picture of that little brown lady, looking up to him, laughing, and loving, is printed indelibly on my mind, alongside her terrible story, and Alastair's part in it.

Twenty-Eight

"Not afraid"

Alastair was 88 when he was struck by the only serious illness of his life, apart from the injuries. He started to have pains in his stomach and chest, which became worse rather than better, and seemed to spread to his legs. Even so, I had to work hard to persuade him to go to the doctor.

The subsequent investigations showed not one tumour but several. There was little point in operating, they said, because the malignancies were growing and spreading. He was offered chemo-therapy but told the consultant he would not have it..

We walked out to the car, hand in hand with my arm almost locked into his. I kept back the outward signs of distress as well as I could. But in the car I could not hold them back any longer. Slumped over the wheel, the tears flowed, racking sobs could not be held back. I had never cried like that in my life, not for Josie, or Bill, or my mother and father. His arm was round me, hugging gently, his voice whispering in my ear. "Angie, my darling, my darling, please ...."

But when speech became possible, all I could say, the only pathetic, selfish words that came, were about me. Why had he refused the treatment, that would have kept him with me for a little longer. A few extra months. Perhaps years.

He said, very gently: "Darling, I believe we've just got to face it. My time has come. I'm eighty-eight years old and I've had a good life. From everything we've been told and what we've seen, we know that no treatment can possibly make me better. I don't think it would even delay .... what has to happen ..... for any worthwhile time. It would leave you nursing an invalid for even longer. It might be different if I was twenty years younger, or even ten. I think I have to accept that it's the end."

And as I cried again:

"My sweetheart, please don't. I don't want to leave you. You know that. But we both know it has to happen. Dying's nothing to be afraid of, when you've had a good life, like I have. Especially the part with you."

For the next two months he was quite active, walked round the farm and the woods, spotted a sick cow that had somehow escaped the eyes of Charles or his stockman. I told all the children, and Peter, and Kathleen, who at 84 and

86 were both in good health, and still are. I spend a lot of time with Kathleen. I wrote to Angus and Jennie, because they seem to prefer a letter to the phone, and had the most wonderfully understanding reply. Erbie, sometimes with Connie, came at least twice a week. Emily Jane and Randall came from America for Christmas, and were surprised to find him so apparently well, after what they had heard from me about his illness.

By February however, he had to have frequent injections of morphine, to keep the pain in check. He refused to go to hospital, so was confined to bed and developed a chest infection, which meant more medication. Doctor Jenkinson, who we knew well because he had treated the Home Farm five for their various disorders, came every day, and towards the end twice a day, and the district nurses the same. I spent most of my time by his bedside, and slept on a divan two feet away.

At the beginning of March, he seemed to improve. Antibiotics appeared to have quelled the chest infection. For a period of three or four weeks, he got out of bed and sat in a sitting room chair, talked farming with Charles and Erbie, heard Edward's business news, listened to radio and read the newspapers, watched television. I allowed myself to hope that the cancers might have gone into remission, as occasionally happens, and Dr Jenkinson agreed it was possible.

Alastair though had no such thought, as he showed when he used the lucid interval to talk about things that were obviously troubling him.

He said: "Darling, one thing I want to ask you. Don't let them take me to hospital. I want to stay here, at Lyndford. My father, and my grandfather and his father all died here, and others further back, I expect. Please, Angie."

I managed to assure him. He should not be taken away. He had not finished, though.

"There's something else. Something I want you to tell the children. I don't think they know and I want them to.

"They know my grandfather lost his mind when Dad married Mother. But what they don't know is that it was me being born that was the last straw – made him take his own life. Dad and Mother never talked about it. I got it from Aunt Billie, when I asked what Grandfather would have thought about my marrying Debra. It seems he – did it – immediately after he was told. She told me as well how awful Dad and Mother felt about it – she was afraid Dad would lose his mind as well. There was no reason why I should feel guilty, I suppose, but I did. I told Deb, but she thought we should keep it between us."

"Why did your Aunt Billie tell you? Would it not have been better forgotten?"

"She didn't think so. She thought secrets like that turned into skeletons in the cupboard, and I think she was right. P'raps I'm wrong, darling, but I'd be glad if you told them. I'll tell them if you don't want to .... but .... it may not be possible ...."

I knew what he meant. I don't know whether his Aunt Billie was right, or not, but if Alastair wanted his sons and daughter to know, they must be told. I gave him that promise, too.

By the end of the month my hopes had been dashed, and the downward spiral had resumed. He was in continual discomfort or worse, or comatose when the morphine was at its most effective. There were only occasional short periods when he could speak lucidly.

In one of them, the last, he said: "Darling, I'm not afraid of ..... what's going to happen. But I don't want to leave a mess behind. Is everything in order?"

It would have been stupid to come out with some banality like urging him not to worry about anything, just to get better. That would have been contrary to everything in his philosophy, and mine. I could only say: "Don't worry, my love, there's no mess, everything's tidy."

He smiled as if to say "Well you would say that, wouldn't you," but actually whispered only: "Thank you, Angie."

Those were the last words he spoke. We both knew the end was near. For two more days he was conscious for only minutes at a time. His three children were all close at hand – Emily Jane had come from America – and he knew them, smiled at them, tried to squeeze their hands.

They were with me, in the room adjoining, when the nurse from the agency we had engaged to help care for him, as well as anyone could, came in to whisper: "I think you should go in, Mrs Jameson." I looked at them, asking the question, but Edward said: "No, you, Angela."

I sat by the bedside, holding his hand. His eyes were closed, his mouth just open. I could see by the ever so slight vibration of his lips, the dear lips that for nearly twenty years had hardly missed a day being pressed on mine, that he was breathing, almost silently. He looked to be peacefully asleep, just as in the hospital all those years before.

The lips went still, and I kissed his forehead, as I had then. Only this time there could be no awakening.